CRASH

JOHN BRADY

CRASH

Copyright © 2018 by John Brady

Cover: JHWB

ISBN: 978-1-988041-13-1

www.johnbradysbooks.com

Also by John Brady

The Inspector Matt Minogue series

A Stone Of The Heart
Unholy Ground
Kaddish In Dublin
All Souls
The Good Life
A Carra King
Wonderland
Islandbridge
The Going Rate
The Coast Road

The Felix Kimmel series

Poacher's Road

For Hanna, with love.

Homo homine lupus.

February

At least Sonia had stopped crying by the time she left. We had made up too - in a way. But I knew it wouldn't last. I knew that something had been broken and that no amount of goodwill or excuses would fix it. No, not this time.

I had leaped out of the bed in a flash, the Sig braced in both hands and covering the angles line by line and zone by zone. But even as it was happening, a part of me knew that the sound that had ripped me from sleep was likely harmless. It was a car back-firing, or something falling off the bed side table. Maybe part of a dream, even.

Bit by bit, the real world slid back into place. The apartment. Islandbridge. Dublin. Financial crisis. February. Rain. And Sonia. 'Petrified' is the word.

Of course, I tried to explain things away. I couldn't help it, love – it was all reflex. Look, I just did the range training last week so .... And so forth. Probably not the smartest thing to say.

She got moving at last. It was like she was learning to walk all over again. I hadn't the heart to look down the hall as she left. I pretty-well knew that I had woken people up. Most of them have been decent about it, but there are limits.

It was coming up to five o'clock by then. I fully intended to give the mindfulness thing a go. After all, the shrink wasn't pushing it at me just to pass the time of day, was she. But it was not to be. I ended up nursing a second too-big glass of duty free Vitamin J while I tried to unwind things in my mind. Then I fell asleep.

So much for February then. A shambles, entirely. I was glad to see the back of it.

1

Four inches – four, no more and no less. That was what it came down to in the end: the space between the accelerator pedal and the brake pedal. Four lousy inches. So? So a turn of the ankle, a dab on the accelerator, and none of this would have happened.

The traffic light ahead was green too. Things might be coming apart at the seams in this country but green was still green. Green didn't mean stop here and do something mad, or stupid.

Yet there I was slotting my Golf into a spot a couple of hundred yards down from Firenza. *Firenza*. What kind of a name was that anyway. Tons of these coffee places had shut down already. Which was why this one caught my eye when I was driving by here last week. Also, because I remember Sonia saying she liked the look of place.

OK then, so when she got back...

When she got back. Like I needed another hint that maybe I was losing the plot. I already had a big, fat glowing one announcing just that – agreeing to meet the wife of a jailed gangster here this morning.

I turned off the engine and let down the window. It was May – finally. The best month of the year bar none. That feeling I'd had, that everything had been crowding in tighter, it had eased. Things had drawn back to a decent distance, or a manageable distance, at least. It felt there was more space around things now. Fresh starts, possibilities. This was May working its magic again.

Or maybe it wasn't May at all. Maybe it was the pills.

Was there stuff the shrink hadn't told me about them? I had checked online, of course. There was every possible side effect you could imagine. It left me wondering if I was making things up. But that feeling that I was overlooking something, or misreading things, it was still there. Things were not quite as they seemed. Every now and then, the most ordinary stuff would give off strong vibes of peculiarity. Looking at something – a window, say, or a lamp shade, or an apple – the familiarity would slowly drain out of it. It was as if things were whispering that you couldn't depend on them. A hint, or a warning, that they mightn't hold up for much longer. They might even turn on you, somehow.

Blame the pills, right. But, sure, half of Ireland was on pills these days. I checked my watch. A few minutes early. I'd give the mindfulness thing another bash. Let my mind into neutral, set it free to wander its own way.

Not a chance. It snapped right back to what it had been chewing on – wondering how I'd gotten shanghaied into this. As if I didn't know. It was the old story: Ma hoking up some notion and somehow I came attached.

I was in the middle of Dublin Bay yesterday when she'd phoned. Literally in the middle of it, half way along the South Bull. I put the reedy voice down to the anniversary. It was seven years for Terry. Seven. It was unbelievable.

"Ma? I can't hear you. I'm out in the wind and everything."

"I said, how come you didn't ring me. The text I sent you?"

I have to have a little chat. ASAP. A very sad situation.

"I was going to, later on."

She said nothing for a while.

"Well how's Sonia, tell us."

"Sonia's in China, Ma. Did I forget to tell you that?"

"God but you're contrary this evening. Look, Tommy. It'll all turn out to the good. Give it time, give it time. I'm very fond of Sonia, Tommy – very."

"Me too Ma. Me too."

Her raspy laugh collapsed into a cough. It had always made me want to put my hands over my ears. Once, when I was nine, I took all her fags and I mashed them up and threw them in the bin. She was doing the office cleaning at the time. I'd sit at the bottom of the stairs waiting on her. Instead of me getting the clattering that I deserved, she cried and cried. I'd never seen her like that before. It scared the living shite out of me. My shirt collar was ringing wet from her tears. And she held me so tight, I thought she'd smother me.

"Where are you in anyway? Up Mount Kilimanjaro is it?"

"Near enough. I'm over at Poolbeg, the Bull Wall there."

"Poolbeg? Out on that ...? You're mad."

"Yeah well I come by it honestly, don't I."

Too late. You can't take back words. If there was a name for that long, crooked road that led Terry to that laneway that night, it wasn't the word 'mad.' Terry was never 'mad.' A twin would know. Twin – it was like a magic word for some people. They sort of thought it was two of the same person. Not so. My temper issue aside, I was more to the Ma side of the ledger. I liked things organized, settled. Terry, it had to be said, was more like our Da – fly-off-the-handle style. An easy mark for the dealers anyway. For the gangs too, of course. For anybody really.

Ma still saw Terry all over town. She knew it wasn't Terry, of course. It was someone Terry's size or with Terry's walk, or with Terry's hair. It was that way for me too. Like I had a Terry-model Sat Nav in my head complete with a ghost map of Dublin. That hollow-eyed, ruined-looking head wandering into traffic? Terry. Just because you don't believe in ghosts doesn't mean you're not going to be seeing one. Another thing I never knew? You could be fierce angry at a ghost.

Another cough from Ma.

"Ma? Them fags, they've got to go. No two ways about it."

"I know, I know."

"Come on now. Seriously."

"I know, I said. It takes time, Tommy. All right?"

She was quiet then. The big thing was still waiting to be said. She knew I'd be heading over to the cemetery before dark.

"So give him my best," she said. "As always."

Her voice was quavering. I hoped to God she wouldn't lose it, because if she did, I would too.

"Make sure and tell him that. You hear?"

That, I liked to hear. Needed to hear, truth be told. It was that same warning tone she used when we were young lads. It meant she'd be okay.

"I always tell him Ma. He knew it too, so he did. Always."

I look out into the Bay. It was cooler here than I'd thought. But the sun had made an appearance at last, sliding in and out from behind the clouds to knock sparkles off the water. There were whitecaps out toward the Kish and Northside, the Hill of Howth performed its sly shimmy across the waves to keep up with me on my run out along the Wall.

It wasn't a run at all. No-one is his right mind would run along the Wall. After centuries of tides and gales battering away at it, and the Liffey trying to shoulder it out of existence, it was as miracle there was any Wall left. If the dodgy surface didn't get you, or the the blinding light off the water, the gusts of wind would. This was a world that swayed and tilted around you, a world where you could twist your ankle in any of a thousand places and tumble into Dublin Bay. So no running. The correct term was shuffle. I was grand with shuffling, actually. It was good training for the ring. No, I wasn't great or anywhere near great back when I was serious about boxing, but at least I could hold my own. I wanted that back.

Ma was still cogitating. I'd just have to wait. It'd be a long day for her too. At least the Wall was weaving its spell today. There was nothing but the sea all around. The swishing of the water had filled my head, washing out all the nonsense: the madness on the job, the crash, the tsunami of bad news every hour of the day – even the fact that Sonia had flown the coop – *poof*. Half-way to the lighthouse and I was in the zone. The whole walking-on-water illusion was complete.

And so, I'd wonder afterwards, was that a sign that I had missed that day? My Ma more or less imagined that I walked on water. Her son the newly-minted sergeant, the white-haired boy himself. The man who could do anything. Sure.

I was long enough waiting.

"All right so, Ma. This too shall pass. Right?"

IOne of her million stand-bys. It used to drive me and Terry up the wall.

"Good lads the both of you." Her voice had firmed up. "But listen, love. Before you go. There's something else. I got bell other day, so I did, out of the blue."

Out of the blue: Ma wouldn't tell a lie. She'd just improve on the facts.

"You remember Bernie Cummins?"

"Well I do and I don't."

"Ah come on. And poor Darren? What happened to him?"

Poor Darren. Darren Cummins was one of Crumlin's more violent criminals – and that was saying something. Wild, violent and incompetent. Off his head basically. One of Darren's quirks was using a nail gun to get his point across. Did that have something to do with Poor Darren encountering a party outside a restaurant one night, a party keen on getting a point of his own across by means of a shotgun fired about eighteen inches from Darren's face? I was working the Murder Squad at the time. Plate-Glass Sheehy showed me scene photos below in Ryans one night. I'd seen plenty, but this one was not something you'd forget. An open case to this very day.

"Bernie's a mother too you know, Tommy."

"A mother. I see. All right, so that qualifies her to...?"

"What ails you? The job, is it? Did you get any leave -"

"Listen, Ma –"

"- my point is, a mother loves her children, no matter what."

'No matter what.' I could hardly miss that one. Terry, of course. This from a woman who 'married for love' the dashing Frank Malone. He dashed, all right. Left her with two boys to rear.

"Ma. What are you telling me this for?"

"Bernie's trying to get in touch with him, but he's not answering. In bits she is, in bits."

A cargo boat I hadn't noticed earlier was moving into the Bay. Gary, I thought. So maybe he wasn't cut from the same crazy cloth as Darren, but he was a bad article in his own right. I came across him years ago in a pub we were clearing. And my God, what a shaper. He was high for sure. He got into my face right away. Say hello to good old Sheila for me will you – his exact words. That was what he called my Ma – good old Sheila. I almost had a go at him then and there.

"Gary's all she has left, Tommy. It's awful, just awful."

The gusts were getting stronger by the minute.

"Jenn, the daughter? She's there all to the good, isn't she?"

"Ah, you remember! All the lads had a crush on her?"

"Not this lad. Your pal Bernie has a husband, does she not."

"Of course she does! But Tony got put away. Remember? A long sentence. Very long."

Tony Cummins had a new barrister: my Ma.

"What does this have to do with me, or you for that matter?"

"Who said it did? I'm not asking for anything."

"Yeah you are. Or you're going to."

"It's just that your name came up, Tommy. That's all."

"My name came up. Now how did that happen, I wonder."

"Ah go away out of that. Look, Tony's not the worst."

"How do you know he's not?"

"Come on now. He's nothing like what's out there these days. No, no, no. Not by a long shot."

A gust raced across the water and pushed me back on my heels. I looked out over the swells. 'Not the worst.' Ma knew right from wrong but her loyalties kept getting in her way. Tony Cummins had managed to stay free of the feuding and the back-stabbing. No mean feat that, all the more so since it had gone completely mad here the past few years.

Memories tip-toed around in my mind. Those First Communion pictures of me and Terry? Gary Cummins was in them too, along with proud, smiling, young-looking mothers Bernadette Cummins and Sheila Malone. Try as I might I couldn't remember Bernie Cummins' face. I didn't recall seeing Tony Cummins in them. As for our Da, he wouldn't be making any appearance. Lazarus, he was not. Me and Terry were well into our teens before Ma let go of her tragic-accident-on-a-building-site-in-London line. It's like they say: the past can be fierce unpredictable.

"The thing is, Tommy, it's not just Bernie asking."

"Who's asking, then?"

"You know who I mean. What I mean, like."

"No I don't."

"Don't be like that now. Her husband I'm talking about."

Everything around me – the sea, the wind, even the aggravation – went on hold.

"Ma. Do you know what are you saying."

"You heard me."

"What you said about Tony Cummins. Are you spoofing?"

"What a thing to say. Your own mother? Listen to me, Bernie kept telling me over and over again. 'Be sure and tell that to Tommy now.' She said it a half dozen times, so she did."

A patch of sunshine opened up over Howth. I had been wrong about the tide. It was coming in.

"The McDonalds there in Clondalkin, across from Dunnes?"

"Bad idea, Ma. Too many eyes out there."

My feet had taken on a mind of their own. They were pawing the stones, like a dog,

"So where will I tell her to meet you then?"

"Who said I was going along with this?"

The long pause was Ma's best card. Eventually, she spoke.

"Are you still there, Tommy?"

"Look, Ma. We're mad busy at work. OK?"

"Just ten minutes would do it. That's all. Any place really."

Some coffee place, was all I could come up with. Somewhere out of the way. That place that Sonia liked, the one I'd noticed the other day was open still.

"There must be a place you have in mind so. Is there?"

I closed my eyes and drew a slow, calming breath. Your Ma's your Ma. That was the be-all and end-all of it.

"There's a café. Firenza it's called. It's in Rathmines."

"Fir what? And why Rathmines?"

"That's the whole point, Ma. Firenza, OK? Ten minutes, tell her. Ten – not a second longer."

And that was that. I stopped well short of the lighthouse and headed back to the car park.

Nothing registered with me as I drove back into town. Not that fierce spooky no-man's land by the Pigeon House with the god-awful stink of sewerage hanging over it, with those freaky sound effects from the generating station coming up through the ground at you. Not even Dear Old Dirty Dublin's famous two-fingered salute to the universe, the huge striped-sock painted chimneys looming up over the road like they were aiming to collapse on you. That conversation with Ma kept nibbling away at my brain. Tony Cummins making an approach to a copper? It just didn't make sense. He was old school to the extreme. You could put him in a crime museum, nearly. If anyone would know the consequences, it'd be Tony Cummins. He'd be a goner if word got out, in prison or out.

*   *   *

Back at the apartment I put the shower to needle-power. To hell with the Cumminses, each and every one of them. I had an appointment this evening, and nothing was going to get in the way of it. Seven years come and gone? There was no getting around it. We'd found Terry huddled in a doorway the back of Abbey Street. You'd have thought he was just nodding out. His face was still blue when we got to him. He couldn't have been gone long. Terry was one of the first of the fentanyl overdoses, a distinction of sorts. Which had left me a distinction of my own. I was now a Detective Sergeant in the Drugs Squad with a brother dead of an overdose.

I had three sausages left over from yesterday. They'd work OK with the day before's spaghetti. Waiting for the microwave, my eyes strayed again to the boxes stacked by the wall. Still pristine in their IKEA cardboard coffins. Still giving off that IKEA stink. Still waiting for me every evening. I pushed away from the table and took my plate to the counter. A second beer would help things along? No. Later, maybe. Today was different.

I finished the spaghetti and looked around for the bag with my gear for the cemetery. Unsurprisingly, it was where I had left it this morning. It felt heavier this year, somehow.

I took my time. I always aimed for the end of the day, just before they close the gates. It was a mental trick, of course. It let me off the hook: sorry Terry, I've got to go–they're closing the place up. Half an hour did the job anyway. I figured on Pacman taking between three and four minutes–if the battery didn't do something weird like last year. It was the identical Pacman that we started out with a million years ago. I still had Avenger and Mario too. Mario was Terry's favourite for ages. I usually brought the DS with me as well, for backup. I could nearly donate it to a museum at this stage.

By the time I was parking next the cemetery, that dull ache in my chest had turned sharp. I hunted around the glove compartment for paper hankies. Then out I got and hefted the bag, and made for the gate.

A powerful whiff of lilac mingled with the dusty, metallic smell you got before rain. The sight of fresh grave loaded up with flowers and wreaths gave me a jolt. The usual doubts commenced their parade. This ritual was just plain weird. Morbid. A form of denial? How many more years would I carry on with it anyway?

I pushed on.

I didn't need to be a highly-trained Garda detective to notice the figure hanging around at a semi-discreet distance, and keeping pace with me. I'd ignore Mr. Christopher Cullinane until I was good and ready. It took time to work up a charitable frame of mind. This was the same Christy who had nearly derailed the funeral. The minute I'd seen him, I'd lost the rag. The gall of that junkie bastard to show up? Talk about out of order. I remembered him running like a starving greyhound, and me sort of admiring the fact that he could run that fast.

We both knew there'd be no re-runs of that. It was mainly Ma's doing. The first Christmas after, Christy had left a box of chocolates and a card at the door, and very wisely made himself scarce. I was not one bit impressed, though. I still wanted to burst him, in actual fact. While I said my piece concerning where Christy could put his chocolates, Ma just stared at the window. Then she got up and walked away.

I came out to the house a few days later to be met with a peculiar sight entirely. The party now cocked up at the kitchen table with a cup of tea in front of him? A nice big plate of Mikados to graze on? Sitting where Terry used to sit? You could hear a pin drop. Ma executed a longish version of her staring at the window routine. I stared hard at Christy. Christy stared at the table. And?

And nothing. We talked about the Eurovision, as I recall.

Later on, Ma asked me if I knew that Christy dreamt about Terry every single night. That he cried every time too? Did I know that Christy had thought of doing away with himself? And – did I think God didn't care about Christy, or people like Christy? These were not questions.

Seven years. Seven.

Making my way over to the big marble yoke next to Terry's I perched on a corner of it. Ma's angel-with-the rosary-hanging-off-it item needed a cleaning. I could feel Christy's eyes burning on my back but I didn't care. The scent of lilac was heavy in the warm evening air. I looked around the graveyard. The light had gone soft, all right.

Out came the Nintendo. I turned the sound right down. I got my little miracle then: all the way to level IV without it crapping out on me. As usual, I could barely get the words out.

"All right Terry. It's your go now."

2

Those monkeys – lemurs? That's what Christy's eyes reminded me of. That leather jacket oh his, it was definitely new. He took it off and pulled his shirt sleeve up to his elbow.

"Four years– four. Not bad, hah? Even if I do so say so myself."

God knows I was trying, but Christy's face, his voice even, gave me a tired feeling.

"Fair play to you, man."

He looked away, trying to hide his smile.

"Look, here's for the flowers."

He eyed at the hundred like it was a miracle at Lourdes.

"Christ, Tommy, I couldn't. No way, man. God, no."

"Just take it, will you. And don't be arguing with me. Eh, no speeches either. All right?"

He winced in a show of reluctance and placed the money reverently in his pocket.

"Straight to the bank, Tommy. Every last penny."

"Every cent, you mean. And you know the banks are bust, right?"

The smile came as a leer. Teeth like baked beans.

For some reason then, my gaze stayed on Christy. Maybe it was the end-of-day quiet or the soft, late evening light. It might even have had something to do with that scent of privet and lilac you get everywhere this time of year. Or maybe it was knowing that Christy could leave here, but that Terry could not.

"Question for you Christy. Remember the Cumminses?"

The smile faded, but he was determined to square up.

"You mean the Cumminses Cumminses?"

"Them's the ones. More Gary though. You know Gary, right?"

"Well Jaysus Tommy, I mean who doesn't know Gary."

"So what do you know?"

Christy frowned and screwed up his eyes.

"Have you seen Gary lately, is what I mean."

He batted away the question with a quick shake of his head.

"What? Big nothing? Little nothing? Or nothing, like I'm-not-saying nothing?"

"Nothing, Tommy. Not, a, bleeding, thing."

I mustered my offended look and waited.

"Sorry Tommy, but come on. Things is dodgy enough these days."

"You know Gary's Ma, right? Mrs. Cummins?"

"Bernie, yeah." He nodded several times. "Tell you one thing. She's a saint, that woman."

My sarcastic eyebrow lift earned me a sly grin.

"But that's the way isn't it," he said "It's the fathers are the sinners. Right?"

"What about Jennifer. Usen't you have a thing for her?"

It was like Christy had been asked his opinion on a bad smell.

"Are you joking me, Tommy?"

"So you did, then. Still do, maybe?"

"God no! Tons of lads had the hots for her, not just me."

Something resembling regret crossed his face. He wrinkled his nose again and looked up at the trees for inspiration. The evening light had turned them mysterious-looking.

"Sure, she's married for ages," he went on. "Jenn is. But she was never a real Cummins like. That was the mother's doing. She made Jenn immune, or something. Ha ha."

"Who's the hub? Jennifer's?"

"Oh I don't know. But I hear she has a nice family thing going now. Somewhere out the North County. Nice big house, all that fresh air and all. Well away from the likes of us riff-raff."

He awarded himself another laugh. I slid the sacred Gameboy back into my bag. A caretaker had caught my eye.

"Better split or they'll keep us here all night, ha ha."

We walked on. May made you forget how crap the Januarys and Februarys were. The freezing pipes, the feeling that anything was liable to turn on you.

"How long did he get anyway, Tommy? Tony C, I mean."

I told him I wasn't sure.

"There's plenty did worse though," Christy said.

"So maybe he wasn't stabbing people in the street. That doesn't mean he's not a bad article."

Christy looked left and right before leaning in.

"Come on Tommy. He's nothing like what Darren was. Seriously? Got to admit."

"Jaysus sakes, Christy. You don't inherit things from your kids. It's the other way around, man."

He drew back and bugged out his eyes and performed a slow, pantomime version of injecting himself. All right: an exposition of how Tony Cummins' male offspring had lost the run of themselves.

"I'll tell you one thing," he said then. "It gets you thinking about karma, and that's a fact."

"Karma. Karma what?"

"Bernie Cummins, is what. Good-living, decent, not a bad bone in her body? But then there's, you know, her husband. So you'd be asking yourself, how does that happen. Right?"

A bird began screeching. We were at the gate now. The last of the daylight wasn't so weak that I couldn't see fresh bird-shit on my Golf. Then I saw the motorbike parked a bit behind. I slipped my hand inside my jacket and felt around for the Sig.

"You like?"

My heartbeats had migrated to my throat. I had to remember to breathe. I stopped looking up and down the avenue. The bike wasn't that big really. It was more your rough-and-tough model, for crossing Africa in the one day, or something. Not a getaway sports bike, at any rate.

"That's yours, that yoke?"

"A big Ten Four there. A beast entirely, I'm telling you. This yoke, it'd take you up The Spike, so it would. Near enough like."

The smile took years off Christy. I imagined him racing up the Spire, all three hundred-and-something foot of it. Christy, cheered on by multitudes of fans in O Connell Street. Christy, my brother's pal. But my copper brain had no off switch. New leather jacket? New (looking) motorbike? He was in better financial order than I'd have thought. But I wouldn't be asking. Part of me needed to go on imagining that he was clean still.

"I do go up the mountains on it," he went on. "Honest to God – I swear. Nature, the environment – all that. That's what I'm into now. No more wrong turns. Cul-de-sacs. Get it?"

Wrong turns. I'd have plenty of time to think about that. I'd have too much time, actually. Time to tell myself that what happened afterward wasn't down to me being careless or preoccupied or stressed out. Wasn't there a thing called free will? So what happened after – I tried to tell myself – was Christy's choice to make. A hundred euro wasn't a huge amount of money. It was only for luck really, for old times' sakes. Let the gods smile on Christy – that was my thinking.

Nope. The truth, the cold hard truth, was that it was me being a copper. Doing the things that a copper did. I knew the money'd make Christy feel that he had to pony up something in return. To show me that he had his act together and that he could hold up his end too – even if he didn't want to.

I watched him open the ugly-looking tin box bolted on the back of the bike and take out a helmet. I really, really didn't like seeing people with motorbike helmets on anywhere near me. A lot of Guards have the same aversion.

Christy lifted his visor to give me the eye.

"I've got your number. Ha ha. Your mobile, I mean."

My mind had emptied. Then I remembered. Gary Cummins, he meant.

Back at the apartment I sank three cans of Fosters. Only the one Jameson, though it was a bit more than it should've been. It was Shark Week on Discovery? I was out the moment I'd hit the pillow. I'd stayed that way until the alarm too. That hadn't happened in months. Did that mean –

So much for my stab at mindfulness.

I was still in Rathmines. Still sitting in my car. Still half-addled. I tried again to put some shape on things. OK, Tony Cummins's missus wanted to talk to me. Bernadette Cummins, 'Bernie,' my Ma's best pal from all the way back to Primary. Long before marriage, long before they'd gone out working or had families of their own. Long before the adult woes and tribulations came looking for them. Bernie who, even in this day and age, apparently went to Mass every day. The obvious question? How come Holy Bernie was still married to the man who was at one time one of Dublin's biggest gangsters?

I checked my phone. Nothing from Ma or from Bernie Cummins to say call it off. No email from Midnight either, my contact in Oz. Midnight, aka ex-Garda Kevin Earley, who was a big part of my Plan B. Not even one of those stupid emails Macker sends around. Slipping my mobile back into my pocket, my fingers brushed against the envelope again. Another sly poke from Destiny, I wondered.

I took the letter out. I really should've left it at home – but I'd been saying that ever since I'd gotten it. I pretty-well knew the contents by heart anyway. It wasn't the full report, but it should have been enough for me anyway. Exonerated. Sometimes, the more you look at a word, the stranger that word becomes in your mind. 'That Day In Dalkey' – right. The shrink, she nailed me on that right away. Not 'the shooting,' or 'the murder' – no: 'that day.' It gave me the pip the way she harped on about it, though. But I didn't let on.

I was still patchy on that day, actually. Odd things stayed. Smells: burning rubber, cordite, diesel exhaust. Colours: white faces, a sky the colour of dirty water. The blinding blue dazzle of the arrays. That bright red stain crawling down the door panel. The Sig that I'd unholstered and half-wedged under my calf, how it flew off into the wheel-well when I'd hit the curb. That sudden crush of knowing that hit like a straight punch to the sternum. The motorbike I'd seen speeding toward town earlier? It must have been the pair who had decided that, if that was Detective Garda Malone's car, it had to be Malone behind the wheel, and their payday for doing a number on him had arrived. 'Doing a number' – right. Killing him.

There were things burned into my mind that I couldn't even have seen that day. I'd thought about that a fair bit since. I knew that brains weren't cameras, or recorders. An out-of-body type of thing? That was too airy-fairy for me. They had to be my version of what the Emergency Response lads were probably saying to themselves as they piled out of their Volvo, ready for World War Three. *OK, lads. We have some head-case armed with a pistol and waving a Garda card, running around shouting like a lunatic.*

Another thing was the quiet. For all the shouting and the sirens, it had been so quiet in my mind. Quiet enough to imagine I could hear someone murmuring the same phrase over and over again.

Will they shoot me, won't they shoot me.

Will they shoot me, won't they shoot me.

They – the investigation team – had thrown tons of man hours at the case. They'd homed in on one of the two they reckoned had been on the motorbike only to have him disappear. It was looking more and more like he'd been made to disappear, and permanently. The other prime had been taken in for questioning five times now. There was no give in him, not one bit. I wasn't supposed to be privy to details, but a little dickey bird had told me that at least the phone taps were still on. Also, they'd found the hours to keep a 24-hour surveillance for another few weeks yet.

Repeat: exoneration. But it wasn't enough. It'd never be enough. I knew what people were thinking: *no way Dalkey just happened out of the blue. It had to be that Joey D business earlier.* Joey D, the criminal mastermind who literally couldn't tie his own shoelaces? The Joey D who tripped over his own laces while I was chasing him across a roof, and took a flyer and landed twenty feet below on his thick, doomed head? Didn't it count that I was cleared for that? The fact that it took less than ten minutes at the Ombudsman's that morning? To any normal copper that should mean one thing – they'd known right from the start that it was an open-and-shut misadventure.

But a dismissal didn't stop tongues wagging. There were coppers -decent, conscientious coppers too – who inclined to the notion that I'd thrown Joey D. off that roof for a reason – to shut him up. That, in their minds, was to allow Garda Malone to keep his operation rolling along. Not just Malone's operation – but the gangster pals he was shielding as well, the self-same blokes he grew up with. You grow up in Crumlin in a 'broken home,' and that was enough for some people. Heaving with gangbangers, right?

I sometimes regretted not kicking up a fuss when I got the heave from the unit I was working at the time. There was no direct mention of the Joey D thing. No, I had 'drawn attention to operations.' Should I've gotten on the blower to the Association? Maybe. Trust is everything. For a copper, it's the only thing. I had to take the long view, to bide my time and wait for things to settle. Lately though, I'd been feeling a wobble. Who hadn't, the way things were going. I'd begun thinking the unthinkable, of just jacking it in and starting fresh – in Oz. Me, the last man in Dublin you'd expect to be making a bee line for the airport. There's a thousand ways to go mad they say. In trying hard not to think about doing a bunk to Oz, I might have found mine.

I looked down Rathmines Road. Empty: thank you very much, financial crisis. Yes, I'd have been over the canal by now, at Christchurch even, maybe even in sight of the quays. Well on the way to where I really should be, back in that manky, stale-fart saturated, unmarked Mondeo next to Macker.

Days away from the raid and we were still short-handed. The months of planning, the man-hours – in Spain and Holland too – and we were still scrambling for bodies to fill the watch shifts. Operation Condor: a bird of prey that swoops down for the kill. The Spanish coppers got to pick it. Our end had twenty-seven suspects targeted. Some collection they were too: nationals from five EU countries, two from the Middle East, three Africans. Bad eggs entirely, every man jack of them. A sort of a mad United Nations come-all-ye.

And killing people was nothing to this crowd. Europol had eleven murders down to them, and as many and more attempted. They put this outfit's share of the drug trade at in-or-around six hundred million in the past year alone. They imported from Mexico and from Colombia and – I still wondered if this was a massive spoof – they even dealt with the Taliban. What was really

17

giving us the willies was intel that they had gotten two Mac 10s and a half dozen AK 47s into Ireland. So there was a lot of moving parts to this operation. Everything had to line up. But how likely was that, these days? Europol, when it worked, was the eighth wonder of the world, but if someone missed a gear along the chain, there was a lot could go wrong, and fast.

Yet here I was this fine May morning about to give time that I didn't have to the wife of a gangster? Who, despite Ma's massively naïve assurances, was in no position to guarantee that us finding her missing waster of a son would make her husband willing to play ball with us?

No, I decided. This was pure madness. Who was to say that this 'little chat' wasn't an out-and-out set-up or a trap of some kind, or a diversion? I wasn't thinking straight yesterday when I'd agreed to this. Distracted, preoccupied, stressed-out – whatever. Maybe a touch of the old self-sabotage rigmarole back in action. Something to bring up again with the shrink.

I jammed the key back into the ignition and clicked in my belt. About five seconds later, I took the key back out. It wasn't about keeping my word to my Ma. Ma'd get over it. I was pretty sure too that Bernie Cummins – if that thin, pale woman perched by one of the tables inside that Firenza gaff really was her – hadn't seen me cruising past. Even if she had, so what? I'd broken a promise to meet her? The wife of a has-been gangster? I could live with that.

What stopped me was something else. It was that bloke with her, her minder. Maybe Bernie Cummins hadn't seen me, but he had. He'd better have – that was his job. He had at least made mental note of someone slowly driving by and looking in the window of the café. He might even have had a picture of me to go on. Dublin gangsters are nothing if not resourceful. I didn't have a name on that wide, lumpy-faced git but immediately I saw him, I knew. If you were wearing a bomber jacket in May, in Ireland, weather was not your concern. So, if I was going to walk away, that would've counted as another failure.

I released my seat belt and closed my eyes and took a long, slow breath. I was still cursing when I heaved myself out of the car.

3

A foreign-looking woman appeared to be running the show here. Her slow murmured conversation faltered while she tracked me making my way down between the tables.

In front of Bernie Cummins was what looked like half of a flat white. There was something odd about her face. Her greeting, if I could've call it that, was a flutter of the lips and a raising and lowering of eyebrows. I drew in a chair.

"Ah Tommy. Thanks very much. Long time and all. How are you?"

"Not too bad thanks, Mrs. Cummins."

I stole a quick close-up as she shifted on her chair. She definitely looked shook. Her skin was a strange colour. If it was make-up doing that, it belonged in Madame Tussaud's. And if she had spent money on that strange-looking hair, that was more money wasted too.

"Yes," she said, pausing to swallow, "thanks for coming. You're great."

I swiveled another look Lug-face's way. The flat eyes looked painted on, dummy eyes with nothing coming through from behind. A bit of a cliché in my line of work, but not to be underestimated all the same.

"Mrs. Cummins. This fella here. He's with you, is he?"

"Well yes. Tony likes him to, you know, help out."

I turned to Lug-face.

"Go be helpful somewhere else then. Out of earshot, like?"

His eyes skipped between Bernie Cummins and me and he looked away. Orders came from Tony, no doubt. She shifted in her seat again.

"I don't mean to be rude now," she said. "But Gerry takes his responsibilities to heart. He's very protective. To a fault, like."

'Gerry.' I considered telling Bernie Cummins to pull the other one. To wit, that I'd bet a week's pay that her 'Gerry' here was currently in possession of a firearm. Thus and therefore, he'd get ten plus for that. More to the point, she'd be up the creek as well.

"Mrs. Cummins? Any talk is between you and me. This fella here is a spoiler. "

She rubbed at the tip of her nose. Gerry slid his eyes back toward her. Something off Discovery Channel, I thought. The eyes of some deep-sea creature gliding over the sea-bed.

"It's okay Gerry," she said then. "Really. I'll be grand. Honest I will."

His parting message was a long slow blink. I noted the twitchy hand as he walked away. In case I missed that, he issued a reminder on his way to the door – a half-hearted kick at one of the stools. The woman on the phone looked from me to Bernadette Cummins and back.

"All business, Tommy. Fair enough." This observation she directed at her cup. She was trying to smile, and failing." Your Ma's so proud of you. Honest to God, so proud."

The manager-woman was preparing to head over to take an order, biting her lip and holding her breath. I waved her off.

"Mrs. Cummins? Just so's you know. I'm not applying for a job here."

She flexed her eyebrows and eyed her half-gone coffee. Through the window I saw that Gerry had found his spot on the footpath outside. He might have a belly on him, all right, but he'd still be bad news if he got in close. I teased up the sleeve of my jacket to check my watch.

"I appreciate your situation," she said. "This is about Gary."

"Gary, your son."

"It's too much for us, what's going on. It's too much."

I'd never be in the running for a Nobel Peace Prize, but at this point I possibly earned one. Proof of that was in what I did not say to Bernie Cummins there and then.

Bernie baby? Son number one was a violent, sadistic criminal. Son number two is a wash-out, a criminal. And now you come crying to the Guards because he maybe got what the universe wants him to get?

"Darren," she said, drawing a breath, "that was bad. Very bad. It couldn't be worse, I used to think. Not a word of a lie, it nearly killed us, what happened."

The phrase thudded in my head. 'Happened.' Did this woman go around with a box on her head? Things just 'happened' in her world? I noted a tremor as she hoisted her gaze from the cup.

"But it is," she whispered. "It's worse."

My brain stuttered trying to recall how long ago Darren Cummins had met his maker.

"It's hitting us very, very hard," she added. "My husband too, like."

And now I thought: my God, this woman, she played my Ma like a Stradivarius. Just then, as though she had a side line in mind rearing too, she looked up.

"I need to tell you something first," she said. "Tony knows we're having this little chat. He said to make sure that I told you that early on. So's you'd know."

I half-closed my eyes to try to hide any show of interest. A thought dropped back into my mind: OK then, here we go. We have now hit part b) of the set-up – the bait.

She was waiting for a response. Her gaze had sharpened up, I noted.

"You're telling me that he's OK with us talking here. Your husband, like."

"That's right," she said. "And Tony wants you to know something else too. That he never, ever had anything to do with what happened to your brother, to Terry. Never."

The 'never' clanged in my mind like saucepans falling down concrete steps. I thought right away: them pills again. Another side effect. They had to go, they just had to.

"Really? Once upon a time, there was a little Duck and his name was Donald."

"Tommy, really. On my word."

"And Donald's best friend was called Goofy."

"Tony is wholeheartedly for this chat," she said, firmly. "Totally, I'm telling you. We need help, is what I'm saying. Me and Tony, we need help."

I gave the café a long, slow, sour survey. It wasn't that bad of a place really. I should just get over this nag I had for the whole fancy coffee thing. The waitress / owner / manager was back on her phone, but she was watching us too.

"For Gary," Bernie Cummins said. "For finding Gary, I mean."

"Phone the Guards, Mrs. Cummins. The Garda Help Line."

"But we need the kind of help that'll get results."

"You could try Crime Call too. Put up posters..."

Her eyes lost the little spark they had had.

"I think you know what I mean, Tommy."

A bus took its time going by. Something about the resigned looks on peoples' faces there reminded me that I needed to cop on here. Because I now had a fight on my hands. Here before me, meek and washed-out looking, sat my Ma's childhood friend. Her lifelong friend. And yes, another Ma who had lost her son. And Ma, she never asked for much.

But I couldn't just give in.

"Listen, Mrs. Cummins -"

"- Bernie, please. Call me Bernie."

"Mrs. Cummins. Listen to me. I am the exact wrong person for you. You mightn't know this, but some of the people I work with, they imagine things. It's to do with my background."

"They look at you twice because you're Crumlin-reared." The faint smile only made her look more wrecked. "But I'm not asking you personally, Tommy. No, no."

"I don't get it. Why am I here then?"

"I'm only – we're only, I should say – asking you to see what can be done to find Gary, and to let them know that we're so worried and all that, and..."

She ran out of harmless-sounding words that don't say death, or kill, or murder.

"You're asking me to make sure that Missing Persons is doing its job?"

She looked out the window as though to reassure Lug-face aka Gerry that she wasn't in danger.

"We want Gary back," she said. "We need him back. That's all that matters to us."

Maybe she thought I was thick, because she didn't wait long to follow up.

"And I'm telling you, Tony's on board. You know what that means, I'm sure."

'On board.' I looked her in the eye but she looked by me.

A couple came in the door of the café. The way Gerry was staring through the glass at them it was a wonder that their backs weren't on fire. Watching them dithering about where to sit gave me time to think, though. I had a bad feeling about this. It was a cod, a well-rehearsed, well-thought-out cod. It was coming from a smart, shrewd woman who'd stayed married to a gangster. A Bernie Cummins that my Ma, God help her, could probably never guess at.

"Approaching the Guards is his idea. That's what you're telling me?"

A bit of life came back into her eyes.

"Not 'the Guards' – you. He says, if you want to chat with him, that's OK. You only, mind."

Her matter-of-fact tone only made it weirder. All I could muster was a blank look.

"You know where Tony is, I'm sure. He's not one to bellyache now, but there's always pressure. Pressure from different quarters." She turned a hazy look on me." People at odds with him, people who'd be looking for an opening. And it happens, doesn't it? The wrong people get put together at the wrong time. The 'scheduling errors?'"

I saw her fail to hide a grimace. A sharp intake of breath followed. She sat very still. When she spoke again, each word came slowly and carefully as though squeezed under a door.

"People think strange things, things about my husband. Stories get put out, all kinds of yarns, about so-and-so talking to someone else. The trouble is, them rumours going around, nobody cares if they're true or not. Right?"

"Sounds to me you know a lot about the inside of a prison."

Unkind, I knew. But it didn't seem to register with her.

"So here we are," she said. "We'd appreciate your help."

My anger had been coming to a slow boil. First the set-up, now the sting. Did they actually take me for such a gobshite?

"Tell me something, Mrs. Cummins. The wire – is it hard to fit? Is it itchy?"

Her eyes narrowed in confusion.

"But maybe it's not your first time. With a wire, I mean."

"What wire?"

"You know that I'm reporting this. This approach."

"My approach?"

"As an attempted bribery of a Garda officer."

I even knew the proper name of the charge to – Prevention of Corruption Act. It had come up in the Sergeants' test.

She sat upright and frowned at me. For the first time, she appeared shocked.

"Here's the thing, Mrs. Cummins. I've been telling you things, see? Now, you appeared to be listening, but I don't know if you actually heard me. So I'll tell you again. I'm not Tommy somebody, whose Ma is an old pal of yours. I'm Garda Detective Sergeant Malone."

"But it's not that," she said. "It's not that at all, no."

"It's not what?"

"No, no," she said again, and she raised her hand in protest. "It's not for you, not personally, no. This can be for everyone's benefit. Everyone, yes."

Something gave way then. I just laughed. It was a real laugh too, the kind I hadn't had for a long, long time. The couple just arrived began eyeing us big-time. The one behind the counter muttered into the phone like she was a ventriloquist, but her eyes remained locked on me.

Oddly, Bernie Cummins didn't seem put out.

"All right," I told her. "Let me make a guess. Criminal Assets are parked in your kitchen. They're putting the heavy word on you. So you know you're bunched. That's why we're having our chat here. Right?"

"I don't know anything about criminal assets."

I wanted to laugh at this one too, but I couldn't.

"Look," she said. Her frown cut deeper. "That's what I'm saying. I – we, we're not trying to give you anything personally like. It's just that Tony says, anything has to come through you, anything he might have to say. Nobody else, just you."

"So he agreed with you getting in touch with my Ma."

"Well not exactly."

"'Not exactly' means what, Mrs. Cummins?"

"It was Tony's idea in the first place. He remembered you."

It felt like everything had suddenly been hoovered out of the space between us.

"We want Gary back. Even if he has to go to jail. We can't take this, we just can't."

Her words hung in the air a while.

"So Tony's ready," she added. "All you have to do is ask."

My full-bore stare wasn't enough to stop her gaze veering away. She looked very shook now. Now I understood why her face looked odd earlier. It wasn't just the pallor. Where her eyebrows were supposed to be, there was just skin.

As hard as Lug-face was staring, it felt he was looking through me too. That look was all too familiar. I used to think it was hatred plain and simple, but after meeting enough like the Gerry model here, I realized there was something else to it. It held a specific message. If it came to the crunch, it said, it wouldn't matter a good God-damn to him whether I was a copper or not.

Bernie Cummins had settled a stare on a portion of wall. Our meeting, our 'chat,' was over.

She rose slowly, pausing twice before straightening up. Lug-Face Gerry held open the door for her, his marine-creature stare clamped on me all the while. I noted how carefully she walked through the doorway. In my mind I played out the little speech that I could've, possibly should've, recited. *Listen here to me now, Mrs. Cummins. A word to the wise. If what you told me here is true, and it's not some stitch-up or a scam, you won't be dictating how this goes. And that washed-up jail bird husband of yours won't either.*

I was wrong about that, very wrong. I wouldn't have long to wait for that revelation to land on me either.

4

Meanwhile, I had made my re-entry back into the real world. I was back in Macker-Land, back across from the rat-run known as e Breffni. Back to that state of ... 'mindful boredom' was the nearest I could get.

Sergeants didn't do surveillance detail of course, but Delaney, my C.O., had O.K.ed it. Circumstances, he called it. But coppers are paid to be suspicious, so I kept a few items handy for any who didn't 100% buy into a short-staffing line. I was out here, I'd say, to get a feel for street-level action again. Or: I wasn't cut out for desk work eight, ten hours a day. Really, so much of the job now was screens and forms and meetings, with a phone stuck to your ear for so long it felt like you'd scraped the side of your head along a brick wall. Yes, pulling a watch shift was part of 'getting back to basics.' 'Sharing the load.' 'Back at the coal face.' They'd dampen down the brain nicely, I figured. Just the ticket to keep conversations moving in the right direction.

What I wouldn't say: I needed out of the Unit office as much as I bloody-well could. Why was because I didn't want to have to keep ignoring stuff there. The looks. The calculated silences. Plus, there had been too many near-misses there. It had been the same bollocks stirring the pot both times – Walshie. I ended up squaring up to him. Told him to straight-out admit it had been him retailing sly remarks about my Joey D troubles and – worse – the Dalkey issue. Bare-faced denied it, he did. Even had the gall to try out his warped sense of humour on me. I was ready for wigs on the green. It was a close-run thing.

Yet even if I'd gone and knocked seven shades out of him, that wouldn't have done much. The problem was, it wasn't just the likes of Walshie who were suspicious. There were brass who wanted me nailed, and if I couldn't be nailed, they wanted me o.u.t. They'd be looking for some way to do it. I wouldn't see it coming either.

All-in-all, much easier on the old nerves to be sitting eyeing the comings-and-goings at the Breffni aka 'The Breffni House Boutique Hotel.' Truth be told, it took us way too long to cop on to how much was going on in the kip. It was a shining example of how things had gone here the past decade. Of how brazen the gangsters had gotten. How crime had gone international. How much money was in the drug trade now. Right under our noses too. Plain-and-simple, we had overlooked the gaff.

There was more than enough going on here on Dorset St. already. The flats and the B and Bs and the guest houses used be chock-full of people of every colour and creed. The languages, the food, the music – all wafting about in the air. Nice. But all the while, Breffni quietly became a port-of-call for every slag, blag and scumbag. Prostitution aka 'the sex trade,' fencing, rent-a-gun – any of those would have been cause enough to have a task force on the place. But the big reason we were here was the drug trade. The Breffni had become a clearing house, one that we were about to nail via Operation Condor.

"We're well on the way now, Skip. Oh yes. Am I right, or am I right?"

Macker and his wind-ups. He sighed, and he began to unkink himself. Bamboozler-in-chief, I called Macker. Well on the way to what, I was supposed to ask. I never did. 'Well on the way' was probably his favourite. Either that or 'business as usual.' All the insane stuff that was coming out – the dodgy banks, the child abuse, the brown envelopes – each and every new scandal? Ah, 'business as usual.' Or, 'we're well on the way.' And repeat. It was like singing Lanigan's Ball: you could make up the words as you went along.

He'd been doing his 'little people' routine more lately. It wasn't the fairies he was talking about, of course. It was us – we were the little people. Us mugs like, the ones getting it in the neck. The law-abiding iijits still paying the bills. The ones with the hours cut and the mad commutes to bogland, out to jerry-built homes that every day were worth less than the insane mortgages hanging around our necks. With the new levies and fees and taxes and surcharges. The ones with the stunned looks on their faces gawking out through the

Departures gates, watching their kids leave. *Them* ones.

Macker didn't come across angry, or bitter. Everybody else might be like that bloke in the film, the one who taps the brakes and – oh-oh – there's no brakes! Not Macker. Like David bloody Attenborough he was, yammering on in that sing-song voice of his about the flora and fauna. Talk about spoiled for choice. The banksters, of course: alcoholics left in charge of the brewery. Clicking keyboards and strutting about in thousand Euro suits. Hand-in-glove with the other poster-boys for the crash, of course, our so-called developers, the spivs and wasters who'd left ghost estates full of half-finished houses all over the place to rot away in the rain.

Not to mention the huge supporting cast and crew. Talk about spoiled for choice. The legions of back-scratchers, all nod-and-wink, say-no-more and whatever-you're-having-yourself. All looking the other way. The TDs and their packs of cute-hoor cronies, snouts at the trough and creaming it like billy-o. The jumped-up nobodies in useless semi-state outfits, busy as beavers filing expenses and lining up for bonuses. PR spoofers and consultants spinning their PowerPoints and catch-phrases for daw-brains further up the greasy pole. Accountants who couldn't account. Auditors who couldn't audit. All the valuers and the estate agents and the advertisers and the witless media smilers and know-it-all – even the tall foreheads in the universities. All massive experts to beat the band. *Mar dheá.* Sure, we'll be grand, was the order of the day. We're great little country, all right. World-class. Punch above our weight. Smoke-and-daggers? That wasn't the half of it. But now? M.I.A. All gone to ground, deep into the keep-the-head-down and the divil take the hindmost mode.

Hence Macker wheeling out his 'little people' routine. The wolves were circling closer? Help was on the way. Our sturdy stalwarts the little people to the rescue. They'd put manners on them. And it'd be the little people who'd carry the can for whatever Frankfurt or Brussels or New York wanted too. Not a bother on them – the backbone of the country, the little people were. There was nothing they couldn't do. Or, as Macker liked to say when he'd reach the end of a sermon – it was all magic. Little people magic.

He'd deliver his sermons in slow, murmured recitations, with the faraway look of a man in a trance. Other times, he'd launch his riddle-type talk with a battery of sly, leading questions thrown in for good measure. He reminded me for all the world of a veteran wig, slowly nailing a witness in cross-examination with innocuous-sounding questions and pleasant little observations.

But sometimes Macker's calmness was downright unnatural. Freaky, actually. *Macker,* I wanted to shout – *just let it rip, will you? Come on man, it's die dog or eat the hatchet here now. We all know the country's gone to the wall. So just get it off your chest for the love of God!*

Maybe that's what he was hoping for. Or maybe it was just Macker playing Macker mind games. One thing I was sure of: there was a lot going on in that noggin of his. Anyway. Hardly a wonder why nobody wanted to do watch shifts with him.

"Right..." he paused to work through a yawn. "OK, right. Today's episode. You ready, Skip? Audi people. Audi drivers, like."

Saying nothing remained my policy. It hadn't worked yet.

"Are they a different species, you reckon? A lost tribe maybe? Or is it maybe more an SUV thing per se... Who can say. But that's the burning issue for today."

The screen on his phone was so cracked that I kept looking at the cracks more than the video. It was his daughter's old iPhone, not even a year old. How could it be 'old?' I'd overheard her talking to him once. A proper little bitch, she sounded.

"Exhibit A, your honour. The M50, yesterday. The Dundrum exit, I do believe, but feel free to correct me there. Anyway. Watch."

There was a white van and a red SUV, an Audi. Said Audi had apparently barged into the exit line. The van driver, a hefty-looking item, got out of the van. Whoever was taking the video said 'oh shite!' Van Man walked briskly up to the back passenger door of the Audi and, without so much as a by-your-leave, took a good hard kick at it. Somebody laughed like a monkey.

"A nice how-do-you-do, isn't it? What's the world coming to at all, at all. Now that there happens to be a Q7 Audi. Panel work, we're talking, five, six hundred easy. OK now – watch."

Audi Man slid smoothly out from behind the wheel. He left his door open. A trim-looking bloke, well put together and suspiciously light on his feet. I noted how he held down his tie as he walked unhurriedly toward the van. He didn't seem at all angry. It was more a preoccupied look. Accountant, I wondered. Barrister. Doctor?

"Watch, Skipper – watch. You don't want to miss this."

And of course I missed it. 'Jaysus!' shouted somebody. 'Did you see that?'

Van Man was now surfacing about ten feet from where I'd last seen him. Macker rubbed his hands together like he was trying to start a fire.

"Locked horns with the wrong fella there, didn't he?"

I checked the volume on the hand-set.

"So now, Skipper. We're the polis, are we not. And therein lies the conundrum, and it is this: what do we do? Section 6 the pair of them? Ding Van man alone, for assault? What?"

"First thing you do is turn that shite off. Jaysus."

Macker leaned against the door and put on a theatrical face.

"Let's say Van Man wants his straightener. Normal reaction, right? So he goes and he grabs hold of a hammer or something, and out he goes and creases Audi Man with it. Now what do you say?"

What to say? *Macker, how do they say shut up in your language?*

"You and Einstein, Macker. Honest to God, I don't know which one of you is cleverer."

A move across the street rescued the situation. Unless the bloke departing the Breffni had an identical twin, wearing identical gear, he was the same bloke who had entered the Breffni not long ago. After I checked the time and logged it, I called the camera man. It was Clancy. We were still using use our mobiles on the job. Four years after it was hailed as the Second Coming, the digital radio network still dropped out in way too many places.

"Already on the way." Uploading, Clancy meant. "Wait a sec, lad. Which folder do ye want it in?"

"What do you mean which folder?"

"Ugly bastard folder? Ugly-as-sin..? Dirty-looking ugly..."

Clancy could be a howl, all right. I had to put this on speaker. After a good bit of over-and-back, we settled on one: fierce dirty-looking ugly low-down fat-face skanger hairy-arsed bastard… section. Macker gave off one of his tinny laughs and went back to his phone, chortling quietly every now and then. The minutes resumed their crawl.

"Christ – I never knew that. Mount Leinster?"

He let down his phone on his lap and looked over.

"Mount Leinster. Half in Carlow, half in Wexford. 1786."

I had been mentally listing the exact nationalities that Operation Condor had spat up.

"Guess what happened there, Skip. Go on."

"Your Ma, she… Ah no. I can't say it. It wouldn't be right."

That effort earned me a broad, artificial grin.

"It's where the last Irish wolf was done in. Hunted down and kilt, so he was -1786. Isn't that something?"

I'd forgotten a Dutch national. He was one of the bag-men.

"1786. Tell me this now, Skip. What is the Irish for wolf?"

Was this what going bonkers was like, I wondered – discussing the Irish for wolf?

"No? My God, you Dublin people – well, no offence. Anyway. It's *mac tíre*. And it means..? It means 'son of the country.' Literally."

He pretended to wait for a question. Or a compliment, maybe.

"Like, back then a wolf was sort of considered… You get it?"

"Macker. There's nothing to get."

"No, what I am trying to get at is – oh oh. Who, whoa, whoa – stop the lights. Hold on everybody. Here we go."

I had noticed them first, actually. The woman was dressed like an old-style nun but without any white. No face, just eyes. The bloke had a bushy number fairly glowing with that henna stuff. His tunic went to his knees. He had a white cap on the crown of his head. Afghanistan? Pakistan?

"First thing came into your head, Skip? Don't think now, just say it."

"Macker. For Jaysus' sake. Not everybody has a face full of freckles and bug rusty heads here. Not anymore."

"Seriously. First thought, come on." The couple stepped into a shop. "Anything, go on. Look, it's brain training, elasticity, use it or lose it."

I trailed a glare by him and returned to watching the street.

"Yes siree," he said. "Well on the way. That's the be-all and end-all of it."

He had parked his phone screen up on his knee. It had dimmed almost completely but I still recognized the page – Daft.ie. Another piece of the Macker jigsaw. Detective Garda McHugh had the old houses and lands for sale itch. Hardly just a hobby either, I figured. It fit snugly with another of his little quirks– the DART. *Ze Dublin Area Rapid Transit* he called it, like he was a tourist. Getting hold of a house on the DART – that was Macker's dream. Culchies the likes of Macker and his missus, they'd be fierce crafty with their money. The way house prices were dropping, they were probably be close to making this DART dream a reality. 'Well on the way,' was right.

So much for that piece of the puzzle. But there was another side to Macker, one I didn't want to know too much about. I didn't want to find out that behind of all that guff of his was one of those types who actually loves bad news, and the grimmer the better. There were people like that. Not just the gawkers at the site of a car accident either. They had a wider view of things. Like it wasn't enough for them that things were going off the rails in this country. What did they actually want? Complete chaos? Total meltdown? They wanted the army on the streets? Who knew. They just enjoyed the mayhem. Cruel? Misanthropic – was that the word? Not people you'd want to be around at any rate. But exist they did and, it had to be said, most of the ones I'd come across were coppers.

I had other pieces of the Macker jigsaw too, smaller pieces. Still, I had picked up a hint that things might not be all joy and bliss in Macker-Land. Phone conversations I shouldn't have overheard. The marriage, I figured, had hit a bad patch. Hardly a surprise that. Coppers have always had it rough in the marriage stakes. But that missus of his appeared to be a particularly hard goer. There was a daughter issue too. Maybe that was normal these days. It might pass when the old hormones came off the boil. Like I'd know, me, the thirty eight and a half year old bachelor more or less living with his mother. The one whose fiancée had done a bunk on him, but he couldn't bring himself to believe it yet.

"'The centre cannot hold.' Remember that one?"

I flicked through my Contacts. It'd be so easy to text Sonia. But a deal's a deal.

"No? Poetry for the Leaving? On the syllabus for ages?"

"I never went to school. None of us Dubs did. All right?"

He nodded away my contribution with a bogus smile of understanding.

"Ah not to worry," he said. "The Inspectorate will set the world to rights any day now."

He pretended to misread my effort to ignore him.

"The big review? Our very own Garda Inspectorate? Top-to-bottom reform?"

I'd had enough.

"Macker. The Chinese, they have this saying. You get a set amount of words, they say, and when they're gone, you shuffle off this mortal coil."

"Right you be." He made a thin smile. "But you can't cod me."

I was instantly on edge. It wasn't the words – it was what was behind them. Throwaway comments like that were sharp reminders that I could never let down my guard. I might like to believe that I had Macker more-or-less figured out, but I'd never let go of the suspicion that he carried on the way he did because... Well, because that was the plan. The mind games, the word association nonsense, the slagging – this wasn't just entertainment. Macker's job was to soften me up. Either he'd get the goods on me or he'd drive me around the twist enough that I'd jack in the job. Whether Internal Review had decided I really was a bent copper or just a permanent aggravation, it didn't matter. They wanted me out.

I'd sometimes imagine spoofing Macker.

This stays between me and you, all right? So here's the thing, I did actually throw Joey D. off that roof. Sure did, yep. I put him a choke on him and then I gave him the old heave-ho. I had to, see?

Oh that's very interesting, Skip. Tell us, why do you say 'had to'?
Otherwise I was bunched. Joey knew everything! He'd use it on me.
God, but you're the hard man entirely.
The means must when the devil drives. Isn't that what they say?
True for you. You have plenty on the go, it sounds like.
That I do. But I'm only what you'd call an information broker.
No way! Passing Garda intel on to the bad guys, is it?
'Bad guys?' Haha. Do you see any bankers in the dock? Priests?
Fair point, Skipper, fair point. Well, does it pay, this gig of yours?
Does it what! The money's brilliant. Come here to me, do you want in? We're talking big money, let me tell you – very big. You'd be on the pig's back, surely. That missus of yours? Strolling down to the DART every morning? Mortgage? Hah. Don't be talking, sure.

That guitar riff was Macker's phone. The message: 'Boris' and the other two had just gone into a pub. This was one of the reasons we were paired up. 'Boris' was one of the skangers at the centre of this. Large, dark and hairy, and a former bouncer to boot, 'Boris' was no more Russian than I was. He was from Serbia. The pressing question: had 'Boris' just gone for a gargle, or was he trying to evade our surveillance? First the waiting game. Then, one of us might have to go on the hoof. Me, of course. If things were ever to go haywire, I was the armed wing of our twosome also.

Macker was still staring at the dashboard and turning his mobile over and over in his hand. The minutes dragged more. I flipped through the laminated watch-photos: a refresher on the gallery of scobes coming and going in the Breffni. Plenty of brown faces in amongst our own sorry-arse home-growns. The two Arabic names still made me think of suicide bombers. The Nigerian with the gleaming forehead who claimed to be king of someplace. Big Fish One and Big Fish Two, the ones we really wanted, hadn't shown in nearly a week. Neither hide nor hair of either one of them. Maybe Belfast was too cozy for them? Or, they knew that we were on to them? And how would -

"Holy God, the state of your man."

A crazy-eyed head was stumbling diagonally by the Breffni. But I wasn't 100% sure if it was pity I'd heard in Macker's voice. You saw addicts everywhere now. Up here, we were seeing more of the far-gone and very much ruined variety. Bright-eyed heroin users lurching along like the walking dead. The hyper-active crack merchants with their Hallowe'eny grins, laughing and oblivious. Lately, we were seeing more flakka heads. Those ones in particular gave me the willies. The way they stalked and marched about, picking at themselves? Like robots they were. As though a mad scientist with a remote control, testing to see how far he could go. The first fentanyl was bad but, with the new lab drugs on the street, it was a fast drop. Only a matter of days for some of them.

Maybe it was that very thought that brought Gary Cummins floating back up in my thoughts then. Was that what we were dealing with? One designer street-drug gone wrong, a trapdoor that opened under him? He could be lying dead in a ditch somewhere for days now. What would Bernie Cummins do then? It was out of my hands. My job was to just file this morning's contact. The chain was totally straightforward – C.O. first. End of story, so. But I wasn't going to drop it on Delaney over the phone. I'd bring it by him, end of shift.

"Macker. I'm going to try a name on you. Cummins. Tony Cummins."

He sighed and began to unkink himself.

"Cummins, Cummins... Dublin?"

"Dublin. Tony, Anthony. What do you know about him?"

"Probably a damned sight less than what you'd know."

"Answer the question. Tony Cummins, yes or no."

"I have to go with a maybe. A very watered-down maybe."

"Come on. And you the man who knows about historical wolves and everything?"

"I know the name," he said, "but wait. Isn't he out of the picture? Done in that big feud a few years back. Wasn't he?"

"No, that was the son. Tony Cummins is in Portlaoise a while now."

Macker stroked under his chin in a thoughtful manner.

"That's all, Skip. Sorry but. History is more my forte."

History, I thought. Tony Cummins would fit the bill now.

"Thanking his lucky stars he's safe in jail, is he?"

Macker's version of a Northern accent was crap: almost as bad as mine. I didn't need the hint anyway. The dogs in the street knew what the IRA were really about. Continuity 'RA, Real 'RA, Mad Maniac 'RA – it didn't matter a damn really. They were all in the same line of work. It wasn't politics they were after, it was money – raw, dirty money. The millions they were making from smuggling fags and robbed cars weren't enough for them. They wanted into any business, legit or otherwise. Night-club 'security' ran to fifty grand a year. People paid. The 'RA also wanted the drug trade. They put the word out to dealers: switch over to us, or it'll be wigs on the green. For them who didn't kowtow, it came hot and heavy. Some of them were left by the side of the road, kneecapped. Some were done outright.

My phone went off just as Macker was about to share some other observation. It was Delaney. It took only a few words from him for the whole of Dorset Street and Macker, and most everything else actually, to evaporate. Delaney had no questions for me. He had only an order.

The call over, I checked the time. I'd left Firenza about eighty ...three minutes ago. That was all it took them.

5

"Aha, Skipper. So they found it at last? The er.... ?"

The paranoia swept back in. But I couldn't read anything into that half-amused, half apologetic leer.

"...snapshot of you with the brassers in, where was it again? Costa Del Sol? Drinking the bubbly off their knockers?"

He had moved on to his gormless smile. Something in his eyes didn't match up, though.

"Come on Skip. There's no hiding nowadays. Facebook? Instagram? It was just a matter of time."

I pretended to study a small man with thick glasses and a small, dog, walking by. 'Senior officer,' Delaney had said. He hadn't said who or from where. Serious Crimes maybe? Gangs? His sparing words were a signal, though. Meeting with Bernie Cummins before clearing it first had landed me in such a big pile of shite that he could barely find the words to tell me how big.

"I have a meeting. You hold the fort on your own for a bit?"

Macker nodded, pretended to consider this. I checked the time again. 'Happens to be in your area,' Delaney had said. Really?

But it was true. With a well-timed U-turn, a new-looking green Avensis swept suddenly alongside. This stunt driver flexed an eyebrow and gave Macker a cheeky look.

"Mother of God." Macker's sly tone had evaporated. "Is that who I think it is? The Golden Boy himself? Deadly."

The Avensis moved on ahead, to a bus stop.

"Is that him you're meeting?"

"Him who."

"Come on Skip. You don't memorize every Garda Review?"

Whoever was in the driver's seat was still on a call.

"I'll give you a clue," Macker said. "On the cover, February's. Ironman or tri-athlete ribbon or something around his neck?"

I shook my head. Macker seemed to enjoy my ignorance.

"Éamonn Nolan," he said. "Hardman Garda *numero uno*."

All right. Now I remembered. So we were in the presence of a legend. Super-cop, the man who lived and breathed the whole war-on-crime stuff. Inspector grade by thirty, with FBI and Europol courses under his belt to boot. The word fast-track had been invented for him. It didn't hurt that he had ace timing too. He got the nod last year, back when the three fellas were shot to bits in Clondalkin in the space of forty-eight hours. Everyone was jumping up and down, screaming about gangs running wild and what in the name of God were we going to do et cetera. The Commissioner went Rambo and let the Organized Crime Unit off the leash. Get in their faces, said he. Get in their faces and take them down.

There was cheering in the stations and the patrol cars that day. This'd be hell for leather, with bells on. No more rounding up shitehawks and calling it proper police work. Whatever the OCU wanted, the OCU got. The whole fandango: coppers cherry-picked from Dublin stations and Special Detective Units. Pursuit Range Rovers, use-of-force cars. Uzis, H and Ks. Special Criminal Court, dockets cleared.

Nolan wasn't waiting long for his Oscar moment. It came one night up in Monaghan with a bust on a diesel-washing outfit. We knew there was IRA behind it, and his task force were ready. It turned into a free-for-all. A getaway car turned into a colander by Garda Uzis, two hard chaws stone dead, and a surviving hard chaw with no fewer than seven rounds in him. This episode and a near-facsimile a month later got Nolan catapulted into 2-I-C of the Organized Crime Unit.

"Skip? Will you get his autograph for me?"

Stepping out on the footpath gave me the fleeting pleasure of slamming shut my door on yet another Macker witticism. The speed of things was doing a number on my head. One minute I was moping around the apartment, or steeling myself for the ritual at the graveyard. Then, not two hours ago, I found myself sitting in a café across the table from the wife of one of Ireland's biggest gangsters ...of recent times, anyway. And now I just got a go-go order from Delaney to drop everything and meet hot-shot Nolan?

My reward for pulling open door of the Avensis was a whiff of leather jacket and tired-smelling aftershave whooshed in my face. Nolan was still on a call. No handshake on offer yet. He was one of the chosen, what we used to call Dubs who joined the Guards, but there was none of the stabby-eyed gurrier look to him. He looked almost international. About time really. Culchies still ruled the roost but we had Polish Guards now. A Chinese one, even.

Nolan thumbed Mute, looked up with a pirate-style smile.

"How's it going there."

"It's going so-so."

"Only so-so?" He slid a print-out from a folder and held it up. "Do you know who belongs to this face?"

A later-model Gary Cummins. He was running to fat. The hazy, withdrawn eyes looked glassy, too stoned maybe to beam out the hatred. The hair was all over the place like a first-arrest snap. I doubted that the fair-sized scratch over Gary's eyebrow came from a cat scrawbing at him. Maybe one of ours had given him a well-deserved clip on the ear. Yet I saw not one feature to tell me that Bernadette Cummins was this man's mother.

"That was eighteen months ago," Nolan said. "And it's been downhill since, I believe. Have you seen him lately?"

"No. I wouldn't be sure if that was Gary or Darren either."

Something about the way Nolan tugged at his nose said to me that I was now conversing with a bloke who had a serious temper. He shrugged off some notion and put the page down. Then he muttered something to the driver, hit Mute again and turned away. His phone conversation gave nothing away. The nearest he came was: 'Santry, for Christ's sakes? *Again?*'

41

We pulled quickly back into traffic. We were soon flaking away down Parnell Street, off in the direction of – well, I had no clue. Shite City, I suspected. He ended his call, eased back against the door and rested a pseudo-friendly stare on me.

"So. Is Bernie Cummins on the level?"

"I have no idea one way or the other."

The timed delay suggested he wasn't thrilled with that.

"You didn't report this approach from Bernie Cummins?"

"I'll do it when I got back to HQ. Not over the phone."

Nolan turned around to look at something.

"See that, Mick?" he said. "Outside the pub?"

The driver nodded like he'd finally gotten his head around Back Holes. 'Mick.' Well 'Mick's' practice of eyeing me in the mirror with massive disdain had given me the pip. Nolan's mobile went off again. I turned away and faked an interest in the street.

We turned into Ship Street, one of the few cobblestone streets that ran along the wall of Dublin Castle. Nolan waved driver Mick to pull over. We waited out a few 'ahas' from him before he dumped the call. He stared at the interior light for a few moments.

"Where were we? Oh, I forgot: congrats on your promotion."

I didn't get a clear hint of sarcasm. But Nolan was a Dub: he'd be past master.

"Remind me," he said, "when did Murder Squad fold?"

"Coming up for four years in October."

"You picked up plenty there, I'll bet you. God, yes."

Was he talking about a virus, I thought of asking.

"Skills, like," he added. "Valuable policing experience?"

I was well-reared. If it was a real question, I would have fetched up some answer, to be polite. Like Nolan didn't already know enough. He'd for damned sure know about my travails with Joey D and the whole Dalkey mess too. One was odd, two was a pattern, like.

"A bit hard to get to, are ya Tommy?"

The Dublin drone, sharp as a rusty blade. But Nolan's put-on heartiness didn't impress me one bit.

"Hell's bells," he went on. "Doesn't play well with others?"

"It depends on the game."

"Ah janey, that's no answer. Aren't we on the same side?"

'Mick' was enjoying this. I stared back for a count of three.

"Look," I said, "If I'm in some kind of shite, just say so."

"Oh, were you are expecting bad news?"

"These days, it's all we're getting."

"Ah, the state of the nation. Is that keeping you up at night?"

"Do you have a lot of those jokes?"

The lips moved like he was enjoying the last of a good pint.

"Let's hear it so, Tommy. What did Mrs. Cummins want?"

I truly hated air-quotes, but for this they were perfect.

"'Help.'"

"Ah, help. Because you're a compassionate person?"

"My Ma knows her. They're pals for ages. Since they were young ones."

"Right, right, right. Clogher Road, yes. Right."

Like he was announcing the half-time score in a fourth division football game. I tried not to give anything away.

"So what did you make of Bernie today?"

"Upset. Distressed would be a good word. She's not well."

"Is she a much different person than she was years ago?"

"I have no idea."

"You knew the Cumminses though. Growing up, like?"

"I knew *of* the Cumminses. Just like half of Dublin did."

"Yes but you grew up around these people, is my point."

'These people.' A phrase I never liked the sound of.

Driver 'Mick' was finally banjaxed by a lorry reversing out. This pleased me. I turned to Nolan.

"It sounds to me you've got some peculiar notions here."

"How so."

"The way you're talking here? For starters, I don't hold with people cocking their snoot at where someone's from."

"Told you Mick, didn't I. Fiver you owe me."

He was smiling, sort of, but the cold eyes never left mine. "De real bleedin' Crumlin style. *Ya know whar am sane, ruyh.*"

If Nolan was waiting for applause, he'd be waiting.

"The Cumminses," he said. "There's Gary and there's Darren. Right?"

"Darren who's dead. And Jennifer, who's not."

"'The one that got away.' Isn't that what they call her?"

"I don't know."

"Another 'I don't know.' What do you know about her?"

"Nothing."

"I see, I see. Tony Cummins' missus asks your ... help. Now tell me something. Do you think she okayed that with the hub first?"

"Who knows. It could have been vice versa for all I know. I'd lay odds he knew, though."

"The kind of 'help' that'd earn you a nice little place in Spain maybe?"

I counted to three in my mind. It didn't help much.

"Or a little brown envelope? Seriously?"

"Go and fuck off with yourself. Far off."

"Fuck off with yourself Inspector Nolan you mean, surely."

I grabbed hold of the door release.

"OK not Spain," I heard then. "How's about China maybe?"

His expression said calm, even relaxed. I tried to remember if martial arts was one of his million talents. It wouldn't much matter in a space like this. But it'd be as ugly as it would be dangerous.

"I thought with your job and all," he went on. "China's where all the big labs are, right? Very talented people them Chinese, I do believe. Go-getters. Of course there's the history and all...."

It wasn't so much the digs that got to me. It was how he landed them from behind this façade. Like we were having a polite by-the-way chat at a bus stop.

Meanwhile, on the other channel: *you're a Sergeant in the Drug Squad, and the only woman you found willing to tie the knot with happens to have been born over there? And furthermore, happens to be back there for a suspiciously long stay?*

But life has its little mysteries – another of Ma's little sayings. Somehow, my gob stayed shut. Maybe it was that part of me that was OK with trouble boiling up. For the clarity it brought, I supposed, and the strange calm.

Nolan finished flicking through menus on his mobile and slipped it into his pocket. He turned to me then as though laying eyes on me for the first time.

"All right, Sergeant Malone. I do believe that you're the very man that we've been looking for."

I said nothing. The merry eyes stayed on mine.

"Think he'll do, Mick?"

"I don't know," the driver said. "Some mouth on him."

Nolan nodded and his eyes snapped back to laser grade.

"One thing. You only get one fuck-off with me. Just the one. OK?"

I could manage a blank stare for quite a while myself.

"So Mick," Nolan said then. "Let us deliver Sergeant Malone back to the front lines of policing where, in these tendentious times, he is so sorely needed. We shall discuss matters en route."

The tires yowled plenty on our way back to Dorset St. We snipped a red light at Thomas Street. Traffic going down the quays was a doddle. Ghost town, all right. Two or three seconds off an amber light, Driver Mick yanked the wheel and launched us down a lane that I thought only the likes of me knew about. Did they drive around like madmen all day, I wondered. At this rate, I'd be back with Macker in minutes.

"Your C.O.'s onside," Nolan said. "Delaney, right? Can't say he's happy though. Prefers to hold onto his good cards, naturally enough. Who wouldn't? Here, I'll tell you what he said. 'If anyone can, Tommy can.' Don't you wish every C.O. was like that?"

Compliments always made me suspicious.

"This operation," he went on. "'Condor?' You're Sergeant. But you're on surveillance details?"

"Times is tough. We all do our bit to even things out."

"Your shift's 'til seven, I believe?"

"Allegedly seven. Unless something breaks."

"How likely would that be, do you think?"

"If I knew that, I'd be telling fortunes below in Moore St."

"Fair enough. So look, you'll find your way over then. Half-past seven, quarter to eight, say?"

"Over where?"

"We're in the Park. Give me a bell when you're coming."

The lack of a response had him turning in his seat again.

"Tony Cummins needs us. And Tony knows you have to give to get."

"It was Bernie Cummins doing the asking."

"What's your point?"

"Talk to him, not her. She's in a bad place. Cancer?"

"I know. I also know this is the makings of a very big deal."

"I'm Drugs Central. There's no find-Gary-Cummins on our to-do list that I saw."

"All to the good. Because we want it to look like you're on your tod, doing a personal favour for Bernie Cummins. On the QT, low-key."

My brain carried on registering things. Nolan's lazy, probably insulting manner of speaking. That cocky bastard driver's fingers impatiently tap-tapping on the wheel.

"You the man, Tommy. It's you she wants."

Nolan's voice had taken on a quasi-pally tone. That sliding sensation came to me then, the feeling that things were giving way under me.

"Build the relationship. Establish rapport. Chat, listen, whatever. Get the ball rolling. Bit by bit, we get to where we need to be. She gets what she wants too. It's a win-win."

"It's Gary she wants. To know he's safe, or alive, at least."

"'Course she does! She's his mammy! We're here to help."

Not once had Nolan so much as hinted at the obvious: was Gary Cummins even alive? And what's more, I wouldn't be one bit surprised if Nolan was holding something back too. Maybe that Gary Cummins had been a snitch? The word dropped images from my old Squad life splat into my mind. A body floating to the surface of a quarry pond. Another one, limbs tied at impossible angles by barbed wire. Mushy corpses, their faces still contorted with agony and fear. You could tell right away: snitch.

"You have a question," Nolan said. "Fire away."

"What if Gary Cummins isn't just lying low?"

"Six feet low, like? Nah. If he was done, it'd be out there."

What made him so sure, I wondered.

"Look," he went on. "Once we get Tony talking, there's no going back. Seriously. What are his options? Zip. He'll be sixty-eight years old when he gets out – *sixty-eight*. If he gets out."

He dipped his forehead like he wanted the spar to get serious.

"Criminal Assets are all over him. Money's gone, or it's locked, or seized. But what Tony does have is something he doesn't need – his so-called friends. You know the story, right? In Tony's world, friends get to be enemies fierce rapid. The wolves are always circling. And the minute you're down, you're a goner. If anyone knows that, it's Tony Cummins."

He extended his index finger next to his outstretched thumb.

"What's he got in his favour? His sons – oh, wait: he doesn't. Well he has Gary. More's the pity, is all you can say about that really. I mean, what is Gary? Maybe he's not the out-and-out psycho that his brother was. But really? Gary's a loser, and ..."

Nolan wouldn't be getting any help from me.

"...and he's an addict. Did she level with you about that?"

"It didn't come up."

"Point is, there was a time when Tony could stonewall us 'til the cows come home. Not anymore. With cancer, no way he's going to deny her."

This echoed silently for a while. I had met a few Nolans in my career. There was an aura about them. Some would make the hair stand up on the back of your neck.

We were on Dorset Street already? Not only was this true, we were pulling in behind Macker. Nolan's hand was on my arm before I could tug at the release. I took in the tight, bogus smile, the cop-eyes flicking around my face.

"See you later on, Tommy. Looking forward."

Then I was on the curb and swinging the door shut. The Avensis catapulted away. Nolan was already back on his mobile.

Something bulldozed all this from my mind in an instant: I was absolutely gumming for a drink. Not just a pint either. It was Vitamin J that I wanted, in quantity, and fast-acting.

A text: Delaney? Again? He wanted to see me. *Now*, like.

6

Delaney carefully closed his office door behind him.

"Tommy. What's the story."

"I think that's my question, boss."

He did a slow eyebrow dance and pretended to eye a print-out on his desk.

"OK," he said then. "Garda Drug Squad Sergeant meets with imprisoned gangster's missus. Nice headline, isn't it?"

"I was going to bring it by you in person, end of shift."

"I believe you. OK. Now, Nolan. What does he want?"

"Best I can make out, he wanted to air some mad notions."

Delaney made a duck-face and blinked slowly, twice.

"Tommy. You're not doing yourself any favours here."

"He had a fantasy that I work for him. That kind of 'mad.'"

"I see. Well now, the same Éamonn Nolan asked me an odd question. He wanted to know if you were as 'candid' with us here. What do you think he meant, 'candid?'"

"Maybe he's used to having yes-men around?"

"Come on now. Since when were you so sensitive?"

"Since a yoyo the name of Nolan got in my face, is when."

"What can I tell you. Anyway. He laughed it off this time."

I sniffed the air and tried to read that print-out.

"You know as well as I do what the OCU is there for. When the Minister calls for war, it's not boy scouts he has in mind."

"Did he call for cowboy tactics? Posers throwing shapes and pulling the type of stunts that'd have the likes of us normal, regulation-bound coppers on the carpet?"

Delaney nodded philosophically and looked by me.

"Working an op with the OCU wouldn't do you any harm," he said. "The old CV department, I'm talking about."

"Boss, if my CV needs a wash, it won't go the Nolan route."

"Jesus, Tommy. An opportunity, is what this is. Networking. A display of adaptability. Relationship building. Would it be so terrible for you to just get on the right side of this?"

'Relationship building.' He and Nolan had talked, all right.

"OK they're hard goers, the OCU. But on the other hand...?"

"On the other hand she had warts. Here, did I mention OCU cowboy carry-on? The dirty work they do be getting up to?"

His gaze swung back. He had a dim, displeased look now.

"Well, you'll know to keep your wits about you so, won't you."

"But this is all hypothetical we're talking. Isn't it?"

"Spare me the song and dance. And keep me in the picture."

"The picture."

"What do you think? Tell me what Nolan gets you doing."

I turned things over in my mind. Delaney was under massive stress too. I sometimes forgot.

"Boss. Condor's near the go-day. We need all hands on deck. And staffing? Sure, we're juggling chainsaws as it is."

"Come on now, Tommy. You know the way it is."

"It sounds like I might need a refresher. Do I?"

"You're a sergeant – that's the way it is. And sergeants read the circulars, do they not? So yes, we're badly stretched. And yes, we have to do more with less. 'We' being 'all of us.' 'All of us' being the Garda Síochána, aka the good guys. Because it's us against them and... because we all swore the same oath."

He eyed his desk-top as though something was missing.

"Try to remember that," he said. "It'll help."

"Go forth in peace?"

Delaney's response was an undertaker's smile. Well, at least I wasn't the only one pissed off.

*   *   *

You smell HQ long before you see it. An old 'joke.' Ha. Ha. Ha.

Dublin Zoo might be a half a mile away but you still got a right good whiff of it here at the gate to HQ, aka 'The Park.' A harmless enough looking place from a distance here at the more picturesque end of the Phoenix Park where all the roads and avenues are overhung by lush stands of trees and well-tended shrubbery to beat the band. All very mannerly and well-behaved looking. Duly noted et cetera – but: a good number of the heads jogging here happened to be fellas from the run-jump-and-shoot units headquartered here, Guards and Army both.

My apartment, which is to say me and Sonia's apartment, was only about a fifteen-minute walk. That wasn't a coincidence. Part of why I liked the apartment was because it was next to The Phoenix Park. It still held fond memories, from back in the St Joe years. We used come by here a fair good bit on our runs. I liked the running-in-a-pack feeling, that we were boxers, athletes. We were going places, like.

Sonia had her own reasons for picking the apartment. For her it was the Luas, the art gallery place, the three klicks or so to O'Connell Bridge. She liked the history bit as well, the Vikings bit and all that. Also, you saw mountains from the balcony. And the Liffey ran by next to us too, looking absolutely nothing like the swill you got by the quays later.

But that evening, I wasn't that 14-year-old maniac who spent almost every evening in St Joe's. I was an adult sitting in his car, an adult very much less than thrilled to be here. I bided my time eyeing HQ through the railings while I took my sweet time with my Salt and Vinegar and my Caramilk. The fish and chips that I really wanted I'd get on my way to Ringsend. Tonight was a regular get-together. No way was I missing that.

These get-togethers were more than just going for a few scoops. I might even have called it 'therapy' if I was so minded, which I wasn't. You shouldn't need a shrink or a book to tell you that to figure out where you're headed, you'd better look over your shoulder at some point. So that was one of the reasons I had made a point of getting back in touch with some of the lads that me and Terry grew up with.

Things were more than a bit dodgy at first. Spots and Gameboy both had similar issues to Terry's. I was hardly one of the lads either: I was a copper, a 'narc.' But we all sort of agreed to draw a veil over that aspect of things. That involved letting sleeping dogs keep sleeping. We only talked about the old days the odd time. The Before Days we called them. Before Days were safe to talk about because they went back to when we were young fellas, back before things went astray.

My Before Days stopped the moment Terry tried cocaine for the first time. It was like an arrow had been aimed at him on the day he was born, and that arrow had finally found him. It changed him right then and there. In short order he was unmanageable. A matter of weeks, if I recall. A total shock.

From then on we got lulls and lies and lots of acting and drama, but things never really got better. The best it got was treatment. Fortune House, Coolmine, Fettercairn – Terry did them all. They slowed him but didn't stop him landing on that square with the name that was soon bandied about everywhere– 'the chaotic drug user.' Hence the ghost appearances. Hence the need to check another bloke lying there on the footpath. Knowing it couldn't be Terry, but needing to check anyway.

Somehow, the likes of Gameboy dodged any arrow of destiny. I had a theory: it was because he was so good at video games. He'd totally lose himself in them. Before he was Gameboy, he was Doctor Who. 'Who's that?' 'Who said that?' 'Who's he looking at?' He couldn't come to Terry's funeral. He was serving his fourth sentence. After his sixth go in prison, he came out clean. 'Something about the number six,' he told me. He got trained to be a crane driver then, and made scads of money during the boom.

Spots was a horse of a different colour. Spots Feeney. With that hair-on-fire look and mad freckles all over spooky, milk-white skin, he couldn't not get the name Spots. The nose on him, though. It was like somebody got ahold of it and pinched it, and then they twisted it, and shoved it back into his face for good measure.

The same Spots was a highly combustible item. A look would set him off. He came by it honestly enough. His Ma had mental issues. His Da was basically a violent dipso. Back when Spots was eleven he stayed with us a few months. I just asked Ma and she said yeah, we'd give it a bash. It wasn't like the Malone clan was in the best of nick ourselves at that juncture. But Spots fitted right in. He just did what we did. Homework done, beds made, school gone to, prayers said. Ma put him in the room above the stairs. Some nights I'd hear him crying.

Then one day, no more Spots. He was out of the picture for ages after. He shot through those years on a raging river of booze and drugs. Robbery, housebreaking, warehouse rob-to-order jobs. Shoplifting and even pickpocketing when he was stuck. He was even hijacking lorries. A near-murder that got kicked back to assault with intent. It was always about drugs. Money to get drugs, things he had to do for people he owed.

Spots had a marriage behind him. Theresa. A daughter too, Jessica, fourteen or so. She was cut out of him too, temperament-wise. His disability got him his place in Ringsend. By rights, the car that creased him should've killed him. He came out of a coma weeks after, not knowing if a) he was alive and b) if he was alive at all, would he ever walk again.

Mainly, how he dealt with that was by staying gargled or high 24/7. That all stopped one day. He never told me how or why. I had an idea, though. January the year he left us, I'd tracked down Terry in a place on the North Strand. He told me he'd had a weird dream, a nightmare actually. Spots Feeney had featured. Spots had got him by the shirt and he was roaring and winding up to give him a clatter. Next thing Terry knew, Spots was holding him tight and crying and shouting at the same time. I never brought up this matter with Spots.

Having umpteen pieces of metal holding him together wasn't going to stop Spots. A skinny runt he was, like a greyhound. Then he started going to a gym. In no time at all then, he was all upper-body and ready to move tall buildings.

He'd kept it up since. The same gym, I learned, was a favourite hangout for at least a half-dozen serious, up-and-coming gangbangers. Coincidence, right, sure.

Spots then decided that it was high time to make a living, and to that end he became a taxi man – taxi man, not taxi *driver*. Taxi man meant professional: a divine calling. Taxi *driver* was a bloke who cut corners, cheated, and generally made life crap for a taxi man and the known world in general. Spots didn't do much taxi-ing, just enough to keep the plate and get out and about. So far so good.

It took me a while to learn what his real gig was. It wasn't getting people to places. It was getting people from places, i.e. out of places they shouldn't be. This often involved well-known people, or well-off people, people busy making massive gobshites of themselves or otherwise putting themselves into stupid, compromising, downright dangerous situations.

Spots was carving out his niche just as the Celtic Tiger was getting going in earnest, back when the money was sloshing around like the water coming into the Titanic. One dark and stormy night, he told me, a young one, fourteen or fifteen, a bit of a rip apparently, went missing. In actual fact, she'd gone on the razzle. Important fact: her people were millionaire-bracket out the Southside. The mother got a garbled phone call from Princess: she hit the panic button. Her hub, he called Spots. Said hub had been one of Spots' fares one night. It was one of those encounters where philosophical sorts of things got said. People tell strangers things they'd never dare say to family.

But somehow, some way, Spots found that kid that night. She was over in a dive off Capel Street, high on something-or-other and in just about in the worst company you could imagine. There was trouble getting her out. The be-all and the end-all of it was Spots doing a number on some party who'd been throwing shapes. Bones broken, concussion, and so forth.

He got the kid home in any event, her puking like the Trevi Fountain all over the back seat. Father met him at the door, forked over five hundred nicker. Not a word said. Another five the next day. Spots never got charged for that night's set-to: someone took care of it. This episode got him known in certain quarters, whereupon certain people kept his number handy. It was all about trust, about keeping things under wraps.

We used slag Spots about writing his memoirs. We even gave him a title – 'Taxi Tales: 1001 Nights in the Big Smoke.' Some of what he told us were so mad that we didn't know if he was spoofing or not. Not that you'd call him a spoofer: he'd rear up on you. Even when he was a young fella, Spots had you wondering. He had all the tricks, all the convincing details. What he said was so real you'd be right there with him. He didn't miss much. Even small stuff got his attention. A quirk, or the way somebody spoke, or looked or walked. Weather even, or the sky itself. I sometimes wondered if there was an Aspie thing going on with him.

Whatever mix of fact and fiction Spots' memoirs would turn out to be, he certainly had the time to write them if he so wanted. Sleep was an issue with him. Some nights he'd drive around at all hours. Mystery Tours, he called them. I went along a few times. He truly knew every crook and nanny in the place. He never once let on that he got a kick out of driving around drinking cans of beer with a copper i.e. the enemy. Once we went as far as Tara – Tara of all places, the whole High King bit. I spent a very peculiar hour wobbling around in the moonlight until –

- A streetlamp by the railings just lit up, yanking me back to here-and-now. I gave up trying to get the last bits of crisps from the bottom of the bag. It was time to 'give a bell' to Nolan. I studied the dark droopy branches of a chestnut tree while I waited for him to answer. Relief began leaking in after three rings: grand, I thought, that was me heading to Ringsend.

"Ah, Tommy. I was wondering."

I kept the cursing in my head. I heard a door opening at his end, and steps.

"Come on up, meet the team. Sound all right?"

It sounded shite, actually. But I was here, wasn't I.

I got a long look from the uniform manning the gate. Maybe I was a bit too interested in the shatter-proof glass set-up, or the anti-ram barriers. I was soon standing next to a vacant reception desk and scowling at the camera in the ceiling. Nolan appeared just as my count got to forty.

He waved his card fob at various sensors each time cocking an ear for the buzzer to the door release. He talked over his shoulder as we climbed the stairs. Halfway up, we turned sharply toward the front of the building, the side that faced onto the Phoenix Park proper, and after a last wave of his pass over a sensor by a door with no name, he yanked on the handle. Sharp smells flooded out and stung in my nose: mortar and adhesive, general new plastic stuff, carpet.

What a set-up. The usual Garda universe of grot and grime had vanished. Here was something you'd see in an ad for Italian office furniture. Glass-topped partitions on the cubicles, proper filing cabinets, acres of table space, ergonomic mesh chairs. Tons of huge monitors. A radio base was set up in one corner, like a tabernacle. Everything was open, bright and colourful. There was nothing to hide, it was a new world. Not a single bit of kit, no tunics or hi-vis gear or ballistic vests or equipment belts or handsets, lying about or slung over chairs or partitions. Not one cardboard box kicked in under a desk. Mugs, dirty or otherwise, none. No postcards or snaps of your kids or your wedding or your football team. Not even a newspaper. It was like a film set.

"Like an IKEA showroom, people tell me. You think?"

"I'm not the man to ask about that IKEA stuff."

A woman, mid-thirties, on a mobile, sat at one of the desks, also attending to her screen in a manner that said she saw big problems reported thereon. Nolan took up station by her desk. She got the message and finished her call, and got up out of her chair.

"Áine," Nolan said.

The direct look said copper, right enough. A reddish-blond crop of hair said 'shower and go about your business,' not 'book me a fancy hair-do every week.' The general ruddiness and the tightness around the eyes suggested sports, or the outdoors.

"This is Tommy." Nolan turned to me." Or do you prefer...?"

"Tommy. Even my Ma refuses to call me by Sergeant."

She had that hard, quick competitor's handshake.

"Áine was Kevin Street," Nolan said. "Tales to be told, right?"

"Never a dull moment," she said. Another bogger. I gave up trying to place bogger accents years ago. Cork, Leitim, whatever.

"Áine's frontline. She'll work with you on this."

Sergeant Áine Somebody had found a perch back on the edge of her desk, one foot pulled up behind her knee.

"Yep," Nolan went on. "Shortlisted for Inspector last week too, so she did. We couldn't be more proud."

She examined the toe of her shoe. A sign of embarrassment, I figured. Or that she was far from thrilled that she'd had to stay late and wait for this Malone tosser to show up. Nolan said something about leaving us to it – and then he was off like a dirty shirt.

My irritation had turned to annoyance.

"Er, Áine? There's a problem. Several, actually."

She looked over, eyes lazily alert.

"Problem A) is I have a pressing engagement – tonight."

I left it hanging there, but there was no reaction.

"Problem B), your boss is under a misunderstanding. This 'working with' thing he just said? It doesn't actually exist."

She had an advanced degree in stone-faced expressions.

"I got sent here for a chat," I went on, "but that's all."

"A walk-around and a briefing is what I heard."

And with that she turned back to her desk, picked up a file folder and handed it to me. A briefing file on Mr. Gary Cummins. I skimmed through the first two pages and closed it again. As I was presenting it back to her, Nolan re-appeared.

"Had a read? Good. Let's go through it, the three of us, and see what comes out of it."

"Sorry, no can do. I have a commitment this evening. I already mentioned this?"

I picked up on a mental exchange between Nolan and Áine.

"Fair enough so." Nolan had put on a bland face. "No bother, Tommy. It can wait 'til the morning."

You'll be waiting, I thought. I walked back through the space-age office. The interruption I braced for never came. Then I was outside, walking through the zoo-smelling dusk to my car. By the time I turned the key in the ignition I was well-and-truly steaming. I was still steaming when I drove out the Park. Steaming when I got to Islandbridge. Steaming when I launched the car down the quays.

By the time I was slowing for the lights by the Four Courts, the air had gone out of all this mental commotion. My anger had evaporated. Coming up to O'Connell Bridge required my usual effort to keep eyes averted from the goings-on along the boardwalk. There were too many Terrys there, day in and day out. So, just as I had learned to do – and God knows it took me long enough to learn it – I got by it. But I realized then that, instead of still being steamed about this whole Gary Gannon thing or getting down in the mouth again about Terry, I had slid into a downer frame of mind. It wasn't so much a downer as it was a feeling that I was missing something. That I was just a passenger, or a spectator.

Part of the mindfulness thing was, allegedly, to let stuff be. To look without judgement. Fat chance of that after flicking through Gary Cummins' woeful record. What a waster. Why couldn't some refugee, some starving African kid say, have a chance instead? Gary's supposed partner's name slid into my mind: Enright, Mary Enright. Easy to remember because of the 'right' bit. 'D.U.' too. No surprise there.

Bernie Cummins, I thought then. She was behind this sinking feeling I had. Hope, illusions, denial – sure. All part of being human. But surely to God someone had levelled with her? *Bernie, my dear, chances are your Gary is no more.* The hows, whys, wheres and whens would surface in due course, but dead meant dead. Nolan might be a certified pain in the face, but that didn't mean he wasn't right. If someone was making an example of Gary, we'd likely have found him by now. He'd have been done out in public, or left out in public at least. As to why hide or bury the body, there'd be no shortage of notions. The 'RA had killed people and never told anyone where to find them. There was planned psychological warfare to that too: a complete disappearance put the fear of God in everyone.

And then there was ...overthinking. Even coppers fell into the trap of constructing grand theories and notions. The world is not some piece of clockwork where you can figure out what fits where and why. Sometimes it's just luck, or chance. Or just chaos. What if Gary's disappearing act hadn't been about anybody owing anybody anything, or double-crossing anyone? No master plan, no grand rationale? It needn't have been a big deal. Say he'd just rubbed someone the wrong way. Something trivial, stupid, childish even. Had he shot his mouth off? Gotten into a scrap? Nursed a grudge to the point of planning revenge, but then it backfired on him? Maybe it got about that Gary had ratted someone out. It didn't need to be true. A rumour'd be enough.

Still my thoughts kept elastic-banding back – back to Bernadette Cummins. One son murdered. Husband in jail. Now son number two was missing. And she was sick, very sick. Who decided that Bernie Cummins be put through this torture? Some God she had going for her. He kept slamming doors in her face. I didn't need a shrink to tell me there was such a thing as the subconscious. Bernie Cummins deserved a tip of the scales back her way, for once. Some fairness in life...

And that was when the fog cleared a bit. No wonder I had this low-burning anger smouldering away inside. My thinking brain had gone AWOL. The truth was, some part of me had already signed on to play Sir Galahad here.

What. A. Colossal. Gobshite.

Something else had been shuffling around in the back of my mind too. It was Nolan: a cocky, arrogant, overbearing bollocks. But then came his 'No bother, Tommy.' No bother? But, sure enough, here I was on my merry way for a few pints with my mates, as planned. This was all too agreeable, all to easy by far. Which must mean that there was something getting by me here. Delaney: he had to be in on it too. Hadn't he just hoofed me over to Nolan will-nilly, here's-your-hat-and-what's-your-hurry style.

That wasn't the last of my revelations then either. Another thought snapped into place, one that sent chills up and down my spine. Sometimes the obvious is so obvious that you don't see it: Garda brass had never stopped believing they had a crooked Guard to root out. So Nolan was just the face of the operation. This Cummins thing was just the bait. The target was me.

The lights changed. I stabbed the pedal and tore away from O Connell Bridge, tires shrieking, I drank in all the noise and the distractions. The rubbery stink of the city mingled with the sour tang of the Liffey at low tide. The heavy crisscross span of the bridge slid up the windscreen as I ploughed down Eden Quay at a rate of knots. My swing around the Custom House spun a quick view down the North Wall. Ground zero as it were, the scene of the crime, site of those shiny, air-conditioned spiders' nests where hedge-fund suits had cooked up the crash over their fifty-euro lunches and lines of coke.

Everything looked gank. The new Sam Beckett with the Liffey dawdling under it out into the Bay? Naw. That harp-y business made no sense. As for that lopsided convention centre we were all supposed to be so proud of? It looked ready to slide back into rubble – and good riddance to it too. The abandoned guts of the Anglo building topped it all off. Bomb it, I thought. Just bomb it. Start fresh – if there'd ever be a chance after all that had happened.

I took the turn off the quays fast enough to draw long banshee, cats-in-heat wails from the tires. I kept up the mad rally driving out to Pearse Street, where I brought the Golf back to law-abiding speed and aimed it at Ringsend. Ringsend was all right. Even with all the new apartments and so forth. Mostly all right. Plenty of people still thought of Ringsend as the place you'd get beat up at the drop of a hat. A place where you'd get the Ringsend Kiss, a head-butt to end all head-butts. Them days were long past, but like so much other stuff in this country, the story hadn't changed.

I got my precious haddock and chips and took it back to the car. The haddock wasn't great. More suspicions slyly presented themselves in my mind as I polished off the last of my chips. Had Bernie Cummins gotten squeezed into some deal, and now I was part of it? If so, by whom? Or this was just a mad film running only in my mind. Produced, directed by and starring T. Malone. Special word of thanks, of course, to the manufacturers of the pills that the shrink had assured T. Malone would 'help.'

I got out of the car, my thoughts considerably darkened by this notion. It was a drink I wanted, and I wanted the damned thing now, not later. I slowed only to listen for the beeps from the alarm. To hell with the crook lock. Let them rob it. I'd buy a new one when I got to Oz, wouldn't I.

7

Gameboy insisted on buying a round. Gameboy, of all people. Wonders never ceased. Crane operators were suddenly back in demand? No, no, no – he'd 'won a few bob on the nags.' Said with a straight face too.

We settled into the usual guff – the slagging, the sorting out, the accusations. *Are you mad? Are you having a laugh? Don't be an iijit.* Gameboy, as always, had issues to air. He wasn't actually on the Internet. The Internet was on him. Morning, noon and night. So now that he knew everything since the dawn of time, he took it as his sworn duty to bore the arse off everybody. Interest rates, Middle East oil wars. Genetically modified crops, the Double Irish, CIA drones, Afghanistan.

"It's only coming out now," he began. "Totally unbelievable, so it is."

We waited. It could be anything.

"They planned right from the start too. The IMF, they -"

"Whoa," said Spots. "Forget it. Not tonight, Josephine."

Gameboy sprouted his indignant look.

"Heard it all before Joe," Spots said. "The bubble, the bail-out, the banks, the bollocks – we know. All right?"

"Oh, so you already know they're planning to put the army guarding the ATMs too then, do you. That they don't even know where – "

"Where'd you hear that?"

"Where? All you have to do is go online, man. There's people there, anonymous like, insiders, and they're putting it out."

"Insiders. Nice. Anonymous too, into the bargain. Lovely."

"Oh to you it's all just a put-on. Is that it?"

"Call it anything you like – swiz, con job, scam."

"A travesty is what it is. And people have had it up to here, I'm telling you. No joking. There's going to be riots any day. Mark my words."

That was not true. It was so not-true that I was sure even Gameboy knew it. But nobody wanted to admit that the whole Irish rebel thing was rubbish. That guff about giving the bond-holders a hair-cut? Giving them the keys of the house, more like. Everyone was keeping their heads down. Them what could bale were baling. I thought of Midnight, now a copper in Queensland somewhere. His missus was nursing there already. Their kids 'loved the beach.' Our winter was their summer too.

After a few more tries, Gameboy opted to take his marbles elsewhere. I watched him head over to a pair of blokes he knew from when they had shared State accommodations together.

"Really," Spots said. "Who wants to keep hearing that shite. The more I listen to that stuff, the stupider I get."

"So he's totally out of order talking about it. Nice."

Spots slid me a pitying glance, but said nothing.

"What if he's right?"

"Yeah well I was righter to put a stop to his gallop."

"That's just hopping the ball. What if I told you you're out of order here?"

"What if I told you that you're just acting the maggot and trying to rise a row here?"

"Gameboy's entitled to his point, is all I'm saying."

"Really now. I save us a lorry-load of bullshit and instead of a wee word of thanks, you start handing out the pay to me."

"All I'm saying is, the man's allowed to have his say."

Spots turned a look of strained patience my way.

"Tommy. I'm not here to be you. OK?"

I turned to watching the barman. Leo. Leo of the lazy eye. He caught my eye and winked. He'd had this weird mannerism since I'd come in first years ago. Always licking his lips.

"You know, I have to say this, Tommy. Seems to me that you've been getting some quare notions lately. This is coming from a friend now."

Friend or foe: I sometimes wondered. But Mr. Spots Feeney, he didn't miss much. Knowing him, he had probably heard the pills rattling around in the box in my pocket once or twice, and put two and two together.

"Don't get me wrong. I know what stress can do. All right?"

No way was I going to let on that he'd hit a nerve.

"Who's to say what's quare these days," I managed. "We're in upside-down land these days, haven't you noticed?"

"Ah, I see. Fair enough so. It's just you getting your jollies here winding me up then. By the way, that's kind of juvenile."

I was a bit surprised. It wasn't often I got to wind Spots up.

"Listen to me," he went on. "You can put a turbo on it, what Gameboy's saying, and you can paint stripes on it and all, but it's still bullshit. There ain't gonna be any marches, or protests, or any of that. No. We're a walkover, so we are, people in this country. We're all talk. The gift of the gab. Some gift. A big, fat nothing."

He waited to see if this was sinking in. I opted for the elevated eyebrow.

"Jaysus Tommy, get up out of that. Really? You know the lie of the land as well as I do. Gameboy and the Internet, I swear. He should stick to the porno like everybody else."

"Here's a man trying to be a better citizen. Trying to get himself better informed and so forth. And your advice is?"

"Yeah yeah yeah," Spots said. "Enjoy your little laugh. Go ahead. But I'll tell you something now. The day your mob starts locking up the real criminals in this country – them robber bankers and raper priests and so on and so forth – *that's* the day you get my full and undivided attention."

He took a long go of his pint. I watched Gameboy advance some issue with his new / old audience.

"Nothing personal of course," I said.

"'Course not. Nobody's blaming you for being a copper."

For that one I gave him a very cool once-over.

"All hot air," he went on. "That's all. Like they say, the dogs they do be barking, but the camels, well they just carry on walking."

Camels, I thought. You could parade down O'Connell Street on a camel – in the nip – and nobody'd notice. Some days it felt like anything could happen.

"Anyway," Spots went on, stretching out an arm as though to lift something non-existent. "How's the sleep situation with you these days."

"It's grand. Sleeping like a baby."

Sure – waking up every two hours, screaming. That was Spots' line from bygone times. It was from his time in the horrors with that mad cold-turkey move of his that no-one believed would work. That was the thing, he told me after, that kept him going.

He began observing a dilapidated -looking bloke standing by the far end of the bar, texting. He had a worn look to him, and he was swaying a bit. A husband I wondered. Didn't want to go home because... The bank called. The doctor says he needs to see me. I got laid off. Or how about: Sorry, honey, I just can't take it anymore. That was happening a lot now.

"Status update. In focking Ringsend. Poiles of focking riff-raff."

Spots had the DART accent down pat. Miles ahead of Macker's efforts. He took a sip of beer and licked his lips.

"I'm going to tell you something now. And it is this. Nobody's going to thank you. Nobody, all right?"

"Nobody thank me for what."

"You know what. A pat on the back, you'll get, a medal, maybe. But that's the best it's going to get. Won't do much to keep the wolf from the door, will it."

The word struck a little spark in my mind. Macker and his wolf. Now Spots? I'd been noticing that more lately, how a word or a phrase kept circling in my mind. Fixated, or something. A sign of going mad, trying to link things that really had no connection?

"So you have to wonder, I think. I mean to say, where is the thanks for a job well done? The appreciation. The reward. The respect, at least. Right?"

I knew where this was going – no-man's land. Every now and then Spots put out a little experimental remark. The message? There were options he, or people he knew could present. I had yet to call him on this. He'd never admit to putting out these feelers. It wouldn't be for himself he'd be asking anyway.

His next sip of beer was for effect.

"Eh, them flowers? Very nice. Tell your Ma. Very nice."

The cemetery, he meant. This was him reminding me that he had made his own visit. Every year.

"And give her an ould hug for me while you're at it."

He wasn't joking. I didn't doubt that he'd check I did it too.

"This brings me to another matter." He allowed several long moments to pass. "Guess who I bumped into today. A new motorbike under him too – new-looking in anyway."

"Christy, yeah. He had it with him at the graveyard."

Spots' eyebrow stayed up a bit too long.

"Some messer that fella. Do you need reminding of that?"

I didn't know why, but I felt a need to stand up for Christy. He always did give Spots the pip anyway.

"At least his heart's in the right place," I said.

Spots rubbed his nose and resumed eyeing the clientele.

"I see," he said. "Well here's an idea, Tommy. You go and have a word with your pal, Mister Big-Heart. About keeping his big gob shut."

Somewhere in a corner of my mind, a little alarm went off.

"Meaning?"

"Meaning *I* know you'd never ask Christy to do stuff. The question is, though, do other people know? Like, not-nice other people?"

"What 'stuff' are you talking about?"

"Come on, Tommy. Don't play the copper with me. You know Christy's coming on like he's the cock of the walk? Like he's your right hand man? Starsky and bleeding Hutch, or something?"

He began to fondle his glass.

"Pulled up next to me so he did. All aflutter, man on a mission style. 'Seen Gary C, have you?' says he. Right out of the blue. I couldn't believe it."

I took another go of my pint.

"There he is, Christy, with them big eyes of his glowing like he's on his knees in Lourdes and he just got his sight back. 'What?' says I. 'What did you say to me?' Did he pick up the hint? Not, a, chance. That fella couldn't pick up nits. 'Gary Cummins,' he asks me – again. 'Have you seen him around the place at all?"

Spots took a few moments to shake his head in wonder.

"Look, I says to him, are you gone completely mental? You watch what you're saying, and who you're saying it to. Unless you want people to think you're a snitch."

In my mind, I could hear this exchange all too clearly.

"'Oh Jaysus, hold your horses now,' says Christy. Like he hadn't stepped in a big enough pile of shite. 'I just thought maybe you and Jennifer stayed in touch and all...?'"

Recalling this made Spots frown.

"Tony Cummins' daughter he's talking about," he said.

"Well did you? Stay in touch with Jennifer?"

"You and Christy. A right bill of goods the pair of you. Jaysus."

"It's just a question. First love, there's no cure."

His eyes narrowed. I'd never been good at figuring when disdain turned to anger with Spots.

"Ancient history, Tommy. It was the last century – the last *millennium*, for God's sakes."

"So you're totally over her. Which explains you rearing up here on me. Obviously."

Spots closed his eyes. A horse-laugh from someone drew them open again. He shook his shoulders as though he'd felt a draught.

"For your information," he said, "I actually met them once, the happy couple, Jennifer and the hub. Liam. It was one of those weird things, like it was fate that we bump into one another – destiny, whatever. And me on the flat of me back out in that place beyond in Sallynoggin. Christ."

"Rehab, you're talking about? Physio, I mean."

"Yeah that kind of rehab. But there she was, Jenn, in visiting someone. Couldn't believe it. Thought it was the, you know? Hallucinating? But that's when I saw it – Jenn had actually turned into her mother. Know what I mean?"

My expression said enough, I reckoned.

"Yep, I was half expecting to see rosary beads. Christ, I thought to myself after, how did I not see that coming."

"You should've had rosary beads with you. Impress her and all."

"Oh but you're the funny fellow."

"What about the hub? Liam Somebody?"

"Why are you asking me?"

"It's not sour grapes now, or anything. Oh God, no."

"Look. He is complete, total straightsville. OK? Murphy, Liam Murphy. Big fella, hardworking. Quiet type, a builder I do believe. Not your quote, unquote, bad boy."

"Tell me then, Mr. Bad Boy. Did you get on with her da?"

He leaned back as though something rotten had been slid under his nose.

"Why or how, exactly, would this be any of your business?"

"He hardly welcomed you with open arms I'd say. No offence."

Instead of a harsh retort he sucked his teeth and looked away. I finished my pint. It wasn't getting the job done. I couldn't hold off the hankering for the hard stuff much longer.

"Back to Christy," Spots said. "I says to him, Christy, that particular party you're asking about? He won't appreciate you going around like this. His family won't either, let me tell you."

"And?"

"And nothing. Christy just looks at me, like: so...? You have to remember he's not all there, so he isn't, sad to say."

Spots wasn't wrong about Christy. But he wasn't sad either.

"That's when he drops his clanger: 'Tommy Malone's looking for him.'"

He was waiting for a reaction. I wasn't sure what to say.

"Makes sense he'd ask you, though," I said, finally. "I mean to say, you want the low-down, Spots Feeney's the man. Right?"

The trademark freckles had faded over the years. They stood out like tiny holes now.

"'The low-down'? Are you out of your tiny mind? Even if I did know anything, you think I'd tell the likes of Christy Cullinane?"

"Fair enough. So tell it to me instead, then."

Grabbing his glass like it was a hand from a lifeboat, Spots drained it and clapped it back on the table. He eased back into his bleak study of proceedings.

Gameboy was tacking back our way. It was his round anyway. After the drinks came, Gameboy felt entitled to edge back into his topics of interest. Government surveillance. He was allowed to proceed – for a while. I wished I'd remembered to power my mobile off. I got to it on the third ring, though. 'Unknown.' Over a background of crappy techno, I got a hoarse-sounding hello. My hello back got me another hello. I gave it a few more tries. Nothing. I ended the call.

"See?" Gameboy said. "Amn't I just after telling you? Way more dropped calls this last while, way more. Know why?"

"Because the network is shite?"

"Ah that's what they *want* you to think."

"Who does."

"Who do you think."

My mobile was buzzing again. Mr. Unknown was back. There was no hello this time. No music in the background now either, but something that sounded like traffic.

"Who's this?"

I heard was hard breathing, a whisper. Then it was gone.

*   *   *

Driving underground to park always gave me heebie jeebies. It's not something a normal human being should be doing.

The IKEA flat packs had not budged. Same for the tiles, and the glue, and the grout. Likewise, the trowel and the spacers and everything else. Everything on pause, occupant included -

- I had a text. At first I didn't believe it. I counted to five and read it again. The words hadn't changed. They hadn't gone away either: Report to OCU in a.m. Text back to confirm order received. 'Order?' Somebody had lit a fire under Delaney. I squeezed an 'OK' out of my fingers and hit Send. So be it, was my thought. But come the morning, by God I'd put a straightener on this nonsense.

I freed a tube of Becks from the fridge and fired up the laptop. Staying away from Facebook was not as hard as Id' expected. I wasn't much of a Facebooker to begin with. A week and more would go by between Sonia's updates. She was very measured about what she'd say too. You'd think she was a copper, herself.

When I saw my inbox then, I didn't believe it. Sonia? Hoax was my first thought, or her account has been hijacked. But it seemed to be the genuine article.

Having funnnn!!! Family soooo older(!) Lots of changes. 'Irish accent'! Sooo many people, sooo small place. Lots of Mainlanders! OMG SHOPPING! PRO shopper…! Miss you, Tom.

Oh my heart. Nobody called me Tom except her. No XX, of course. But was there something else to it? Maybe it was the old subconscious at work, her pushing back against what she really wanted, which was the old fare-thee-well-and-fuck-far-off plan. I tried to snuff that notion out.

I re-read the email. Even the 'sent from my iPhone' was adorable. The picture she attached had a forest of skyscrapers in the background. Kowloon? If that was her cousin Jenny… there was no nice way to say it: Jenny was daw-faced. One of those flat, disc-shaped faces that put you in mind of a saucepan lid. The small eyes didn't help. Plus, Cousin Jenny had caught the Burberry fever. But since when was I so pass-remarkable? My heart twisted and heaved.

"Tom misses you too, Sonia."

I liked the sound of that. I said it again. I tried to say it in Mandarin. My interest in learning Mandarin only went so far. About as far as that small mole on Sonia's thigh. The thought made me reel with lust. I sat back. I couldn't blame the Becks beer, or the pints of Bud or the two Jemmys either, or the stink off the IKEA for that matter – for the number of efforts I needed to come up with a reply to Sonia's email. Still, I managed to stick to my policy. Messages had to be brief and low-key. Restrained. I didn't even make a crack about the latest shit to hit the fan here. She didn't need updates on the shambles here. Er, worse by the day?

It was after midnight when I conked out. I knew this because I had unplugged the clock so I wouldn't end up looking at it when I woke up. The nocturnal episodes had kept themselves to a fairly short loop lately. It was still me running down an alley or between things, or out in traffic. But that night was good. I didn't wake up with my heart leaping out of my chest, and leaping/falling out of the bed to fight the world.

The Dublin that I woke up to was technically in daylight, but also a Dublin under bunched up, grubby-looking clouds. A feed of pints came at a cost: feeling rough as a badger's arse the morning after. That's the deal. In the shower, I tried to forecast what the day might bring. Going to the wall with Nolan? There'd be a cost to that too. How much, I couldn't tell. Later, over corn flakes, I looked around the apartment and tried to figure what I'd miss about it. Not much. The twenty grand I've lost on the place, of course. God knows, I'd waited long enough to buy my own place, but if Sonia wasn't – I got up from the table like it had caught on fire. The final item before locking up was always the same. I'd always be OCD about the Sig: holster release, safety, chamber, clip and... Three times I checked it.

It felt weird not to be behind the wheel. I had decided that I might as well walk over to the OCU. Fifteen minutes would get me there. Brisk walk. Clear the head. Standing next to the light to cross Conyngham Rd was a shaky-looking character, draped in what looked like a sleeping bag. Slept rough in the Park, I surmised. His beady eyes stayed on me as I approached, eyes that were unnervingly clear and off-kilter at the same time. I thought of Christy

Cullinane. Spots was right to be worked up. If Christy was going around blathering his head off, he needed that talking-to, ASAP. It had to be me.

*　　*　　*

Sergeant Áine intercepted me on my way to Nolan.

"The meeting's at ten," she said. "Éamonn's office."

She waited for a response. Not for long, however.

"I can show you around in the meantime."

Ah don't bother, you're grand, I beamed out mentally. I'll just stand here like a complete tool. But something about her brisk manner got to me. Next thing I knew, I was walking around after her. She introduced me to some OCU coppers amongst whom was that bollocks of a driver from yesterday. 'Mick' was a Detective Mick Quinn. Was 'Mick' less of a poser here? Judging by the thin smile, apparently not.

We were soon back by her pod. She waved at a spare chair. I preferred to stand. Macker had emailed. It was one of his cryptic efforts. *Item A: Seán D sub U, WTF?* But I got it: Seán Devine was standing in – 'subbing' – for me. Item B: *WYB*. No need to translate that one: Watch Your Back.

Áine took out a file folder and placed it on the desk, and nudged it in my direction.

"If you're curious," she said.

There were about a dozen pages of PULSE print-outs. Tony Cummins' name was at the top of each.

"That one's not that long ago," she said. The photo was from two years back. Cummins looking a bit shop-worn in it.

"Maybe you knew him to see already?"

"Me? Because I'm from Crumlin too, like?"

She nodded as though this was of no interest and moved off. I did a quick march through the pages. Tony Cummins was a bit of a time capsule really. A relic. His Dublin was history, a Dublin where if you asked for espresso, they'd send you to the post office.

Cummins made his debut with Eighty-Seven Kelly out of Walkinstown, a colourful but clumsy gouger of long standing remembered in name because of his answers in court about how many times he'd been arrested. Whatever Tony Cummins did or didn't learn from Kelly, it wasn't enough to keep him out of prison. He was married to Bernadette Cummins by then, née Rooney. I couldn't help reading things into the face in that long-ago arrest photo: defiance, amusement. The usual quiet hatred.

It was entirely possible that, like Kelly, Tony Cummins had started out regarding the drug business as dirty. But after a stay in prison, and after looking around and sniffing the winds of change, he'd changed his tune. Parting company from the Kellys – they were soon gone to the wall anyway – Cummins appeared to sail through probation. He was a husband (Bernie) father (Darren), an a 'house painter.'

It wasn't paint jobs kept Tony busy for the next nine years or so. His name came up over and over again in criminal investigations. Nothing stuck – this in spite of a half dozen arrests and serious interviews by serious coppers too. Armed robberies of security vans, post offices, banks. Linked to gun smuggling, vehicle theft, hijackings, extortion. First-tier suspect in several shootings and pipe bombings. Believed to have disappeared someone who'd been paid to shoot him. Undertook witness intimidation or directed persons to do so. Even surveillance on him and his cohorts never got up material that could put Tony Cummins behind bars.

Then the day came when he decided he'd go after the Guards. Not 'go after' as in shoot at. He'd sue them. Two Albanians had been found with identical injuries up by the canal, one of them dead already. One of the first places raided was the Cummins home. Darren came out of it with a dislocated shoulder and cuts, Tony with a black eye that he was only too happy to parade like lepers' sores before each and every camera he could find. It ended in a stalemate. I half-remembered a picture of him from back then, a big smile plastered to his face as he left a courthouse.

Even as he dug himself into the drug trade, the white van full of painter's tools was parked outside the Cummins': Anthony Cummins, family man, painter by trade. He didn't take after the other scobes by moving out a mini-fortress place out Kildare way. No Ferraris in Marbella, no blow-out weekends in London. Was this Bernie Cummins' doing, I wondered. A promise she dragged out of him, to let her fantasize that they were a normal family? Did she never once ask him: Tony, is it true what I'm after hearing, that you ordered a man kneecapped? Oh and pass the salt will you, love.

What did for Tony Cummins in the end was a combination of things. We'd made serious inroads with proceeds of crime and joint task force stuff. Cummins had always had competition, but it got so's it wasn't just sorting out the next crop of upstarts from Bluebell or Inchicore. Things had gone global. Bad guys were coming to our fair isle from all over. A lot of them were very bad articles too. It wasn't just the drugs trade they wanted. They were after everything – thieving, brothels, smuggling, fraud, money laundering. They didn't bat an eye at killing people either.

And then of course there was the North. People didn't expect the Good Friday thing to last, but last it did. The 'RA already had their rackets, but a bunch of them took a serious look South, and decided it was time. Time to set up shop in hard-done areas of Dublin and in towns down the country. Time to scatter the bits-and-bobs of gangs who were there already, even former 'RA pals and their hangers-on.

In a couple of years, it was all theirs. They left some longtime Dublin gangsters alone – to keep them on edge and biddable. Better that than all-out gang war on the streets. Tony Cummins was the exception – an independent of sorts who was let carry on some of his ventures. The talk was that he had connections. That he had done one of the Nordie hardmen a favour years back. God knows there was more than enough guff to go around. He was paying his passage like everyone else, I'd bet. Whether or which, there were – there *are* – massively temperamental heads involved, and the wheels were liable to come off at any given moment.

Still, Cummins managed. He had the rep of keeping a cool head when it came to working things out, i.e. not taking mad excursions into RamboLand. But heroin was tearing through every working class area of Dublin like a tornado, shredding everything in its path: lives, marriages, families. The old loyalties were out the window. The savage feuding and the street shootings

73

didn't stop either. It got so that even the likes of Tony Cummins couldn't be sure that he wouldn't step out his hall door one fine morning and meet the proverbial strung-out seventeen-year-old Grand Theft Auto maestro with the balaclava and the gun.

Yet he could've come through this, even The Boom was still booming. He had money, he had people working for him, he had connections. He could've worked out a new alliance, for a while at least. He could've bowed out even, left the country like other skangers did, for Costa del Sol or the like. But there was that karma thing again. It was known that Darren Cummins had a sadistic turn of mind. Also, he was liable to say and do mad stuff when he was off his face. It came as no great surprise that he stepped out of a restaurant one night and into a double shotgun blast.

Nothing in these pages so much as hinted at what effect that had on Tony Cummins. Nor Bernie Cummins, for that matter. For a moment then, I saw her wan face and her flinching smile again. What made this woman tick? Bernie, I said then in silent conversation with her, *come here to me, I know we all live on the banks of denial. It doesn't mean we have to go swimming in it every single day!*

...what finally got Tony Cummins off the streets came in a short summary. Destiny sent a shaper the name of Adam Gibbons, him and a chef turned restaurant owner. Gibbons, who was known to work for Tony Cummins, one day announced to this restaurant owner that, as Darren Cummins had just been to his restaurant, this fact surely played some part in Darren getting kilt. In other words, this restaurant bloke must have tipped off the killers. Thus and therefore, said restaurateur could only get out of this situation by coughing up serious money, i.e. fifty grand. Otherwise, it was face Tony Cummins.

Completely bogus. It was this Gibbons head trying to hoke up some runaway money. He'd worked for Tony Cummins for years but now he was jumpy. He wanted out before –his words – 'Tony turned on me.' Cummins, he claimed, had 'lost his rag with him' over Darren's murder. Tony had told him he should've seen it coming and kept Darren out of harm's way. Or worse, Cummins suspected that Gibbons might've tipped off to the killers. Either way, that to Gibbons meant that Tony Cummins was liable to do for him.

This extortion effort spooked the restaurateur / chef so much that he ran straight to the Guards. We steered him through it and, along with wire recordings and what Gibbons was to spill later on, it was enough to get Tony Cummins' arse into judge-only trial in the Special Criminal Court. He got hit good and hard: 12 to 15.

- That ringing was coming from this extension there. Áine.

"OK we're up," she said. "Éamonn's office."

Nolan waved us in but continued his phone conversation, just listening. Áine had a notebook open and resting on her knee. While we waited for Nolan to wrap up his call she watched a screensaver, photos of somewhere that wasn't Ireland. After Nolan finished his call, he took a few moments to eye something he had written on a pad. Then he looked from me to Áine and back.

"Anything jump out at you in that report Tommy?"

"Maybe not so much Cummins. More his missus really."

Nolan's smile was a slight twisting of his mouth.

"Right," he said. "As in she's our key here? So we need to make things easy for her. What she wants she gets. But it's time to see what Tony thinks of how matters are moving now, though."

He glanced at his watch and back at me. I had a pretty good idea of what was coming.

"Portlaoise," Nolan said. "Time to chew the fat with Tony."

"Is he expecting a visit?"

He nodded and squared his mobile with the edge of a folder.

"Just Cummins himself? Or will he have representation?"

"Just him, and your good self, of course. OK?"

Not OK. I said nothing.

"We're there to help," Nolan went on, "that's the message. Yes, we'll commit serious resources to finding his son. But Tony baby needs to know that we need his buy-in. So it's 'Look Tony, without your help finding this son of yours is a no-go.'"

Was he waiting for a sign that I'd memorize these lines?

"It's Bernie'll make or break this. He can't deny her."

75

Again he paused. He obviously didn't like waiting.

"You know she's starting more chemo?" he asked.

I told Nolan that I did not. Something sour and ugly had begun burrowing around in my mind.

"That's confidential, by the way. I mention it because Tony knows it's not looking good for her right now."

This item stayed hanging in the room a while.

"Now," he continued, "bearing in mind that he knows this, we still don't have much of a picture of Tony Cummins' mental state at the present time. You'll be sussing that out today also. He may *say* he's ready to deal, but when it comes time to follow through?"

"Say he gets bollicky with me What's the drill?"

"Back off, of course. But... if you feel it'll work, you remind him that it's him came to us, or his wife did. Also –" he turned to Áine. "Missing Persons? How many again, Cat?"

"Two thousand plus so far this year," she said. "Outstandings are seven hundred thirty something."

Did this Áine one really keep facts like that at her fingertips? But there was trickery in that figure, I knew. There was 'missing' and there was missing. What she was doing was plugging in this year's outstandings to the carry-forward number that went back all the way to the Seventies. Not to begin to factor in all the immigrants and refugees and failed asylums that poured in since.

"You hear that?" Nolan asked. "That's how you remind Tony that we can't perform miracles. Oh, you could maybe ask him if he's aware of all the cutbacks, the effect they're having on us?"

This might have been as close as Nolan got to 'funny.'

He placed a hand on his mobile, a signal that we were finished. I followed Áine down a hallway, out into a small, enclosed car park. She stopped and poked her key in her palm.

"Anything you need before we hit the road?"

Need? Christ, I thought. Where to start.

8

The car key that Áine was toting around went with a newish, dusty-looking Octavia. I got in and put on my belt. Said nothing.

She didn't feel any need to share what route she'd take to get out to the M7. Didn't feel any need to talk at all actually. I guessed right anyway: we were out the Chapelizod gate and poking along the South Circ in no time. She put Kilmainham behind us right quick and proceeded to make short work of the Inchicore Road. We came a cropper with road works on a stretch of Tyrconnel Road. Still, we were on the bridge over the M50 in no time.

Soon, the signs were slipping by: Newcastle, Belgard, Kingswood. Áine seemed to relax a bit. She was a culchie, so by definition had a yen for fields and hills and cows etc. Maybe not. It'd be a while before I got a fix on her. Getting ordered to drop what she was doing and partner up some loolah parachuted in wasn't the best intro.

"Rathcoole," she said as the sign drew nearer.

"Right. Rathcoole you have to watch."

She looked over as though to air a grievance.

"Some serious heavies there," I said. "That's all."

"There's a Rathcoole in Sligo as well."

We were actually having a conversation?

"Sligo, nice."

"You know Sligo? County Sligo?"

"I heard it's nice. Mountains, lakes. Sea and stuff. Right?"

The flicker around her mouth might've been that thing they call chagrin. Whatever loolah was driving the lorry ahead didn't get the concept of lanes. As smooth as silk Áine slid into fourth and the Octavia took off like the clappers. Hills – not clouds as I'd thought – slid across the window as she eased back into our lane. The Welcome to County Kildare sign flew by

"Have you been to Portlaoise before? The prison?"

I told her I hadn't. All I knew was that it was high security, home to hard-core gangsters and IRA heads. We passed a longish line of cars. One had a dog half-out the window. Comical, what the air rushing by does to a dog's face. It made her smile too. A remark on dogs opened up a careful-enough chat. People and dogs, dogs and people, and so forth. I told her about an auld fella we knew growing up, Sailor Kelly. How he had a face like a scotch terrier and we'd bark at him sometimes.

Dogs moved us on to dog owners. It turned out she and I knew people in common. Plate Glass Sheehy, Murder Squad vet, kept greyhounds. Typical Kerryman: in the revolving door behind you, out ahead of you. She knew Paddy Toner in Drugs Central. Paddy, the only man left on the planet who listened to Bob Geldof's records. He actually enjoyed the slagging he got for it.

Bit by bit, the conversation tacked over toward the personal side. I offered a presentable version of Tommy Malone's life and times to date. The apartment thing, of course, and how I was still of two minds about it. The 'fiancée traveling in Asia' item got by without comment. The phrase sounded weird to me, even.

By the time we get the first sign for Portlaoise, I had learned that Áine had a separation ongoing. The hub worked in one of the banks, but being as the banks were wrecked and laying off left right and centre, the situation was dodgy. The stress had brought out issues, she said. He wanted out, out of Ireland. The problem was, she didn't. At least they didn't have kids, she said.

We eased out of that before it got heavy. Holiday stuff: France was always nice (her contribution). Austria was gorgeous (Sonia's description that I hijacked). Car insurance, the VHI. Restaurants that didn't cost an arm and a leg, and sports teams and what-have-you. She took a call at the exact moment we were Welcomed to County Laois. The phone conversation had something to do with food? It turned out to be dog food.

"My sister," she said, after the call.

I went back to pretending to be interested in the passing hedges and fields. We flew by trailers plastered with ads, parked near the road. A cluster of unfinished houses, one of the famous/infamous ghost estates, flashed by. A few Vegas style monstrosities appeared, all columns and interlock.

Bits of our conversation drifted back into my mind. She was working on human trafficking and prostitution, mostly to do with knocking shops down Waterford and Cork way. The crash hasn't made any difference. Kids were still smuggled in from all over. Africa, China, even from Iraq. So, I thought: a marriage a gone bad. A job where she dealt with the absolute worst of humanity. This Áine one was really up against it.

"A question," I said then. "What's Nolan's plan here?"

"His plan..? Have you asked him?"

She pretended the horizon required her keen scrutiny. So the small talk had been camouflage. The icebergs were still there. The motorway swung away from us and we slowed for a roundabout. Fields, the odd house, hedges, flowed by. A long, straight road, patchy-wet from showers, led us into town proper. Killeshin Hotel – Great Weekend Deals! The road narrowed again. I was thinking about Bernie Cummins.

"Whatever it takes. Is that his style? Nolan's?"

"Aren't you being a bit dramatic there?"

"What I mean is, he knows Bernie Cummins is sick."

"Yes, but who made the approach? Us or them?"

The party line. Her gaze didn't budge from the road ahead.

"And Quinn. Mick Quinn, is it?"

She looked over. I had asked a stupid question?

"He's tight with Nolan, is he?"

"They go back," she said. "So yes, they're pretty tight."

We coasted by newish apartments, a car dealership. Open fields behind a low stone wall. Older terraces, clues that we were close to the town centre, began to run along to the driver's side. This was the main Dublin road back then. We came through here on an outing with the other altar boys, to a place near Galway, an amusement arcade and swim place. It could've been that trip when it started. Terry and Father ...

"That's part of the prison, that place?"

"It's the visitors' centre," she said. "Is all this new to you?"

"If it's more than ten mile out of Dublin, it's new to me."

Then I spotted them, the two old prison towers, rising above the hedges. The front of the prison had been cleared of the sheds and bungalow that I remember. It looked like a little park now, with grass and shrubs and pavers and what-have-you. The railings would be right at home around a posh house. They had even managed to make the lines of anti-ram bollards behind them look normal. The makeover had exposed old prison walls. They didn't look that high any more. That old Lord of the Rings type door that I remembered between the towers was left as it was, though.

"The army's here somewhere? Guarding the place, I mean."

"They patrol on the roof more, I believe."

She made a U-turn back to the visitors' centre. There were two cars at the gate ahead of us. I was getting a clammy, claustrophobic feeling. And I hadn't even left the car yet.

There was nary a Guard or prison officer to be seen. Áine took out her card got out and walked to what looked like a video-link station by the gate. I tried to count the cameras. The second car was let in. Áine said something to the camera, nodded and headed back to the car.

"They'll want your mobile," she said. "No exceptions, since well, you know."

I did know. The wild booze-and-drugs Christmas parties in the prison had turned up on YouTube, and caused ructions.

The gate swung open. I saw vans, a single Garda car, two paddy-wagons. There were plenty of parking spots. We climbed out, closing our doors at the same time. From a door-opening next to some kind of a guard house, a bloke in a prison guard uniform appeared. Owl-eyed, fortyish, sagging a bit, he held my card at face level to compare it with the real item. He looked from me to Áine and back.

"First time here?"

"That's right."

"We'll release you in due course. But only as long as you behave yourself."

This comedian then pointed us toward a door. I was all too aware of the cameras, of the mass of the buildings around us, of what went on here. A piercing stink of disinfectant brought me back. Terry spent a total of four and a half years in a place like this, the sum of his two episodes of imprisonment. OK, not as severe as here, but still I hated every single second of the visits. Hated Terry. Hated myself for hating Terry.

A mirrored one-way ran a section the length of the narrow room ahead. Not much more than a corridor really, it reminded me of the security checks at the airport. In here it was just me and a near-retirement-looking prison officer who was separating a plastic tray from a stack.

I switched off my phone, met his eye.

"Just so's you know? I'm front-line, so I'm armed."

It took a moment for him to get it. He looked over at the one-way. Prison Officer Friendly Enough was no more. Prison Officer Pissed-Off took over.

"Take off the jacket first."

I treated the performance as though I was doing my exit test for the gun card all over again. Fellas failed it because they took their eyes off the pistol for a second when they were disarming it. I slid the clip slowly and precisely to a a a corner of the tray like a magician about to disappear a coin.

"Your personal items will be secured until your departure."

The arrival of someone in civvies at the other end of the room curtailed my effort to see anything through the one-way. New arrival was not friendly, and he wanted me to know that.

"John Mulhern," he said. "This way. I've a room booked."

We stopped at the end of a passageway by a blind metal security door. Mulhern looked up at the camera. The pay-off was a loud, harsh buzz. The motorized door swung open, stopping with a final-sounding, railway-shunting calibre clank. Inside were metal grilles, serious-looking locks, all backed up by heavily painted cement everywhere. Another uniform needed to check us here.

"Your Garda card?"

Mulhern was already very correctly holding his own ID up. Then we were through yet another door. Every door we passed had numbers on them. Mulhern stopped by a 'D14' and pulled it open. A stale smell wafted out: a match for an empty biscuit tin. There was no one-way glass, just a table and cloth-covered chairs. We could be in an office, almost. Mulhern made his way to the far side of the table. He grasped the back of a chair and stared at me.

"You're meeting Anthony for the first time?"

"I am."

"OK. Smiler, they call him around here. Have you've been briefed on him?"

Tony Cummins' arrest photo dropped into my mind.

"Some."

A northwards move of eyebrows hinted that this 'briefing' was by Mulhern's standards decidedly pissant.

"He has his place the pecking order here. C Block. You know how the blocks are divided up here?"

"Sort of. You put the IRA crowd in E Block?"

"'The subversives.' That's right, yes."

"Next to the bank directors and the politicians, is it? Or the Father O'Paedophiles?"

Mulhern received my wit poorly. He went on, tonelessly.

"You'll need to be extra cautious with Cummins. Extra wary. He'll test you."

He paused then, waited for questions. I hadn't come up on the last bus. I knew what he wanted – an excuse to slap another snooty retort on me. I studied his receding hair line instead.

"He has a strong personality," he went on. "A lot of the inmates here do. They try to condition the staff, to make everything seem friendly. Then they see their opening. But Anthony Cummins, he could give the psychology people a run for their money."

"Thanks," I said. "I have some experience in the stuff."

Mulhern's eyes lost focus and his forehead wrinkled, like he was dealing with trapped wind.

"I have to tell you," he said, "we were surprised he agreed to this. He's running a huge risk. If word were to get out?"

"Do you think word will get out?"

He couldn't carry a hard stare. He knew it too, I figured, and it bothered him. He nodded toward a black bubble on the ceiling.

"Your encounter will be recorded."

He released his grip on the chair and stood up straight, and waited. Another chance for me to ask questions that he could hit with a stick? Or maybe he just wanted to get a last look at this big-shot super-cop down from Dublin. The gobshite about to stumble into a trap set by 'Anthony' Cummins. He scraped both corners of his gob, a delicate gesture that always reminded me of cats.

"OK, Sergeant, work away. He's all yours, 'Smiler.' Just remember, like we say here, sharks have a smile too."

9

Tony Cummins was an eye-opener. He was younger-looking, and fresher-looking, than I'd expected. You'd have thought that he had just stepped in off the street for a little chat. Strangely, this only made me feel the prison wrapping itself around me tighter. Distracting details buzzed in my mind. The open-necked shirt was too white. Were inmates actually allowed to wearing a watch?

Mulhern waited by the door for us to settle. Cummins smiled up at him.

"Double cappuccino for me. Not sure what this man wants."

The Dublin twang was where it should be, so far up his *no-az*, it's almost in his *eye-az*.

"A sense of humour makes all the difference," said Cummins, staring at the door after Mulhern left. "Don't you think, Tommy?"

I took my time flipping open my notebook.

"Sergeant," I said.

"Still using them things? No little computery yokes at all?"

My pencil needed attention too. I heard him shift in the chair.

"Come on, you just watch it all on video later on anyways."

I let my eyes go flat before looking up. Left arm on the armrest, he was leaning a little that way, stroking his lip with his little finger. I kicked away a sudden thought: was I on the losing side here?

"So thanks for dropping by," he said. "Just so's you know from the kick-off here. I've got no axe to grind with you or yours. OK?"

I stayed with my stone-face.

"How is Sheila anyway?"

"I don't know a Sheila."

There was a flicker in his eye but the smile stayed firm.

"It's your Ma I'm referring to. A true friend to Bernie."

He threw back his head then and laughed softly.

"Come on," he said. "You have to laugh. The women mate for life. Pals, I mean, not the other business. They made their First Communion together, your mother and Bernie, right?"

"I'm not sure."

He lifted his arm to stroke the back of his neck, eyeing me all the while. He wanted me to notice that he has been moving iron around? Message received.

"Friends," he murmured. "Oh yes. Through thick and thin."

Trew tick an' tin. Platinum Dub, all right.

"Ever wonder about your old pals? Where are they now, like?"

My answer was a shrug. It felt like the room was shrinking.

"No? Really? Remember so-and-so? Is he in jail? Gone straight? Is he on the dole on a beach in Spain? In the ground...?"

"You probably know more about the subject than I do."

Cummins seemed to like this answer. He blinked and smiled.

"Look, I respect loyalty, I do. Loyalty plain and simple."

Eyes locked on mine, he made two philosophical nods.

"So tell your Ma she has my respect. No matter what."

I thought about the people watching this a room or two over, and wondered if they could feel the same chill as I did. Cummins stopped stroking the back of his neck.

"Everything okay there Tommy – Sergeant, I mean?"

"This 'no matter what' of ours. It means what?"

"Oh come on now. It's just an expression. English as she is spoken, and all that."

"A person might think it's a plan. Or a threat."

"Dear oh dear." The smile looked genuine. "Someone got out the wrong side of the bed."

"There's something you want. But I haven't heard what it is yet."

He let down his arm and began a study of the table top. When he looked up again, the smile had become more of a grimace.

"This is your game plan?"

"There is no game plan. I'm here to listen, is all."

He slid down a little in the chair.

"Well well well. We have the new-style copper here, do we. Wakes up, slides out of his designer apartment – oh by the way, meant to ask you. You like living in one of those? To me, they'd be like living in a glasshouse. Get the feeling people can see in? But sure, I suppose they're used to them over there, aren't they."

I already knew what was coming.

"Hong Kong, is it? Pictures I seen, it's wall to wall skyscrapers. Jesus. Anyway. Where were we? The new-style copper – hey, did you used to have an old banger? An Escort, a red one? I nearly forgot. God, what a tragedy. Out of commission now I suppose."

I put down my pencil and stared back into the recessed eyes. Somewhere in there, I might pick up a signal that Tony Cummins had a part in what was to be my murder that day in Dalkey.

"What exactly is it you want."

"Nobody told you? All right. What I want is Gary found, and put in a safe place. Do you need a minute to write that down?"

"Will that be all?"

"He needs detox. Treatment, counselling. He needs anger-management stuff too, if you're asking."

"Did you forget anything?"

"If you have to give him a clatter, I wouldn't mind too much."

"Right. You don't have Darren to put order on him for you."

The twinkle in his eyes froze.

"They should do a study of you. How someone can turn out the way you did. Compared to that brother of yours."

His words had no effect. I had been ready for this in some way that I hadn't even realized.

"Yeah I do know," I said. "How, is because I'm the one gets to walk out of here and head back to Dublin. Have a bit of dinner, maybe a Quarter Pounder – with cheese. A pint or two. Or ten. Sleep in me own bed. Is that the sort of thing you mean?"

He made another, slower blink. The eyes reminded me of when we'd be messing around when we were kids, pretending to be hypnotized. I had shifted onto the balls of my feet, ready to jump.

"You think you can talk to me any way you want? Do –"

The door swinging open cut off the rest. It was Mulhern and by God he was in a dander. He wanted me out. I was in no hurry, however. I had a notebook to close, an elastic band to arrange. The door swung closed faster than I expected. Nolan's face was suddenly about eighteen inches from mine. I didn't even get a chance to pretend I wasn't shocked. Mulhern slid by us, so close I had to step out of his way.

"What's the plan here, Tommy? What is the fucking *plan*?"

So this was Nolan being livid. His stare skipped between my eyes like he was watching tennis.

"Because whatever it is, I need to be in on it. *In advance.*"

The far door opened. I caught sight of Cat, and Mick Quinn.

"We need to communicate here, Sergeant. Yes?"

I found a small scratch on the wall to silently rehearse my response. *The Plan, Arse-face, is this: a) you get out of my light here before I puck the lugs off you, and b) I go back to Dublin where I resume my duties with normal, civilized people. That is The Plan.*

"What in the name of God are you poking Cummins for?"

"Er, because he was trying to run the show?"

"Of course he is! But you can handle that, right?"

"Two, he threatened a Garda officer. A Garda Sergeant."

Nolan looked away, took a few steps over and back.

"OK," he said, like he needed to be sure. "OK. Next step?"

"There is no next step."

Nolan stared at me like I was the Virgin Mary at Fatima.

"You mean, let all this crash and burn?"

"If he wants us," I said, "he'll come around. But if all he was doing was cat-farting around, well so what then."

Nolan, for the first time, looked shocked.

"Cat-farting around? Look, Tony Cummins wants the meet and it's you he wants to talk to."

I had caught Áine's eye at last. I was betting she could read thought-waves too. You drove me here, I beamed out. Keeping the fact from me that you and Nolan and even Quinn were going to be in the audience here. Words would be had.

"You just have to get the ball rolling," Nolan went on. "You enable, see? Establish a comfort level. And if that involves a bit of his mind games, or slagging, well you can deal with that I am sure."

Slagging, I thought. 'No matter what' didn't sound like a slag.

"After you get him on the hook you can step back."

"I sit there and let him threaten me?"

"That's just him feeling you out. You know that."

"He knew about my fiancée, about where I live. About the shooting back in Dalkey – he even knew the car I was driving."

"He's trying to run you a bit. So? What did you expect?"

He gestured toward the closed door.

"Look, he knows we have him by the hasp. That's why he's messing with your head. He's looking to see what he can salvage all the same. We play him, he doesn't play us. At the end of the day, he knows that he's cornered."

Surely to God, I thought, even Nolan knew what a cornered animal could do. Buy he seemed to have moved on a different track now. He dropped his head and came back up and chortling. He stopped soon enough and caught my eye, and winked.

"So let's try round two, Tommy. OK?"

I looked over at the door again. If I looked long enough, maybe I'd see Tony Cummins' fist and forearm sticking through it.

*   *   *

"What were we saying? Before we were so rudely interrupted."

Cummins was a lot less smiley now. Still, he was trying.

"You were talking about your son."

He turned to look directly at the camera. It was like he was looking for approval of his display of great patience dealing with this thicko copper here.

"What do they want, do you think? Them out there watching."

"They want progress."

He dropped his voice to a stage whisper and leaned in a tad.

"You mean they want me to rat people out. Just say it."

He leaned back and eyed the camera again.

"Oh yes," he said, "we have Tony Cummins where we want him now. Now we'll get what we couldn't get at the trial, with our deals and our inducements and ..."

He turned to examining the wall. Maybe it was badly painted?

"Now correct me if I'm wrong, but I do believe that is extortion? Maybe even hostage-taking? What would you call it?"

A big part of good interview technique is the copper knowing when to keep his trap shut. Cummins was keen to talk, though.

"Your plea bargain circus didn't work. The stoolie deals didn't either. God knows you tried but. Months, it went on."

His gaze swung back my way, narrow and hard.

"So what are the chances of me snitching, would you say?"

"I'd say they're pretty good in actual fact."

I did not get the reaction I expected. He began to study his nails. When he spoke it was so low I almost missed the first words.

"Bernie's a good-living, decent person. A lady. You understand that. You were reared proper, Bernie said. Is that right?"

"My Ma would be the one to ask."

"Your Ma's all right. Bernie deserves good things to happen to her. Especially now. Just like your Ma does too. Don't get me wrong. What I'm saying is, nobody deserves to lose a son."

A patch of skin on Cummins' forehead gave off a dull shine.

"Look, I know what people say. 'How could Bernie have married that Cummins fella?' I don't care. Nobody can judge Bernie – nobody. What's done is done. That's life. C'est la vie."

He looked up from his nails.

"You don't believe me about a certain matter, do you. A matter relating to your family."

I knew where he'd take this. I got that sharp, almost black and white vision thing rightaway. Edges, shapes – everything – felt so distinct, so near. If he said Terry's name, I might lose it.

"Get the ball rolling," I said. "Give us something to work with."

He offered a bashful smile but his eyes grew fixed again.

"All right. Firm but fair, as they say. No kiss first though? Not even a cuddle?"

"Let me ask you something then. Gary's gone missing but no-one's called Missing Persons Bureau. Can you explain that?"

"You mean to the two lazy, fat coppers and the fat, lazy, culchie secretary there in 'Missing Persons'? Not one of whom give a flying shite about Gary? That 'Missing Persons Bureau'?"

"If you want to get things moving here, that's not the way."

"OK. So what exactly does your 'get things moving' look like?"

"It means we look for Gary. Where should we start?"

Cummins' eyes shed their intensity and came to rest on the wall behind me. Something had given way in him – I hoped.

"You're asking the wrong man, I'm sorry to say."

"You're telling me that you're not in touch with Gary?"

He shook his head.

"Every family has their thing," he said. "The way of the world."

"I know – we know – that Gary has problems."

"'Problems?' You can say that again. You've been through the mill yourself, with your own situation. You learn a lot of things you never wanted to learn though. Right?"

"You're talking about addiction? Or is it something else?"

Again there was that confusion between smiling and rage.

"Can you tell me where Gary's staying then? Or who with?"

Cummins shook his head again. He resumed his wall-stare. When eventually he spoke, his words came in a slow monotone.

"I put Gary out. Out of the house. This was a while back."

"How long ago was that?"

"Last July. You can only do so much. Know what I mean?"

I opted for stalling. His gaze moved from the wall back to me.

"I had to. Bernie, she could never do something like that. Gary was out of order, out of control really."

"So where did he go?"

He drew in a breath, and let it out his nose in a slow, soft whistle.

"Did he head for Jennifer's maybe?"

He seemed to have taken a vow of silence.

"His sister, I'm asking you. Did Gary go to Jennifer's?"

Cummins began to shake his head.

"Why wouldn't he go to her?"

He seemed to wrestle with bothering to answer.

"Did Bernie talk to you about this?" he asked instead.

"No. Should she have?"

"You know what Downs is? Of course you do."

"This is your granddaughter you're talking about? Maria?"

I wondered if the camera caught the sudden flash in his eyes. His jaw slid over and back like he had taken a punch.

"That is correct."

"Does Gary visit? Stay with her maybe? It's a big place, I hear."

The jaw went still. He waited until I met his gaze fully.

"I'm going to tell you something now, OK? And if it's the only thing you remember from this conversation, well that'll be a job well done. So here it is. My daughter, Jennifer, and her family, they are in a completely different world to what you're thinking."

"I'm not thinking anything. I'm asking for some basic info."

"No you're not. You're playing to the gallery out there. Your copper pals, a pack of – no, not even wolves. Jackals they are, looking to drag people into this and to mess them up. Listen to me now. Jennifer, she's cut out of her mother. Jennifer is Bernie, and Bernie is Jennifer. Got that?"

He studied the knuckles on his left and began stroking them.

"That might mean nothing to you," he went on. "Or that shower out there watching. But your Ma, she'd know what I'm saying. She'd know there's nothing fake about Bernie."

He stopped stroking his knuckles and flexed his fingers.

"The day Jenn was born, Bernie told me the way things was going to be. It had to be that way. She had the plan from day one."

He glanced my way as though for verification.

"And that's exactly how she was reared, my daughter. My wife laid down the law, and I did what I was told. You're getting this from the horse's mouth. You and your cronies out there can have a good laugh over that now. I don't care."

The frown cut deeper between his eyebrows.

"So Jennifer does not come into this matter. And if I hear that you, or any of the monkeys watching us here hassles Jennifer, there'll be no go on anything. Not an inch. See?"

This warranted at least a mild nod from me.

"But just so's you don't go away with a flea in your ear about this, and because you had the decency to answer the call for my wife, I will tell you something else here. Jennifer and Maria are away. They're in Spain, so they are. It's a break for the both of them. They go over five or six times a year. Maria loves the sea side, right? And Jennifer has friends there. They help her out with Maria, so they do. Good people. Decent people."

He settled back in his chair and reignited his stare. I mulled over what I wanted to say, and couldn't. First off, this bullshit about good and decent people was a complete non-starter with me. I knew good and decent people. And as for the 'friends' that Jennifer allegedly had in Spain I'd bet good money that numbered among them were wives and girlfriends of Dublin gangsters who had transplanted themselves to the Costa.

"So where might he go then, Gary. Give us some start on it."

"Here and there. I tried to keep tabs. I actually had people looking in on him for a while. I tried to keep channels open. It looked good for a bit, I had hope, I really did. But it's a disease."

"Gary was – is – on Methadone?"

Cummins looked from me to the camera and back.

"I don't know. All I know is he'd got a bit calmer. I met him, and we talked. It was the first talk I had with him really, man to man like. Yeah, that's another one for youse to have a giggle over."

He slid a thumbnail along his lower lip.

"You want to know what I told Gary? I'll tell you. I told him that he had no right to break his mother's heart. I also told him I'd be ready to take him back on board, but I needed proof. I needed time to go by too, to see him staying clean."

I wondered: did this fella here ever hear his own words the way that other people heard them? 'Back on board.' Back learning how to be a proper criminal again, under his father's guiding hand.

"So I take it that this has not yet come to pass."

"Correct, Sergeant. That has not come to pass."

He paused mid-stretch, and fixed me with a look that was not unkind.

"Your turn now. Explain to me what's on offer finding Gary."

"I'm not here to make offers."

"Says you. Well I say you better change your tune on that score."

I imagined Nolan out there, rolling his eyes and cursing.

"So tell me then. How are you going to go about it?"

"First is we canvas. Talk to people close to Gary. He has a girl friend?"

"I don't know any more. He did, and that's what I was talking about here when I was saying that things had been looking up for a while. She was good for him, I was told."

"Her name?"

"I forget." Cummins didn't seem to care that his lie was obvious. Maybe he was even proud of it. "Where else would you go looking?"

"His associates. Do you know any of them, I wonder?"

Another shake of the head. I couldn't tell if he got the sarcasm.

"We'd see if he has come in contact with us recently."

"The Guards, like? Arrested and that?"

"That, yeh, or questioned. Or, seen with certain parties in certain places. Associates, meetings, get-togethers. Pubs and clubs."

Cummins nodded a few times. I supposed it meant go on.

"We'd track his bank stuff, his cards. His online activity, of course. That gets more and more important every year now. More useful, like."

"People are iijits, aren't they? The Internet stuff, I mean."

For a moment, I thought he was about to give me a dig about Sonia.

"It's like they leave a trail everywhere. Right? Them new phones too, that they call smart phones? 'Smart? I ask you. More like 'stupid.' Right?"

"Maybe so."

"Definitely, you mean. Go on, about the plan. What else."

"Gary's mobile phone trail. Clinics, doctor visits. Casualty admissions. Dole office. Social Protection interactions."

I stopped when I saw him frown.

"Social welfare, I'm talking about."

"Right, yeh. The new name, OK. Go on."

"Well there are other sources."

"Cameras like? CCTV, right?"

"We probably wouldn't make that first thing."

"Why not? If he's on a camera..?"

"If it's a follow-up on a sighting in a given place, sure. Especially a place we could expect him to be coming back to."

Cummins scratched his chin. Had I just given him instructions for how to find Gary himself? Or for him to pass on to Gary , so he could evade us coppers who'd soon be looking for him?

"What else?"

I left it unanswered. Cummins got the hint, but pressed on.

"Cameras in buses, in taxis, right? Shops, pubs even?"

"Does your son be taking taxis a lot?"

"Well there's no way he's running a car of his own, I'll bet you. C'mere, you have that recognition stuff too, I heard. Is that true?"

"I don't know."

He threw me a disbelieving glance and turned to studying his cuticles.

"The aim is to track Gary's routines," I said. "To put him on a timeline and map out things that way. Patterns, routines. Predictions."

"I see," he said. He turned over his hand. "Yeh. Sort of."

"This's if he is really a missing person. Which is not clear yet."

Cummins' head tilted slowly up. His eyes had almost completely disappeared. A muscle moved by his jaw.

"You'll do better than 'track' Gary. You'll find him."

"It takes time, this stuff. Rome wasn't burned in a day."

But Tony Cummins' train of thought had no stops.

"Find him," he repeated. "You hear me? Find him and bring him to Bernie – or Bernie to him. And like I said, I don't care what you do with him after that. Charge him, hold him over, put him in next to the monkeys above in the zoo. You want a minute to write that down?"

All I could do was wait.

"Something else. This is very important. None of this in the papers. No telly either. No Garda appeal stuff. And not on that website of yours either, that Missing Persons thing. And most definitely not on any Facebook Tweet whatever thing – no way."

Placing his hands flat on the table, he glared up at me from under his eyebrows. He flicked a quick over up toward the glass.

"I don't want 'them' running the show. I want you doing it."

"I can't do this on my own."

"But you'd have the inside track, so you would."

Inside track? I thought of Macker and his epistles.

"There is no inside track."

"You have to say that, I know. But you know what I'm talking about."

"If you mean you want somebody to upend procedures, I can't."

"Don't tell me what you can't do. You find a way, with our without them out there. It's not on them. It's on you."

I kept my waiting face intact, and listened to his breathing.

"So now you want your bag of sweets, I suppose. Right?"

He didn't expect a reply.

"Of course you do. All right, youse listening in out there, my fans in the audience. Are you listening? 17 Clonmore Villas. For all you culchies, that's The Blanch, spitting distance of Corduff. Second last house there."

"Blanchardstown," I said, also for the audience. "A house?"

"Yeah a house. You think it's just a tinker's camp out there?"

"Who – "

"There's a fella. You know him – you should know him, at least. It's his granny's place. The age of Methuselah she is, and she's lost the tun of herself. Doesn't know one day from the next. Like some of the lads in here, ha ha. In anyway, there's a shed down the back. Pull up two slabs in the walk there, right in front of the shed. You go down two, three feet."

"Who's involved?"

"Nobody, is who. God's honest truth, the fella, he doesn't know anything about what's there any more than his granny does. He's banged up for the last four year – that's how he doesn't. So don't bother trying to fit him up over it. They just used the gaff. So go and do a bit of digging."

"Digging for what?"

"For making the streets safer, is what. Isn't that what youse are supposed to be doing? And no, they're not loaded. They were wrapped by an expert."

"Who owns them? Who put them there?"

"Does this look like a confession box to you?

His eyes had lost interest in anything around him. It seemed to be the door he was addressing.

"Eh. One last thing? Phone Bernie. Tell her it's started. Don't forget."

And that, apparently, was that. I waited anyway. He might cough up another bona-fide? But all I saw in the end, or all I believed I saw, was a Tony Cummins already telling himself whatever story he needed to. Whatever it would take to explain away what he had just done.

10

Mulhern held open the door like he was trying to pull it off its hinges. Outside at last, I could breathe again. The air was soft and moist, and smelled of hay and other farmy matters. I watched Quinn strut off in a showy manner alongside Áine, toward the Octavia.

"Walk to the car with me will you," Nolan said. I thought about it, but I went anyway.

"'Tell Bernie it's started,'" he said. "'Tell her... it's started...'?"

OK, so maybe it was a code. All I took from it was that Tony Cummins was bracing himself for something bad, and that his missus should too. Nolan answered his own question.

"Well that did it," he said. "No going back now. So I've called in a watch on this Clonmore Villas place. See who we can bag coming and going before we pounce. Not too long but."

A van started up and coughed a mini-cloud of diesel exhaust our way. We were at Nolan's car now. Quinn stood waiting, arms folded like he had just taken the world title. Áine had havered off toward the Octavia. She did not look around.

"You and Áine make a list what you need and fire it over to me."

"Need for... what?"

Nolan stopped. I kept going a few steps on, just for pig iron.

"This operation," he said. "We're on the move now."

I had come in range of a Quinn look. I stared right back.

"But Cummins is on board now. So that's my part over."

It took Quinn a few moments to pry his pseudo-humorous stare off me.

"Talk to Doherty," Nolan said. "Delaney, I mean. Your C.O."

With that he was off like a dirty shirt. Furthermore, unless I intended to walk back to Dublin, I'd better make my way over to Áine.

Nary a word passed between us as she pulled out onto the road and aimed the Octavia in the general direction of the M7. We were out of Portlaoise quicker than we had come in. At the entrance to the motorway, she put the boot down hard. I waited until she settled into top gear.

"That was a mistake," I said. "Surprises like that are bad ju-ju. OK?"

She pursed her lips and pretended to look around at the countryside. Yet, as the miles began to tick by, I felt something shift. Maybe it was the patches of sun lighting up the fields now. More likely it was realizing that she had to take orders too. By Kildare, the burn had gone off my anger. I tested the waters with a morsel of shop talk. Has she heard how gummed up the State Lab was lately? 11,000 plus items of evidence last year? Overflow, overtime? Crisis? She had heard. She agreed that the fur would fly when charges got dropped et cetera.

But it took a bollocks on his phone to finally brake the ice, a bollocks piloting an old banger with a Longford registration, drifting over and back across the line. Catríona geared down, swung out, and we surged by. Longford bastard, I heard her whisper.

"Sounds to me you have it in for Longford people. Áine?"

"Not Longford people. Longford bastards. Thomas?"

Not bad. But it wasn't enough just to make smiley faces and swap witty remarks. Damage had been done.

"Level with me," I said. "You're all over Bernie Cummins' phone. Yes?"

She adjusted her grip on the steering wheel.

"I'll try different English then. The OCU is a) tracking Bernie Cummins and/or b) monitoring Bernie Cummins' phone?"

"Bernadette Cummins is the wife of a high-profile gangster."

"So you know who she's phoning then. Is she in contact with Gary?"

"Didn't you ask her that?"

"I did. Should I believe the, ah, wife of a high profile gangster?"

She wove her head a little to see around traffic ahead.

"Áine, listen to me. I don't get why Gary Cummins would take a powder. You don't either, to be honest. But we both know how hard that is to do, disappearing like that. OK, Gary may go through a rake of burners phones but still, there has to be a mobile he keeps for priorities. Fix, finance, family. So......?"

If someone was needed to act the part of the priest in confession hearing about a bad habit for the fiftieth time, she'd have aced it.

"What are you saying?"

"You know more about the Cumminses that you're letting on."

She frowned in disapproval. She was willing to give a little, though.

"A week ago, Gary used a land line. A pub out Clondalkin, not a regular spot for him."

"OK, so I can rephrase that then. You do keep an eye on them, Gary Cummins included."

The two-second glare was a bit much. We were doing eighty.

"OCU is gangs." She spoke as though to a child. "Gary Cummins is a small time hoodlum nobody. He's station work."

"Come on. He's on your radar then. 'Seen with?' 'Spoken of?'"

"Of course his name surfaces – along with a million other names. It's called data. It's there on PULSE, if you care to read it."

"Is Gary in with serious gougers? Hanging with? Auditioning?"

She adjusted the mirror while she calibrated an answer.

"As a matter of fact, back in March Gary Cummins was logged talking with two Real IRA heads in a pub in Tempelogue."

Now *that* I had not expected. Wouldn't these be the very ones who had taken over Tony Cummins' territory? Maybe that's that what Cummins had been hinting at with his guff about loyalty.

"Does Tony Cummins know any of this?"

"It's hard to say. Word gets around handy enough."

"Why would Real IRA want anything to do with Gary?"

101

For a reply, she lifted a hand off the wheel and stretched out her fingers.

"Is that another 'you need to take it up with Éamonn?'"

She drew a knuckle along her eyebrow and focused more on driving.

"Not that you asked," I went on, "but here's my guess. Tony Cummins got to stay alive, and got to keep making his crust, because the 'RA let him do so – but for a price. Everybody pays, sooner or later."

Her hands tightened on the wheel.

"So here's Gary, maybe trying to get mileage out of that connection?"

Her phone rang. The sister again. The shop had run out of whatever type of food the dog got. Áine said it was OK to try a tin of something else. The call seemed to have irritated her, and for a moment, I got the mad idea that she might be about to scream. I watched the Dublin and Wicklow Mountains rise over the hedges. The Octavia ploughed into a long curve, at speed. Flecks of rain hit the windscreen. She fiddled with the mist cycle. The wipers squeaked and she turned them off again.

"Gary's dead," she said then. "That's your thinking?"

"It's hard not to think it. You?"

"The notion is there, all right. But I'm not going to dwell on it. Have you heard of confirmation bias?"

"I think so. I'd be more First Communion biased, meself."

"Ah. The money, I suppose?"

I'd kept my eyes on the broken line segments flashing by below. But I had heard a softening clear in her tone. Maybe even a smile.

"'Course it was. Everybody pays, sooner or later."

The showers that had been forecast finally got to us at the Naas bypass. Áine still got us onto the South Circ just shy of three o'clock. Fifteen minutes later, she was key-passing us through to the OCU. The spiffy IKEA vibe had given way more to the look of a regular coppers' den. A smell of tea relieved the background stink of plastics and solvents, and that sharp, nagging smell you got from the insides of a new computer.

There were coppers about now, about a dozen so far's I could make out anyway, three of them Banners.[1]. All of them were younger than me. I spotted

1 · *Bean Garda*, female Garda Officer. Discontinued, but still in colloquial use.

one bloke I thought I knew from the Boat Club. The other OCU coppers? 'In the field,' no doubt. 'Operational.' A heavy-set fella with black hair and a five-o-clock situation up to his eyes asked Áine if she had booked a court. A squash court he meant.

"I'll try getting ahold of Mary Enright," Áine said, when we got next to Nolan's office. He was not back yet. "The girlfriend."

"Not 'partner?'"

"It's not clear yet. You'll phone Mrs. Cummins?"

She could hardly miss my lack of enthusiasm.

"And tell us how it goes? What her reaction is?"

The ironic tone was barely a titch short of out-and-out sarcasm. It was a good time for me to exit anyway. I found a spot behind a row of cabinets. Delaney answered on the first ring.

"Boss? Get me out of this. They're trying to rope me into more stuff."

"They're not *trying* to do anything, Tommy."

"Look, I did what they wanted. The bloke they want, he committed."

"Great. Good work. So now comes the follow-through."

"Wait. It's mission accomplished, boss. Where's it say follow-through?"

"I wish I'd recorded the phone call I got an hour ago. I' play it to you."

"Phone call. About what?"

"The one from HQ that said 'second Sergeant Malone for as long as..'"

"Orders? To you?"

"From higher-up than you'd imagine. I'm not joking you."

"So Nolan is now in charge of Drugs Central? Since when?"

"Are you telling me you don't know there's staff getting yanked here there and everywhere? That we all have to do our bit until things stabilize? You want me to tell you again, Tommy?"

"But this is different. We're almost there, the operation? My name is on it, boss. I want in. And for the record, I haven't gotten a solid week off since last summer either. Remember we talked, how when -"

"Jesus Christ, would you just give over?"

What day was it today? Let's Everybody Turn Turk On Tommy Malone Day? I hadn't heard Delaney this put-out for a long time.

"Are you hearing me at all, Tommy? Divisional Chief, phones me? Says they absolutely need – wait, I'll use the word *require* – you as a liaison? Apparently because of them knowing you, your families or something."

"But for how long?"

"You think I have a say? Look, it's sorted. Done. Nolan has plenty of pull, so he does. So if I were you, I'd be minding my ps and qs here."

"Nolan is a grade A bollocks. He's not the only one here either."

"Tommy? Get a hold of yourself. You've hardly have your Sergeant's, for the love of God. Repeat: turn this around in your head. Think opportunity, man. Come on now. You know how good an OCU op'd look on your ticket."

My mind swarmed and buzzed: Operation Condor without me in on the day. Holiday out the window. Sonia. Oz –

"I'll keep your spot next to Macker for you. Will that do you?"

As a peace offering it was fierce lame.

*   *   *

The number Bernie Cummins had given me to contact her went straight to voice mail. I wandered back to check on Nolan. The fecker still wasn't back? I was mulling over alternatives when my phone went. The 'hello?' was the just woken up, not quite awake kind.

"Mrs. Cummins?"

"Yes. Have you got news, tell me?"

"Not concerning Gary, I don't. Look, I've been down the country, to a meeting."

"All right, I understand. So he filled you in then."

"Well he voiced his agreement with what you're asking."

"Of course he did. What did you expect?"

The sharp tone surprised me. Maybe she was in pain?

"He can't help on where Gary might be," I continued. "That's another reason I'm phoning. Mobile numbers for Gary. He switches SIMs, right?"

"Yes, I mean no, I don't know. He phones from, well, wherever he happens to be."

"Those are on your mobile then. In your Calls, or your Contacts."

"I don't think so. No, I'm telling you..."

"Well where do you think Gary could've gone?"

She took her time with a reply. I heard what sounded like a wheeze.

"I don't know. I wish I did, but I don't."

"Mrs. Cummins. There's nothing to be gained by holding back stuff."

"I truly, truly don't."

"Your husband said he gave Gary the heave-ho a while back."

"That's right, sadly."

"This was before he went to prison? Two years, or more?"

"Well it wasn't exactly that way. Tony, well, he left instructions."

"What's 'left instructions?'"

"He sent word. And Gary was told."

"So was it you kicked – sorry, told Gary he had to go?"

"No. Tony asked Gerry to have a word with him."

Gerry ... OK – Lugface. Her hammer-headed, silent guardian.

"How did your husband know Gary was causing trouble at home?"

It was a question she didn't feel a need to answer.

"When did you see Gary last?'

"It was last Tuesday – no, the Wednesday. He showed up at the clinic where I go to for me treatment. In the waiting area there."

"Has he met you there before?"

She thought about her answer.

"Once before, yes. But I wasn't expecting him either time."

Well duh, I felt like saying. Gary knew it'd be just him and his Ma, with no Lug-face present to fend him off.

"Anyone with him on either visit?"

"No. Not that I saw."

"And how did Gary look to you?"

"He was out of sorts. Tired, like he wasn't sleeping."

"Just tired?"

"He didn't appear to be high, if that's what you're asking."

"Did he tell you anything about what was going on in his life? His worries –"

"It was a bad day. It didn't go well."

"A disagreement, you mean?"

"No. He didn't argue. He knows I'm right. He even admits it. The thing is, he can't stand to hear it. He's heard it all before."

"Telling him to get his act together, that sort of thing?"

"Something like that, yes. That would be about the size of it."

"So where is home for Gary these days? He has his own place?"

"He did, a while ago, but I don't know. He stays with people, I'm not sure who. He'll sleep here the very odd time. I don't tell Tony. He'll sneak into the bed, and then there he is in the morning. He comes by every now and then too, for clothes, or something to eat. And, before you ask, yes, looking for money."

I let the conversation hang again.

"I mean, this isn't his actual home," she said then. "Gary is thirty-two years of age."

She had been doing the sidestepping routine so long that it was second nature to her. I scribbled down a few words. – Dinner – Clothes – Mammy's boy – Scared shitless. – On the run?

"I was requested not to ask about Jennifer," I began. "But that's just not going to wash. Whatever it is, it'll have to be out in open eventually. I say we get to it now. OK?"

She hesitated before replying.

"There's issues there, that's all I can say."

If it were possible for a voice to shrink, hers had done just that.

"Has Gary, say, contacted Jennifer? Asked her for help?"

"She would've told me. We talk, every day."

"No way he'd go visit her even? Jennifer's place, I mean?"

"Believe me," she said at last, "there's no cause to drag Jennifer into this. She has more than enough on her hands, Jenn does."

The moments stretched out longer.

"Are you still there?"

"I am for now. Look, Mrs. Cummins. The way I see is I have to go to my C.O., my boss like, and tell him that this is going to go nowhere."

"But why do you say that?"

"Because you and your husband ... I don't want to actually say 'withholding information,' but that's what it amounts to."

I thought I heard her swallow.

"Go ahead then, just ask your questions."

"Has anyone come looking for Gary? Phoning the house?"

"No, no, they haven't."

"Nobody?"

"People know not to be looking for Gary here."

I wondered about that. This woman might have her hopes and her beliefs mixed up here. Anything goes these days, I felt like reminding her. A free-for-all. The Cumminses' humble abode might not be as off-limits to criminals looking for her son as she might like to imagine.

"Texts, emails? Messaging? Facebook? Voice mail? Messages on an answering machine, even?"

"No, I should try that stuff you said, but... I send the odd email, is all."

"Tell me about Mary Enright."

"That's over and done with. They split up months ago."

The way her voice went up at the end struck me as odd.

"I bear her no ill-will now. For giving Gary the push, I mean."

"Do you know her, or did you know her, like?"

"No I don't. But I know she's an – God, I shouldn't be..."

"An addict?"

"I don't know it one hundred percent. She had it rough, that much I know. She had a husband, he was violent, but then he was killed in a car crash a few years ago. A lot of troubles, yes."

Maybe, hearing herself say these things, she felt a need to even things out more then.

"Let's not cod ourselves," she said. "Gary's not easy. I'm his mother, so I know."

"Has he found another interest since? An old flame maybe?"

"God, I don't know. He was always secretive, Gary. Always. You think he tells his mother what he's up to, everything? With a girl-friend? A grown man?"

My instinct was to push. But when I next heard her speak, any firmness in her voice had gone under.

"Another thing needs saying. Him getting told to, well, to find his own place? That was partly my doing. It had to be done."

She paused then, as though she knew that any more talk would be a waste.

"Could Gary could be ... aggressive? With you, at home?"

I recognized that catch in her breath. It was the same as Ma made when she was trying not to cry.

"I'm not trying to blackguard anyone here, Mrs. Cummins. But I know there's things a family don't like other people to know. There's the shame thing and all. You know what I'm getting at?"

She did not answer.

"But an addict turns into someone else, don't they. A stranger, like. That's how I had to start looking at it anyway. A stranger who could turn on you. This is not just talk now. It happened in my family, so it did. And, to tell you the God's honest truth, we ended up doing the same as what you told me. We never wanted to, but."

"I know what you're saying Tom... Sergeant." She sounded like a kid who was almost asleep but still able to manage a few words. "I do, yes. And that was why Tony felt he had to, you know."

"And there's bad feeling now, is there? Over this falling-out?"

"It's like you said. Every family has their.... It's just... Well you know what I mean, I am sure."

She took a long, heaved-out breath. I was surprised when she took up the threads again.

"Can you imagine me going to the Garda station? Me? What they'd say to me? What they'd think, anyway? So that's why we had to find someone we could work with."

I tried to imagine what a row between Gary and his mother looked like. Bernie Cummins might be a decent, good-living person, but I doubted she was a pushover. If she was half the woman my Ma was, she'd be a serious proposition.

"He wasn't always this way," I heard her say next. "I have to remind myself. Yes he did some bad things, but he was getting better. He really was, but after what happened to Darren, he was never the same. Never."

What I heard next was definitely a stifled sob.

"I actually wish you'd put him away. Then he'd get the help."

I wouldn't be the one to tell her that there was no real 'help' in prison. That too often what you got in prison were home-brew replacements that could kill you.

"Is Gary in a program? Save me phoning around to find out."

"I know he started one last summer, but then, when I'd ask him, he'd tell me he'd beat it by himself. And if I'd ask him if he wanted me to ... well, he'd get fierce... Look, I don't know if you'd know this, but Gary has this.... this tendency."

Tendency? It sounded like she was quietly blowing her nose. The wait was nearly too much, but I managed to hold my whisht.

"...so when things get to be too much for him – for Gary – well he just ups and runs off somewhere, and hides. It's a panic thing, the doctor told me years ago. Like, he does it to calm himself."

A ping went off in my mind. Was she already preparing a defence for Gary? Because she knew he had done something?

"A very anxious child he was. Sensitive, like. Things got to him more than other lads. But he'd hide it and not let on. We only found out about his learning disability later on. There's a part of Gary still a little boy. He gets so scared he loses the run of himself."

'Sensitive.' 'Scared.' 'Little boy?' You could build another Ha'penny Bridge with all the irony in that – ten of them. I wrote ' does a runner' in my notebook next to 'learning disability?!' which I underlined twice.

"Does Gary be asking you for money?"

"He does, sometimes, yes. But he gets nothing, a lot of the time."

Her voice had dropped back to that flat, monotonous tone.

"When was the last time he asked?"

"It was that day at the clinic. Tony doesn't know I do it. Or he lets on he doesn't know."

The talk was tiring her. I still had plenty of questions.

What did she know of any of Gary's haunts? Little enough, it seemed. A couple of pubs he liked, or used to like. The Flying Dutchman – I remembered passing it a few times, out in Walkinstown. Doyles, a pub I couldn't place right off, somewhere down the quays. The Duke, if he was flush. He liked the kebab take-out from.. she couldn't remember the name of it... down off North Earl St. Some clubs she'd heard him mention over the years. Copperface Jacks of course, where else. Some place D1..? D2? Dicey Reillys, was that one? Was she imagining it?

She she wasn't trying mess with me. Who hadn't heard of chemo fog.

"What about Gary's mates?"

She did not answer right away. The question had upset her, I thought. It was a reminder of how little she knew of her son's life now. Her surviving son. Her kicked-out junkie of a surviving son. I was more angry than I'd realized.

"Well I have to say, I don't know. You were saying yourself how things slide, like? The business about a stranger?"

"Right. But whatever about pals he has had for years, maybe there was someone he mentioned more recently?"

Another long delay. The chemo left people knackered, I'd heard.

"There was some fella out Neilstown way," she said at last. "I only remembered because Gary'd mentioned him recently. Some fella he was thinking of getting in with, or had gotten in with."

"What would 'getting in with' mean?"

"Motorbikes, I think he said. Yes."

"Is Gary into motorbikes?"

"Well he has an interest in them," she said. "He did before, in anyway. The thrills and that, I suppose."

"Did he maybe mean it more as a, let's say, a business venture then?"

She sighed before replying.

"I don't know. Sorry, I just don't. Things Gary says, you wouldn't know whether to... Well you know what I mean."

"Would you have a name for me? This motorbike thing?"

"Hay... wait. Har – no. God, I should be better at this – Wait: Hynes. 'Dec' I think, yes. Dec is Declan. Declan Hynes?"

I heard a yawn then. She hadn't tried cover it up it either.

"You have my number, Mrs. Cummins."

The words, or the idea, seemed to startle her.

"That's it, is it? Isn't there, you know..?"

"There will be, yes. Look, if you remember something, or you hear something? Names, places, that sort of thing? Just scribble them down right away too. Fair enough?"

"That's a good idea. I will. A good idea, yes."

"I'll be in touch. All right?"

I didn't hang up right away. I just looked at the phone in my hand. Was I hoping she'd say something more? That the end of the call would prompt her to pry some item from her weary, chemical-dampened brain?

Or was because I had suddenly felt a need to apologize to her? Ludicrous – me, apologize to her? For what?

There was a cold aftertaste to it. Was that yet another sign of some quiet mental slide about to pick up speed?

It was she who hung up first.

11

I headed over to Áine's desk – her 'pod.'

"I just talked with Bernie Cummins. It's slim pickings."

If she was thrilled by this news, she hid it well.

"But I got a name – Hynes. H-Y-N-E-S, Declan. Allegedly a friend of Gary's. She thinks Gary was maybe planning something with him. Hynes is, or was, in the motorbike business."

"Motorbike business," she repeated.

She was eyeing the screen like it was a suspicious object. The system was as slow as ever. The usual 'Network Issues.'

"She might have issues remembering," I said. "I'll try again with her later on."

Áine swivelled around and wrote 'Hynes – friend G?' on a pad. Quinn's voice from over the way grew louder. Funny the way ears work. Mine glommed onto stuff that was pissing me off the most.

"This Haynes as 'friend,' I'd have me doubts."

Áine turned back, let her expression ask the question. Behind the partition, I noticed Quinn was on the move.

"He'll have gone through any friends he had a long time ago."

She seemed to consider the notion.

"An addict will screw anyone, and I mean anyone. Friends – real friends, non-addict friends – they disappear. Whoever Gary gets with now wouldn't be ones he'd tell his Ma about."

Quinn had worked his way behind us, and he was looking down at the screen.

"It's like that all day," he declared. Áine kept ignoring him. I could see it was work for her. "The way things are going, we'll be back to the carrier pigeons and the messenger boys."

I tilted my head to look up at him. I wasn't here to cure Quinn of being Quinn. That didn't mean it was open house for gobshites.

"You have some matter to communicate here?"

The question sort of amused him. He gave Áine what looked like an I-told-you-so look, and then he winked at me.

"Anyway. You make a lovely couple, the pair of you."

She kept her gaze fastened on the screen. At last, the fields began to fill in. She keyed in Hynes' name. He showed up fifth.

"Okay," she said, "....nine years ago. What else for him?"

"The motorbikes thing. Is that showing?"

"There's notes here from somebody Gormley, in Swords station. He questioned Hynes about ... stolen parts? No charges. Hynes has, had, a place, 'The Fast Lane.' The Long Mile Road."

I pulled it up on my mobile. There was no web site to it, but I had a phone number right away. Two rings went by before it was picked up. Was it sales or service I wanted? A bloke, youngish, with a semi sanded-down Dub accent. I asked if Declan was available.

"Who's calling?"

"Tom, tell him. Tom."

I listened to him cover the mouthpiece and yell Hynes' name. Áine tilted the monitor more my way so I could see the map. Twenty minutes or so would do it.

Then came Hynes. How could he help me, he wanted to know.

"Well thank you for offering. You can help me by meeting me for a chat."

"A chat? This is motorbikes here. Who're you in anyway?"

"I'm a Guard who wants to talk to you."

"Really. Any looper can pick up the phone and say that."

"Fair enough, but I'm not just any looper. I can prove it too."

"You can take a running jump at yourself, is what you can do."

"I'll give you a shout later on, at home? That work better?"

"Drop dead."

"Nah, I'm busy. I'll probably end up sending a squad car."

I could hear Hynes thinking, almost.

"How do I know you're a copper?"

"Give me twenty minutes. Then I'll show you, in person."

"Lookit, I don't have time for this shite."

"Me neither, to tell you the God's honest truth. See you soon."

"If you really are a copper, you better be bringing a warrant."

"A warrant? I see. Quick question for you. Do you get many visits from the Revenue?"

"The Revenue? What does this have to do with anything?"

"I'll tell you when I get there. You'll make a point of staying put there now until I show, OK?"

Áine had a pad of paper. She was ready to start following up on Gary Cummins' 'old' associates. I looked down Hynes's record again.

"You're going there?" she asked." Now? Who with?"

"Me, myself and I. Staff shortage, remember? 'More with less?'"

Once outside, I could actually breathe. I waited in the car to settle my head a bit and get my bearings. Australia, emigrate. Delaney, turn-coat. That sly bastard Quinn. And as for Nolan –

Áine, for some reason, had stepped outside now too. She looked different here. Taller? She was on her mobile, and she looked like she had a lot on her mind. I made up imaginary conversations. Talking to the separated husband? No, planning something for after work. Calling a pal for a get-together, squash, a night out, but there was some glitch....

Something about her standing there, it bothered me. She finished her call and looked at her phone a while as though it belonged to someone else, and then she headed back.

By the time I wheeled into the industrial estate where Hynes' motorbike place was supposed to be, Áine Nugent had more or less faded from my mind – but not before a visitation from a sharp and mortifying notion. I had overlooked a simple explanation for Sergeant Nugent appearing to seem 'weird:' it was a perfectly normal reaction to being with a genuine weirdo – me.

All right – The Fast Lane. It didn't look that fast. Mind you, it did look relatively fast compared to a To Let place next to it with huge chains on the door and a faded sign telling drivers to report to the office. Hynes' place seemed to consist of a roll-up door next to a companion normal steel-clad door. Showroom? Display window? Maybe it was for assembly or repairs only. I looked up and down the car park, and the one across the road. One well-used van with an underinflated tire.

Pushing open the door set off a buzzer and drew out a subdued, pleasant niff of oil and solvents. But this wasn't the greasy skanger-ama hangout I had predicted. Facing me instead was a fancy office table with two leather chairs that broke a view of a longish, stone-effect section of wall. The wall opposite had three framed posters of very pricey-looking bikes at rest and in motion. A brace of BMWs with two up, taking it rapid through some glittery city at night. A Ducati complete with moody-looking models arranged against stonework and stucco. A Moto Guzzi facing up a corkscrew mountain road whose name I couldn't remember. A security cam peeped out of the ceiling title from the far corner. I stared back at it for a count of five.

A soft squeak signalled a door opening, and in leaked a dose of rap-sounding stuff. Somebody called out to somebody else to turn down the 'music.' Hynes crooked his arm around the edge of the door and studied his visitor. He was different from his old mug-shot. A strangely-tanned face emerged like an orange fruit from an open-necked, striped shirt. The skanger inclination for bling was in evidence. The ear studs might be small, but the gold neck chain and the wrist watch were not.

"You're the one phoned? The alleged copper?"

"None other."

I had my card ready. Hynes eyed it but made no effort to come any closer so he could actually read it. He shifted his weight a little. I heard the tink of a tool being put down on cement

"So what's the point of coming ... to hassle me for no reason?"

His eyes were baggier than I'd noticed earlier. The hair could well be dyed.

"Don't tell me you object to assisting the Garda Síochána."

He let go the door and folded his arms over his chest.

"I do, as a matter of fact. So don't be taking me for a gobshite."

"Is the word 'gobshite' actually written on your file? Maybe I missed it."

"Oh, they sent a comedian."

The eyes, already squinched, narrowed more. He gave me an up and down look, the one says a barney is in the offing. As if. The whole hard-chaw Dub thing, it's just play-acting a lot of the time.

"For your information," he said. "I know the score. I give you the bum's rush like you deserve, strange things start to happen. Hassles, nuisances. Inspections. That's how youse operate."

I eyed another poster of a BMW in a race. It looked like a cross between a U-boat and a surgical instrument.

"Just get it over with," he said. "ASAP."

"OK. It's about someone you know. Gary Cummins."

Hynes shook his head.

"What are you shaking your head for?"

"I'm a tax-payer, trying to make a living, that's what for."

"You know him, yes or no?"

"I know Gary Cummins – a bit. Next?"

"When did you see him last?"

"A while ago."

"How much of a while ago."

"Hard to remember."

"How hard? Hard enough to need to do an interview down at the station?"

"I have a lot on me mind. Country's going down the drain, have you noticed?"

"Talk with Gary? Text him? Email? Tweet, Facebook? Write him a letter?"

He snorted and issued a smirk crossed with a pout. The frown returned, stronger.

"Sure you want to leave it at that? We know Gary does be in touch with you."

"Oh does he now. And how do 'we' know that?"

"He used your phone here is how. Last week."

"Maybe I wasn't here."

"You mean Gary has the run of the place? Just shows up, borrows a motorbike when he feels like it? Sure why not, I suppose, when they don't cost him anything."

"Whatever that means." He rolled his eyes, unconvincingly.

"What it means is that this gaff needs to be gone over. For tax issues. Health and safety probably. Oh, for stolen property too."

Hynes unfolded his arms, tilted his head and squinted at me. I nodded toward the door.

"It only takes one, one tiny, eenchy-weenchy item. A washer, a bolt. Anything."

He canted his head the other way and slid his watch up his arm.

"This here is a clean, legit business. Everything run proper."

"To the best of your knowledge, maybe. But what about people working here? What items do they bring through here? Chopped parts are a third, a quarter, the price."

"There's nothing for you here. Nothing, as in bugger-all."

"Only way to find out is to look. Something to watch, no?"

"That's called a search warrant. Have you got one?"

"It's not 'search warrant.' It's your-business-takes-a-nap-while-we-do-an-itemized-inventory. Eh, how long do you think that'd take? And what if they put an audit on you for the last five years?"

"People can sue the Guards now, you know."

"Sue? Said the bloke with a record for receiving stolen goods."

"That was eight years ago!"

His shout echoed longer than it should have. The door opened, and a gawky-looking bloke leaned in. A ferret-faced skanger from central casting – complete with the number one cut and the fag behind his ear. He slid a lazy glance from Hynes to me and back.

"What," Hynes half-shouted. He sucked in a breath and rubbed at his chin. "Look," he said next, "it's OK. I'll handle it."

We eyed one another again, the mechanic and I. He let go the door, and he was gone. While Hynes was mentally regrouping I examined a Harley poster. If you wanted proof of just how cracked the Celtic Tiger years had been, the mere fact that these colossal pieces of shite started showing up on Irish roads said plenty.

"So what do you really want." Hynes's voice had dropped to a murmur. "How much?"

"Trying to corrupt a Garda officer?"

"What Garda officer? You're coming on like a gangster."

"Keep digging, you're almost there. You'll know when you hit."

"I have no clue what's going on in that head of yours. You're making it up by the minute. I swear that's what you're doing."

"All right so. Gary isn't hiding under a chair here. Where do I find him then?"

Hynes looked at the floor between us. To spit? He just might.

"How would I know where he is."

"Your last contact with him."

He found a mark on the floor that needed his deep study. His reply ground out between his teeth.

"Last week. Like you told me you know about, already?"

"Was he on his own that day?"

"Yeah, he was."

"How'd he get here?"

Hynes shrugged.

119

"You keep your tapes, or whatever, from those cameras?"

"No I don't. Not that it's any of your business."

"Why not?"

"There's no need to. Not unless there's an issue."

"Well this is an issue, an issue in the making."

"Do the paper work so. See how that goes."

"How'd Gary seem to you?"

"I don't know. How should he seem?"

"Was he high?"

"High? Really? God, I've got no idea."

"Did it look to you that Gary was doing all right for himself?"

"How people get by is none of my business. Jobseekers, nixers – who knows what people do these days. Live and let live, I say."

"Did he make any other phone calls?"

His response was another shrug.

"Is Gary dropping by here a regular event?"

"No. Maybe a while ago, he would have come by a fair bit. But that was before things went belly up for him and his Da. Before your crowd went after them."

A droning burr started up in the garage, spreading across the floor and up my bones into my teeth. An ugly sound that made me think of bad things, of what a power tool could do to a bone.

Hynes raised his eyebrows and let a smirk take shape.

"Youse wish Tony Cummins was still running things. Right?"

"What makes you say that?"

"And you're a detective? Jaysus, man. Because it was easier for you coppers, clearer. Like you knew him. And he knew you."

His smirk was in full flower now, loaded to the brim with contempt.

"Ah drop the acting. Youse must be fierce hard-up in copper-land these days to be putting the squeeze on the likes of me."

"'The squeeze?' You're still not getting this. I can tell."

"Ah come on. Just tell me out straight – what's the deal? You want to move stuff? Launder cash? Just tell me."

"That's the second time. I'll file it with the other one."

His lips tightened into an open sneer.

"Oh how silly of me. Now I get it -you're on the needle. Well I beg your pardon for not knowing sooner. Runs in the family as they say, like wooden legs. What was his name, that brother of –"

I tried over the years, I really tried. What bothered me most was that I got no warning myself. Not to speak of the surprise that Hynes got. All that came into my head when I saw him go over was: not bad – caught him completely off-guard. It had only been a slap, but the surprise had sent him back a step. That's where a chair got him tottering, and over he went.

"Well done. All on camera. Nice. That's you going to prison."

The grinder started up again, cutting off his opinionating. He got up slowly, dusting himself off like he won a prize, and he set the chair back up. The grinder stopped.

"They'll be waiting on the cell block for you. Something for you to look forward to."

"You'll be busy listening to the clay banging on your coffin."

Hynes' eyes darted all around my face. A redness was starting where I had slapped him.

"You are some wally," I said. "The person you should be worried about, he isn't going to care a damn about any set-to here."

Confusion flickered in his eyes.

"Lookit, Mastermind. Tony Cummins? He's no fan of ours, but if he hears you're complicating things? Not smart."

I was expecting a move, even if it was just to stalk off or to grab a phone. He stayed put, however. I'd run with that.

"OK then. Let's get stuff done and I'll be on our merry way. Here's the replay, so be ready this time. OK: Gary dropped by here last week. The question again: dropped by for what?"

I had only his stare to work with.

"What are you dithering for still? Look, I get it. Me, I wouldn't want to be one of the 'friends' that Gary comes calling on for favours. Who knows what he'll do these days. Right?"

Hynes was permanently in a trance? Scheming, more likely.

"We're just trying to locate him," I said. "It's the job, we have to do it whether we want to or not. There's no come-back on you."

Hynes glanced flicked his head toward the the door to his left.

"I have a sort of an office in there."

He waited for me and closed the door behind me. A studio photo had a chubby-looking kid with a Chelsea shirt and a recent quiff sitting on Hynes' knee. Next to family-man Hynes was a happy-looking, hefty-looking, significant other. The tanning bed was much in favour with her also.

He pointed his index finger down at the desk between us and lowered it like a drill press onto the desktop.

"Before I say one word to you, get this straight. Whatever I say to you is only stuff you'd hear off other people anyway. That's the only reason I'm doing this. Right?"

He opened his eyes wide like he was choking on his own sincerity. I could afford a nod.

"OK yes, I do know Gary Cummins. And yes, we were mates once upon a time. Sort-of, in so far as you could be mates with Gary. Now get this – I'm not in the kind of a life where I'd see Gary, or meet Gary. We don't do business, we don't socialize. Nada. And no, don't beat about the bush with me. Because you know why. You know what drugs do a fella. The person Gary was, he's not there anymore."

This off his chest, he leaned back into the chair.

"Yes, Gary Cummins has dropped in here in the past. Do I want him dropping in here? No, I do not want him dropping in here. So write that down, and remember that. It's not by choice."

"When he came last week, what did he want?"

"Who knows what he wanted. A chat, a few bob."

"A chat. A chat about what?"

"You trying to turn this into an interrogation, or what?"

"What do you want an interrogation maybe? Look. You talked, the two of you -"

"- Wrong. Gary talked, and I pretended to listen. I worked on a bike, he yapped."

"So what did you talk about?"

"What did *he* talk about, you mean."

"He wanted you to get involved in something?"

"'Involved,' huh. Well, OK, so maybe he did. Involved in yapping about old times, all that stuff. Old escapades, who did what, do you remember so-and-so. All that old shite."

"You're telling me Gary came all the way out here just for a trip down memory lane. Really? Why didn't you just give him the bum's rush so?"

Hynes folded his arms and ran his tongue across his front teeth.

"You couldn't run him out because he happens to have the name Cummins. Yes?"

He shaped a word elaborately on his lips before enunciating it.

"'Volatile.' You familiar with the word?"

"Gary wanted something, more than a chat."

He gave me a benevolent look that in Dublin meant contempt.

"Cor-rect. And that is what I did. I gave him forty something Euro. Just to get rid of him."

"To get rid of your pal, who came here in need."

"I told you, the person Gary is now, he's no friend of mine."

"That wasn't all he wanted off you."

"He wanted things a 'friend' wouldn't ask for in the first place."

"Like what?"

Hynes breathed in deeply, and let it out slow and steady through his nostrils.

"He asked about moving stuff. Said that he could, quote unquote, get stuff."

"'Stuff. What stuff? What 'moving stuff'?"

"What do you think, IKEA furniture? Robbing motorbikes, he meant. Motorbike parts, all that."

"And where did this discussion go?"

"Nowhere. Why is because there was no discussion. This is a place of business. It's not a drop-in centre for headers to come by and waste my time with mad dreams-and-schemes shite."

"Who's Gary in with, with this 'moving stuff?'"

"Think I asked him? That he'd tell me, if I did? Get serious."

I tried to find a better part of this plastic chair to sit on.

"Did Gary air his problems with you?"

"Gary has problems?"

"I see. Tell me something now. Who scares you more, Gary or his Da?"

He eyed the open doorway behind me and looked around the room.

"I mind my own business," he said. "Right now, I have a garage to run."

"You're too chicken, so I'll say it. Gary tried to sign you up – that's what he did. Tried to tap you, to put his hand in the till. To sign you up for insurance. For the old 'protection' bit."

"Rubbish. Is there someplace I can sign on for protection from madmen coppers?"

"You better not be expecting an Oscar for this."

Hynes chortled and made a lazy wave of his hand.

"What are they feeding you," he said. "This is all a frigment of your imagination. I'll say it again: no crime committed here. Nobody robbed. No bikes missing, no tools. No-thing. OK?"

"Not OK. You're trying to tell me me you can't recall one single, concrete issue from his visit?"

He tugged at his nose and pretended to hold back a smirk.

"What? Was it the 'concrete?'"

His shrug annoyed me as much as his bogus amusement.

"Concrete shoes, is that what you're saying?"

"It's a joke, man – relax, will you. I'm just getting in the spirit of this, this, 'visit.' That's all. Look, it was you started the comedy."

I stared and watched his fake amusement fade.

"Oh for Christ's sakes," he said. "Get real. People talk, that's all I meant. Who knows."

"Gary's run afoul of somebody. Is that what you're telling me?"

"I'm not telling you anything. You're just trying to put words in my mouth. That's an expression, a joke, whatever."

An engine came to life, revved twice, and puttered out. A light spanner fell clanking to the concrete. That young lad who had leaned in the door could pass for sixteen or seventeen.

"OK, so," I said then. "This is how it looks to a normal person. Right now is not best time to be trying to flog pricey bikes. Matter of fact, your business could go to the wall any day. But a captain of industry like yourself, you'd be looking for new opportunities. Resorting to stuff you never thought you'd have to try. You and Gary, now that'd be some team."

Hynes had taken to examining some item on the wall.

"Do you have any idea how many people Gary pissed off?"

"Is that what he did? Tried to put the heavy word on you, and you...?"

He gaze slid back. Hatred is not dramatic. It's calm and cold.

"You clobbered Gary didn't you. A real clatter? Or just a friendly tap?"

"There's nothing to clobber. Gary's a junkie. It'd be like trying to clobber a ghost."

Ah. A bloke who'd push away a drowning man from a lifeboat.

"OK. Aside from you, who else has Gary pissed off?"

"What a question. And you the detective and all."

"Let's try an answer in English. Who?"

"Well who do you think, sunshine?"

It was a poor enough effort, but he did nail the 'you.' '*Yuy.*' Uncooked Nordy English at its very best.

"The North? IRA fellas? Is that what you're saying?"

Hynes sighed and took out a folder and flipped the cover. He began to thumb through papers. They looked to me to be bills, invoices I supposed, for parts.

125

"Lucky Gary has you, though. A friend in need, and all that?"

He kept looking through his bits of paper. I wanted to wait, to have another go. But I'd had enough. The North, I thought on my way out. Why was I at all surprised that looking for a half-arsed, drug-addled criminal had led me to the letters IRA?

12

Áine Nugent's number wasn't where it was supposed to be. I was still stumbling through Contacts when Macker called.

"My God Skip but you've no idea what you're missing. No idea."

This was a recital, not a conversation. I waited.

"Me and Seán, God, the laugh we had? There was a fella got thrown down the stairs in the Breffni here."

"Better not have been one of ours."

"Ha ha, no. Some punter he was, but he was put out about the quality of his massage, and he stepped over the line with one of the ladies. So listen. Guess how long it took for a squad car to show?"

"I have to go."

"Here's a clue: manpower crisis, response times in the bin –"

"– Macker? Really – "

"– Honest to God, Skip. I timed it. Response time thirty-one minutes. Thirty one minutes. In the middle of Dublin city, thirty one minutes."

I told him again. He ignored me again. Would I be interested in going out for a pint sometime. 'Sometime'? And I thought: how does 'never' sound. I gave him a 'maybe later' and ended the call.

I had put Áine Nugent it under K, for some reason. She picked up immediately. I told her about my session with Hynes.

Her first question: did Hynes back up this IRA talk? The doubt in her voice was clear. Fair enough. 'IRA' was a catch-all for a lot of stuff now. Real IRA, Continuity IRA. UnReal IRA, Delusional IRA – it was all the same gig: guns, drugs, robberies, extortion, fuel laundering, money laundering, prostitution, feuding, rowing....more feuding, more rowing. Whatever you're having yourself, like.

"He's messing with us then," she said. "You reckon?"

"I've got no idea. Let's say stranger things have happened. Wasn't there mention of possible associations in that file you prepped? Tony Cummins meeting IRA fellas? Or was I dreaming?"

She wanted a minute to track that down again, to see if she'd missed anything. Her keyboard clacking in the background was a strangely OK accompaniment to the soft hum-and-hush of the Long Mile Road traffic and the now-and-again snores and snorts of artics pulling their loads out to the M7.

"All right," she said, decisively. "From what I'm reading here..." Her mouse clicked once in the pause. '...older intel, Tony Cummins ... reported meeting with a known IRA member. A C.I. reports he heard Tony Cummins might've been working on a way they could get along with them, or with some faction of them anyway. That was three months before his last arrest."

"Do you want to chase that one?"

All right, she said. She'd look into it. The cagey tone was back.

"That was only round one for Hynes by the way," I said then. "I'll file a summary. I'll dig in hard when round two comes along."

"That sounds like a plan."

Our odd, stumbling conversation staggered on.

"What's the story on his ex?" I asked. "The Enright woman?"

Áine had an address, a phone number. Aughavannagh Rd: Crumlin, just off the canal.

"It's her parents' place," she said. "I spoke with her mother."

"Did you ask her mother for her version of Gary Cummins?"

"No. I was using the Social Protection route with her."

Posing as a civil servant wasn't the most creative way of getting info. Too bad it worked so well.

"She's back living there with her mother," Áine went on. "Mother says Mary lost her job there last month. Hair dresser?"

Áine could hardly have yet asked Mary Enright's Ma if she knew her daughter had worked on and off – so to speak – in the sex trade aka 'escort services.' Or if, the way things were going now, her daughter might well be back in the same line of work.

"Mary has form going back," she added. "She was quite the goer. Shoplifting, disorderly. Assaulting a Guard even. Damage to property, twice. Possession stolen property, receiving. Paying for her fix has to be part of that. I read a bit from a pre-sentencing, her counsel saying how a boyfriend got her hooked. But her latest run-in is nearly five years back."

"Mended her ways?"

"She's is in the program four years. That could be it."

Four years in a methadone program said something, right enough. But who knew. There were plenty who still took heroin on the side. It was only out in CASP in Clondalkin, where they had the staff, that they were 100% on top of sample swappers.

"Here's an interesting thing. She's in an outfit that fires in complaints to GSOC on a regular basis. *'Slán Abhaile'* Do you know them?"

I did. 'Safe home' – one of the few bits of Irish that stayed in my head. Women in the sex trade, and a good smattering of nose-rings and graduate degrees into the bargain. Sisterhood stuff.

"I got as far as her voice mail. But according to her mother, Mary switches her mobile off sometimes."

One covering for the other, I couldn't help thinking. But there was something off-key about this get-hold-of-Mary-Enright thing. Me, I'd have let the mother know in no uncertain terms that she had better get ahold of Mary herself, and fast. Either that or one or both of this mother-daughter tag team would wind up in an interview room somewhere late into the night hours.

"I'll keep trying," Áine said. And that, apparently, was that.

What was going on with her, I wondered then. Was she actually dragging her heels on this? Because? OK, getting inconveniently shunted off her promotional trajectory to work next to Thomas Malone had put her in a snit.

What a tragedy. Well I knew what passive-aggressive was. Maybe it was time I told her that.

And that was when my belly commenced to growl like a cat. I wasn't far from the McDonalds in Phibsboro. What a coincidence.

*   *   *

Something about McDonalds' fries: they always left grease on your fingertips. You could wipe your fingers, lick them even, but short of chopping them off, you were stuck with that grease.

I could see it here on my screen. I was monkeying around with the Hong Kong street map again, trying to see how much of it I remembered. When Sonia'd get back, I'd be ready to talk intelligently to her about places she'd visited. To that end, I sometimes ran practice future conversations through my mind: 'I bet you that was spectacular, that Ma On Shan place …'

An incoming call vaporized my daydream. It was Áine: she had gotten the mother to nail down a meet with this Mary Enright. Then came unexpected diversion.

"As long iz you-az are not try-an' to stitch her up for sumtin.'"

This was her trying to mend fences?

"Not bad. Not bad for a Sligo person, I mean."

"Ah, it needs work. Anyway, there's a catch. Mary doesn't want us coming to the house, on account the locals would see us. She had a compromise place in Fairview, a pub there. I went with it."

Áine wasn't asking. Fairview? Nothing wrong with Fairview – except that there are serious gangsters running businesses there. Businesses as in fronts. One was the Commodore pub. I chased a Latvian bloke into the place two years back. It was like running into a colony of penguins, or something, the way the regulars started scattering their baggies and their aluminium packages and their plastic packs all over the kip.

"Not a kip called the Commodore, I hope."

"No, Dolans."

She was heading over now. We'd meet there in, say, fifteen? The brisk tone had me on the back foot. There was some kind of a snakes and ladders thing going on here between us – most def. One minute I could hardly get a word out of her, but the next it was all business: we'll do this, that and the other – right now too.

Such were my thoughts as I coasted on down Gardiner St with my foot poised over the brake pedal and trying not to keep looking up the copper-edged clouds crowding the sky. Down to the turn onto Summerhill. That was close enough to the belly of the beast.

I'd been here last week, to collect the Ma. She had bought some big plastic hamper things on sale. I'd had plenty to look at while I sat waiting. A head in a torn soccer jersey doing his Riverdance about a metre from my front bumper. The fella curled up by the security railings to a shop. The pair sitting dopily on the footpath staring out at nothing. At least I wasn't swarmed by one of those roving packs of kids who go around putting the fear of God in everyone, Guards included. 10 and 11 years old – younger, some of them. Our other 'untouchables.' Lightning quick they were, and fearless. High, some of them too. Pull a knife as quick as look at you. Feral, was the word people were using now.

I made it out to Fairview unscathed. Big surprise, not. Fairview was nothing to me really, just a place to drive through. Oddly, for this hour, a kebab place seemed busy. Trust the foreigners to make a go of things no matter what. Dolans was on the quiet side of the junction for the Malahide Road. Parking was easier than I had expected. A dosser attached by his shoulder to the wall of a newsagents got my interest then. A scout, was my first thought. I didn't have time to decide if he was actually having an actual conversation on his mobile. I stepped out onto the footpath just in time to get a text from Áine: she was already in the pub? Odd.

Stepping into Dolans I right away saw Áine talking with a woman. Mary Enright? A quick scope of the clientele offered up three able-bodied but possibly work-shy characters half-watching a Liga match on Sky. The seven or eight others on the premises, geezers all, appeared to have all the time in the world.

131

I had expected a shifty, run-down Mary Enright, not this placid-looking, put-together person. The methadone maybe, I thought, the way it flattened you out. There was make-up in evidence, and she had done something with her hair. Her glass was almost full of what could be cider. I noted how her eyes went into wandering mode when she spotted me. I noticed something else too. First chance I got, I caught Áine's eye and touched my forehead in the same spot that, on Mary Enright's face, looked awfully like a bruise.

"Mary and I were just chatting," Áine said.

"Right," said Mary Enright. She sat up a bit straighter and looked me directly in the eyes. "I'm going to say to you what I said to her, and it's this: I'm only here for one reason, and one reason only. It's for Mrs. Cummins. For Bernie, like."

"I see," was all I could think to say. I was getting my bearings yet. It looked like Áine had decided on a softly-softly approach here. The barman was waiting. I added a 7 Up to the order.

"We were saying how Dublin's changed," said Áine.

Mary Enright nodded vigorously. She began laying down the law on this topic. Cuts to Social Welfare. People losing their medical cards. Rent allowances cut. The arrival of the barman didn't slow her. A visit to the doctor, not to mind the price of filling a prescription? And the wait for to be seen by a hospital doctor? I started chewing on the slice of lemon. Was it nerves had turned her so yappy, I wondered.

"And it's the foreigners too," she said, swinging a look from Áine to me. "How is it they're getting the houses and the jobs, and getting money for having their kids, and everything?"

I saw no sign of Áine putting a halt to her gallop. I tugged out the lemon rind from between my teeth.

"You know why we're meeting here, I take it."

"Well I do, yeah. But I've got questions for you too, you know."

"Great. Fire away so."

"OK. About Gary, is he really 'missing?' How do I know youse're not out to nail him for something?"

I slid my gaze up toward her forehead.

"After seeing that present there, maybe we should be."

She bit at the corner of her mouth and reached for her drink.

"Where do you reckon Gary's gone?" I asked

She tilted the glass to move the ice around.

"Has he got any wheels? Or the use of wheels?"

"'The use of wheels.' Hah. That's a good way of putting it. So is it robbing cars he's at?"

"I don't know. Is it something Gary does be at, robbing cars?"

She toyed more with her glass.

"Oh I don't know about that," she said.

Her drink held poised by her lips, she examined Áine's face.

"Are you really a Guard? No."

"I showed you my card, didn't I?"

"Ah go on. You can't be. You're too pretty."

Embarrassment seemed to make Áine freeze, eyes fixed on nothing. Her uneasy stillness stirred something in me. I saw myself slagging her later on with a re-run: *Yar te-oooh prihhy.*

"Me," said Mary Enright then, still chortling, "I wanted to be a Guard. No joking now – I swear to God I did."

This admission made her throw her head back and laugh. If it was meant to be funny, I wasn't getting it. What I got was a glimpse of a long-gone little girl, a kid with no cares, with no clue of what her future was to be. Before drugs blighted her, before her body would be claimed by strangers.

She shook the remains of her drink hard.

"Probably them cop shows on the telly, right? L.A. though, not this hole. Who knows though? It's never too late, that's what I say – as long as you have a goal and you don't give up."

"You mean applying to be a Guard?" Áine asked.

For a moment I thought Mary Enright was going to rear up.

"No, no," she said instead. "I mean *acting* a Guard. A series, like? Talent is one thing, but you have to work on it. You know?"

Acting? The conversation had wandered off into the bushes.

"You have to build up to it. Getting yourself out there, trying things, all that. Even being a contestant is enough, that's what I say. It's true. You don't have to win everything to get ahead."

I was pretty sure that confusion had landed on Áine too. There was no sign of her wanting to interrupt, though.

"People will remember you. That's how it works."

More and more, this had that off-key air of someone with mental troubles. A conversation but we were just here incidentally.

"Presence, that's what it's called. It's an attitude, right? How you carry yourself. A way of doing something."

She looked from Áine to me and back. Did she see us?

"That opens doors, you know. And you have to go out of your comfort zone. A bit of luck too, of course. Nobody'd deny that. But – the right time and the right place and the right people – boom. Lights, cameras, action. That's how it happens."

She smiled then, as though she had re-entered the present and was noticing Áine and me for the first time.

"Television, is it?" Áine asked.

"Oh, it's not just the telly. That's the thing, you see? I mean, the All Ireland Talent type of thing, there's nothing wrong with that, not a bit. It's grand for a certain type of person, but there's auditioning going on all over. Film, ads, a bit of modelling. Not a lot of people know that, but it's true."

"Mary?"

Áine offered her a measured but not unsympathetic look.

"You and Gary? You get together still?"

The glass went still in her hand, but the ice cubes continued their half-hearted drift.

"No. That's history."

"Was it Gary did that? Your forehead? He has a temper, I hear."

This earned Áine a burning glance. Then Mary Enright dropped her eyes to the glass and resumed her glass-twirling.

"Yeah well," she said. "I set him straight on that, so I did."

"When? When did it happen, I mean?"

"Two weeks ago. But then I waited, see? I let him do the whole rigmarole, the sorry bit. How he was going to get clean and we'd go to Australia the two of us and start all over– all that. And him crying like a baby. Blaming the drugs, saying how he always loved me, how I was the only one for him – that I inspired him. Inspired!"

She darted a look at Áine and then at me.

"Then what," Áine said. "You say you waited. For what?"

"What do you think? Waited until I could give him a right good kick in the goolies, is what. And I says to him, you're a lying, thieving junkie, I says. You won't face up to it, so you won't."

"When was this?"

Mary Enright stared at the ceiling, nodding as she counted.

"Sunday night. Saying how I was the love of his life."

"You weren't scared of him?"

"What, Gary? No. I knew he'd get back in touch. Sure enough he texted me, wanted to come to the house, my Ma's place, like. I said no way, meet me by the side of the shops. It was gone nine, it was getting dark. He came by, walking. He might have got a lift or a bus or a taxi, I don't know."

"Did he tell you what he was up to these days?"

She screwed up her eyes.

"Where he stays," Áine explained. "Where he was coming from. Where he was going after?"

Mary Enright shook her head.

"He appears out of thin air," she said, "and then disappears again. Like Harry Potter, he was."

"How did he look to you?"

"Funny you ask. He looked like shite, actually. And he stank."

"Was he high? A smell of drink off him?"

"Probably – I don't know. He was like a tramp, what do you call – homeless person. Down and out, like. Honest to God I mightn't have recognized him if I'd just seen him across the road."

"You were a couple for a long while."

The plucked and penciled eyebrows formed lazy capital Vs. She was really surprised that I actually could talk?

"Why do you say that? I mean, the way you said it."

"Did you meet any of his family?"

"As I mentioned earlier," she began, slowing more with each word to stare at me, as though daring me to argue," I met Mrs. Cummins. And I consider it a privilege."

"Where did you meet her? At the house? Cummins' I mean."

"No," she said. I heard a tightly-held breath escape. "Look, I'm not stupid. I got it why Gary wouldn't do that, wouldn't bring me to the house, like. His Ma'd know, right?"

"She'd know what?"

Her eyes dulled, as if she was entangled in too many notions.

"She'd know what I do be up to – what I *used* to be up to. No, I met her once, in town, in a café, with Gary. He must have told her a bit about my situation. She didn't say much, to be honest. But she never let on for a second that she thought I was a lower form of life. Not a bit of it, no way."

She blinked several times, rapidly.

"Never give up she told me. God was watching out for me, she said."

Her eyes were intense now, and searching.

"That woman, she knows heartache. You can tell. A real lady."

Eyes prickling with tears, she turned away. I parked a stare on one of the dossers at the bar, my way to announce that he needn't trouble himself to pretend that he wasn't trying to eavesdrop.

"She knows, you know," I hear Mary Enright say then. She poked her eyes with her knuckles and rolled her eyes around to clear her eyes of the tears. "He's her son, for God's sake."

"'She knows?' What does she know?"

For such a combustible question, I got a meek reaction.

"She knows he won't kick until, well who knows. There's nothing she can do to make him. Sure she wasn't able to get Darren off the road he went on, was she."

She took her time blowing her nose.

"God, what she must be going through. Like, all she can do is wait? And wait for what? But still she has the good word for the likes of me."

Her eyes skipped to Áine, wiped her nose again.

"A tragedy is what this is. A complete tragedy."

"You met Gary's father?" I asked. She shook her head.

"The brother, Darren?"

"No. But I knew about him. He was ... well that's all I'll say."

"What else do you know about Gary's family?"

"He has a sister, but I never met her. Jennifer's her name. All I know is she's not part of, well she's not in the picture."

"Gary's on the outs with her, is that what you mean?"

"How would I know? Why are you asking me?"

With that, she sat up and rearranged herself on the seat like she was pushing herself away from what had been crowding her. Another shift, I thought. More and more, they're finding out that there's something else behind drug abuse. Some diagnosis.

But other notions were scratching away in my mind. Had Mary Enright set out to meet Gary one fine day, but stopped to make a little phone call first. The tip-off, yes. For money, and maybe for revenge. She had admitted he beat her. Would she throw him to the wolves for that?

"Back to Gary," Áine said. "Was he in trouble? Scared?"

The answer this time was a shake of the head.

"I'll tell you something now," Mary Enright said then. "I still can't get over the fact I stuck with him so long. You know that battered wife thing? How they stay, even after?"

She swished a mouthful of her drink as if that'd wash the words away. Her gaze slid across the table-top and dropped into the space below. After a few moments, she snapped back to attention.

"Let's face it," she said, eyes back on Áine again. "Gary needs to be in a facility. To get him away from everything, right? Then he wouldn't keep rubbing up against, well, you know the type of people I mean."

She eyed her glass, felt the heft of it on her palm.

"Like the people he gets his gear from, you mean?"

Slight as it was, a shrug, it was not a good enough answer. I sent out what I hoped were eyebrow signals to Áine: a) Enough's enough, and b) Time to wheel out some sharp, pointy questions.

I was about to pitch my first when a tinny burst of music cut me off. Coldplay? Mary Enright drew out a new-looking phone, fluttered her free hand as she got up and slipped around the edge of the table. She picked her spot several paces away, her back to us. I raised an eyebrow to match Áine's. Agreement on something at last? Yep. There indeed appeared to be more than the one Mary Enright present.

13

"Sorry about that."

She sat down slowly like it was a hot bath she was getting into.

"That's the biz for you, isn't it."

Her smile was a bit too acrobatic. She enjoyed seeing that she had two cops waiting on her?

"Auditions I'm talking about," she said.

Auditions? Right, sure. I weighed the notion of calling her on it. No. Not now. She was trying to get her life back from addiction.

"You get a call any time, day or night. I have a few minutes yet though."

"Great," I said "So let's move to details. To some specifics?"

"Specific what?"

The smile had tightened some. She was more nervous than cheeky. Was a performance on the way? *The* performance, maybe?

"Gary. He considered himself close to you still, you were saying. That to me suggests he'd tell you stuff, some stuff at least, whether you wanted to hear it or not. Have I got that right?"

She blinked and refreshed her smile, and said nothing.

"For example, was he avoiding certain places, or people? Topics of conversation? Like, did he refuse to answer a question?"

She looked out across the floor of the pub like it was beginning to fill with water, and then by Áine back to me.

"Funny you say that. Because Gary never actually said anything like that to me, but there was something. It was something I saw, or heard, I should say."

Her gaze, when she drew it back, went to Áine. Away from the one who had asked the question, the one she knew would be the hard sell. I mentally added that item to my suspicions.

"I was going along Pearse Street," she began, "just after Easter. I was only after getting off the phone to him actually – to Gary like. He was in good order, I remember, telling me how he'd just gone two days without using."

She turned up that sympathetic-pal-in-confidence look she had latched onto Áine.

"I don't know if you'd know this, but for someone heavy into something, two days is like, eternity."

Áine had borrowed that steady, cool gaze from a statue.

"Anyway," Mary Enright went on, "he'd been telling me how he how was handling better than he'd thought he would. Cold turkey, you know? It's pure hell. You can't imagine."

She risked a glance my way.

"Anyway. You know the clinic there on Pearse Street?"

I nodded.

"So I seen some fellas there, hanging around like. Now, to me they're on the lookout. They're waiting, like. First I've got them for cops, actually. There's foreigners in the Guards now, right?"

"Foreigners," Áine said. "How'd you know they were?"

"I'm getting to that, OK? So I start to see, no they can't be cops. Narcs, like. Real cops wouldn't be standing there drawing attention to themselves like that. And anyway, it's a treatment centre, it's a disease. Cops aren't just out to get people. Right?"

She squinted at Áine then, as though for a go-ahead.

"How many fellas?" Áine asked.

"Sorry, two. So, I says to myself, there's something about them. Nasty-looking, like? And then I got it, what they were doing. Some of those people. You know what I'm talking about?"

There was a new confidence in her eyes. Well, I thought. I had acting skills of my own. I'd play along.

"Drug dealers, you're saying?"

"Worse," she said, quickly. "The ones what do the dirty work for them. You know what I'm saying?"

I resurrected the lemon rind from my 7 Up. Not bad, I thought. She maybe even enlisted Áine some with that old female solidarity bit, common cause, suffering sisters thing. But Mary Enright probably hadn't gotten drama coaching where they'd have told her what not to do. Like now. Trying Too Hard, it was called.

"Did you know them?" Áine asked then. "These two?"

"God, no. But I could *feel* it. That vibe off them, like *violent*. You know, like?"

"OK. Back to how you knew they were foreigners."

She seemed relieved to be asked the question.

"I heard them, is how. They were having a row – an argument. Only one of them though. The other one was, like, 'I've heard it all before.'"

"What language?"

"Russian it sounded like. You hear it in films."

I asked her if it wasn't Polish.

"OK. Russian-sounding then."

The barman was a moment late in yanking a look off of us. I put back down my 7 Up.

"So there they were, these two fellas. They went down the lane a bit, where they could look out and keep sketch. Then, these two other lads, they come up the footpath. You can tell they're headed for the clinic, right? So doesn't one of the two foreign blokes march out onto path, blocking the way like, and starts firing questions at them. I hear the other lads answering back. They're normal, Irish fellas. Yeah they're a bit spaced, a bit the worst for wear and all. But they're arguing with this Russian or whatever guy, telling him to fu – you know. So that guy, he gives one of them a shove."

She grabbed her straw and poked it around in her drink.

"Next thing is, they're all shouting and roaring, and then, one of the Irish lads, he lashes out with a boot. That's when the other fella, the Russian type, he pulls a knife."

She stopped poking and eyed something in the drink.

"Oh my God," she continued then. "Pandemonium, or what. Fellas running into the traffic, cars skidding, horns going mad. Everything. And them foreigners, they just took off across Pearse St. Just like that, gone. They knew their way around."

She sucked up the remains of her drink

"How does this relate to Gary Cummins?" Áine asked.

"Right, OK. So I'm headed on toward D'Olier St. But then, down the way a bit, don't I see one of the lads from that set-to. So I ask him, what happened there I says, back at the clinic?"

Gathering herself, she looked at Áine again and then back at me.

"'Oh them head-cases,' – well I left out the curse-words there, you know – 'them headers,' says he, 'they were looking for Gary.'"

"Gary who," Áine said.

"That's what I said! 'Gary Cummins,' one of them said."

"And why were the other fellas looking for him?"

"Ah come on, you tell me. No offence. But here's the thing. It turns out that one of them foreigners, he wasn't Russian at all!"

"Maybe I missed that part," Áine said.

"Remember me saying that one of them throwing shapes, and then he pulled a knife? The other one I'm talking about now, the second fella. The quieter one, for lack of a better word?"

Mary Enright paused to draw in a breath.

"Well the fella I spoke to, he said he heard that guy talking to the other fella, the mentaller who was doing the arguing earlier, and then pulled the knife. Trying to calm him down, like."

She touched her hair like it was a wig she was adjusting.

"Things is going mad around here – you don't need to tell me. But that bit, I mean that really took the biscuit. Like, what would two fellas like that be up to? It didn't make sense. Whatever about the Russian or Polish or whatever, you hear that other accent, it's not good things you do be thinking of, is it?"

"You lost me," I said. "What accent? Russian accent?"

"God no." She paused, eyes wide. "The *North*, I'm saying! Didn't I say that already? The fella trying to put order on Knife Guy, he had a *Northern* accent." Eyes straining, she flipped a look between me and Áine. "That's why I'm saying mad, like. I mean, a Russian or whatever? And he's hanging around with some fella from the wee North?"

My thoughts ran to Hynes, of course. Hynes and his hint about the IRA. It wouldn't take much for an apparently witless gobshite like Gary Cummins to stir up the wide world of trouble with IRA heads. That was almost guaranteed to be severely injurious to his health – and to others, like his father. Tony Cummins was currently under the same roof, more or less, as IRA hardmen. Being locked up didn't stop them issuing orders.

From Áine now, a questioning glance. Whatever that meant. Push the conversation more? Or wind it up and get out of here? Maybe it was both – nail a few more details, or try to verify or tease out more from what Mary Enright'd already said. She seemed willing to carry on. She was well able to talk, anyway.

But, I thought then, for all her talk, there was a dull feel to the conversation. A hollowness. Like we were going through the motions. The more we'd tried to nail down a detail, the vaguer she became. Time of day? People who'd seen this row outside the clinic? Clearer descriptions? Who'd know these characters? The name of the bloke who gave her the wee North line...? Hum, ho, er maybe, sorry – and repeat, with a semi-embarrassed smile of regret thrown in. To be fair, though, wasn't this a good sign in an interview, that someone wasn't trying to pretend to be a hundred percent sure of something?

So: a performance? I couldn't decide. All I knew was that I'd moved pretty quickly from mild bafflement to impatience, and then to frustration. I half-listened while Áine tried to make inroads again on this 'Russian' / IRA angle. Mary Enright frowned and closed her eyes like a kid trying to come up with the perfect answer. When they opened again, it was as if she had come from somewhere far away. And still that faint, even sympathetic, smile.

Human nature being what it is, the straightforward proposition always arrives late. OK, I thought, Mary Enright was high – *duh*. But I'd actually seen no signs of that at all. I should know. Furthermore, if she and Bernie Cummins were to be believed, she'd stuck with the treatment program and kicked street drugs. I believed it. The way she'd called Gary's bluff about being ready to quit? That was the brutal straight talk you heard from people who got on with recovery. Mary Enright knew as well as I knew that most every addict you'd ever meet would always be 'ready to quit.'

So no. There was something else going on here. This wasn't just someone with a criminal background talking to two coppers, and trying to palm off attractive-looking parcels of bullshit on them. Mary Enright was not completely with us here because .... Mary Enright was not all there to begin with. Not the full round of the clock.

'Dissociative' – that was the word, yes: it had bounced around the courtroom every single day of that trial like a mad golf ball. This was back on my second case on the Squad, that fella in Carlow who'd killed his mother. It came down as expected in the finish-up, acquittal by insanity and an indefinite in Dundrum. Dissociation: the word stuck with me so much that for a while I began to see 'dissociation' everywhere. We were all a bit dissociated, I decided.

Some more than others, though. It would account for the detached feel to the conversation here. That sense that I was merely incidental to the situation here, in the audience as it were, or behind glass. Or the even weirder feeling: that there seemed to be more than one Mary Enright here.

Just as I was settling on this notion, I felt that landslide in my mind again. As though I was suddenly teetering over the edge of a cliff had that had appeared by my feet, with a world of doubts opening up under me. Maybe this feeling of things being so off-kilter here wasn't about Mary Enright, or Áine, or this pub or anything else. Maybe it was me. Misreading the situation? Building up a big nothing in my mind? The goddamned pills.

My best move was to just attend to the small things for a while, and let this feeling go by. I sat back and half-listened to Mary Enright describe the horrors of withdrawal. How Gary could never manage on his own. How he could barely boil an egg. How he got confused and violent and then how he'd cry and get aggro and ...

That was when I stopped my quasi-meditative flexing of toes and fingers. No, I hadn't imagined it. This vibe I was picking up on, it was real. Mary Enight might not be the full shilling, but she wasn't barking mad. Meeting here had been her idea, in actual fact. Áine, for some reason, had gone along with it. Not something I'd have entertained. Letting me know that she'd pull her own moves to match my going off solo to see Hynes?

Whatever. But actors don't get to pick where to go: they get told. Mary Enright was here to do a job. And she was playing to somebody else besides me and Áine too, I'd bet. It wasn't an imaginary audience either. And so, unless this dump was rigged for studio quality audio and video – and it wasn't, because I'd had this habit for years of sussing out CCTV – that audience was somewhere right here in this pub.

I faked a yawn and let it blossom into a long, slow stretch, but leaving just enough of a gap in my eyelids for a scope of the loafers at that table again. They didn't look like app developers or start-up ninjas launching IPOs. Might be some fine-tuned disability gigs in operation there, all the same.

I tuned into Mary Enright's talk again. The same phrases were cropping up more and more. *Know what I mean? Wait 'til I tell you. You won't believe this now.* Áine would likely pull back soon enough, I figured. But before we split, I wanted a look at every one of the clients on the premises here. To that end, I formed a plan. A bit of the old pitch and toss – that was the ticket.

I'd already gathered change in my hand. I rose from the chair as though heading to the bar. The moment I felt my knuckles slide by the top of my pocket, I let fly. The coins hit the floor with a swoosh and crash, a good portion of them immediately skittering madly and rolling in fine fashion in all directions. So many were in motion, it was madness to try to keep track of them.

"Jaysus," one droned. "There's the housekeeping – gone."

Two of them had budged already, to help forage. I headed over. The last of them, the one I was most curious about, remained a hold-out, sipping philosophically at his drink and looking away. I noted again the cut of the jacket, and the shoes. Not Pennys finest merchandise, not by a long shot.

"Thanks, lads."

The one nearest me, a shovel-faced item, had grey-white brillo-pad hair and a shiny lumpy-looking forehead.

"Save me having to go to the pawn again."

Witty quips didn't move him. But it got me what I wanted – a chance to settle a while on Mr. Not Stooping To Help. His hand was half-over an iPhone next to his drink. Lager, it looked like. With hardly anything gone from it. The lads next to him were pints and black-and-white pudding fellas: this character was a misfit. A local bloke made good, I wondered? The type who feels comfortable in his old haunts and doesn't forget his mates? Hardly. Not these days, sunshine. It was every man for himself these days.

Spilling coins all over the floor had had another effect. It shunted the conversation between Áine and Mary Enright off track. That was no harm, I figured. The expression on Áine's face was telling me that she too reckoned that this session was past its sell-by date. As for Mary Enright, I couldn't tell. She seemed a bit unsettled by the episode. I caught Áine's eye as I headed back to the table.

"We'll be in touch," I said to Mary Enright. Maybe it was relief I saw on her face then. "By the way, best of luck with that career."

Something flickered in her eyes. Then a thin, not-sure smile.

That cantankerous-looking sky from earlier was gone: the sun had decided to visit Fairview. Traffic moved away smartly from the lights and picked up speed on the Clontarf Road. I was already sussing out a spot to fade into, from where I could watch the door.

"A bit abrupt," Áine said. "And what was that 'career' bit?"

"'Well there I was, skipping along Pearse Street one fine day and...' Sure you were, Mary. And I'm the Archbishop of Dublin."

"What makes you so sure?"

"I'm not sure. So that's what I'm doing now. I'm going to see who comes out of there with her."

She was impatient now, tipping into vexation.

"You wouldn't have noticed," I said. "Your back was to them."

"Hey!"

The anger contorted her face mightily. Her head was shaking a little too, like she had tremors. For a moment I thought she might actually have a go at me.

"Don't you god-damned condescend to me. You hear?"

I was useless with an angry woman. I fold, plain and simple.

"You didn't strike me as one," she went on. "But maybe my radar's on the fritz."

"Radar. I don't get it."

She looked at the traffic like it was Nazi tanks rolling into Paris.

"That you were another Neanderthal," she said.

"Hold your horses. No call to be throwing gender shite at me."

"This from the one who wasn't really in the conversation back there? Because you never wanted to be in on it in the first place?"

"Really in on a conversation? But it was your gig. Your lead?"

"That part you got right. Yes, I did get Mary Enright, who to my mind needs a softly, softly approach to get anything out of her. Then you go and drop some strange, sarcastic comment on her?"

"Nothing strange about it, Áine. I just wanted her to know that I wouldn't be taken up the garden path."

Was she stuck for words? I kept my eye on the door of the pub.

"As for the other thing that got your goat, what I was trying to say was that you weren't in a position to see, the way the seating was. That's all. Lookit, it took me long enough, and I was the one who actually had a view of him."

"Him who?"

"There's a bloke in the pub who didn't match the furniture. The demographic, whatever."

For this valuable pointer I got a display of Áine looking around cruelly at nothing in particular.

"All right, here's what has me thinking this way. Mary Enright has her issues, OK? What they are I do not know. But she is under somebody's thumb. Willingly or not, I don't know."

"You just decided this? Oh, I forgot. The legendary Murder Squad, where you make perfect assessments in ten minutes."

"Prove me wrong, so. But give this a few minutes first."

"How come your glorious Murder Squad is no more anyway?"

"We were too glorious, is how come. Politics too. Plus, we were a victim of your own success. We trained the mules too well. They went back to their divisions and did us out of a job, the feckers."

Again she eyed the traffic coming out from the city end.

"I heard good things about Sligo," I said. "How friendly the people are there. Allegedly."

She heaved off some comment with a flick of her head, and started scanning the shops.

"No doubt you've picked your hide already," she said then.

'Hide?' I nearly laughed. It was her advertising that she knew the lingo, that she had training. I nodded toward the newsagents. There was a bit of window not covered in lotto posters and ads.

She nodded grimly and poked in her Bluetooth, and was gone.

The shop smelled of the usual: sour milk, the sugary tang of sweets and fruit, and a cardboardy stink. That burned coffee that nobody ever buys. I looked out. Where the hell was Áine? Then I saw her. She had taken off her jacket and tied it by the sleeves around her waist. Her hair was out from whatever had been holding it in at the back. She had a good spot next to a bus shelter, with two fogeys for company there. A bus blocked my view just as I got her number up. She answered as the bus engine surged.

"You all right there boss?"

It was the fella behind the counter: Mr. Goatee Nose-Ring. I slid out my wallet and held up my warrant card.

"Jaysus, whoa. Is that real?"

The pub door was opening. And there he was: Mr. Shoes.

"That's him," I said to Áine. "You see him yet?"

"There who is?"

Mr. Goatee wanted to be part of our conversation?

"I'm talking to someone. All right? So gimme space here."

"Is that real, that thing? There's no badge or anything."

"No badge. Yes, real card. Give me space, I said."

Mr. Shoes held the door half-open and looked both ways. Out peeped Mary Enright, frowning against the sunlight and darting looks everywhere. What was she expecting, paparazzi?

"OK," Áine said. "I see them now. What's our move?"

"Take the both of them you. I want to see who else comes out."

"Keys in his hand. Fiddling with them..."

"A reg number will do for now."

"They're sort of talking. Can you see them?"

"Not as well as you can. Have you got a zoom on that phone?"

"...she's doing the talking. He's not interested. Wait – he just said something to her. Something not nice, I think? See her?"

No I bloody well couldn't. But between here and a hairdressers two doors down there was bugger-all in the line of places to fade, where I could take a look and not be spotted.

"She looks nervous. Well, serious anyway."

Oh my *Jaysus*: another bus? Cursing wouldn't make it vanish.

"OK so," Áine said. "Yes. We're in luck."

I broke into a jog. Free of the bus, I caught sight of Mary Enright. She was arguing, it looked like. Mr. Shoes stopped at a smaller, late model Audi and looked at her, and wagged the keys. She slumped her shoulders, and slid into the front passenger seat, and sat there like a dummy.

"Are you getting the number?"

I thumbed in the reg that Áine recited.

"... going, going... Gone."

149

The Audi slipped easily into the city-bound traffic. Macker, I thought. Macker and his Audi Theory of Life. Maybe the man was onto something after all.

14

We stood by Áine's car. She: slowly scraping the edge of her sole on the curb. Me: scraping my mind for some neutral parting words. We both wanted the same thing, I figured. a) To get out of here. Also: b) diplomatically affirm that we'd be able to work together without tearing anyone's eyes out over it.

"I thought I'd heard that name before, all right."

This Corcoran character, she was referring to: Brendan Corcoran. Audi Man, Mr. Shoes. Sure enough, there was nothing local about Corcoran. Nothing that'd have him dropping into a Fairview pub here for a jar with the locals, or quasi-locals. For a drink that he had hardly touched in anyhow. And he had paid a round for those blokes he'd been sitting with. Who turned out to be the most disobliging contrary bastards. No, nobody knew his name. No, they didn't know who he was. No, nobody knew if it was night or day at the moment. Fairview, I thought. Who knew there were that many bollockses in Fairview.

"What does a promoter promote anyway?"

I offered my guess, i.e. that it probably covered a multitude. Áine scraped her shoe some more.

"A solicitor *and* a promoter," she added. "Don't solicitors make enough dosh already?"

It was a decent effort to smooth over our squabble.

"Bear in mind that this is the legal profession we're talking about," I said. "Sure, the Vatican's only trotting after them."

Shoe-work apparently complete now, she looked across the traffic toward Fairview Park.

"It's nearly a job requirement, isn't it," she said. "Not having a good word to say about them."

It took me a moment. Ah – what Guards in general thought of barristers and solicitors, she meant.

"But where do you start, like."

Those words suddenly cleared my mind. Still, she read my expression as proof of a less-than-sharp brain behind it.

"It's the whole system of course," she added. "Isn't it."

Suspicion had one thing going for it – it made you focus. This conversational poking around of hers, it wasn't just to pass the time of day. Like Macker and his sly bamboozling, it was giving me an opening. These casual-sounding remarks about lawyers and crookery were anything but casual. A great opportunity for Tommy Malone here to show just how cynical he had gotten? Some tell-tale signs he had indeed changed sides?

"You sound a bit down on the old legal profession there."

She was caught between offence and confusion.

"Come on," she said. "It's just that sometimes, when you see how cases end up? You can't help but think they're working against you – sometimes anyway. That's all I'm saying. Is that news?"

Sure, we're all pals here. Right?

Like hell. It did not help one bit that I was always the familiar recital ready to roll out. All I had to do was drop in the name 'Áine.' *Nail on head there, Áine. Yep, the whole system's rigged. Top to bottom. We're the gobshites aren't we, chasing robbers and addicts. Meanwhile the big crimes aren't even crimes. God, no. With the old boy network, you'll always be grand. Snug as a bug. Penalty points? Hah. Grants? Secured. Land rezoned? Done. Predator priests? Shuffled out of sight. God's honest truth.* And so forth.

Or not. Was there a word 'misheard?' Mis-thought? It was time to choke off the paranoia here. Áine's comments were nothing new. I'd be hearing the same and more since Adam was a boy. And yet again I had missed the obvious: Áine had worked in people trafficking. Jesus. What drugs did was a horror-show, but buying and selling human beings? Brutalizing them? That was lower still. Whatever that work did to the coppers lifting the lid on it might go a bit of the way to account for Áine's take on matters.

"That stuff you were working on," I said. "I don't think I could handle that at all. I'd go mad, so I would. So fair dues to you."

Her eyes clouded again.

"Trafficking, right? Why's it called that, anyway. Call it slavery, or kidnapping, or something."

Her blinked several times, but her expression stayed set.

"Back to Mary Enright," she said. "This talent thing she talks about. You don't buy it, do you?"

"Who knows. Let's find out."

How elastic a term could 'talent' be. Mary Enright had been in the escort racket, working the hotels for several years. Hardly the entertainment quotient that talent shows were trying to drum up?

"And this mysterious 'Russian' gangster. Plausible to you?"

"I want to say no. But these days? Anything goes."

I turned my attention to a leaf trapped by the wiper blade. It was fresh and entire: it deserved to be still on its tree. Whatever Áine Nugent here thought, I had looked at Mary Enright and what I'd seen was an easy mark. Especially if she was doubling up on methadone with her own habit. Which I indeed suspected. Detox was one thing. Rehab was another. Everything'd be in the mix – debt, extortion. Blackmail.

Áine had been waiting for me to meet her gaze.

"Look," she said. "That issue earlier. The misunderstanding?"

"I don't recall any misunderstanding."

"Nice try."

This close, her face looked different. Embarrassment sure, but I saw a hint of mischief too. It was my turn to watch traffic. Not enough, I realized. She had put herself out. I should say something.

"Newsflash. I'm not the model colleague. No big secret, OK?"

"What are you saying," she said. "It's me's trying to apologize."

"What do they say in Sligo when they want to go. Now, like."

153

"Same as they say in Dublin."

I couldn't tell. Probably I'd messed up. Again.

Lets ger oura here in de name a Jaysus. That's what they say in Sligo too, Sergeant Malone."

I looked over anyway. It was a mistake. Something was going on in her eyes. I didn't know what it was, but I had a feeling that I was, or shortly would be, in some sort of trouble.

*　　*　　*

Nolan leaned back in his chair while Áine reeled off the gist of the Mary Enright session. I eyed the notes I'd made from my file search after we'd gotten back. When Áine finished, Nolan hauled himself upright and made a church-and-steeple with his fingers.

"This Corcoran item," he said, "a 'promoter.' What gives?"

Áine scratched the crown of her head with her little finger before she began.

"So far, blank. He has a few hats. But he is a solicitor, and yes, there actually is such a thing as entertainment law. He has been involved in film and television stuff for years. It's to do with money-men, producers. I had it explained to me as 'helps round up production money.'"

"Does he now. Did I hear you say launder?"

Nolan enjoyed his own wit, I suppose. Áine shrugged.

"If that's the case, it's not showing up yet," she said.

"Is there any film work going on these days?" Nolan asked. "What with things the way they are here?"

Áine had no answer.

"He's listed as owner of two apartments," she said instead. "Which makes him a landlord. Ballsbridge. Pretty posh."

"Posh? It better be on the DART, for proper posh."

Where the hell had that come from? Macker-talk it had taken over some part of my brain. It was no use being gobsmacked, though. Áine's eyes stayed on me a few moments.

"He's also listed as founder and CEO," she went on, seeing her dim view had been duly noted. "An outfit called Spotlight Talent."

"Any website to it?"

"Yep. The way it sounds. No spaces, dot IE. Not much there."

Nolan let his church spire dig deeper into his chin.

"Is he married?" I asked." Family?"

"Nope," she replied. "Gay, I don't know – yet. He has a brother, very successful out in Dubai. Financials, broker, or the like."

"Back to Ms Enright," said Nolan. "Tommy. Your take?"

"My first thought was, she'd prepped. She came with a script."

"Is that the IRA, Russian thing you're referring to?"

"That'd be a big part of it. Somebody gave her pointers."

"Did you see signs she was there under duress?"

"Not me," Áine said. "But I've been fooled before."

From Nolan a brief, mysterious smile. An inside joke?

"All right," he said. "So we have Gary's ex, Mary Enright. And now we hear that Gary clobbered her. OK, so the question has to be asked. Has Mary Enright got payback in mind here. Tommy?"

I had been eyeing the way Áine moved her foot in semi circles, like stretching before a run.

"Hard to say without knowing her better."

Nolan shuttled looks between me and Áine.

"Did she set Gary up? Did she get *paid* to set Gary up?"

He knew neither Áine nor I would hook that one.

"They're things to bear in mind," he continued, "going forward, as they say. But back to basics for now. Gary Cummins has a habit, and we need to attend to the usual suspects. Gary owes somebody, he cut somebody short -and all the rest of it. We've seen that movie before. Haven't we Tommy?"

The remark came out flat, even stupid-sounding.

"A recurring theme in drugs and addiction, I mean. Right?"

"Recurring would be the word for it, right enough."

"Now we also have to keep in mind the other possibility, and that is, are we too late for Mr. Gary Cummins."

Áine's foot-twirling stopped.

"I'm sticking with alive," she said.

Nolan nodded unconvincingly and began rebuilding his church and steeple.

"Gary's mammy says he's prone to doing a runner when he's under pressure," he said. "No sign of him on flight lists? Ferries?"

Áine shook her head. Nolan eased back into his thinking-out-loud mode.

"OK, so our Gary does not appear to have gone on the continent or to the UK. But how long is too long for him to be hiding in the bushes, or under someone's bed? As a matter of interest, here is a number: forty two."

Áine took it as her job to ask him what he meant.

"Presumed foul play," replied Nolan, "remains not yet found. Forty-two. Did you know it was that many?"

I didn't. But I did remember Macker mentioning a memo last month. It had to do with a new push to locate murder victims. There had been stuff in the news, distraught parents and so forth. Macker had made some out-of-order comment about detectives being issued special shovels. Classic Macker.

Nolan sat up and elbowing onto his desk, he made a duck's head with his hand and promptly clapped the duck's bill shut tight

"A reminder," he said, looking between Áine and me. "Nothing of this outside of this office. Because, if indeed the mortal remains of Gary Cummins do come floating in off Dublin Bay, or turn up in a ditch or a barrel or the like, Tony Cummins will have no further need of us. And that we do not want."

He put away his duck, rested his forearms on his desk and shared a non-smile with us.

"OK, we broaden it out. So show me your shopping list, Cat. What staff do you reckon you'd need? Going full tilt, I mean."

"Six to eight," she said. "To get good momentum going."

That's when I made another discovery: my new colleague Áine Nugent had already thought this out. She began the task-list on her fingers. It started with working back through the supposed barney outside the methadone clinic. There was getting into the layers around Gary Cummins, sifting through layers of cronies and routines, and hang-outs.

"Tommy's role," Nolan said as she finished. "Just to be clear?"

"Operational staffing is above me," she said, tonelessly. Something possibly related to humour glimmered in Nolan's eyes. I was suddenly tired of being a spectator.

"I'm easy," I said. "Turf me out any time. Now'd be good."

"Jesus Christ in heaven!" Nolan's fake jollity had an edge to it. "Our trump card? Look, it's Sergeant Malone the Cumminses want, and by God it's Sergeant Malone they're going to -"

The phone was in his hand before the extension glowed again.

"He's back? Yep, tell him I want him – need him. Right away."

"Tom the Bomb," he said as replaced the receiver. He turned to me. "Tom Kennedy's the man'll get things up to speed. A workhorse, entirely."

As though some actor had been waiting in the wings for a cue, a sound of whistling between teeth started up. It quickly grew louder and within a matter of moments, said Kennedy had arrived. Half-baldy, with a few years on me, he had a rolling gait that hinted he'd be handy enough in a set-to. The aggressive handshake was a clear enough sign that the happy-go-lucky air was likely fake. I listened while Kennedy and Nolan threw comments around about holidays and Kerry and Cork and other culchie stuff. Workhorse, I thought, He looked a bit like a horse, the long face on him, the toss of hair. He might sleep standing up, even.

I stole a glance at Áine as Kennedy settled himself next to her. She had a blank, inward look, the look a person mulling over something that she had overlooked and now probably regretted.

*   *   *

It was gone half past six by the time we'd hashed out an operational plan.

Kennedy and a detective the name of McGinn would start compiling and mapping out people linked to Gary Cummins, hostiles and friendlies both, and we'd work out from there. Kennedy would divvy up the jobs and set up a work-space too, and then we'd fetch up our first team meeting.

"Is that Daly?" he asked me, craning his neck over my list. "That word, that name, there?"

I read out the other names that Bernie Cummins had given me.

"I'll brief Seánie first," he said. McGinn, he meant. "Get him started on Gary's ports of call. Then it'll be all hands on deck to get out and start covering the ground and getting ahold of heads. Fionnula and Smithie will row in first thing in the morning."

The names meant nothing. I took a gawk at where I had scribbled their names: 'Finnoula' was Finnoula Balfe. Had I seen her over at a desk near the window? Was Smithie the red-headed bloke I had seen by the door, the coolio with those retro specs?

"I'll do the searches before I head home," Kennedy said. "Have them ready for the morning, and hit the ground running first thing. We'll be sucking diesel then. Zero to sixty in no time at all."

"Thanks," Áine said. It sounded genuine.

Kennedy lingered, consulting his notes, and then cantered off, his head sliding and bobbing along the top of the cubicles. His whistling faded and then stopped. The awkwardness that I had sensed earlier seemed to ease. Kennedy, I wondered. Was he one of Áine's 'Neanderthals'?

"Mrs. -" A yawn had interrupted her. Something about her closing her eyes, or the way she stifled a stretch made a soft pop in my mind. "Sorry, excuse me. Mrs. Cummins – Bernie. You'll call her and let her in on this? That we've task-forced the search now?"

"You reckon we should tell her? Now, like?"

"Wouldn't she'd like to hear it? Pass it on to you-know-who?"

"I don't know. The less said the better, I reckon."

Her eyes went big for a moment. She stifled a follow-up yawn then, snapped her notebook shut and started gathering folders.

"Have you worked with 'Tom the Bomb' before?" I asked.

She settled the edges of her papers on the table top again.

"Why are you asking me that?"

Her glance reminded me of the one you get from an opponent right after the ref gives you the sportsmanship guff. Right before you try to knock the living shite out of one another.

"Because I'd like to know if Kennedy working for us. Or, if Bossman put him in to keep an eye on us."

She tilted her head and gave me a scientific look.

"Important case like this, Nolan figures you need minding?"

There was no explosion. She returned to settling the file folders, clapping their edges on the table again and again. Eventually, she pretended to notice that I had been staring all the while.

"Here's one for you then, Sergeant Malone. Is your career affected because you were born male?"

Ah. No. There was no answer that'd work. I eyed the postcards pinned to the partition. A fierce orderly arrangement it was. Crete? The sea was so blue it just had to be fake. One of them wasn't a post card, it was a snapshot. It was definitely Ireland. Sligo, I decided. Where complicated people came from.

*　　*　　*

Bernie Cummins sounded like she'd just woken up. Or maybe had never gone to sleep. I took it slow. She had only a few questions. Was it a round-the-clock thing, people out looking for Gary? I told her it was not. Also, that we were only getting going in an organized fashion, and the search could ramp up to that. Was I running the search? I was, I told her. Me and another Guard. She sounded beyond tired. Relieved and defeated at the same time. Her next question I had expected. I couldn't have prepared for it.

"So what do you think? Really think, like."

"It's just police work, Mrs. Cummins. Procedures, techniques, information sharing. Nothing too startling."

159

She was maybe too tired to call me on this. Or maybe too smart. I filed the call right after. It took me a while to come up with a word to describe Bernie Cummins' manner during the conversation. I settled on 'weak.' Then I went back to filing my session with Hynes earlier. Looking it over after, I had adjective trouble with him too. 'Misleading?' In the end, I left 'evasive.'

I checked for email, personal email. Waiting for it to load, I imagined my fingers taking on a life of their own and just logging into Facebook and getting it over with. There was nothing anyway, nothing except two ads for car insurance that got by the spam filter. Spam has plenty. Tatiana had 'hottttt XXX pitcures' to share with me, and me ONLY. Clearly so smitten with me that her spelling was gone astray on her.

Áine was ahead of me, rising already. By the time I was tucking in my chair, she was sliding shut a cabinet. The lock appeared to be bollicky. She was patient and methodical. Fancy new furniture and fittings, I thought, and the locks are crap?

"Is that the mysterious Sligo place you mentioned earlier?"

She stopped trying to coax the key and she followed my nod toward the non-postcard.

"Even more mysterious. Limerick."

"Right. I went there once. Came home though. It was closed."

My 'joke' had a magical effect on the lock. She turned the key and pocketed it. I told her I was heading out. How about her?

"No, I have a deadline, a CEPOL thing. It's online."

"CEPOL? They're a lot more popular these days, I believe."

It was well-meant, but it was still two lies in a row. A lot of the CEPOL courses were dead boring. I knew of only one guy, Kev Deasy in the drugs unit in Sundrive Road, who'd finished one.

I made a stop at the jacks on my way out and, job done, I meandered off to the canteen to get a big, long go of water. I drank it leaning against a cabinet, and looking around. A showroom, this place all right. A model you'd imagine could only be in some posh place in, say, Zurich. or Berlin. Imagine if this was how all the Garda offices were furnished? Morale...?

It didn't take long for the sour notions to roll in, of course. Nolan: a jumped-up bollocks. But he was as jumped-up bollocks with pull, and he knew how to use it. Everyone else was fighting just to keep bodies on shift and begging for more at the same time. Not Nolan. He just clicked his fingers – lo and behold, instant task force. Kennedy, McGinn, Finnoula What's-Her-Name.... more in the pipeline too. I looked down into the mug. Was that where I then saw what I'd missed earlier? Those people were Nolan's picks, not Áine's. Did she even want or need them yet? That had never come up. Nolan just slotted them in, and that was that.

A cold, knife-sharp notion caught me then, like the winds that come at you if you're anywhere near the quays on a Winter's day, and cut the face off you. Maybe I had got it all backwards – again.

I lowered the mug. That's what was going on, I thought: I had become one of them. A begrudger. Only seeing the bad in people. Looking for the low-down, the dirt. Because...? Because that's what the job did to you. No doubt there'd be others who'd want Nolan taken down a peg or two just because he was successful. It was old story too – spite, plain and simple. I'd had a lens over my eyes for so long that I'd forgotten it was there.

I put my philosophical investigation on hold and took a long drink from the mug. The water tasted different this time. Yes, I realized, I had signed up with the begrudger brigade without even realizing it. I had another go of water and started some mental backpedaling.

Item 1: Nolan was going to these lengths for one simple reason: *he wanted it to work.* It wasn't just the glory he was after, and the CV boost. Snagging Tony Cummins really was a big deal. It could be a massive opener for Garda operations all across the board. So why wouldn't Nolan throw everything he could get at it?

Item 2: So Nolan was a prize bollocks. So what? Like Delaney said, since when was I so thin-skinned? Nolan wasn't a bollocks for the sake of being bollicky: it was part of the package. Kilmartin, for example, was the back of the neck a lot of the time in the Squad. We put up with it. We knew he was a cop and a half.

Item 3: Another situation I was getting wrong? This Áine Nugent. What if Nolan wasn't actually carrying her, or playing the tender gender quota game with her? What if he was actually backing her to the hilt? As in he really wanted her to win this one, but at the same time he needed to keep a close eye on things. That was his job, for God's sake. He couldn't just let her have the run of everything. She was new to it, she'd miss stuff. If the operation went skew-ways. it was Nolan who'd have to answer for it all.

This mental excursion left me more than a bit morto. Tired too. I moved to a spot that offered a half-decent view of a real world outside. The light had gone pale and things were flattening out and losing their colours in preparation for the night. I had things to do. One was to get my shopping list out of my head and into actual food. Milk and eggs, and sausages, and whatever fruit I could commit to when I saw it there in front of me. And I couldn't dodge doing laundry one more day.

Yet I found myself taking another mug of water from the tap and returning to my long gawk out that window. My mind had slid further, all the way to China, to that town where Sonia should be heading to around now, the village her grandfather had started out from. Damned if I could remember the name of it. The more I tried, the more annoying it got. Which was what sent me back down the hallway again to find a decent sized screen to Google it.

The place was quiet. No sign of Áine. Her screen had timed out. The glass panel over Nolan's office door was dark also. Maybe everyone was out on the prowl at the same time? Then there was a noise. So, not everybody was gone home, or out on an op. It sounded like the groan you make as you stretch. Whoever was the author seemed to like it or, if it was pain, he or she hadn't gotten through it yet, because it repeated. The next one was like someone was catching their breath. I heard harsh whispers then, one of them a 'no.' A hoarse whisper then, said like it was a curse: 'here.'

And then the real cursing started. It was a man, and he was trying not to raise his voice. I backtracked the few steps to get a better notion of where this was coming from. I didn't need to put my ear to the door. This so-called conversation was coming from Nolan's office. I knew what skin on skin sounded like, skin slapping against skin that is to say. This was by no means

162

a scrap. No, there was some how's-your-father afoot. More cursing then. But that was the way it went sometimes when there were people going at it hammer and tongs.

The dirty talk tapered off. Somebody grunted, I couldn't tell who, and then came panting and words I couldn't make head nor tail of, at all. Then, as if mother nature wanted to remind us that humans weren't half as important as they thought, a couple of squeaks got added to the orchestra. Part of me didn't want to know the who was who here. The other part of me, the one not born yesterday, already knew. I turned away – and then I freaked.

Five, six feet from me was Quinn, standing there. Arms folded and feet spread, he was announcing that he meant business. He might have imagined that he was smiling but all that came to me from between those eyelids was contempt. He tilted his head and swivelled his eyes in a lazy fashion toward Nolan's door, and back. Then, opening wide his eyes, he looked me over like I was covered in shite. My heart began slowing. I got my breathing better under control. I didn't care that he had seen me reacting this way, or that he'd likely guessed why my hand had instinctively dived inside my jacket.

He stepped to the side with a mock politeness as I went by. I'd say he picked up on the fact that I was close to having a go at him. He grabbed the door behind me before it swung shut.

"Were you looking for someone there, head-the-ball?"

"Maybe I was," I said, half-over my shoulder. "I'm not any more though. ... Micro mickey."

15

I ended up chickening out of going into Supervalu. No surprise there. The results were 100% predictable too – me ending up back at the apartment picking at what I'd grabbed at the Centra instead. A 'baguette.' I right away got involved with a can of beer, stopping only when my tonsils were about to explode. The second can took time.

Useless phrases kept spinning around in my head: *People are complicated. Don't make assumptions. You're missing something here.*

I tried to take a logical line. A) I hadn't *seen* something. I'd only *heard* something. B) Who's to say that it really was Áine in there, or even Nolan? C) These people were adults anyway. And so forth. But all it took to explode all this was recall of Quinn hanging around by the door. Like a dog waiting for his owner.

I even did a few laps of the excuse route. That 'Neanderthals' comment of Áine's? How many years had she been wading through a swamp of boys-club coppers the likes of Quinn? Sure, promotion would get her into a better situation but that was the very thing that became a weak point. That was what got her cornered. And then her personal life. Who knew what way her separation was going. All that going on? It'd wear anyone down.

So the more I thought, the less I knew. The not-messed up part of my brain kept issuing feeble commands all the while. Go pound a bag down at St Joe's. Go for a run in the Park. Go do what you've been avoiding here: dishes, hoover, the rake of laundry that still hadn't magically washed and dried itself, and then hung itself up.

I was draining the second can and thinking about a third when Sonia appeared. Yep, there she was, right by the banks of one of those paddy fields that she loved to take snaps of. Peasants wading and stooping and smiling.

China – full of happy, happy people. Yeah right sure. Sonia was smiling, of course. Well why wouldn't she? She was reconnecting with her ancestors.

But I just couldn't hang on to that face, that smile. Another face was intruding. Bernie Cummins. Not smiling. She was sitting in front of a window or a doorway, like she as waiting for someone. I didn't doubt that she was in pain, with nothing facing her but the prospect of more of this. Her lips moved. She wasn't praying for herself. She was praying for a person no-one else would pray for – Gary. Bernie Cummins and my Ma, pals for fifty something years. Was there a prize for something like this?

Ghosts. Could you be haunted by ghosts of living people too?

Then I remembered: I'd told Ma I'd be in touch. I took a go of the third can, and keyed in her number.

"How'd she look? Tell me – Bernie, how'd she look?"

"Well she looked older than the last time I saw her."

"Come on. This is your mother you're talking to."

I poked at the beer can that I'd just flattened. Fair City was rolling on in the background. She always got drawn back to it.

"Just think of the peace of mind you're giving her," she said.

The yoghurt ad came on, the happy belly one.

"Tommy?" The tightness in her voice made me sit up, literally.

"Now I know you do be busy all day....."

She definitely sounded flustered now, and confused.

"I thought maybe you knew already," she went on, "and that's why you were phoning? Why you sound a bit low? Me, I heard it off Theresa Cooney down the road. But I haven't seen the news ... maybe... I don't know. I don't want to see it, in actual fact."

"Ma? In the name of Jaysus –"

"The poor divil," she said, suddenly. "If it's really him, I mean. God look down on him! Terry had such a soft spot for him. That's all I can think about. Back when you know, before things went ..."

She drew in a long raspy breath.

"There's bits of it all over the road, his motorbike. Barry, you know,

Theresa's hub? He saw it. Belongings scattered all over the road. Like, I don't know, a bomb. A hit and run, they're saying."

My eyes had locked on the picture over the table, the one of the Yellow River at sunset that Sonia put up the week before she left. My throat was so tight that my voice came in a squeak.

"Ma. Who are you talking about? Is it Christy?"

"So you heard already! Lord a' mercy on the poor divil! I thought it could have been some lad who robbed the motorbike on him. Joyriding, you know?"

My neck and shoulders had seized up. There was a familiar tightening at the base of my skull. Without thinking about it, I had already opened up my laptop. I was waiting for the stupid Wi-Fi to stop its stupid searching. I checked the time. Still twenty minutes still to the radio news.

"Barry, he sort of knows Christy too. He knew him, I mean."

Finally. Breaking News – if ever there was a more stupid name for a thing. And there was something: motorcyclist, Crumlin. There was no name. Spots' words dropped into my mind: Christy should know better than to be playing with matches.

There wasn't enough air in the room.

"What are you doing there, Tommy? I hear you typing ..."

*   *   *

It took me eleven minutes to find that what Ma had said was true. I'd kept trying online, but 'updated' and 'breaking' don't mean what they say they mean. A call to Johnny Murtagh, who had transferred to Traffic Services a few years back, worked the oracle. I was patched into an on-scene Traffic Corps mule. A van, said the mule, it was seen speeding off. And yes, the wallet ID said Christy.

That image that had stuck in my mind of Bernie Cummins agonizing over her missing son? Gone. What I had instead was worse. It came with a sound track too. The shriek, the sizzle of tires under locked wheels. The thump like an explosion, a sound you feel more than you hear. Then the grinding screeching of a motorbike skittering across the road as it comes apart. But

167

worst of all, that sound you can't get any other way but when a body's hurled against something hard and unmoving.

My stomach gave a sharp tug and then I was scrambling for the jacks. The heaves stopped the moment I knelt by the toilet bowl. Cold, hard notions slid into my mind. This was Christy's own doing, not mine. And Christy is –was? – no angel. That guff out of him at the graveyard, Nature-Boy going up the mountains to get away from it all? Coppers weren't lie detectors, but still. The truth was, lying came easy to Christy. Who was to say he hadn't gone back on the needle? Or that it had never stopped in the first place? Drinking too maybe, even showing off...

No. No amount of Jameson's finest was going to turn this around. I eased back onto my heels and stared at the tiles above the bath. It was me who had turned Christy into a target. It didn't matter that he had made himself my fantasy sidekick, Christy Cullinane 007. Him showing up at the graveyard had always got my goat, but I still expected him to be there. I had even gone to the money-out-of-the-wall for him earlier. Money for what? An offering? I didn't fork over money every year to Christy to persuade a God that I didn't believe in to let Terry out of a Purgatory that I didn't believe in either. The money thing was just something Terry'd have done.

Another dry heave corkscrewed around in my guts. I get up on my hunkers and reached for the cold tap on the bath. Dowsing cold water over my face wasn't going to fix this, though. I got back on my feet and filled the hand basin, and I took one of Sonia's facecloths and massaged my face and eyes with it. Just as I let down the face cloth to reach for the hot tap again, everything stopped.

Something in the mirror just changed? There had been a movement: I was sure of it. Yet everything looked the same. The same boring view of our tiny hallway as ever. I'd noticed that little gap under the hall door from the first day I'd moved into the place. But slight as it was, it was enough to show a faint shadow from something lying against it, or standing close to the door, outside.

My eyes burned. Possibilities popped up but evaporated almost instantly. Sonia – she'd come back early and was going to surprise me. Repair man, inspection, somebody collecting door-to-door for the Vincent de Paul? A neighbour, a cup of sugar. Nope.

My Sig was where I'd left it, on the couch. But crossing the hallway meant being directly exposed to the door. For a few insane moments I considered The Alternative. Yes, it'd take time to get it into usable mode, but I wouldn't need to cross that no-man's land. The parts were in that dummy space I'd made behind Sonia's Bose, above the microwave I had only the one clip for it, a rare seventeen rounder that was its former owner's pride and joy, now set snugly into my stash box cut-out cookbook.

Said party, a highly volatile shaper the name of Shiny O'Neill, had done a runner from a house we were raiding. Iijit that I am, I'd gone after him. I saw him throw something in a flower-bed: the something turned out to be this Beretta. Shiny got away from me that day, and went off our radar for months. He turned up again, tangled up in the wreckage of a stolen X5 on the M1 somewhere near Leicester after a chase that wound up to 140 – miles – while he tried to outrun the law and deliver his half mill worth of heroin.

I still felt the same about keeping that pistol, even more so. If there was going to be a roll-back on pistols, and I got deprived of the take-home protection, that wouldn't wash. I had racked up plenty of haters and grudges, and what-have-you. Dublin is still not that big of a place. Better to be alive and facing charges than to have to to people say nice things at your funeral.

My mind was definitely not running the show here: panic was. However long it'd take me to assemble the Beretta was too long. Anyway, I was already darting over to the couch to grab hold of the Sig. Then I was on one knee by the couch with the Sig trained on the door, concentrating on breathing right. The quiet was driving me mad. It took me a minute to get up. It took another minute to get in position by the door to the kitchen. From there I took a look along that gap at the bottom of the door. Nothing. Had I imagined it?

I turned the other way, toward the windows. Maybe that was what had happened: a change of something in my peripheral vision had set me off. My eye went straight to that one apartment across the yard. It had been dark there for months, with the curtains drawn. Now, in the glaring light from a bare bulb, I made out bits and bobs of furniture, and boxes and bags piled up higgledy-piggledy. So someone was moving in. I watched a man in a blue T shirt and then a woman in a white one amble in and look around and drink something. A bank repo, maybe. My mind slid back to Christy, and then veered toward Áine Nugent and Nolan. On it lurched, with growing irritation, to Ma and to Bernie Cummins, and to the self-satisfied, half-sneering face of Tony Cummins.

I came to with a jolt. I had a savage cramp in my hand now. Squeezing the hell out of the grip on the Sig was liable to do that.

*   *   *

That very light rain that had been falling when I came up the ramp lingered as a haze under the streetlights, and then flaring and glowing with the blue roof array on the Traffic Corps Pajero.

The cordon ran a fair good distance, with flashers on the pylons catching the plastic and glass sprayed across the roadway. I figured on a couple of dozen gawkers in three loose groups, eyed by two fairly alert-looking uniforms at each end of the cordon. The beam thrown low across the tarmacadam from one of the light set-ups made it look like a huge dark hole lay next to the cordon. Two techs, his or her boiler suits reflecting the lights with an almost luminous intensity. A pair of well-turned out fellas in civvies stood away to the side, clipboards to their chests like riot shields. In my mind, I already saw the page open on their clipboards. The page-at-a-glance reconstruction summaries. The rows of tick-boxes and the diagrams. The arrows and question marks for entries and exits.

And there it was, the bulk of Christy's motorbike. It looked small here. The handlebars were all wrong and the pedals didn't stick out like they should. About twenty feet beyond, almost at the edge of a floodlit area, were the bits of clothing I'd expected, what the paramedics slice and tear as they go all-out to keep someone breathing. No leather jacket in sight yet.

One of the mules at the tape had had his eye on me all the while. He hauled up in front of me as I approached, and pulled out a madly powerful LED to see my card better. If he was at all impressed, he didn't let on.

"So what's the story here?" I tried.

He eyed me cagily. Just because I couldn't smell my own breath didn't mean that he couldn't.

"A van, I heard?" I hadn't spotted any tire marks yet.

"You heard right," he said.

"Witnesses?"

For an answer, he inclined his head in the general direction of the two plainclothes.

"Was he known to you," he said then, like he was opening an interview. "The victim?"

"In a manner of speaking."

I watched him rearrange his hi-vis and stare back at a car full of people cruising by. His nostrils stirred and he cocked his head sideways. Eyeing me again, he rationed his words in a halting culchie manner.

"All right now Sergeant. I can tell you have had a few jars."

"I'm off duty. Is the ID solid? Photo? Matched up the bike?"

His stare sharpened and turned challenging.

"You brought a fierce big pile of questions with you. For someone who's off-duty. Sergeant?"

A trio of young lads had arrived. They were edging close to the tape. The mule gave me a stay-put look and strode over. They were tame enough, which surprised me. I lifted the tape. It took the mule a few moments.

"Oi," I heard him call out behind. "You can't just walk in there, Sergeant or no Sergeant."

I had certainly gotten the two plainclothes' attention. One of them handed his clipboard to the other and stepped into my path, muttering all the while. He cupped a hand around his ear to hear the Guard behind me calling out again.

He gave my card a look-over like it was a stool sample.

"Drug Squad Central," he announced, like it was a reading test. He looked sideways at me. "A Sergeant to boot. Who'd surely know you never, ever walk through a crime scene."

I gave him a selective story of my connection to Christy, all the while trying to ignore the baggy eyes and the long, suspicious nose that led up to them.

"OK," he said. He'd was in belligerent territory now. "So?"

"So it matters to our case who did this and why."

"Well of course it would. But that to me says you have information for us too, perhaps?"

His slow blinking stare was getting to me.

"It's possible somebody sussed him, and decided to do this."

"Is that a fact now. Continue?"

"The issue is why here, and why now."

"Well," he announced grandly, looking about with a pantomime squint, "this particular bit of road here, you'll have noticed, Sergeant, is the class of location from which you can run out in fifty five different ways. A coincidence, do you think?"

"Was he chased here? Followed, I mean?"

He shuffled his feet a little and looked out over the road again.

"I heard that someone went through his stuff, or tried to."

"You heard that, did you? Well I'd be very interested to find you who told you this."

"Was there anything taken?"

He almost smiled.

"Taken? But you're Drug Squad Central are you not, where it all comes together? So you'd be the one to know what, if anything, would be worth chasing him for, and taking from him."

I was suddenly pierced by the recall of how proud Christy had been of his damned motorbike. Maybe he had been telling the truth about his new clean future, his 'nature.'

"Best you be off now, and leave us to do our job here."

"Have we – have you – found his mobile?"

It was like asking the Pope if the whole crucifixion thing had actually happened at all.

"Well can I do a quick check of his effects?"

172

His look dissolved into a mixture of pity and sarcasm.

"No can do. As you'd know, if you were in your right mind?"

"Just a look, not to go through them or anything."

"Are you out of your bloody mind? Do you realize that I – "

"This is hot and ongoing. OK?" If his eyebrows went up any higher, they'd pull back his hair. "The victim here was trying to contact me. That's the issue, and it needs action now."

His eyes bulged some more before easing back into that glazed, can't-surprise-me model that us coppers are probably born with.

"Listen to me," he said next. "What we have here is a crime scene. We have a male, deceased. We have evidence to gather. And the plain fact of the matter is that you should –"

" – But he was on his way to meet me."

"On his way to meet you. Was he now. Ah."

I heard a scuff of footsteps. His partner was on the way over.

"Did you find his mobile?"

"You're stepping in it here. Git, before things get out of hand."

My mind had drained anyway, drained of questions, of ideas – of words, even. All I had was the wet shine off the roadway, the tape stirring in the faint breeze.

One of the mules had sidled over now too.

"Do we have a problem," he said. Any of the sarcasm he had deducted from his tone he had piled onto his stare. The three of them stood facing me now, in a small but suggestive arc.

"Best we go by the book," the detective said. "OK Sergeant?"

I walked back to the Golf and slid in behind the wheel and – nothing. Nothing more than sitting in a trance. Thoughts – they weren't even thoughts – flew everywhere and nowhere. Numbly, I sat staring, not through the windscreen even, but at the drizzled glass itself. Something about it reminded me of the grille on a confession box. Strange scenes began to leak into my mind.

Bless me Father, for I have sinned. Here is my confession. I'm after killing Christy Cullinane! I mean, I might as well have killed him.

This mad imagining even came with a priest.

Ah, my son. Have you forgotten? Man has free will.

But Christy lost the run of himself years ago! I knew that too!

My imaginary priest stood his ground.

Now listen, my child. Let's be candid here. Christy was past master of the old self-sabotage himself, was he not? And you know what that is, I'm sure. Being as you're no slouch in that regard yourself, now.

My mind swerved into madder, weirder regions: now I was giving Christy a serious dressing-down.

What in the name of Jaysus were you trying to do? Going around like a fart in a bottle, dropping my name everywhere? What were you thinking? Didn't you realize what...

Then I remembered: those phone calls that had gone nowhere. Christy trying to get through? If so, what was he ringing about if it wasn't about Gary Cummins? No, I told myself and repeated it over and over: this was a murder case. It had its own rules, its own path. What's more, it wasn't in my hands. They'd be on to me soon enough. Nolan'd want to know too. And if it got out that there was a mini-task force of coppers looking for Gary Cummins, he'd blow a gasket. Let him, then. I'd had enough.

I was two or three sets of lights away before I had any clue about where I might be headed. I wasn't going back to the apartment. All I'd do there would be sit in front of the goggle box and get plastered. Not a pub either, to get almost as plastered. But the urge to blot things out, to just be away from this, it was getting stronger.

Spots' text back was quick: OK – OK to my proposal to go on a Mystery Tour. Just by me asking him, he'd have sussed that something was out of kilter. I wondered if he had gotten wind yet of what had happened to Christy. My guess see-sawed more to the no side. I stopped at an off-licence and paid far too much for cans of the German beer he favoured, a bottle of Bacardi, and six Pepsis.

Spots was standing by the hall door when I arrived. He eyed the bag of drink under my arm. He was a bit wheezy walking out. With a few half-stifled grunts, he climbed into his Merc.

"Not that I'm asking," he said, rubbing the key between his thumb and forefinger, "but just for the record, you look like shite."

"Just drive, will you. Is that too much to ask?"

"Maybe it is. A question. Is this some kind of entrapment gig?"

"You're not worth entrapping, if that's a proper word even. Want me to drive instead?"

"Full of surprises you are," he said and turned the key.

Sliding the gear stick over and back, he eyed the gauges and listened to the engine. Spots had restored the Merc until it was in A 1 nick, but diesels this old gave off a lot of smoke anyway.

Some of our tours had led to unexpected happenings, and unwelcome events. Two years back, I was in such rag order that I'd actually started carrying The Alternative around with me. It wasn't just paranoia. I hadn't been carded yet for carrying off-duty, for personal protection, so I had taken matters into my own hands.

Long story short, Spots had noticed said Alternative poking out of my jacket pocket. He waited until after the gargle and the joints had done their work before bringing up the topic. The end result was me letting Spots Feeney fire off rounds from it into a very out-of-the-way bog hole up the mountains.

I'd thought about that foray many times since. Couldn't have dreamed up a worse SNAFU. I had just driven a coach-and-horses through Garda regulations. Put myself in a compromising position with a fella who had a criminal record and an odd way of life. All this while en route to potentially chalking up a half-dozen serious criminal charges. Self-sabotage? Hah. Self-explosion, more like it.

"Any particular destination in mind?"

I said nothing. He let in the clutch and the diesel gave a shudder, and we were off.

"Watch you don't get that anywhere."

175

So much for trying to open a can on the sly. I passed it to him.

At the traffic lights, some exhaust found its way in the window. Soon we were going along the canal. We turned for Rathmines and my guesses about destinations dwindled. He had a weird yen for godforsaken places. I felt around for the Bacardi. A problem with Bacardi and Pepsi was that the first one never tastes boozy enough. But Spots wasn't complaining.

We hit Ballyboden and began the climb in earnest. Over the Parkway we went. Soon our headlights lit up the sign for Edmondstown and the road commenced its spaghetti-style twists and turns. Beyond Rockbrook they'd be even tighter. Skirting Kilakee I got a long look back down at the city, glowing like it was on fire, all the way out to where it got dark again over the sea.

After a couple of miles, Spots geared down and gave the wheel a sharp tug. The Merc pulled through the curve and onto to the road up. I had guessed right – The Featherbed. Dublin's own Gobi Desert – nothing but mile upon mile of bog with the odd bush. Eventually, we'd came down off the mountain into the Wicklow end of things, down by the old reformatory and into Glencree.

I watched through the side mirror the red-orange glow of the sidelights sweeping along the rushes and the scouch grass crowding the margins of the road. Spots slowed but we still came close to bottoming the springs. He reached for his ear, to press his hundred Euro Bluetooth earpiece. I eavesdropped the best I could. Pauses between pronouncements were brief.

"He's a bollocks, is why. No I don't care. Tell him yourself."

"People," he grumbled after. "Bray he wanted me to go to. Bray, that's full of you-know-whats? Where you'd get knifed as quick as kiss hands. For two hundred nicker?"

A bit harsh, fair enough. I was no fan of Bray myself. It had been heaving with serious gougers forever. Much more to the point, the one time I was ever shot was in Bray. That was eleven years already. Christ.

We were well into the bog now. Spots geared down for an S bend. As heavy as the old Merc was, it still held tight. Nazis, I thought, Poland.

"Not that you're asking now Tommy." A fiendish glow from the instrument panel lit up his ugly mug. "But the solution's staring you in the face. It's the same old story. Simple."

The Bacardi had kicked in, but I wasn't getting value out of it.

"Story, answer. Face. Staring? What are you on about?"

"The old love life, is what. God knows I told you enough. But did you listen? No you didn't."

He geared down to second, tapped the brakes and turned off the road. The lights bobbed over a track ahead, with puddles. He took it slow around the dug-out, a little arena where they'd cut turf years ago, that hid us from the road. He found his place and stopped and reversed, and aimed the Merc back the way we came. He took out a joint and examined it under the roof light.

"Medicinal," he muttered, before maneuvering himself out.

It was cold up here even for May. The Merc had a good-sized bumper at the front. He gasped a few times while he located his perch on it. Spots still insisted on trying to be normal about sitting around like this, though it probably crucified him.

"100% Irish," he said. He put the joint to his lips. "Nothing skunky either, by God. And highly efficacious it is too."

"Illegal, you mean."

"That's a contentious matter. And anyway, look who's talking."

He struck his lighter and fired up the j and took a draw on it.

"Yes," he said then, breath held. "A work of art from a nice little patch under glass in the county of Wexford, if you're wondering. Save you the bother of waterboarding me."

Spots emitting all this banter here was his effort to try to lighten things, I knew. Terry's anniversary, he was thinking probably.

The breeze was away from me but I still caught plenty of the tang, half fart and half burning hay. He took two more quick pulls and handed it over. He wasn't spoofing. The tingling started almost right away, and then the eye stuff. For some reason I always got twitchy eyes.

"Someday they'll wonder what kind of iijits we were." He had already dropped into contemplative mode. "That we couldn't just use it as God intended. As proper medicine."

He wasn't wrong. It was the stupidest law really.

The tingling had started already and was morphing into a vague, gentle excitement. Things were loosening, expanding. My mind was free of that mad blue-bottle against the glass routine.

Spots let out a volley of smoke and pinched off the joint.

"I'll tell you something," he said, waving it around for the last of the sparks. "It's time to shed. To let go of baggage. You know?"

Sonia, he probably meant. Terry too, probably.

"Yes, you can't do enough shedding in my view. Especially these days. I mean to say, just look around. So much crap carried around? Things could be so much simpler."

He raised his arms to scratch out air-quotes, twice.

"'The rules.' 'The system.' All the stuff you're fed. School, at home, on the job. Propaganda – everywhere. Mind control."

He drew out a tiny LED light and examined the tip of the joint.

"But then one day, there it is." He was turning the joint around like he was a forensic technician. "Right in front of your eyes. And you think: everything they told me is wrong. And after that? Well you wonder: how the hell did I not see this before? Am I blind? Gullible? Am I a thick, am I –"

"With you on the thick bit. Look, give over with the sermon, will you. I hear enough of it."

"I hope you're not going tell me the system's working grand?"

That dry, pasty numbness had spread all across my tongue now. This was not exactly the buzz I'd wanted. In point of fact, the dope had made parts of my mind razor sharp. 'The system,' huh. This could be the time he asks, I thought. Any moment now he'd ask me straight out for 'a little favour.' That's how it'd start.

"Where's the folleyer-upper," I said. "The gargle?"

"What're you asking me for? You're the one in charge of that."

I took out the paper cups, the environmentally moral ones that Sonia had bought for our picnics in the Phoenix Park. I spilled a bit of Bacardi, pouring it. An altar boy again? It was sort-of funny.

This sip of the Bacardi was good. That knot in my neck and my shoulders had gone but I rubbed at it anyway and listened to the breeze hissing across the bog. Christy Cullinane hadn't disappeared from my mind. He'd faded a bit, gone off-stage. Far enough back that he wasn't clawing at me. For now anyway.

Spots made a gassy belch and issued a sigh of contentment. He got awkwardly to his feet then and shuffled into the dark. I thought I heard humming. Maybe it was the wind. In no time at all, he was picking his way back around the bonnet of the Merc.

"I'm telling you. Your problem? You need the ride."

"Ah no thanks. I've got a bit of a headache."

"Funny, you are not. Listen to me, this is science. Biology. This is a pillar of normal, healthy functioning we're talking about. Everybody needs a rub of the relic. Here, did I tell about a new place opened up in Stoneybatter, where – "

"Give over with that shite will you."

He took up a crooked lean against the front side panel.

"Well," he said. "Any word? The land of the rising sun?"

"China she went to, not Japan. You do know they're two different countries?"

"There's another sign right there. Sense of humour – MIA."

He took a longish sip of the rum. Yet again I wondered why smoking a joint never brought me the easy laughs that everyone else seemed to get, no problem. Not so much as a smile even.

"I got an idea the other day," he said then, after belching out a half-hearted version of a wolf howling. "Tycoon Tours. Their houses, I mean. You think?"

"Not my line of work."

"Like a Discovery thing. 'Palaces of Celtic Tiger Tycoons.' Or 'Celtic Tigers – where are they now.' Yes?"

"Have you got it in a PowerPoint? No, wait – send me a PDF."

"God you're contrary tonight. Anyway. I'd be doing myself out of a job."

It took me a moment. Ah: he meant nobody phoning him and begging him to rescue their tosser spouses or parasitic offspring from whatever steaming pile of shite they'd landed themselves in.

I tried to remember why and when it was Bacardi we started on. Who knows. We were thirteen or so. Spots sighed and cleared his throat and spat into the darkness. I took another go at the Bacardi. Spots took out a cigarillo.

"You remember years ago, the camping thing ..." His hand went to his earpiece. I was surprised. Mobile coverage was fierce hit and miss up here.

"Again?" he said. "Didn't you hear me the first time? Listen."

But the other party did not listen. Even over the rustling of the rushes next to me, I could hear him shouting at Spots to shut up. A highly unusual event, this. Long moments passed.

Spots had been working his way slowly upright. He was up now, and unmoving. I hoped this wasn't one of his episodes, when he got locked into what he called a Meccano Man Situation and had to move around like a crab.

"If you," he began, but interrupted himself.

He finished the call with a whispered yeah. Half-crouched, he stumped his way to the driver's side and grabbing the door handle, he stared at that little piece of rain gully they don't have on car roofs any more. I was to my feet and trying not to appear 'helpful.'

"I just heard something. A fella ... heard it a minute ago."

He used his grip on the door handle to lever himself almost to standing. Like a poorly built robot, he slowly swung my way.

"You," he said, the word turning to a snarl. "You knew?"

He didn't want any input. It wasn't answers he was after.

"You did. That's why you're in the state you're in."

Another drag on his cigarillo showed eyes narrowed to slits.

"And here I was almost feeling sorry for you. Terry's on his mind, I thought, the anniversary and all. But look what you've gone and done. You stupid, careless, two-faced copper bastard."

He was too angry, too stunned probably, to say more. I swirled my Bacardi again and downed the last of it. I'd be needing it.

16

Ten minutes slid by. It might as well have been an hour. Spots was still fumbling and stumbling around at the back of the car, cursing non-stop. I couldn't settle on a plan. Not even a thought.

He made his way back to where I sat. We were down to two cans of beer. Spots grabbed his off the roof and pointed it at me.

"God know I warned him!" It was his tenth time, probably, saying it. "I did. You stay to hell away from anything to do with the Cumminses, I told him. You pull one string – just one! – and it'll all come down on top of you, the whole shebang. There's more than enough trigger-happy nut jobs out there, I told him, especially these days. You never know what'll -"

Whatever cut short his speech also put him into a trance. He stared into the night for a bit.

"And you knew too," he said, addressing the big nothing that was the bog and darkness. "You did. You knew bloody well Christy wasn't thinking straight." He pivoted slowly back to face me. "That he *can't* think straight. Tell me different, I dare you."

He jabbed the air between us like he was slowly stabbing everything in sight.

"Whatever about the hard stuff, Christy never stopped toking. And we all knew that – *you* knew that."

I took a go of beer. It had no taste to it. Spots crushed his can.

"And the irony of it is? I'll bet you Christy got further than you ever could. But now you're washing your hands of him. You couldn't care less about the likes of Christy, youse cops. *Bastards.*"

He twisted the can before ripping it cleanly in two. He held one piece up against the sky.

"Put your thinking cap on now," he went on, "if Christy came to me like he did, shaping up like you and him were Batman and Robin.... You go on now and finish that sentence."

"Spell it out for me. You obviously – "

"Typical. All right, who else did Christy do his name-dropping on. That's the issue."

"Funny you mention it. I was wondering the self-same thing."

It took him a moment, but then he reeled back like he got slapped across the face. I seldom saw Spots speechless. It usually preceded trouble. But I didn't care.

"Wait," he said, quietly. "Did I hear you right?"

"Since when was that an answer. Did you, or didn't you?"

"Did I or didn't I what?"

"It was you told me about Christy. How he asking you about Gary Cummins. So who else did you tell?"

I could make out that Spots was shaking his head.

"Disgusting," he said. "Just disgusting. I can't believe you'd actually say that."

"I'm not saying you'd have done it on purpose."

"To think for one second I'd shop Christy around? Even for a laugh? 'Listen lads, you'll never believe what that gobshite Christy is going around asking.'"

He pushed against the door pillar, drawing squeaks from the suspension.

"OK let me turn that one back on you," he said. "What if someone sees me having a jar with you. What'll they make of that? See? Where do I stand now? Someone decides that I'm Christy Cullinane 2.0, nosing around and grassing to mastermind copper Tommy Malone. Thought about that, have you?"

"That's not even thinking. That's just being thick."

"'Being thick?' You putting a big, fat target on my back?"

I turned away and attended to the whispers from the grasses. A faint cooing carried on the breeze. Someday I'd Google night-birds of the Irish bogs.

"That's it?" I said. "You give me dog's abuse, end of story?"

From Spots came a growling, bitter laugh.

"I already did my bit," he said. "Over and above, on the phone to Christy."

"Oh now you tell me. Christy actually phoned you?"

"No, you hopeless tool. *I phoned Christy.*"

"What else are you forgetting to tell me?"

"Listen to you. You think I get up every morning asking myself, oh Janey, how can I assist the forces of law and order today? Like, who can I rat out to my old pal Garda Tommy today?"

The breeze was getting different tunes out of the grass.

"Honest to God," he said. "The nerve of you? Unbelievable. And there's me thinking, 'ah Jaysus, poor Tommy, Terry's -'"

"- All right, all right. You said that already, Mother Theresa"

He turned his gaze from one part of the sky to the next, like he was at the helm of a sailing ship of old. He was muttering now, loud enough for me to hear, of course.

"That's what cops do, of course. They use people. They use them up and then they throw 'em in the bin."

"So you tried to put Christy off. What else did you tell him?"

"That you're a magnet for flying shite. And wasn't I right?"

"You said 'the whole shebang,' earlier on, concerning the Cumminses. What did you mean?"

Even with the dark, I knew I had hit something. Spots' silence only sealed it.

"Christy told you something. That's why you lost your rag."

I heard a wheeze as he shifted his stance.

"Christy thought you'd be the go-to guy to go to because -"

"Shut up. Sure, Christy had questions. The man thought he'd just turn me on like a tap."

He was holding his breath. Something to get off his chest?

"...he has – had had... strange notions about stuff I might do. People I might know."

"*Might* do? *Might* know?"

"Give over. This is no time for your smart remarks. Yes I do know people, and yes, I do get the odd straw in the wind. Hearing about goings-on in this town is no big achievement, let me tell you. But I get to wake up in one piece every morning for a reason. It's because people trust me to know the diff between being in the know, and being a blabbermouth."

Undecided about taking a slug from his can, he lowered again.

"So yes, Christy had done a bit of digging,"

"And?"

"Someone said Gary was, quote, trying to start his own gig."

"Gig. What gig?"

Spots ignored my question and answered it at the same time.

"What gig are you talking about, says I. The last anyone heard of Gary Cummins is that he's so far gone that he's splitting fixes with tossers in the toilet of some pub. He might even be down-and-out, on the street. So don't be an iijit, I says. There is no gig. There never will be a gig."

"Did Christy say who told him this, about Gary and some gig?"

Spots let the can swing between his thumb and forefinger.

"You reckon he was just making this up?"

He half-heartedly waved that one off.

"Look," he said then. "The floor went out from under the Cumminses when Tony got put away. Every dog and divil know that. But I'll tell you this. I don't lose any sleep over the likes of Gary Cummins having to live with the Apache stuff that's going on the streets. The leg-breakers and the stabbers and the whackos? No sir. It's dog eat dog, Tommy. You know that much, at least."

"You think someone was winding Christy up? This talk of Gary starting up on his own?"

"Let's just say stranger things have happened."

He took out another cigarillo. The flame in his cupped hand lit up a face cut deep with perplexity.

"Christy?" he said, after a bout of coughing. "Making it up? Come on. You know the story. Heroin, Christ, the damage is done. It's their life for so long. That's how the brain is wired. Everything breaks down, goes haywire. Real, not real. Fantasy, reality. True, false – whatever. So who knows? Christy never said where he heard that about Gary Cummins, and I never asked. Why? I'll tell you why. Because I didn't believe him, is why. So nobody knows. Nobody."

More smoke batted back my way. Spots spat out into the night.

"Yeah right," he said, and turned to me again. "Sure, it's our national motto, isn't it. 'Nobody knew a thing. I swear!'"

"What are you talking about?"

"The whole 'T.O'D.O.D' rigmarole? You forgot already?"

He growled low in his throat and spat again.

"Overdose? Tom O'Dea?! Shock, horror! 'Nobody knew!' Day in and day out, that's all you heard. Like, a celebrity would never, ever, ever get mixed up in that stuff – God, no. Right. And nobody knew – except they all did. All of O'Dea's so-called pals, they knew from day one. But it doesn't matter if you're an insider, does it. No, it only matters if you're from Artane or Tallaght or Finglas or –"

"Spare me, will you. I didn't come up on the last bus, OK?"

Spots ignored me, as I knew he would.

"It covers everything, doesn't it – 'nobody knew!' Priests raping kids? 'Oops, nobody knew.' Bank's taking your home, putting you out on the street? Oh dear – nobody knew. The crash? Oh, nobody knew it was coming.' Nobody knew.... Nobody."

He nodded away the rest. Last year felt like ages ago now, but O'Dea's face was clear in my mind. He had turned up dead of an overdose on a hotel room floor. Ireland's big television star, the boy next door. Lovely fella, as nice a lad as ever stepped in shoe leather. Family man, decent skin. No airs to T.O.D., no sir. But it came out eventually. Coked up for a decade. Full bottle of vodka before mid-day. Girlfriend on the QT. But...? But nobody knew.

The constant flicking of his cigarillo told me Spots had grown restless. Restless and tetchy.

"Ah who cares," he declared and yanked himself upright. "What the hell use is it, this... Degrading is what it is. Like badgers we are up here in some bog hole, drinking and arguing...?"

His shoe must have stirred against one of the tins. It was enough to send him ape-shit, stomping on it over and over again. When he was finished, he picked up the debris and threw it on the floor in the back. Any buzz I had had was long ago turned sour. It had left me addled and giddy too, but giddy in a bad way: spaced, heavy-hearted, and suddenly very, very tired.

We headed back to town the same way we came. The lights of the city slid into view, its carpet of orange and white twinkling spreading across the horizon. The road took a turn and the banks swallowed the lights up again.

"So that's it then. Another chapter, and close the book. Is it?"

Spots wasn't biting.

"That's the be-all and end-all of it, as far as you're concerned. Christy's just another statistic, right? Too bad, so sad. That's it for you. Is it?"

He took the Merc hard into a curve. His lips barely moved when he spoke.

"You're the polis, so do your job. Is that too much to ask."

When he heard no reply, he looked over again.

"Did you get that? You need to write it down maybe?"

"They reversed over him, did you know? Christy, they ran over him again. Did you pal tell you that?"

Spots stiffened and stared hard ahead, his knuckles tight and pale as he squeezed the wheel.

"All I get's bellyaching and speeches. You're all talk, so you are."

He turned to me with a wild-eyed look. Just as he was about to let fly, his mobile went off. He eyed the screen and then braked hard, whacking the curb as the Merc's tires sizzled to a thudding halt. I could make out a man's voice. The same one who'd called earlier? Spots' glare dulled and then dissolved entirely.

"OK," he said, in a tight monotone. And hit End.

He kept tight hold of the phone, his hand bobbing slowly like he was about to lob a stone. More cars passed, some flashing their hi-beams. Spots watched them as though he wasn't looking through a windscreen but watching a television instead. The twitching around his mouth reminded me of a cat. Diesel exhaust began to seep into the cabin.

"What, you're waiting for the breathalyzer to come to you?"

He slipped the mobile into his jacket and found first gear. Soon we were passing pricey-looking places behind wrought iron gates, with interlock and landscape lighting to beat the band. Lots of German wheels, lots of SUVs – and yes, Macker: lots of Audis too.

Spots accelerated hard away from of one of those tiny roundabouts they had dumped on Sandymount. We were snagged then at the lights by a huge artic chugging up toward the Port of Dublin. It sent my thoughts skidding again: Christy taking his last terrified look out at this world, at the van bearing down on him.

By the time he pulled up short of the house, Spots had the air of a man who had made a decision. I'd been noting the fingers flexing over the rim of the wheel, the frowns that came and went.

"Well," I said.

He looked over sideways like I'd just appeared out of nowhere.

"Well what? You've done enough damage, I do believe."

"So that's it for you then, is it. Make you pronouncements, give me some fake outrage, and leave it at that. Must be nice."

Spots appeared to be composing a thoughtful, or scathing, response. He said nothing though. He looked by me to the window, but the thinking went on. I waited.

"And you're going on the batter now I suppose," he said then. "Right? Try and forget what you done?"

"Wrong. I'm going home. The apartment, like. I'm knackered."

Spots nodded gently. His eyes regained their focus. He looked down at some instrument on the dash and moved the gear stick over and back across neutral. I heard a faint snort. Did the tachometer or something not agree with him? Was he annoyed to see the time on the clock maybe?

Another thing everybody else supposedly gets from smoking a joint? Some all-knowing feeling. Some 'oh now I get it' revelation type thing. Not me. What you never had you never missed, maybe. But tonight, I realized, there might be a little change coming in that. Without being given any word or sign, I now decided that I could read Spots' intentions.

"Eh. Do I need to hit the button for the ejector seat?"

He'd asked me for a reason. I'd head home and wait for his call.

I slid out without a word, and walked back to my car.

*   *   *

A loud car-horn ejected me out of my trance. I had somehow teleported myself to the lights by the canal. When did traffic light turn green?

I had an easy run from there. Then I was home, the apartment that is, waiting for the garage door to roll up. 'The Wellington.' Well for once the name might suit: I'd be needing rubber boots for this mess.

As always, I took the stairs. Lifts had always given me a trapped feeling. I stopped in the last stairwell before my floor and waited, and listened. Coming home gargled didn't make me any less edgy. It just made me slower and clumsier. I drew open the door and looked down the hallway. The usual smells wafted in: cooking past and present. Crud from the carpet. Laundry detergent. The hallway ran like a normal hallway should run, light to light, doorway to doorway. I paraded my neighbours through my mind. 403: those students. 400: that couple studying in the College of Surgeons. Pakistani? Indian? Her: drop-dead gorgeous but always seemed nervous. Him, a gawk but friendly. Excessively so. The gay-for-sure civil servant in 402. Then my hardly-ever-there neighbour Martina, nursing her Ma somewhere in Tipperary.

I pressed close up to the door, my fingertips lightly on the grip of the Sig. I still did the hair in the door-jamb test when the humour took me. I even go so far as to dust and black-lit every now and then. Tricky enough acts to keep up, so they were, after Sonia moved in. Those rituals had started even before I was getting put through the wringer over you-know-who taking his fatal flyer off that roof. Conventional wisdom said that only a complete lunatic would go after a Guard, especially an armed Guard. Conventional wisdom never really worked for me. Drugs in Ireland is a billion-plus racket.

Inside at last, all seemed well – well as in normal. I noted the usual musty not-sure-what-that-is smell. The IKEA perfume also, of course. The microwave was still scrolling its stupid ad. The timer on the lamp had done its duty and the digital doo-dads were doing their slow blinking. I spent some time throwing handfuls of water from the running cold tap over my face. Then I made my way over to leather sofa that I didn't like but couldn't get rid of, and washed down a couple of Anadin.

My brain was revving like mad but the brakes were still on. I kept repeating: there was nothing I could do right now. Tomorrow I'd make inquiries – if someone on the investigation team hadn't already come looking for me, that is. How long it'd take for them to pull my mobile number off Christy's log, or his contacts, I couldn't guess. But, however long it took, your average copper would conclude that something stank here. Rightfully so too. All of which could shape up very ugly indeed. And, if Internal Review really was living up to my paranoid version of them, they could take a fierce nasty line here. I'd been exploiting an undocumented informant. Who was to say I hadn't gotten him killed too?

The vision of that duty-free under the sink began to throw its weight around in earnest now. The excuses surfaced quickly, as usual. It was better than heading out again, to Molloys or somewhere, and getting myself into more shite. It'd keep me here at least. It'd help me fall asleep. Still, I pushed back. I turned the telly back on. It was something to do with oceans. Then it was whales were being chased by a Japanese boat. I was about to lose the fight against the under-the-sink urge.

My mobile broke into its whirring dance on the counter.

"Just listen. No blather out of you. Yes or no."

It was Spots. A perfect attention-getting five rendition of his patented wired and wary tone.

"Maybe."

"Why I even bother, I do not know."

"All right – yes."

"OK then. Two simple words: drop it."

"'Drop it' what?"

"You heard me. Drop. It."

"Wait wait wait – whose idea is this?"

"Lose the arguing thing, will you. A little dickey bird is who."

"Well let's meet somewhere then."

"No we won't 'meet somewhere then.' Pay attention here, and follow the plan. Hit the scratcher and sleep it off. That's it."

"Sleep it off? Christy got killed. That's murder, and I'm a cop."

"Nice speech – for a class of Senior Infants. I told you before and I'll tell you again. You're not thinking straight. Something's going astray with you, and it's getting in the way of your brain."

"You found something. Come on."

I braced for Spots to hang up. The news feed crawling along the bottom of the screen started up another repeat cycle. A factory in Waterford was closing.

"Do the smart thing here," he said. "Not the Tommy thing."

"Means what?"

"It means, let someone else worry about this."

"Look the other way, you mean. Do the make-believe thing."

"Call it what you like. There's your way of going about things and then there's normal peoples' way of going about them."

"It's not me. It's the law you're talking about there, the Guards. OK, so we're not perfect. But the other way is no way at all."

"It was your way of doing things got Christy Cullinane kilt."

I heard his breath whistling in his nostrils.

"This is about Gary Cummins, isn't it. Tell me it's not."

"So you're gone deaf now." He spoke in a droning monotone now. "Listen. All them plans? You still have them, right? Sonia?"

The mention of her name worked as he'd probably planned.

"That family bit you told me you'd like? All that happy-ever-after shite? Well that's the stuff that matters – and hey, think of your Ma. That woman, she thinks you walk on water. So ask yourself, does she need more trouble? So don't be an iijit."

"The kind of iijit who won't join the chorus? 'Nobody knew?'"

"Tommy. Last time? Walk away. Everybody does it, sooner or later."

"Oh sure. 'Kick the can down the road.'"

"Can, road, kick – yeah yeah yeah. Whatever. Just walk."

"And where should I walk, according to you?"

"Anywhere. Walk to bleeding China why don't you. Get a few days off. Tell 'em you got the pox or something. Prague's nice. There's always Amsterdam. Point is, stop asking stupid questions."

I barely noticed him hanging up. After a while, I got up and went to the cupboard under the sink. The sink aka the duty-free.

My first go of the Vitamin J tasted like liquid chipboard. I took the second one back to the couch and I tried to think. Breathing exercises? A lorry with a clapped-out exhaust crawled by on the South Circ. Then, the long, slow squeal of brakes and the muffled thumps of trains in the shunting yards. The fridge went off again.

Staring at a blank TV screen while counting breaths and sipping Jemmy wasn't bringing on revelations. I got hold of my laptop and aimed it at Facebook. A godsend to us coppers, Facebook. I had a separate account for creeping: Gurrier1010. The Gurrier bit was obvious. 1010 meant fight going on. We didn't use radio code crap on the job, but lots of us made up our own codes. A 10-20, when I worked uniform in Swords eons ago, was pizza. 10-99 meant session over at Grogan's after the shift.

Keying in 'Mary Enright' gave me, worldwide, no less than thirty-four persons. This sort of stunned me. I narrowed down to the Irish ones. Last to go was a Mary Enright in Donegal, an assistant manager at an auctioneers. I was left with the one that was just a name, but no details. The notion of sending a friend request 'by mistake' had gained traction. I held off for now. Back to Google. Even basic searches were getting better by every day. A dozen mouse clicks landed me at an outfit called Flare Talent. Another click got me a studio photo of a Mary Enright of some years past. They didn't put her age.

191

I didn't recall seeing chestnut hair like she had in this photo. I wasn't really on the ball in that department. 165 cm sounded right. 'Eyes: blue.' A huge help.

Her talents? 'Vocal.' Maybe liked to belt out 'You're Beautiful' in a karaoke session? 'Dance and movement training.' This CV stuff was on the flakey side. 'Parts in productions, film and stage.' 'Misc. modelling' hardly referred to gluing model plane kits together. Nothing to shift me away from my take of Mary Enright from earlier. You didn't need a degree in criminology to figure that someone with an addiction had to find ways to finance it. Getting your paws on the two hundred Euro a day to put into your arm will throw any decent family upbringing under the bus, and so fast you wouldn't believe it. I'd seen it.

I flicked through more pages on this Flare site. To me, no offence to anyone, it was a lorry-load of nobodies. Three quarters – rough guess – were girls, women. One of the men looked like a picture Ma used have of Elvis Presley. Mime and street performance experience. Worked with kids in drama therapy classes. I counted eight non-white faces in total, all women. A few had names of shows or events that I recognized. There were two claiming they'd gotten on to Ireland's Got Talent.

And I wondered. This stuff was just a hobby. Right? A thing you'd chance your arm at. Maybe not. Maybe they were serious. But wasn't this whole fame / celebrity thing basically a crap-shoot? I turned to look for behind-the-scenes stuff about Flare. Domain owner info held at a hosting company. Not unusual. I went back to the site and trawled some more. View Source told me nothing about when the page had been updated. Contact Us: no phone number? I had a site grabber utility, but I didn't like using it. There'd be a record kept somewhere, I reckoned, or it'd be flagged. I'd maybe look again in the morning. Better yet, I'd get Áine or one of the 'team' we apparently had now, to do the looking.

I turned to Brendan Corcoran. Being Mary Enright's chauffeur was hardly his day job. Brendan Corcoran, promoter. One minute on PULSE earlier this evening had told me that Corcoran was, or seemed to be, clean as a whistle. A complete blank. Not even for incidents, or links, or associates or refs.

My first hop from the search list brought up a photo on a site for ... a bloodstock company? It was some class of shindig. 'Fillies & Follies,' a charity thing. OK. So Corcoran wasn't a horse. But why didn't his face jump out at me? I didn't have a clear picture of his face in my mind to begin with. A page linked to another photo brought me to a list of names. Corcoran was in a tux complete with one of those belts, a cummerbund they're called. He was by no means a natural smiler. He made it worse by trying too hard. I magnified the photo until it was a mucky puddle of pixels, and backed out again.

Bloodstock. It had a bad sound to it, but that was just ignorance on my part. Horse breeding was a better title, entirely. But what did I know about this stuff anyway? SFA. I knew there was money involved, and that sheiks used step out of helicopters in Kildare and drop a few million in a half an hour and fly out again. Whether that was still going on though, I had no idea.

That Follies and Fillies charity dinner tuxedo item was from two years ago. I opened another tab and put Fillies & Follies in a search. All right then – an annual dinner for charity. Spinal cord injuries. The story went back to an accident years ago, someone semi-famous had gotten paralyzed. I returned to the other tab and scrolled on. The faces were those shiny agricultural-looking models I'd associate with horses. Everyone was looking fierce pleased with themselves. Not a single one of the names meant anything to me.

I scrolled down. More people I'd never heard of. Then came a smaller group, where everyone was laughing their heads off. What was so funny? They seemed to be gathered around some bloke leaning in between the bouquets. I could see it was a tux but the photos had been taken from the side, and whoever's head belonged to the tux it was only showing ninety percent hair instead.

Instead of zooming in, I leaned closer to the screen. When I drew back again, that slice of face in profile had taken on a vaguely familiar look. I closed my eyes for a few seconds. As crappy an angle as that photo had, I knew that face. I did.

There were no names listed. The caption? *'Ah go on, will ya! Tell us another one!!'* I studied it again. Still stupid, still useless. The buzz from the dope had worn off. So was it just the gargle making me believe I recognized that guy? Stare at something long enough and it gets to be anything you want it to be.

I put in a new search for Fillies & Follies, this time dated two years back. Then I went to Images and worked down through them. I had gone over the better part of fifty or more before I got what I hoped for. It must have been that trademark bit of hair that had cued me in, the way it hung over his forehead. The patented O' Dea naughty-boy look that the oul ones mooned over. No doubt the laughing woman next to him was hanging on his every word too.

But really? It was all lost on me. That whole salt-of-the-earth, *daycent* man thing, it rubbed me the wrong way. To me, it was a complete cod from Day One. A put-on. He no more spoke for ordinary people than Mick Jagger spoke for the sacrament of marriage. I'd had rows about this with Ma, of course. Ma, the Tom O'Dea groupie. All of which made me totally unfit to grasp what celebrity actually was. T.O.D indeed. T.O.D. O.D. T.O.D. R.I.P.

I dropped a shortcut on the desktop and returned to Corcoran. Us Irish certainly do get around. A fair few Brendan Corcorans lived on the planet currently. A Sydney version looked to be quite the character. I was soon out of matches for the Brendan Corcoran that I wanted, however. A page link that'd been spinning for a while finally came through, but the photos on it were clogging up everything. I was back to The Web, circa 1994. Should I wait? Looking down into the amber treachery that was the last of the glass of whiskey, I decided – or the whiskey decided – I could.

Even before half the photos had come in, I recognized faces. The one drawing in – *crawling* in – next to Corcoran's was that actor, what's-his-name. The one who started out on RTÉ years ago, ended up in the UK. More of the photo filled in. Next to him was a young one awkwardly aboard of a big motorbike. Huge aviators covered half her face, and big red lips the size of party balloons took care of the other half. The skimpy leather kit she had on took care of little enough really. The bike itself was huge, a mad conglomeration of chrome and headlights and handlebars and fat, sweeping exhausts. All-in-all, an ugly-looking a heap of shite if ever I saw one. Not an item you'd see Irish roads much anymore, thank God, the Harley Davidson.

The sound of a door from down the hall got me out of the chair like a scalded cat. I listened hard. Then I got out of my shoes and began a slow, silent patrol of the apartment. I've always had that feeling of being surrounded by glass here. After my fifth round I stopped and woke up the screen on my mobile. Who would I call?

Nobody, is who. I wasn't going to relay news of Christy's murder to Áine tonight. Certainly not to Nolan. As for Spots' dramatic 'drop it' talk, I'd keep that to myself. All I needed right now was for the looney merry-go-round in my head to stop.

I plugged in my mobile and waited to see it was charging. After repeating the process with the laptop, I put a serious go of Jameson in my glass and shoved the bottle back in behind the pipe. That mightn't last. Discovery had Amazon week. Tonight's was some lunatic paddling the length of the river... on his own? That would probably do it, all right. It'd be mad enough to keep me from prowling the apartment like a demented Jack Russell, my mind whirring and rattling with unanswerable questions. Gary Cummins, Mary Enright, Brendan Corcoran, Declan Hynes, Spots Feeney, Christy Cullinane, Bernie Cummins...

Things soon slowed. Like a croc moving through the muddy Amazon, I slid into the soft numbness of not caring, and bit by bit, even the mighty Amazon river itself quietened and commenced to fade.

17

That was my mobile ringing? Here, in Hong Kong? It was my mobile, right enough. I wasn't in Hong Kong though.

Whatever crooked position I'd slid into had left my neck destroyed. It was dark still. There was something about tropical storms on the telly. I hit mute and rubbed at the dried spit that had clotted down to my chin.

Ma? At this hour?

"So where are you love?"

Her breath sounded even raspier.

"It's one o'clock in the morning. Where do you think I am."

"Oh I know, I know," she said. "I'm sorry!"

"You want to tell me you won the jackpot at the bingo. Right?"

"I wish!" Ma was always a dab hand at working the pretend humour into her voice. "No they ganged up on me last time, the numbers."

OK: it was about Christy. It had thrown Ma straight into worrying about her little Tommy. I guessed right.

"They still don't have the name on the news," she said.

"Well that's kind of normal. Next of kin, you see."

"I'm still in shock. I said a decade for him. I put your name in it too. What else can I do?"

The graphics on Discovery had gone completely mad this past year or so: spinning, streaking, exploding.

"You're going to work in the morning I suppose."

"No actually. Bono and me, we're flying to Cannes."

"So will you drop by the house on your way so?"

She hadn't heard me?

"I will, but you know work is the other direction. Right?"

She hadn't. Something heavy-feeling swung in my mind.

"Is everything all right there, Tommy?"

"Don't mind me. Are you all right?"

"You're upset about, you know, poor Christy?"

"Don't be asking me that. Eh, how come you're not in the scratcher?"

"Why are you asking me?"

"Because you're the worst actress on the planet, is why."

"Since when do you start talking to your mother like that?"

Conversations like this would be comical – if it wasn't my life.

"Are you okay, is what I want to know. Are you?"

"I'm grand! And you're there in your own nice place. So that's grand too. Yes it is."

"Ma? You're giving me the creeps here."

"Look, it can wait. Now I can hear your voice and I know that you're home, it'll wait, yes."

Ma taking a detour down the old passive-aggressive route was a rare event.

"I'm heading over," I said. "Give me twenty minutes or so."

Again she protested that it could wait. I could tell her heart wasn't in it. My throat had been sandblasted by the gargle or the gob-wide-open snoring. I filled a glass from the kitchen tap.

"'It,'" I said. "This 'It can wait' of yours. What exactly is 'it'?"

"Be careful driving over, Tommy. Will you?"

"Just tell me. I'm going to find out when I get there in anyway."

After a few words her voice cracked and turned into coughing. But I had heard 'envelope.'

"Envelope. What kind of an envelope?"

"It's sealed," she said, hoarsely. "But I can feel them, so I know."

Something cold and sharp slid up my spine.

"What can you feel?"

I heard her swallow and then clear her throat.

"Two of them, rolling around in there. I can even hear them."

I hit the stool on my way by, rushing for the door.

"My God!" Ma yelled. "What was that, Tommy?"

"It's just a chair. We're going to keep talking, so don't hang up on me. If the call's dropped, just wait, and I'll ring you back. OK?"

Like a gobshite, a drunken gobshite, I almost forgot my keys.

"So tell us again about this envelope thing."

All I heard was her breathing. It had gone ragged, but she was still trying to pretend it was normal. The back of my neck felt like someone was rubbing live electric wires along it.

"Did it come in the post?"

"No. Somebody must have dropped it here by the door, late."

"And have you touched it?"

I was shouting. Bellowing, actually.

"Of course I have! How else would I've pick it up and brought it in with me?"

"Big, small, fat skinny? Heavy, light...?"

I visualized a manila envelope not much bigger than letter sized. The problem was, I could also visualize what was in it too.

"Address too?"

"No."

"Printed or done by hand?"

"By hand. A biro, it looks like. 'T Malone.'"

"That's all? On the outside, I mean."

Her hesitation said that she was faking it again.

"Ma!"

"No!"

I heard her catch a sob. Her voice, small like a kid's, stopped me dead in my tracks.

"It says 'T Malone c/o Sheila Malone.'"

I pulled open the door to the car park hard enough for it to bounce back.

"That was a door, Ma. Keep talking, I'm getting into the car."

"Keep talking about what?"

"Anything! God, it's not like you're ever stuck for talk."

"The way I knew is to do with your grandfather," she began. "He was in the, what do you call it? The LDF, yes, during the Emergency. God, is it ... seventy years ago now?"

She was on auto-pilot now, about old family stuff.

"... joined up just to get the boots...the few shillings too of course. But he got hold of some of those things, I don't know how, and he brought them home one night... thinking that'd impress old Johnny, his Da. Old Johnny was in the 1916 thing, you see, the Rising and that... God, he used to laugh at the LDF fellas... 'Wait'll Hitler sees you, he'll die laughing...'"

A shriek from the tires told me that I'd hit the ramp too fast.

"... so what did Old Johnny do, but beat the ears off him. Old Johnny was a passivist, you see. Oh yes, he'd seen enough. ... the Royal Irish he was with, in the trenches, in the first war, the muck and bullets. He kept that quiet though. He had to, you see. In them days..."

She stopped in mid-sentence.

"That's how I know. I remember what ammunition feels like."

Ammunition. She couldn't bring herself to say 'bullets.'

"Are you in the car now? Is that someone beeping at you?"

"Let's talk about something else."

But now she had run out of words.

"Chinese food, Ma. Them egg rolls, you still like them?"

*   *   *

I still had some left-over evidence bags along and specimen gloves up in our room. Me and Terry's old room. I dropped in the rounds and drew the seal. The rounds were 9mm. No great surprise there, but they were much more heavily lacquered than what we were issued. I had no clue what the code numbers stamped onto the rims meant. Maybe 115 meant the grain? That notion set me wondering about that ammo cache we'd found last year up near the Border, all that old Warsaw Pact stuff.

Ma looked ropey still, and just as pale. I counted seven butts in the ashtray.

"You catch them with that? DNA in the spit, on the envelope?"

"Ma, come on. That's CSI."

She squinched her eyes and drew hard on the cigarette. My sandy-eyed gaze followed the wiry column of smoke until it flattened against the ceiling. On its way back to earth, it lodged a few moments on the photos on the shelf. The famous wedding photo she insisted on displaying there. No wonder she fell for Da. He did look like John Lennon, actually. I tried to skip the one next to it, of Terry in Torremolinos. Valerie, the girl he nearly married. Last I heard, Valerie had been resuscitated four times. The methadone was keeping her going, but she was still sinking.

Ma shuddered then.

"What do we do? Get the Guards in? The real Guards like?"

"I am a real Guard, Ma. No, not yet."

"You're not going to tell them at work, even?"

"I'm thinking about it. I'll have to, at some point. Meanwhile, I'm going to get this looked at."

With the in that I'd kept since Murder Squad days, I could get a quick-and-dirty Ballistics report on these rounds in hours.

She took another long pull on her Silk Cut. I often wondered if being on her own here was making her go a bit dotty.

"She came by the shop. Bernie. I wasn't going to tell you."

"Your work? What did she talk about?"

"Ah it was only to say thanks. And what a nice lad you were."

"Ma? Stay away from her until this thing is sorted. If ever it does get settled, that is."

"What? You mean you don't think Gary will ...?"

I filled up my cup half way. The tea was lukewarm now. It had tasted poxy to begin with.

"If only you'd seen her, Tommy. My God."

Ma didn't remember I'd sat across from Bernie Cummins?

"Shocked, I was. A shadow of the woman she was. My God!"

She bit her lip. Her eyes remained fixed on the microwave.

"She kept talking, Tommy, I couldn't stop her. What could I do? She's on her own."

I wondered if that lug Blake stayed in the house with her.

"So I says to her, Bernie, I says, you need to be somewhere they can take care of you properly. Peace and quiet, you know? But she says to me back that no, she won't go. She's going to wait for Gary, she told me. 'Like a candle in the window,' she said. My God."

She paused as though to hold tight a mental image of candles and windows.

"The little one Tommy? Remember? Maria. Things are so much better for that nowadays. You're too young to remember. Mongoloid, they were called. I sometimes wondered if..."

Her face turned rubbery with sadness.

"You wondered if what."

"No, I wouldn't want you to get the wrong idea."

"Come on. That's my job, getting the wrong idea."

"Ah, stop. It's not nice to think about."

The whiskey had left my throat half-wrecked. This tea was still a trial, but. Ma went into whispering mode.

"It's about little Maria. Bernie took it as a sign, so she did. She told me that. That God had entrusted Maria to them."

Ma searched my face like she was dealing with a Martian.

"A sign," I said.

But her eyes glistened, like she was hearing a tune she loved.

"She loves that little one to bits. They all do. And Jennifer's hub's a lovely fella, Bernie told me. Solid like, you know? Now I'd never say this to her, but God fits the back to the burden."

She eyed me to see if this got a respectful reception. Hardly. It was this noble suffering shite that soured me on the whole God caper in the first place.

"Tell us Ma. How do you think Jennifer got her big mansion?"

202

"Oh come on. Don't tell me you forgot. The boom, the whole Celtic Tiger thing? Sure, there was scads of money flying around. Making money hand over fist, the builders were."

She took another drag of the cigarette and looked off again through the twisting smoke. Was now the time to introduce my mother to the topic of money laundering? No, it could wait.

"Even if it is true what you're saying," she went on, "is that so bad? Tony dotes on that little one, she told me. Look, Tommy, I've said it a thousand times. God works in mysterious ways."

All right, I thought. So maybe Bernie Cummins had gotten her hub to shell out for a good home for their daughter. That'd let her believe that she had gotten one soul saved anyway.

"Bernie's going to wait. Like a vigil. As long as it takes, yes."

"Ma, I have to say this. It looks to me she's on the way out."

I might as well have poked her in the eye with a fork.

"What kind of a thing is that to say? Chemo's brutal. Brutal!"

I eyed the evidence bag again. The bag dulled the shine off the alloys, but the curves of the rims cut sharp against the plastic. There were always ballistic spec photos of shells and fragments around the Squad office. We used to get upwards of two dozen gunshot murders a year back then. I never got over the notion of how something so small could end a life. Which notion somehow brought me back to Tony Cummins. He'd let me know that he knew where I lived. What had he said about apartment living again? Too much glass for his liking? But what if it hadn't been meant as a threat. What if it had been a warning instead?

Ma was sagging in her chair. Back to staring at nothing and rubbing her thumbnail across her lip.

"So what do I do now, Tommy?"

"You listen to me for once in your life. You go stay with Mary."

She looked over but didn't see me. Her sister, my Auntie Mary, was out by Mulhuddart.

"I'd say come to my place, the apartment, but you never know."

A look of alarm came to her face. She took a pull of her Silk Cut.

"Should I be thinking that way too then?"

"Better you think that way than you don't. I'm staying here tonight."

She looked down at her cigarette as though she'd just realized that, yes, it was actually dangerous.

"We'll gather up a few duds and head over to Mary's first thing. Fair enough?"

Ma seemed to need time to come up with an answer. Finally, she nodded.

*　　*　　*

If I added up the time that I'd been awake and subtracted that from the times I'd gotten up to look out the windows ... Well, it'd be a stupid waste of time. Oddly, I wasn't wrecked. I might crash later on but for now, I'd apparently slept enough. More interesting by far? I didn't have the hangover that I richly deserved.

I finished my tea, proper tea that I'd made myself, and moseyed back upstairs to check the back of the house again. Nothing looked different. Ma's flowerbeds were where they should be. Ditto the patches she had cleared for her precious scallions. The flagstones I had put down for her 'patio set' were as flat as ever. No strange bottles with stranger liquids inside. No packages with wires. The day was even shaping up to be sunny. I checked my watch again.

Ma was packed. I took her case down and put it by the hall door. I'd go out on my own first though, and give the place a good look-round. A faint scent of lavender collided with the smell of rashers cooking. A curtain went back on a bedroom across the way. The Donohoes. Well so be it. Let it be one of those Donohoe wasters wondering if that actually was Tommy Malone holding a pistol Napoleon-style inside his jacket. Wait 'til I got rolling around on the road to look under my car.

I opened the back doors first, and then the passenger door. It took some tricky balancing and groping to reach the bonnet release. I did the best I could checking around the inside of the driver's door. No sign of tampering that I recognized. I tugged the gearshift out of first and let down the handbrake. I wanted another slow, careful 360 of the car before pushing it, though.

"You all right right there, chief?"

His eyes had locked onto the Sig. It was reflex, but he wouldn't know that. Some bloke I didn't know. The eyes came up slowly, a glaze over them. I took a deep breath and slid my hand back under the flap of my jacket again. I had trouble getting the words out: no thanks, I was grand. He blinked, and an expression of tender regret took over his face, and he walked away stiffly, like a robot.

There wasn't the space to push the car a full length ahead. I got it to within inches of the Renault ahead, put on the handbrake and got my phone light on. I took my time looking around and then I dropped down to begin my check of the underside. It wasn't going to be 100%, but it'd be enough to spot hasty work. All I came up with was star bursts across my vision and a bitch of an ache in my left shoulder from where I'd over-stretched it.

Ma had been eyeing proceedings from the front room. Her hands were shaking when she stepped out, and she dropped her keys. The suitcase was packed tight. She threw an imploring look to the house as we headed off.

"We should've phoned," she said. "Really, Mary will freak."

"She'll be grand. Aunt Mary likes surprises, remember?"

An old joke. Ma didn't give any sign that she clued in, though. Mary had won a hundred grand in the Lotto years ago. When they phoned to tell her, she lit into them, thinking they were messing.

Off we went, Ma doing that low hum version of Norwegian Wood she did when she was trying project calm. What she made of my ducking and gawking and twitchy turns of the wheel, or my mad looking around, I did not know. But there was no drama. We got to the M50 handy enough. I handed her my mobile. She had phone numbers written on a piece of paper. She phoned Phil first, at the shop. There was hemming and hawing, but it seemed to work. Mary next. The old Ma surfaced then, the living, breathing Oscar contender. Always the smile, even when things were going over the edge. I was so busy eavesdropping that the time flew by. Ma was still talking to Mary as we turned on to the avenue. And there she was, Mary, at the gate, phone in her hand and waving.

It wasn't Aunt Mary's fault that she looked like Prince Charles' wife, what's-her-name. Mary's version of Prince Charles was Frank Buckley – 'Frankly.' A tee-totaller, epic handyman to beat the band, but the man bored for Ireland, though. Mary made a decent fuss over Ma, playing along with the pretence that everything was grand. Sure, of course her sister, the one with the 'family troubles' always dropped by at this hour of the day, a work-day, looking as white as a sheet and needing to stay over. Sheila Malone wasn't the only one who could take the Oscar.

It took me a while to extricate myself. But Aunt Mary was no daw. She was after me like a bloodhound, that corkscrew eye of hers fixed on me. Er, what was going on? I pulled my 'highly confidential' one and gave her my one-eyed nod of trust and deep complicity. She wasn't happy, but it was enough to get me out the door. After a quick scope up and down the road, I slipped in behind the wheel and, like a getaway driver I was g.o.n.e.

I pulled over the first chance I got, on the Navan Road proper. I'd try Áine first. She'd have some idea of how this situation might play with Nolan, for when I did phone him – eventually.

"Yourself," she said. Like I was an annoyance. A Sligo thing?

"Have you got a minute? On your own there?"

She did not answer right away. Could it wait, she asked. Suspicions flew in and out of my head like cartoon bats. She'd phone me back in a minute. A minute? Me, full-on twitchy, out here on the side of the road? Whoever had sent those rounds could've done a lot worse if they'd wanted. So much for logic. It didn't stop me palming the grip on the Sig again and again.

The ring startled me: so damned *loud*? I didn't remember that being one of the side-effects. I asked if she was on her own there.

"Because," I explained, "this is between me and you. All right?"

She said OK. OK, like what-bloody-choice-do-I-have-here-OK. I went ahead anyway, relating the visitation to the Malone household last night. A few simple sentences was all it took. No comment from her, however.

"So what do you think?"

"Well, you can't keep this just between me and you."

"And?"

"And," she said, like she had gotten to the last page of the dictionary but hadn't found the word she wanted. "I don't know what else to say."

I watched two teenagers get off a bus and look around. Shouldn't they be in school? My heart began to make its move up chest toward my neck. I closed my hand around the grip again. One of them took out a packet of cigarettes. They trudged on. The relief was like a leak of air from my chest.

"Are you still there?"

"Yeah. I – sorry, what?"

"You think it had to do with the work we're on?"

"Well Jaysus, how would I *not* think that."

"So that means you have to report it."

I pretended to reflect on her advice.

"OK," I said. "I'll check back in. Give me an hour or so."

"Wait. How is she, your mother?"

How do you think, I wanted to say. You think my Ma had a hobby collecting bullets? Knitting ganseys with them?

"She's shook. She's gone away until this gets sorted."

"Right," Áine said, like she was answering a question nobody had asked. "You'll keep in touch, won't you?"

Well that was different. I told her that I would. I stared at the screen afterwards. Would that explain the weird vibe to our conversation? Her reminder to be in touch: that was her being a normal human being, showing concern. Or was it a giveaway that there was scheming afoot at her end?

I pulled out onto the road and moved smartly through the gearbox. As if I could outrun the confusion. Not to speak of that feeling I was fighting to keep from view, that of a slowly rising fear.

207

18

A strange thing: all the years I'd been coming to The Park, and up and down the North Circ and Infirmary Road? I'd never paid attention to the little streets and lanes here. I found a spot to park, a tight enough one, and another across from it, for Blinky to use.

He rolled up about ten minutes after. The same old Corolla? My God it was. He had new glasses though. Not a good move. They made him look like a fat Harry Potter had mated with a turnip. Maybe the crap style advice had come courtesy of his son, Blinky Carroll Junior, aka Conor. A sneaky act of revenge, like. As a favour to Blinky I had taken Conor on the rounds with me one day in the Squad. The upshot was me coming within inches of giving him a clip on the ear. More than once.

Trying to slip an item under the fence to the Lab was now considered bad juju – officially. But I'd made it my business to inherit Blinky from Murder Squad days. A bottle of Black Bush at the Christmas never did anyone any harm. Also, I had occasionally extended a listening ear over a pint or two in Ryans, where Blinky came every now and then to chew the fat with Minogue and sometimes talk Murder Squad cases –always from the forensic side.

"Very smoke and daggers here, Tommy."

"Couldn't think of a place, sorry."

'Couldn't think' – full stop. Spots' comments had wicked into my mind. Blinky's goldfish-eyed scrutiny was brief.

"Anything," I said to him. "Source, origins. Any print of course. Please and thank you."

Blinky turned the bag over and slid it into his jacket pocket.

"Crime scene? Might you have the, er, actual device itself also?"

"No, and no again. And I'll bet good money there's no prints."

Somewhere in those strained, red-rimmed eyes a sly glow came to life. What I liked about Blinky was the way he reacted to stuff that looked impossible, or downright outlandish.

"Maybe you're not busy enough at the Bureau," I said.

It had the desired effect. Blink lowered his head and looked over the rim of his expensive new crap glasses. With a little twitch around the mouth he shrugged and headed off. As did I.

I waited a few minutes before driving back out to Infirmary Road. I turned right and up to the North Road gate into the Park. It wasn't just to be contrary. The longer route was to give me time to clear my head. All it got me in the end was an extra five minutes of driving and a semi-soothing run along the tree-lined avenues before I had to turn in.

Using my new swipe card gave me a strange feeling. I almost expected it to be rejected on account I had screwed up. Not so, alas. Even odder? I actually got a few howiyas and nods en route to my perch next to Áine. Who was currently on a call. The gist of it seemed to be her trying to get records from a mobile company faster than what the phone company said it could, or would do. I eyed the files on her desk. There was a page from Tony Cummins, going back fifteen years. She told someone she appreciated something and, after a few more remarks, repeated it.

This office chair was suddenly very comfy. I slid and slouched, and let go of a yawn as politely as I could. Should I phone Ma, see how she was getting settled there. Or not? It was too early yet.

"Well," said Áine. "You're managing? What's the story?"

"Look, I want to rewind things. Forget I said anything."

She eased back in her chair, tilted her head like you'd see a cat do before it took a swipe at something. Finally, she spoke.

"That does not strike me as the right option here."

"I need time to figure things out first."

"But this incident, it has a bearing on our work here."

"It has a bearing on me first. So let me decide."

"We don't work that way."

I let the 'we' roll around a bit in my mind.

"And with all due respect," she added. "You mightn't be thinking straight right now."

She wasn't wrong. I hid my reaction in a long stretch. If I had a brain, I'd call the shrink right now and head over ASAP. Áine was still there when I opened my eyes again, still adamant.

"We've dealt with something like this before," she said.

"Threats to officers, you're saying?"

"Right. Someone put a pig's head on the bonnet of one of ours' car." She nodded twice in recollection. "He had a young family. He got his transfer out. He got the twenty-four-hour watch for a while too. It worked out. He's doing grand. Says he doesn't miss the stress, by the way."

I kept up my inspection of the finer details of the edge of the desk. If Áine Nugent's idea of 'worked out' was a transfer to Ballybejaysus, I'd way prefer to take my chances with the stress.

She had rested her chin on a T formed by her thumb and forefinger. Her stare was direct but, far as I could tell, she was not in a dander. Was it only now that I noticed dark patches under her eyes? She had turned back the cuffs of her shirt, or blouse. Powder Blue, they called that blue. Below her wrist were several freckles and fair hairs so fine you'd barely see them.

"So Éamonn has to know. And he has to know now."

*　　*　　*

Nolan's reaction put me on the back foot. He was subdued. Downright sympathetic even. No sharp comments, no digs, no orders disguised as discussion. Not a single sign that it was an act either. All of which set the doubts coursing in my mind again.

He nodded a lot, asked only a few questions. Unlike the priest in confession though, he never took his eyes off mine.

"Desperate," he said. "Disgusting. Is she managing, I hope?"

"She'll manage soon enough, with knobs on."

"Great. But listen, Tommy. There are protocols in place."

"Maybe them protocols work for the ones making the threats."

"I know what you're getting at. What's your thinking?"

"We don't play ball. We play it back on them instead."

Nolan's expression had settled into a version of sympathetic. It suddenly sharpened.

"We keep it under wraps," I explained. "So then, the first one mentions it, the spotlight goes on him. Canary move."

Nolan stretched his neck left and then right.

"I could live with that," he said. "For a while maybe. But the big question is your safety, you and your family. I'm presuming you'll want to go the protection route."

"I do and I don't. It's my Ma I'm worried about. She has a place to go for now. The problem is, they know where she lives, and that's not going to change."

"'They?' Are we supposing that the Gary Cummins business is at the root of this?"

"Well I bloody-well am. Christy Cullinane gets run down. Now my Ma gets bullets left by her door."

"What if it's something else?"

"Something else like what?"

"Well there are people who believe you threw a man off a roof."

Said so quickly, so easily, it threw me. But not for long.

"There are people who believe in fairies and unicorns -"

"My point is, I have to be blunt here, Tommy. We don't know if that's ongoing still, that issue. Do we?"

"We do. It's over. It got the full going-over from the Ombudsman. I was cleared. OK?"

Nolan frowned like he has tasted something that was a bit off.

"A sore point, that issue. I can see that much anyway."

I began a study of a photo on his shelf.

"Malaga," Nolan said. "Do you know the place at all?"

A deceptively calm look had come over his face. Was he now looking for an out-and-out row here?

"This started as me reporting a threat to my family."

"Right. And all I'm asking if it's something other than the Cummins business."

Nolan, so expressionless, had become a shop window model.

"Here's the plan," I said. "Email me your questions. Your observations, or insinuations. I'll answer them and post the results up on Facebook. Save people asking the same thicko questions."

"What answers would those be?"

The same grave, blank-but-attentive expression.

"For one, I am not a bent copper. Two, I don't collude with criminals, or protect criminals, not in any way, shape or form. I don't aid or abet criminals. I don't socialize with criminals."

"Would, say, Vincent Feeney be covered by that? 'Spots?'"

I was up out of the chair now.

"Sit down," Nolan said. "We're talking."

"No we're not. This isn't 'talking.' This is you throwing shite."

He was up quick. In one step he was between me and the door.

"Sit down, Tommy. We'll work through this."

I dimly recognized what that tilt of the chin and the slitty eyes might mean. But, martial arts or not, Nolan was no iijit. Any row here would be a brawl, and Christ knows it'd be an ugly one.

The sound of whistling eased his frown. He looked surprised to discover a biro between his fingers.

"The basics," he said. "Safety first – always. We need to decide how to proceed. It can't be 100% your say-so in the finish-up."

It sounded like an opening. I took it.

"How would it work, me going the protective route?"

"Security detail and twenty-four hour armed watch, to start. A safe house – I'm not saying it'd be in Dublin though. Armed detail when you'd travel."

"What about my Ma?"

"Same. We'll wise up the shop manager, make sure her job is kept for her."

He'd told me he knew I hung out with Spots by times. Now he wanted me to know that he knew where Ma worked.

"Of course we put a team on this right away, find who sent that envelope. We getting the word out in no uncertain fashion too."

I couldn't argue with that. Gangsters had no time for apaches either. Someone going after a copper stirred up a lot of trouble. That meant money lost, coppers nosing around. A gangster will 'anonymously' turn in a name just to get the heat down.

"So get advice," Nolan said. "But I need an answer soon."

Whatever was on my face told him he couldn't leave it at that.

"Look. It won't damage the case as badly as it might appear. OK?" He didn't wait for me to say yea or nay. "We've been walking on eggshells around Bernie. What Bernie wants, Bernie gets. She pretty-well has her own personal Garda detective on call."

If that was him trying to switch to funny, it was not working.

"But now," he went on, "we're in a different world, aren't we. Someone asks about Gary, he gets run over and killed. Now someone wants you off the job. Bernie Cummins needs to be made aware of this, as does her husband."

He widened his eyes then and blinked very slowly.

"So we lay it on the line for her," he said. "Tell her what happened here. How things are on the slide and where they end up, we don't know. What this does to the chances of finding Gary in one piece – that's the question she has to focus on. Unless..."

If I concentrated, or stared, hard enough Nolan could read my mind: putting the boots to a woman with cancer?

"Unless....? Unless she gets Tony to turn on the tap, and turn it on now. Not installments either, bits of this and bits of that when it suits him. We need the full accounting. Open the books, see? Like: what does Gary know about, that would put him in danger. What parts of the Cummins family business does Gary do, or did he do. Who'd have it in for him because of that. So let's hear it – that's if Bernie wants you to find her kid, before it's too late."

The 'Bernie' echoed in my mind. He pressed his finger into the desktop and gave me a theatrical version of a hardman look-over.

"Pony up the goods. Before things are out of hand, entirely."

His extension lit up. He didn't even glance at it. I stared at it until he picked it up. He said 'ten minutes' and hung up. I began my getting-up-and-getting-out-of-here moves.

"One last thing, Tommy? Don't over-think this. Sure, it's you they want, the Cumminses. But that cuts both ways. They don't want you to have to step out of the frame."

He effort to force his frown into a smile was stuck half-way.

"The truth is, they need you more than you need them."

I was at the door now: escape was at hand.

"So let me know."

Some bouts you win with your feet. You're just trying to get to the end of the round anyway. I headed back to Áine's corner.

"Sorted?"

"I don't know." It was only the truth. "I've got thinking to do."

She waited for more info that would never come.

"Tell me something," I said to her. "Is he always like that?"

Her eyes stayed accusingly on mine. I noted a faint flaring about her nose.

"You'll phone Bernie Cummins," she said. "Right?"

"I will get to that – in a bit."

"In a bit?" The words flew out of her, like she was relieved to get back to business. "You do know that we have a team to brief?"

"A team put together? Already? How many?"

"Eight. Eight detectives who were busy enough to begin with. So are you ready?"

*   *   *

Paying attention in the briefing was hard going. For starters, the cup of tea I brought turned out to be poxy. More to the point, I'd slid into a swamp full of notions. I was arguing with myself.

1. *Stay*: loyalty – that's what mattered, nowadays more than ever. Oh sure. To a bollocks who'd sell his own mother at auction?

2. *Run*: the smart option. Family first. Nobody'd gainsay that. Wasn't that plain old chickening out?

3. *Fight*: instinct had a lot going for it. Yes, put the heavy word on Tony, via Bernie. But Christ, didn't she have cancer?

The meeting was slowed by people checking mobile numbers on the board. Kennedy announced that he had made some strides, at least. Given that Gary probably went through a fair share of burner phones, Kennedy was working from numbers Bernie Cummins had given me, tracking IMEIs from any mobiles that Gary was known to have been used in the past five years. There were two marginally worth following, both Vodafone, both from five years ago. Another from O2, of similar vintage.

Yet the obvious question wasn't being asked and if my head had been at ground level, I'd have come out with it: wasn't it beyond strange that not a single mobile phone had been fixed to Gary yet? If there was one thing an addict relied on, it was his mobile phone. I thought of Terry. Terry Million Phones, I used to call him sometimes. Years after he was gone, I was still finding them.

"They'll run numbers tomorrow, they said. They hope."

He tossed a look over in the general direction of Smithie and Finnoula Balfe. A few similar looks earlier had told me that neither of them was massively thrilled to be here. No doubt they had some epically important case or operation elsewhere. And she and Smithie had indeed drawn a tough one. They were heading out on the prowl at clinics, starting with where Gary Cummins was known to have visited in the recent past. Part of that meant trawling the various and sundry laneways, alleyways and premises around the clinics. A more depressing task you couldn't imagine.

We were all looking over the board again, like dogs watching traffic. As if gawking at arrows and words and phone numbers on fuzzy greyscale print-outs would magically produce 'the answer.'

"I have to say, he looks strangely short of mates, Gary does."

It was McGinn. A quick check of the task lists reminded me that he'd been paired up with Kennedy. They were doing a canvas of pubs for anyone willing to admit to knowing Gary Cummins, or –too much to hope for? – having actually been in contact with him in the recent past.

"Can that Hynes fella be described as a mate of Gary's?"

"He might've been," I said. "He claims to be severely allergic to him now. According to him, Gary is after pissing off everybody."

Smithie held his hands open in a beseeching pose.

"He gave me a pretend Nordy accent at one point too," I added. "Hynes did. He wouldn't elaborate."

"IRA?" Was Smithie only pretending to look surprised? "Gary running with them loolahs?"

"Who knows. Maybe it's pure pig iron, to screw us around."

McGinn nodded like I had just confirmed for him that it'd be raining all week. A bout of consulting notebooks, eyeing mobiles and glancing at the board ensued.

"This fella who got run over." It was McGinn again. "He must have a hit a nerve, then? Asking around after Gary Cummins?"

The question was to me. I felt suddenly angry, but sick too.

"He may well have been, all right."

"You reckon he'd have known where to go looking for Gary?"

"I don't know. But I doubt it."

The follow-up question that nobody asked was the same one that lay in my gut like a cement block: why the hell did I ask Christy Cullinane to keep an eye out for Gary Cummins in the first place?

"Point of info," Áine said. "They called it about a quarter of an hour ago. It's off hit-and-run now and gone to murder. Sundrive Road station is carrying it. They have the Bureau in. All I have at the moment is that they're focusing on a mobile. There are signs that somebody took the victim's stuff from the scene."

Smithie took a break from his highly annoying rat-a-tat with a biro on his knuckles to ask if Christy's mobile was showing on the grid. Áine shook her head.

"This Mary Enright one," said Kennedy, stirring again. "What're the prospects there?"

Why were all the questions coming to me?

"Hard to say yet. She's his ex a while now, is what she told us."

"And there's a history to her?"

"Maybe. Modelling, talent shows. Escort services. Likely she was working the hotels, on order."

There were no follow-ups. Áine pointed at the board.

"Corcoran drove her away after our get-together. So I'm assuming for now that he drove her to the place too. And he was in the pub already when we got there, sitting with what looked like a few locals. Tommy had an eye for him though."

"Do we have a fix on him," Kennedy tried. "This Corcoran?"

Áine glanced at me first, and then took over.

"He's a legal eagle, a solicitor."

"Smell a rat right there," Kennedy said.

"I don't know yet if he actually keeps a practice," Áine went on. "He's Dublin, Clontarf. Married, now separated. No kids. Google says he did legal stuff for film and television back in the day. Also a money man, if that's the word for getting production money, or deals. His website says talent agency and events management. It hasn't been updated in about a year, though. As for contact with us, all I can find on the system is a caution given him years ago, something about an issue in a hotel, with drink."

"Events," said Kennedy, with a far-too-obvious irony. "Is that a fancy name for something else? Like escorts? Brassers?"

"No signs so far." Áine was playing it straight. "It is, or could be, a going concern, though. He did what look like large corporate gigs and stuff like that, in recent years. If there's much life in an events management business these days, I don't know."

Her business-like replies only seemed to goad Kennedy.

"Events," he said, like a robot recently switched on. "Sure. Like anyone could manage events in this country these days."

He got not so much as a single smile for it.

"The mother." It was Smithie again. "Mrs. Cummins. I mean, come on. She's got to have some way of contacting her own son. At least an idea of where he'd be?"

"I think she's playing straight." It was all I could think to say. "She knows Gary's off the rails."

Smithie renewed his scowl at the boards. He and McGinn seemed to be tag-partners in the glares and questions department.

"This sister," he said. "Jennifer. Shouldn't she feature more?"

"We'll get to her at some point. She's in Spain right now."

"The Cumminses have a place there? Like, with a nice big washing machine?"

I gave Smithie my you're-not-a-comedian look.

"If they do have a place, it's not in a Cummins name. But the Cumminses aren't budging: leave Jennifer out of this, is the deal. According to them, she never was in of the picture as regards family carry-on – and it's this way on purpose."

"And we're buying that shite?" Scorn sent McGinn's voice higher. "Her brothers are lunatics, her ould lad is or was one of the biggest gangsters in Ireland.... but Jennifer's an angel?"

"At this point, we're just trying to keep people happy. But, so far as we can see, she's pretty well spotless. She's married and living out the country."

"What about her husband," said McGinn, like an accusation. He nodded at the copy of the passport photo we had gotten for Liam Murphy. "Another angel into the bargain?"

I wanted this over. There was stuff to be done – whether I wanted to do it or not. I didn't much give a fiddler's fart whether this crew was happy in their work or not.

"What can I tell you," I said. "He's NCR. He's a builder, is all we know right now. Maybe that'll change, maybe it won't."

On that dodgy note, the briefing ended. Smithie got up slowly, sliding a measured look he had on Áine over to me. No translation required. I could've said it for him. a) we're not gobshites b) this is a dog's breakfast and c) there is something fierce bent and bogey about all this.

Who was I to argue. Certainly not with the man who'd just scored 3/3.

19

I headed for the hallway that led in into the general office. I hadn't imagined it: there was indeed a window there.

Minogue answered after three. I kept it general. Did he have a few minutes to chat? Call him back in ten? It had to be on his mobile, though. I knew he'd get it. Next was Ma. She answered even before the first ring was complete. For someone who'd had live ammunition planted on the doorstep of her house, she sounded quite chipper. I heard someone else in the background, and a tea cup or a plate. I asked Ma if things were working out.

"Oh it couldn't be better, Tommy. Couldn't be better!"

Which meant she had an audience.

"Listen, Ma. I don't want anyone there listening in."

I heard her hand rubbing over the mouthpiece. Next came muffled talk and a door closing. She announced she was out in the back porch.

"You haven't let on the real reason you showed up. Have you?"

"No, no, no. No worries there."

"Good. Look, I told my so-called boss here what happened. There's directives and stuff, for situations like this. So we need to think things through. Figure out what needs to get done."

"Done for who? Me, is it?"

"Yes, you, for starters. Let me hear what you think first."

This set Ma back on her heels a bit.

"Well don't do anything for my sake," she said.

"You're involved, Ma, like it or not. Can't have you going back home, waiting and worrying about this whole thing."

That was when she threw me for a loop.

"What? Worry? Now you listen to me. And listen good."

That tone was a clock-stopper, a voice from many years ago. The one that'd stop me and Terry dead in our tracks. The sound of Ma at the end of her tether.

"Are you listening to me? Are you? How old are you now?"

"Old enough – older by the second. Why are you rearing up?"

"Listen to me now. Don't think about me, or what you think I'm thinking. And don't beat about the bush either when I ask you this. What would you do if you had a free hand? Go on, tell me."

I waited for a bloke to go by. There was a bit of a swagger to him. A cool nod. I hadn't seen him before. He tugged his belt up as he passed, hiking his jacket enough to offer a glimpse of a holster. Was there a message in that? Maybe there was. Several maybe. That I was losing it? That the pills were driving me mad?

"Go on, I said. Tell me what you'd do."

"Ma. I don't live in what-if land. You don't either."

"Oh give over. Do I have to spell it out for you? What about that poor girl shot dead there last year, that girl out in Tallaght? Sixteen years of age, not even starting her life? What about her?"

I had no answer. There was no answer.

"I'm telling you I've had it, Tommy. Had it – up to here!"

"We all have. But now's not the time to go on the warpath."

"Well when in God's name is the right time? Will you tell me that? Or are ye just going to let the gangsters run the country?"

There was no let-up. Any chance I might've had to interrupt her went by the wayside with Áine Nugent's appearance in the doorway. She wasn't just passing through either. She settled against the wall and proceeded to study the floor. Ma was in full spate now: ...poor girl shot stone dead ... law of the jungle...allowing this to happen ...for the love of God...

"- Later Ma, OK? –"

"Don't 'Later Ma' me! Enough is enough! I reared my boys. I done my bit. Now some bast – some *hoodlum* – is trying to run me out of me own home?

222

Me, who grew up here? Raised my boys here? Well let me tell you something. It's the mothers keep the show on the road. And this here mother has had it."

There was a tense vibe to Áine. I waited for a hint but she maintained her gaze on the floor. Just as Ma was winding up again, I hit End.

"My Ma," I said. "Fierce het-up, she is. She gets going and…"

Áine abandoned her mission of holding up the wall.

"We just got word from Portlaoise," she said.

But she was addressing someone with his brain on spin cycle. It took a moment to connect 'Portlaoise' with anything.

"Portlaoise. You mean Tony Cummins?"

"Someone went after him, attacked him. About an hour ago."

"How bad?"

"An inmate, armed with something like a knife. But it looks like he'll make it. Éamonn's trying to find out more." She nodded in the vague direction of Nolan's office. "He wants a word."

Nolan was pacing the room in a cat-like fashion. Eye contact was very much off the menu. He paused to flex his free arm before easing his death-grip on the mobile jammed against his head.

"Sure," he said, like it was a declaration of war. His arm made a wide, slow arc around his head before he extended a baby finger to stroke his scalp. "Okay," he said and closed the call. He studied his mobile as though it had just got pulled from a pharaoh's tomb.

"He's going to be okay. Just missed an artery."

This was when Minogue's call came in. I told him I'd call him back. Nolan had put away his mobile. He had turned thoughtful.

"Well we warned him," he said. "That we did."

The word registered with me, but they made no sense. Then, suddenly, they did.

"'We,'" I said. "'We' warned him? When?"

Nolan's response was a vague wave of his hand.

"You're in contact with Tony Cummins already. Outside of what me and her are doing."

He sat back up, and grabbed a paperclip from next to his mobile.

"Correct," he said. "We are in contact with Tony Cummins."

My follow-up question took the form of a scathing assessment of Nolan's face.

"All right," he said, and started to unbend the paper clip. "There are things in play here. New to you, I know – but."

"Maybe not as new as you imagine."

Up went an eyebrow.

"Don't be letting on that this is news to you," I went on. "You and your crew have the rep. Stitch-ups, entrapment. Using prison inmates? General skullduggery and cowboy moves?"

Nolan's expression relapsed into that strange composure that had me extra suspicious, earlier. He sat back and smiled.

"As bad as schoolgirls aren't we, us Guards? For the old gossip? But that's the way, isn't it, when you're winning, and getting results. Out march the begrudgers. Legions of them."

The smile dissolved back into that bland expression.

"Yep, we've been trying to open up Tony Cummins for a while. So now that we have an opening, we're going to go for it. Not pretty maybe, but it's basic police work, all the same."

"Police work? What about that thick you dragged in here to do the dirty work of browbeating Bernie Cummins? Malone, is that his name? When were you planning to let him in on this?"

"Totally misconstrued, Tommy. There's a need to keep things in separate boxes. OPSEC?"

"I know what operational security is. But you're putting the boots to someone. Someone who's not a criminal and who, by the way, is ill, and worried sick about her son – if he's alive at all."

I looked at Áine. Keeping that robot-face on must've been hard work. When I looked back, Nolan had a dead-eyed, under-the-eyebrow glare waiting. Yet his tone was almost light-hearted.

"OK then. Fair dues to you. But we are where we are. But you know and well I do that we have to look at the big picture. Right?"

A phrase I had added to my Dictionary of Bullshit years ago.

"No?" he asked. "Come on. We don't need to dress up the facts here. Gang crime, international gang crime? Syndicates? Yes, highly organized, cross continent, ruthless, well-resourced syndicates. You know all this. And you know that things are close to out of control. Blender's on full and there ain't no lid. OK, so this Gary Cummins situation. It came sideways at us, and it came with you attached. Bernie Cummins wants you. Tony Cummins too. So we go with that. But it's not the full story."

He eyed the paper clip and let it fall on his desk. Then he picked it up again. His eyes popped wide as he pretended to scrutinize it.

"What we want from Tony Cummins is not your run-of-the-mill stoolie effort. Sure we'd like to get a list of who did what when, and all the rest of it. Wouldn't turn that down – oh God no."

Wrenching his stare from the paper-clip he glanced over.

"By the way. You know Tony does his book-keeping in his head? The man has a phenomenal memory. Every deal and scam going back to Methusalah, chapter and verse."

I thought: *And how exactly would you know that*?

"But you see the catch, I'm sure. Any info he'd give would be after the event. Yes, history. So – a mug's game."

He paused, and smiled like he regretted something. Whatever he hoped to see on his tortured paper clip wasn't materializing.

"But the thing we really want, I haven't told you. So now I will. Because? Well, because this is about you too."

He beamed a look of serene and superior wisdom at me.

"The thing is, Tommy, you have history. Issues. Real or not, it's not for me to say. Like, is it a crime to grow up next door to lads who go on to be gangbangers? As for one's personal life, the tragedies and so forth. Don't even go there. Right?"

Terry. Who else could he mean. I put more ice into my stare.

"But that's coppers for you, isn't it. Jesus but we're a hard crew. No coincidences for us, no sir. Everything's suspicious. So that's what brings us back to our OPSEC issue, that need-to-know that's got you so het-up. Because what I'm about to tell you, you'll see why we tread so carefully here, to the point of outright paranoia."

He hoisted his gaze from the paper clip again.

"Long story short, Tony Cummins got to stay Tony Cummins, and to do Tony Cummins things for so many years, because .... Because he got help. Yep. Tony Cummins got insider help."

A great opportunity to say absolutely nothing.

"Tony Cummins had, and probably still has, a shield. You understand what I'm saying?"

'Shield.' He could've used a normal word. Informant. 'Dirty cop.' 'Cop on the take.' But no. I'd always associate 'shield' with that day in the Ombudsman's office. *There are long-standing rumours that Detective Garda Malone has acted as an agent, a shield if you will, for a leader of a criminal gang based in Dublin West …*

If I wasn't going to talk, Nolan was willing to do it for me.

"And I don't mean Garda Jimmy-Joe Pat out there manning the speed trap in the back end of Tipperary," he said. "Whoever Tony Cummins' shield is, he or she is well up. Years in the Force."

People don't always ask the obvious question, I've discovered.

"So who is it?"

He flipped up his eyelids for a big-eyed, isn't-that-a-howl look.

"Great question, Tommy – great question. Here's my answer: damned if I know." He leaned in over his desk. "But by the living Jesus I am going to find out. *We* are going to find him – or her. Will it be easy? Uh uh. Tony got to walk the streets all these years, and to sleep in his own bed, to go to his daughter's wedding even because …? Because he paid to do so. Paid big too, I bet. But now, this thing today in Portlaoise? As clear a wake-up call as Tony will ever get. There's no place to hide now."

He waited. To let this sink in, I supposed. He didn't wait long.

"Of course we want to help Mrs. Cummins get that son of hers back, and in one piece if that's possible. And of course we'll tread softly on her sensibilities. We're not out to get her. Tony Cummins is still the lock. Bernie Cummins is still the key. But this'll serve to wake her up too, this go at Tony today. You see?"

"I get what you said. The 'see' bit, probably not."

"What I said earlier? This being crunch-time?"

The smile said: *we're grand, sure.* But the eyes? *Fight.*

"So Bernie had better be seeing the light now herself as well."

Words – names – are strange things, I thought.

"We need to be sure she got the message, Tommy. Time to call her. To tell her it's showtime. And now."

His stare eased. Paper-clip time was over.

"Tell her we'll drive her down to Portlaoise at a moment's notice. Unmarked, totally discreet, the presidential treatment. But remind her too in no uncertain terms that someone's got Tony in their sights. Now's the time, tell her. Tony's got to come clean."

I eyed Áine. She pretended not to notice.

"The other matter," I heard Nolan say then. "This business at your mother's house? Somebody's telling you that they know you met with Bernie Cummins. There's procedures, but you got a bit of time to think how best to work it. So what do you think?"

"Things'll be clearer after I've gotten my Ma somewhere safe. Which is happening as we speak."

"You're arranging protective for her yourself? Really?"

"Better I do it. Not to freak her out more than she already is."

"Fair enough." He let a few moments slip by. "So here's an idea. You can make calls to Bernie from anywhere. You don't even have to be working this op. It can look like you've been – what's the word? Intimidated? Bernie hearing that can work in our favour. You get my drift?"

"You want to use this to up the pressure on Mrs. Cummins."

If I didn't recognize the look that Nolan glommed onto me then, Áine's tense stillness gave me a hint: Nolan was daring me to disagree.

I got my feet under me and grabbed the arms of the chair

"None of this leaves this room. Hardly need to remind you?"

"I get it."

"Good. But you must have a question, or two. Do you?"

"Maybe. Tell me, who else in this office knows about this?"

"Fair question. OK – nobody. Now they'd know that Tony Cummins used to be big on our trophy list, and that we nailed him and got him imprisoned. But they wouldn't know we're resurrecting him and that we have an eye on him, ongoing. Or that we're hell-bent on rooting out his insider here from amongst us."

Nolan seemed pleased now, but as cagey as ever. I stood up.

"Tommy? There's a lot at stake. The real deal, the one that's going to count. And by God it'll look good on us –all of us."

To anyone who wasn't me, Nolan's parting words would've sounded all right. Morale boosting is something a good C.O. does. But there was another message wrapped inside. To this gurrier cop, the one with the dubious honour of being born and reared in Crumlin, Nolan was dangling the promise of rehabilitation.

Áine took her time finding her way back to her desk. I sensed she had something to say, but that it'd stay MIA. Well so what. I wasn't a candidate for talk myself. It felt like I had a foot-thick layer of wet cotton wool wrapped around my brain.

The notion of downing a belt of Jemmy hit me like a rogue wave.

Kennedy called out something about CCTV. It was from down by that clinic that Mary Enright had been rabbiting on about, where those nasties had been on the prowl for Gary. Allegedly.

"Anyone fancy going to the pictures with me? *For* me, I mean?"

A comedian in the making, this Kennedy. It'd be more like six hours poking through footage. I flopped down in the spare chair. Áine swivelled a bit but she did not look over.

"By God it'll look good on us."

She wasn't having any of it.

"You'll make that call to Bernie Cummins?"

The way she said it, it sounded like 'Eight to ten, no parole,'

"Soon. I have to sort out what needs doing as regards my Ma."

She looked like she was trying to name a tune she'd heard.

"I see," she said then, almost cheerfully. "OK. Well, I'm going to push on with setting up round two for Mary Enright. Bring her in, and we can get the unscripted version."

"I'd be more interested in that Corcoran item. As in, why's he driving Mary Enright around. Eh, I ran across a picture of him online. Hob-nobbing with...? It was none other than the late, great Irish radio superstar Tom O'Dea."

Her eyes narrowed. I hoped my gentle stare was telling her that I hadn't filed that factoid on the system yet. Actually, I didn't care.

"Tom O'Dea," she said. "Sure, half the country probably, got their picture taken with him."

"I wouldn't doubt it. There's another photo too, though. It's with our friend out the Long Mile Road. Hynes, the motorbike fella? And there's O'Dea sitting on a motorbike. This one's three or four years back. But the type of bike is interesting. A Harley."

She pretended to consider this matter.

"And if you look closely, as I did and nearly blinded myself in the process, you will also see Corcoran in that same photo. It looks like a showroom. Maybe a product launch, if that's the proper term. Hynes sells, or he sold Harleys."

"Is Corcoran the motorbike type?"

"Who knows. Did he know O'Dea? 'Mr. Promoter' et cetera?"

"Back to Hynes. Is he what you call a biker? Biker-gangster..?"

"That I do not know either. But to all appearances, he has been clean for years."

"I know there are Irish bikers," she said. "We did a bust on one in Athlone two years back. The Ds ... D something."

"Double Ds?"

"You ran into them too?"

"We sure did. There's different sets, but. Freewheelers, Alliance, Vikings. Vikings – I ask you. But the ones that we found doing the damage up here were the Double Ds."

"Double D stands for....? I forget."

"Devil's Disciples. Also: Deal Drugs. Deliver Death, we said"

"You know," she said, eyebrows dipping into a frown, "I didn't see any of this entered on the case file."

"Right, I'll get to it soon enough. When the dust settles a bit. But I have a question for you. It's about Bernie Cummins."

Her gaze hardened.

"What does she know?"

"Know....?"

"What Nolan was talking about in there. Cummins' quote, unquote shield. His insider. You reckon she knows who it is?"

Her nostrils twitched. For a moment I believed she'd let loose.

"All I know is we're tasked with finding her son. But if you asked me a similar question, about holding back..."

"Like?" She seemed to be rethinking the notion.

"Like, is Gary's stuff parked over at her house all along, but she doesn't feel like telling us? Maybe he's even based at home? Sometimes, at least?"

"And she knows that if we were to set foot inside her house...?"

"We'll going to find something to incriminate Gary, or her husband – or even her."

"Incriminate," I said. "Have you met Bernie Cummins?"

Áine's reply was a tightening of the lips.

"You think she's an angel or something," she said. "Do you?"

"That's hardly even a question. Come on now."

"You believe that she's got no clue where her son could possibly be. No clue in the wide world? Her only son?"

"Look. You know what addicts do to their families?"

"Look, yourself. This is Dublin we're in. You can't just 'hide.'"

"Well I'll tell you anyway. Heroin, it takes everything – everything – and smashes it. Things you never thought could be broken – family, marriage, plans, home, love – it leaves them in flitters. Shreds, smithereens, tiny bits. A mother's love, even."

Áine started fidgeting with papers on her desk.

"All you get's lies," I continued, "And after a while it all sounds like lies anyway. They assault you, they rob you. They bring scumbags home, people who'll steal from you and assault you. They turn into strangers, dangerous, secretive, paranoid, violent strangers. And yes, they do hide. They're bloody good at it too."

Up came her gaze, like an artillery piece being wound up. There was a severe impatience in it. A notion crashed into my mind.

"Hold on a sec," I said. "You're on the same page as Nolan?"

"I don't know what you're on about. Do you?"

"Putting the boots to Bernie Cummins isn't just a dirty move. It won't wash."

She needlessly turned over a page on her desk. My mobile interrupted proceedings: Minogue. Áine was already pretending to read the next page of something. I wandered over to a quiet corner.

"Boss," I began. "I have a situation. Can I sound you out?"

"Fire away – but in English I'll be able to understand."

I managed a short summary and waited for Minogue to conjugate matters in his head.

"What advice are you getting there?" he asked, eventually.

"The protective services move."

"And what would you want to do here. Or wish you could do?"

"Want? Wish? Wake up on a beach in, say, Bali – the real Bali, not Bally Manure or someplace. With a certain person."

"So what's holding you back. Go."

"Do a runner and feck off? To Bali? That's your expert advice?"

"Your family's under threat. You're astray in the head."

231

Another so-called pal telling me I wasn't right in the head? Just because Minogue spoke in his customary bogger way didn't meant he was wrong.

"This Bali talk of yours," he added, "that's as I roved out."

"What does that mean in normal English?"

"It means I have a good notion of what you really want to do."

"Is this your speech about me being an excitement addict?"

"Well one more time won't singe your ears so. You're itching to take on all the gangsters in Dublin. To go to war entirely."

"Yeah, well whatever. The leopard can't change his stripes."

"Speaking of stripes, is pursuing some mad notion like that what got you your Sergeant's? What I'm saying is, bow out. Follow the protocols and bow out."

With Spots' dramatic 'Drop it,' that made the score two nil.

"How's your Ma anyway, with all this *rí-rá?*"

"She's fierce het-up, so she is. Ready to go Rambo, in actual fact.."

I heard him chuckle. In all our time together, I didn't remember hearing him laugh outright.

"You should coax her out of Dublin for a while."

"Good luck with that caper. She thinks if you go beyond Lucan, you'll never be let back."

"Really now. It so happens that your timing is good. Herself and myself are off down to Clare this afternoon, to the farm. I'm taking a few days. Remember that brother of mine there?"

"He got the farm, you got the bus. That one?"

"*Sin é*. He's out of the hospital. And apparently I'm supposed to 'talk to him.' Your Ma'll come with us."

"My ma? For a minute I thought you were serious."

Minogue's way of answering this was to ignore it.

"Kathleen'll be glad of reinforcements, so she will. Two Dubs against all of West Clare? Let me know when you're on your way."

I kept my mobile parked against my head after the call was over, and let the rest of the day unveil itself in my mind. It'd actually work, this go-to-Clare thing. Having Kathleen, a sidekick from Dublin, Ma'd definitely go for it. That meant me going out to Aunt Mary's at some point, getting hold of the Ma, and then stopping by the house on our way Southside to Minogue's gaff, so she could kit out a weekend suitcase. I'd go to the apartment later on and take an overnight kit to have ready in the car. And yes, I'd get that damned call to Bernie Cummins over with.

Quinn, striding by a gap between cabinets, theatrically skidded to a halt and performed a clown walk back.

"Look a bit lost there Tommy boy. Need pointers?"

My courtroom stare only earned me a half-smile.

"Wish you were back chasing smack heads. Right?"

The words froze me. Quinn had chosen that particular term for a reason. 'Smack head' was precisely what had gotten me into a massive row years ago with an off-duty Coyle. There was drink involved of course, but I lost the rag when I overheard him refer to Terry as 'a smack head.' Coyle considered himself the dog's bollocks in the hand-to-hand department. Right enough, he hit me two good ones in the side of the head. It must have been the gargle let me absorb them. I set him up with my right, and when he bought it, I put him away with a straight, hard left.

"You landed in quite the spot of bother too, I heard."

Quinn was still there. Waiting for a friendship to blossom?

"Did you now. Ears like that, you must be an elephant."

He looked up and down, faked a smile, and made off.

Well, at least I could give up wondering if Nolan or one of his crew had been rooting around in Thomas Malone's career record and personal issues. I could just take it as a given.

Now – it was Bernie Cummins time. I'd been avoiding it long enough. I gave it four rings before I dumped the call. When she hadn't called back, I dialled again and this time I let it go to voice mail. But I couldn't think what to say. What the hell what was there to say anyway? Not to worry, Mrs. Cummins, I'm leaving the case in good hands? Or: Look, there's a whole bunch of collateral damage happening here – I'm out.

Damage: the word set my mind on a hopscotch course. Right away, up bobbed Christy Cullinane. That go-by-the-wall walk of his. Those stupid puppy-eyes. I could hear the van's tires on the wet asphalt and then that thump – I pushed free of that only for Spots to come barreling in. Spitting with fury, yelling in my face about how I'd used Christy. How I'd thrown him to the wolves.

Or not? Minogue had just reminded me: I couldn't think straight. So what I was missing here? Were there warning signs I'd ignored? I remembered Macker's *Watch Your Back* comment. Was than just his usual poxy pseudo-wit? And now Minogue. He had a nose for stuff. 'Bow out'? It meant he had smelled a rat. And to top it all off, there was Spots and his *drop it*. It wasn't just a by-the-way remark. He had made calls. He'd never tell me the ins-and-outs of why he said it. That was the deal between us.

My mind lurched back to Nolan. He made a show of tolerating me because he had to. He'd still keep me in the dark as much as he could. Fair enough, nailing some dirty cop behind Tony Cummins really would be a massive thing. But what exactly was the point of Nolan putting the gobshite hat on me and pretending it was OpSec?

And yet. I couldn't fault him for going after this like a terrier. Ruthless? I could live with 'ruthless.' We were up against out-and-out psychopaths. But was it something beyond ruthless though? He had no qualms about using me to put the squeeze on Bernie Cummins. No qualms about risks to Tony Cummins either. His crew would follow his lead too, no doubt.

And what a crew. That yoyo, Quinn. He was more than just a cheeky muppet. He was going out of his way to be a bollocks. Because...? Because he had Nolan's go-ahead to do so. To go within a hair of provoking a row with me. But for what? To put me in my place, a reminder that I wasn't one of the chosen here? That I was a suspect? Maybe all of the above.

Áine Nugent appeared out of the fog then. That semi-detached, hard-to-read manner? I really had no clue. So what if it was her and Nolan involved in that how's-your-father session last night, in his office. Maybe she was the one wanted that stuff. And she hadn't gotten to where she was by being a push-over, had she. She really put herself into the job too. So of course she'd want her team, her C.O., to land Tony Cummins and his insider. But now with this Malone guy entangled, came unknowns. No wonder she came across as quietly and continuously pissed-off.

I wasn't just spinning me wheels, I was sliding backwards. The simple fact was, I was hanging in the wind. Nobody had my back.

I took out my mobile again. Just as I brought up Ma's number, something went pop in my mind. I almost heard it. It made me step back – literally. My mind-fog suddenly cleared. I had missed the most important thing of all. It was simple: Nolan had something. He knew something. Whatever that something was, I was the very last person he wanted to know about it. I was probably the third last person – after Bernie Cummins and Tony Cummins.

Nolan knew where Gary was.

I let notions roll out in my mind: Gary was in a drawer below in Store Street. He was dead and buried already, ideally never to be found. But Gary was no use dead, so Nolan was using of the ghost of Gary Cummins to get what he wanted. More notions dripped in. Nolan wasn't going down this road alone – he had the quiet blessing of Garda brass. Right from the top. The public were screaming for push-back, weren't they? It wasn't just angels you'd want on your side when the fight was dirty.

Things began to click together more. I could see more now. How things had been humming along grand for Nolan until Bernie Cummins made that call to my Ma and thrown things for a loop. The call had come with Tony Cummins on a leash. Also, unfortunately, yours truly, Malone. Which of course meant Nolan'd hold his nose and make nice. He'd keep close tabs on me, but not so close that I'd suss out the fact that he was holding back something about Gary so's he could screw the Cumminses over.

Another notion slid in: Áine Nugent, she knew all this. She knew, and she couldn't tell. Couldn't, or wouldn't... tell Tommy Malone that he was getting the run-around? Was that too much to ask? Apparently it was.

I tried cursing then but I had no heart for it. Nolan was a conniving loolah. Schemes inside of schemes inside of more schemes. My role, apparently, was to be Captain Clueless, straight out of the Dept. of Colossal Gobshites. To wander around like a battery-operated toy and do what the remote control told me to do. . No wonder Quinn was smirking away any time he'd see me.

Fair enough, I thought then. So I had a schemer, a bollocks and a traitor giving me the run-around. I'd come up with a plan of my own, wouldn't I. It might be a mad plan, a downright dangerous plan even. I didn't doubt that they'd be the self same words I'd get thrown back in my face. Along with whatever else Spots would throw, when I told him.

20

"I think you made the right decision, standing down."

Nolan had put on his most sincere look. It didn't matter.

"Not an easy decision, I'd say. But the right one nonetheless."

I'd headed into his office with no idea which way the cat would jump. I was loaded for trouble all the same, with my lines ready. Number one: the safety and security of my family. Two: even if I wanted to stay on the job, focus and performance were out the window now. I was a liability. A drag on the operation.

I had other items in reserve too. We'd broken the ice with Tony Cummins. There was no going back for him – even with me sidelined. His best move, his only move, was to break loose right now and name names. I'd even use the nuclear option if Nolan came the heavy. The whole protective services protocol was there for a reason. So, if Nolan was going to try for a bit of wiggle-room on that 'officer's discretion' bit, I'd be good and ready. 'Discretion' did not equal veto, and if he thought it did, I'd get AGSI on the blower for him to sort that one out.

"I'm not saying I like it. Of course I don't. But I know where you're coming from."

He made a series of long, slow sympathetic-looking nods.

"Better safe than sorry," I said.

"Damned right, Tommy. I hear you, man. Family first."

I'd wondered how he'd react when I told him that I intended to organize my own lay-low. Didn't bat an eye. I'd already gotten my Ma sorted, I told him. At this, he made to say something but he held back and went to a few questions instead. I gave him the answers he seemed to want. Of course I'd keep in touch. Of course I'd keep up the communications with Bernie Cummins. Of course, I'd relay everything back to Áine. In the business of spoofing, I had always been able to hold my own.

"Well let's not drag things out," he said. The vice-grip handshake and the searching, hawk-eye look held a clear-enough message. Any suspicions he had, he wouldn't be sharing with me.

I almost dodged out of going to see Áine. That made no sense, I realized. She was by no means running the show here at all. The boogey man here was Nolan.

It was like talking through glass. She was just as brief, just as neutral-sounding as Nolan.

"That's too bad," she said. "You've thought it out, I'm sure."

"Not an easy decision."

Maybe it was the way I said it, but it earned me a more peculiar look than I'd expected.

"I'll let the team know," she said. "It'll get their dander up."

"Nolan told me he expects us to be in touch – a lot."

She nodded.

"It might be emails to start with, until I can get some clean gear up and running, phone-wise."

Another few nods. Like this was perfectly normal for one detective to have a conversation with another about getting a burner phone so's they could stay in touch with one another. I suddenly had that feeling again, that I was looking through a glass at everything. That I was one step back, or away, from reality.

Maybe it was that, or maybe it was the sight of an official-looking face on her that goaded me into opening my gob.

"Remember," I said. "There'll be decent postings opening up."

"What," she said. "What's this about?"

"I'm saying you don't have to stay here. You're got prospects."

238

Seeing the colour rise in her cheeks brought me unruly feelings.

"Seriously," I went on. "There will. Don't mind this austerity crisis, stuff. They'll find the money. Senior ranks are piling out."

"Wait, wait, wait. Did I ask you for career guidance?"

"No worries – I don't charge. Look, I always had decent C.Os. Yeah, there were ups and downs but I'll tell you one thing. Nary a one of them thought they were entitled to make up the rules."

Her surprise shot clear through indignation into plain anger.

"Why are you talking like this?"

Whoever'd make air-quotes illegal would get my vote. I didn't even consider trying to return her wild-eyed stare. Yet, as though we'd both suddenly decided that we were going to act as adults for a change, we exchanged parting remarks, one as bogus as the other.

I tried Spots' number again. Still no go. I left the same message, edition number three.

Doubts had been leaking in. Now they were waves. Had I lost the head entirely? Just like that, I'd persuaded myself that Spots would set me up with a place to stay? He'd be suspicious, to say the very least. But he didn't know wouldn't hurt him, would it.

The traffic was so light that I was soon bombing down the quays. I gave Spots another go: same result. This time I didn't bother with any message. Passing Capel St Bridge, I connected with Ma. She sounded downright lively, like she had just stepped out of a party. Whatever I'd suggest was grand by her. 'Grand?'

"C'mere to me with your 'grand.' Did you hear a word I said?"

"Of course I did. But I love going down the country. Love it."

That was Ma for you. Falls into a bucket of shite, comes up a rose. I told her I'd be by to collect her. Then we'd drop by the house to fill a suitcase, and we'd head out to the Minogues in Kilmacud. Fantastic, she said. I bit back the urge to reintroduce her to reality: how she should be on the lookout all the time, and not let down her guard for a moment.

Sheets of sunshine from the windows along the quays flashed in over the river, painting the flat and sluggish water the colour of milky tea. Dinghies moored next the road swayed gently in the full tide, masts drawing lazy arcs across the sky. A ratty-looking cargo boat was unloading beyond the toll bridge. Containers from China – of course they were from China. Everything was from China. There were no line-ups for the toll. I had no change anyway.

And I didn't have a clear plan of action either, did I. But I did have one firm notion. So Nolan wanted his Tony Cummins trophy up on the wall of his IKEA office, did he. Well, I was going to find out just how far he was willing to go to get there. Yes, it was a dicey enough proposition. Maybe that's was why I was now a couple of minutes away from the residence of Mr. Spots Feeney.

*　　*　　*

Whatever I'd been expecting at Spot's place vanished the moment I rounded the bend and the lights filled up my windscreen. There were two fire engines, a squad car, and an ambulance. Neighbours watched from windows across the way, and there were gawkers galore, and cars slowing to look. Alarmingly, there was no Spots.

They had knocked down the garage door to get at the fire. Bent and buckled and torn at the edges, said door now rested crookedly over the bonnet of Spots' Mercedes. Of what had been a Mercedes. One hose still played on the blackened shambles. Weak clouds of steam and smoke stirred lazily about and were soon enticed outside where, after a lazy start at freedom, they eventually vanished.

A fully kitted fireperson holding what looked like an axe was setting down some kind of equipment on the footpath. Fifty feet behind, the door of the ambulance hung half-open. A paramedic, a woman with a tight bun of wiry red hair, was attending to somebody sitting on the edge of a bed. Her partner, an older chap who should be doing do something about his weight, was on a mobile up front, asking someone if someone else would OK something. The conversation seemed very disagreeable to him.

Spots' left hand was already in bandages. The black and grey streaks across his face looked wet. There was a strange look about his eyes like you got when you were drunk and fell asleep and got a fierce sunburn. The eyebrows, I saw then, were burned. He was muttering away in that dogged, monotonous way he used when he didn't want to argue – and that'd he'd clobber anyone who'd try. He stopped when he saw me. He looked more through me than at me and turned away again. The paramedic worked a piece of gauze around his elbow.

"What's going on?"

"Family, are you?" the red-haired one asked. *Demanded.*

"Not quite, no."

I had my photo card out already. She was less than impressed. I waited for words from Spots. The flat glare would be all that'd be on offer, for now. The large paramedic found his way around the side of the ambulance and stood in the doorway.

"This man needs to go to hospital," he announced.

"Not a chance," Spots said. "Give me something to sign."

Red-hair looked at me and then at her partner.

"He has a thing about hospitals," I said. "Let me talk to him."

Red-hair continued winding the gauze. Spots closed his eyes for several seconds. Then he opened them wide, and looked over.

"Look –"

"Shut up. What did I tell you? About being a magnet?"

"All I'm trying to ask is what happened here."

"What does it look like? There was a fire."

"That I can see. But how, when?"

He watched the paramedic finish a last wind of the gauze and tape it down.

"Don't be a thick," I said. "It's not just burns, it's infection and stuff. You know all this. So go get it seen to."

"I already looked at it. I'll take care of it myself."

"Have you given a statement to the Guards?"

He was not interested in this matter either.

Two mules sidled over. A lifer, with a fresh-looking sidekick. I intercepted them.

"Is there a bit of a story to this?" '*Shtory.*' A bogger, of course. The hat tilted up the forehead a bit, the tunic overdue a visit to the dry-cleaners. "This character here and his antique car?"

"Well what did he tell you?"

Senior bloke nodded to the rookie.

"He said he heard something. He went out, the car was on fire."

"What did he hear?"

"He didn't say."

"A device going off maybe?"

Senior paused to compose an even more sarcastic look.

"Well now, Sergeant. It so happens that I've seen the results of a pipe bomb before." He looked over my shoulder. "Ka-boom, is how it goes. Much like what you'd see here. Sergeant."

I'd been working around to the self-same notion. Put a pipe bomb next to a jam-jar of petrol and you got yourself a hell of a fireball, all right. Senior bloke pushed back his hat up a bit more.

"Some pain in the arse he is," he said. "This Free, Frawley?"

"Feeney. The car meant a lot to him."

A smile – of the wrong sort – flickered for a few moments.

"He is skanger, is what I'm hearing. You know that, do you?"

Any account of the several chambers of hells that Spots had been in, and yet climbed out of, would be wasted on these patrol-car culchie know-it-alls.

"Things is different now," I told Senior. "The man is sound. All right?"

Senior wasn't about to give up being a last-worder though.

"Different, is he, your Mr. Feeney? And that's why you're here? The Drug Squad? Because he is sound? A quare class of 'sound.'"

Eyes fixed, and with his expression still very much the abandoned-and-ruined-house model, Spots stepped down from the open door of the ambulance. Red-hair and her partner were putting things in order. The partner folded a piece of paper, a form of some sort, and put it on a clipboard.

"Talk him into going to the Emerg," he said. "Or go to a clinic at least. You're his pal, aren't you?"

*   *   *

Half an hour, forty minutes – they flew by.

Ma phoning broke the spell. Where was I?

"Sorry. Something came up. I'll be over soon's I can."

I left my mobile on the table between us. Spots hadn't budged. He was still staring at the door of his fridge. The whiskey remained untouched.

"Anything else?"

"Anything else what. I already told you. So stop asking."

"You want to deal with them yourself?"

Spots gave me a cloudy look.

"The Guards, I'm talking about. This here is a crime scene."

"I know what it is. Don't come the high cockalorum with me."

"You do, do you. 'Youse cops are useless tools.' And now, when the Guards try to do their job, you want nothing to do with them. Well there's a word for that."

"Youse cops are the problem. You should know that at least."

It was hard to argue with that. Getting the Guards involved would only make life more complicated for Spots. And for me.

"Fine and well for you to be talking, but remember the deal we made? They'd split and leave you alone as long as I got a statement out of you and filed it? Remember?"

"Make something up, can't you. You'll get paid either way."

"You're in the house. You hear something. You go out. You see flames under the garage door. The door won't open, so you try going in the back, but the car's on fire."

Spots blinked.

"No bang? No loud sound at all?"

"I don't know. I had music on. Metal. I like it loud."

243

I made sure that Spots saw me staring at the bandage running from his knuckles to his wrist.

"OK so you want to sort your own issues. But you don't get to run the universe here."

Spots' eyes took on a bit of life.

"Whatever you said there, it makes no sense. You know I really, really don't want youse coppers crawling all over the gaff here."

"Technical Bureau? Forensics? To help us find who did this?"

"They wouldn't be helping me one bit. And by God if they show up, they're getting the bum's rush, and rapid."

He had not strayed from his calm tone.

"Was the garage door open? Locked?"

"The garage door is electric. I came home last night, hit the remote to open."

"Came home from a business call?"

"None of your business, but yes. And don't put that in your notes either. Anyway, it'll give you a laugh. I had to bring someone home from the A and E. What they like to call 'Emerg' now."

"Did you spend the night at an A and E, waiting?"

"Are you mad? No way. No, I got a request. A certain person had gone on the batter, and he needed roping in. I know the bloke. He's done it before. It's a manic depressive scenario."

"Manic depressive, you mean bipolar."

"Bipolar, tripolar – whatever. Look, I dealt with him before. I have a technique, all right? It took a while to get hold of him."

"What's 'got hold of him?' It needed a detour to the A and E?"

"Shut up with that sort of talk. You'd think you were the one got set fire to here. The point is, ten o clock or so I got home. So, between ten and one is the time to figure this thing out. Unless there was a timer and it was attached to the car before."

I waited for Spots to get into this a bit. He didn't. I took the last of the Jameson. Spots maneuvered himself up onto a stool. He still had a rough time of it with normal chairs. You did not dare to offer help, either.

"Look. Is this down to some client of yours? A spat you had?"

"You came all the way out here to ask something so stupid?"

"People who lose the run of themselves, it's your line of work."

"Really," he said, his voice rising a little. "Well I'm beginning to think that the real problem here is you, pal. You and *your* line of work. You're injurious to my health and well-being."

He rubbed delicately along his eyebrows.

"I can read your mind anyway," I said. "It's not that hard."

"Old copper trick, your 'mind-reading.' As old as the hills."

"There's a Cummins in the woodpile here somewhere. That's what you're thinking – Eh. Where'd you park?"

"Around the corner."

"How far 'around the corner'?"

"That's your biggest concern right now, where I parked?"

"Easy for you to say. You're the one carries a gun. Any word?"

"Any word about...?"

"The price of Mullingar heifers, what do you think? Any word on Christy, or the murdering bastards what ran him over, is what."

"It's a murder case now."

"So you didn't come out here just to – OK. You're here as a copper, on a case. About Christy? Am I being, ah, 'interviewed?'"

"I'm not working it. This is you and me talking, That's all."

"A social call? And you the one telling me how you're run off your feet?"

"I'm off-duty. I flew the coop. I had to."

Disbelief erased Spots' frown, but it quickly reassembled itself.

"You jacked in the job? Finally got something in OZ? No way. I don't believe you."

"I didn't jack in the job. I'm off duty, and I will be for a bit."

He intensified his study of the gauze on his hand.

245

"They caught you doing something. What?"

"Someone left items at the front door yesterday. At my Ma's."

He lifted his gaze, placed his arm down gently on the table top.

"'Items.' On your Ma's doorstep. Did I hear you right?"

"Ask me what the items were."

Spots raised his bandaged arm and eyed it. He shook his head.

"Two live rounds and a note. To 'Sheila Malone and Family.'"

He closed his eyes tight. Several moments passed before they snapped back open. There was a kind of whirring in them now. A frown came and went, as did a twitch of the lips. He turned away. Whatever he'd been about to say slid under the surface.

21

We were still knocking off Heinekens. It had gone six. Spots gave off a big, strained sigh.

"So. You need to lie low, you're telling me. A place to crash."

I pulled a lapel up to my nose. The fire stink was deep in it.

"Correct."

"Otherwise?"

"Otherwise? I don't know otherwise. I'd probably have to get on a plane and go somewhere."

"And what's the story with your Ma."

"I'm getting her away for a bit."

"And that means...?"

"Down the country. So far down, even the culchies get lost."

Spots picked up a long screwdriver and began rolling it over a folded tea-towel, over and back.

"And this top-secret James Bondy shite you're at?"

Right as I'd told him about getting snagged in the find-Gary-Cummins nonsense, I'd felt the cold truth of remorse. But there was no going back. Was that why I'd told him?

"Others take over. It's all team-work. Signals go out, of course."

Spots stopped rolling the screwdriver.

"'Signals go out,'" he said, with a half-ironic cringe.

"We want whoever did this. That's the message."

"Oh. You tell the bad guys to grass whoever put the item at your Ma's doorstep. That's brilliant, Tommy."

This was just Spots playing to the gallery. He well knew that we sometimes relied on criminals to police their own. We just didn't broadcast it. Sometimes the choice is between bad and worse. Apaches going after a copper pulled down massive trouble. Raids, searches, general bollicking and knocking heads. That cost.

"So here's you shoved out. And you're calling this a win?"

I attended to my Heineken. Not my favourite by a long shot.

"It's not just taking a powder. I have ideas of my own."

Spots stopped rolling the screwdriver and peered over.

"Do you now. Well I don't want to know about your ideas."

"Just so's you know. Lying low is different from running away."

"Is it, now. And what's wrong with running away?"

"Did you not get my speech about the bad guys not winning?"

Spots resumed rolling the screwdriver. He reminded me of someone working a lathe.

"That's a great story," he said. "'Daddy, daddy! Tell us about how the bad guys never win! Yeah, the one about how the boys in blue always finish on top.'"

I took my time downing the last of the Heineken.

"You taking on a crowd of gangsters, single-handed. How can that not work. Fabulous." He could have been talking about how to fix a puncture. "I almost forgot you can be such a tool. Almost."

"I'm not in the habit of looking the other way. Not like some."

"Aha. And what channel is all this on again? The Cartoon Channel? Wait, what are you again? Gobshite Man? Dublin's champion crime-buster of the next minnel- min – millill –"

"Millennium, you thick. *Millen -*"

I'd seen videos on YouTube that were something like what I saw next – what I didn't see, actually. On YouTube it's speeded up, tricked, edited, and so forth. But here in Spots' kitchen, I got a live demo. A savage, deadly demo of movement and speed.

I'd still swear that the sound of the screwdriver rolling off the dishcloth and bouncing off the table into his hand came to me after. 'After:' when I found myself staring at the screwdriver tip three inches from my nose. Noting how Spots' hand did not waver. The look didn't say anger, or confusion. It was just the neutral look of a person I might or might not have met before.

"Mister Dictionary here. Mister I Have Ideas Of My Own."

He darted a look in the direction of his garage. It was his holy of holies where he communed with his idols. The tools so meticulously arranged. The posters of the Ireland side that beat Italy years ago. Nelson's Pillar before it got blown up. That poster of a weird-looking 1950s Merc that no-one bothered to paint.

"Someone tries to burn me house down. Your 'ideas' at work."

He sucked in a breath through his teeth and slowly lowered his arm, and carefully laid the screwdriver on the towel. My hand shook as I moved the empty can about.

"I told you, leave it alone. Walk. But did you listen?"

"Fill me in on where you got your tip. Your 'drop it' moment."

"That's not how things work sunshine, and well you know it. Now just because you woke up one morning and decided to go messing around in the Cumminses' business -"

"- it's not business. It's crime. People maimed and murdered."

"Newsflash, Tommy? You can't win, OK? You can't. Everything they told you is wrong. So wake up. Life is life. That's how it is. Have you noticed? Things is on the slide. Hit the skids, banjoed, falling apart. All over Dublin – what am I saying – all over Ireland! So you can make your speeches until the cows come home, but this is the way things are going to be. That's the way things always *have* been. Make your arrangements accordingly."

I crushed my can slowly and noisily and laid it on the counter.

"And by the way," he added, "I have yet to hear from you how you landed in the middle of all this in the first place."

"I was born and reared in Crumlin."

"Wait a minute. Just because you were what, seven doors down from the Cumminses? Pull the other one, it's got bells on it."

I let my gaze rove the room. Spots shifted a little on the stool.

"There's the perfect example," he said. "Just typical. Here's you asking all kinds of info, but then, I ask you a simple question? Smart-alec comments, dodges. Always the swiz, always."

"You want me to spill about a Garda operation? Dream on."

"Oooh, a Garda operation. So that's why me place went up in flames. A Garda operation."

"Blame the Guards. You're going around in rings. Look, it's not like you wouldn't have scumbag clients who'd turn on you."

"Tactic number fifty, toss in the decoy. Nice. Very original."

"You're all talk. All I know is we have to go after them."

"There you go again – 'we' and 'them.' Comical, so you are."

"It's not just about you. My Ma got run out of her home too."

"You told me that. Who brought that down on her, I wonder?"

"How do you know it wasn't the other way around?"

I could tell that Spots got it right off the bat. I must've been coming to a slow boil already. The drink, of course.

"What does that mean exactly, 'The other way around'?"

I kept up my stare at the screwdriver. He reached for the Vitamin J. I didn't protest the refill.

"You're telling me it was your Ma got this thing rolling?"

Spots' eyes were half-shut, like he was facing into a breeze.

"I'll give you the basics," I said. "But that's all."

What I did give him was maybe a quarter of the full story to date. That was how I justified it to myself anyway. My basic line: a desperate and sick Bernie Cummins was asking anyone she could think of for help. Ma happened to be one of the anyones.

We tended our glasses awhile.

"So you saw her," he said. "Mrs. Cummins. You met with her."

I let the whiskey rest on the back of my tongue a while.

"No way you'd have gone to her house. Your Ma's neither."

I put down the tumbler and edged off the stool.

"She doesn't drive," Spots said.

"How do you know?"

"The somebody who drove her, was he in on your little 'meeting' too?"

"He who?"

"Looks like a bowling ball with bumps? Bad eyes? Like an Alsatian, the way they stare...?"

He didn't seem to expect an answer. He sat up and stretched.

"And yet, here you are. You just happen to show up here at my place. Just as this thing is going down. Can you explain that?"

My Heineken buzz was rolling over into being half-drunk.

"You're one of them weirdoes who just follows ambulances and fire engines? I doubt it. So how'd you know to come -"

A ring tone cut him off. He looked down his nose at his mobile. Unknown. He looked up and locked eyes with me a moment and looked down at the mobile again. Then he took the call.

He offered no greeting. I could hear only the faintest of tones leaking out of the earpiece. The caller was speaking slowly and quietly. Then I heard what sounded like a question.

"Wait – how did you get this number?"

I saw the familiar tightening in his features, the wariness hardening into something more serious.

"Hold on. Who told you that?"

His strained eyes ran by me as he edged off the stool. Tucking his mobile tighter to his head, he began a processional walk out to the hall. "That's right," I heard him say. He had tipped into belligerent now. "Why should I..." he began, but left off. That marked the last of his conversational input. He closed the door behind him. I finished the Jemmy. Time passed. He'd never get the stink of smoke out of this house, I thought.

I jumped when the door handle turned. Spots was rubbing carefully at his singed eyebrows. He looked around as though baffled that he had ended up in this strange place. He stared at me then, but it felt like he was staring through me. I remembered too well how Spots the younger used to lose it without warning.

"Are you all right?"

"Am I all right." He repeated it like it was an in-joke. "Me, am I all right. Jesus." His stare weakened into a far-away look. Sensing my close study maybe, his eyes snapped back into focus.

"Your Ma. Safe and sound somewhere. Did I hear right?"

I nodded.

"You on the loose, of course. As per usual, I might add. Now. You never answered my question. Which was why, at this particular moment in time, are you after showing up at my place? Feeling guilty that you put this in motion, are you?"

"You think I knew this was going to happen? You're cracked."

"Really now. Says the copper who's on the run from gangsters."

"Lose the drama there. I'm not 'on the run.'"

"Yeah right sure. Some country we're living in, when it's the cops who have to go on the run."

There was no point in arguing. Especially because I had just spotted a tell-tale item. It was that brief glint in the Feeney eye that said wheels were in motion.

"All right. Come here to me. Howth."

"Howth. What about Howth."

"There is a place there. I do be looking in on every now and again. Keeping an eye on it, for a party that I've done work for."

"Oh he's in jail, all right. That kind of party?"

"You wish. The thing about Howth is, it's near enough and far enough away. You agree?"

"You're saying you'd put me up there?"

"This is not just about you. I'm in the picture too. Do I want to be? Did I ask to be? No, and no again. One thousand percent no. OK now. If you say yes to Howth, that car of yours is not the way to go. Park it, tip it off the quays, bury it, I don't care. Just get rid of it. Find your way to the end of the DART, to Howth like."

"I have to drive my Ma somewhere. I'm already late getting to her too. And I need to get a few things from my own place too."

Spots trailed a long, insolent look by me.

"Naturally," he said, "there's conditions, so listen. This is about you minding your manners. No, it's not a crack house we're going to, so take down your cop antenna. But nothing's for nothing. I ask a reasonable-type question, I expect a reasonable-type answer."

He soon got it that he wouldn't get a yea or nay out of me.

"Tommy? I need to know we're on the same wavelength here."

"You said you had questions."

"You didn't just decide to drop by for a social call. Yes, or no?"

I shook my head.

"So spell it out for me."

"I came by because I need a go-ahead."

"A go-ahead. Jesus. Have I heard that one before?"

"I imagined you'd have some interest, some slight sliver of interest in helping me track down who ran Christy Cullinane down in the street like a dog. That you wouldn't just let it go by."

Spots lifted his bandaged arm and flexed it. Then he froze. I heard a voice talking outside now too. I felt around for the grip of my pistol. A fireman's helmet slid by the window.

"This started out being about Gary Cummins," he said then. "Is that still the way?"

"It is. But nobody actually gives a fiddler's about Gary per se."

"Shocked, I am. Shocked."

Spots was never much good at playing the iijit. But only a complete gobshite wouldn't see how valuable Gary Cummins could be as a crowbar on his father.

"The thing is," I said, "I actually do want to find Gary."

"Well of course you do. Look, if I was Snow White, I'd feel Happy too. But like you said, there's more than just you doing this find-Gary-Cummins lark. Right? – and no shilly-shallying here."

He dipped his brow and leaned in a little.

"Did they put you up this? Roping me into this shemozzle?"

Half-gargled or not, I still should've seen this coming. I shook my head.

"But they'd know me, right? Your copper pals?"

"They know *of* you. I got accused of being a mate of yours."

"A serious allegation, all right. But look, we know that youse cops do be pulling quare stunts with the rule book when it suits you. So answer me this. Is somebody twisting your arm?"

The smell of burned stuff had grown very strong again, stinging the top of my nose.

"Such a stupid question, I couldn't even begin to answer it."

"What kind of cops are they, the ones you're working with?"

"You think I'm such an iijit that I'd get used, and not know it?"

He turned away with a shake of his head. I began itemizing what to grab from the apartment when I'd duck in on the way to Aunt Mary's. Laptop, chargers, passport. A few clothes of course... Better not forget the pills, of course. Or should I just swear off...? I was addled. I'd know what needed doing when I'd get there.

"You cops never learn. You don't even ask the right questions."

"So pretend I was as smart as you."

"Huh. If you were, then you wouldn't be screwing around here, would you. Listen to yourself. 'Spots, where's Gary Cummins?' 'Spots, any idea who'd want to do a number on Gary Cummins?' 'Spots, what day is it today?' Jaysus a two-year-old child could come up with better questions."

"Try one of your smart questions on me so."

Spots hesitated. I heard that voice outside again, the fireman.

"Here's one," he said then. "Where's Tony Cummins' stuff? His loot. His, ah, 'proceeds.'"

"That'd be looked into already. You know Criminal Assets?"

"I do. But what did they find? Bet you I know. Bugger-all."

"And you know this for certain, of course. Because...?"

"Hah, everybody knows it. You think Tony Cummins is the only one? You think crime is all about putting on masks and robbing banks and then blowing cash all over the gaff? How much do you think he has gone through over the years anyway?"

"I've got no idea. But Criminal Assets are tough and – "

"- No they're not. OK, ever seen the Cumminses' place? New windows yeah, nice porch and everything. But is it a castle? Does it look like a million?"

"Maybe they're not the showy type."

"Says you. Well I'll say it: the Cumminses, you'd never know from the look of that house that he had money. Now here's another question: do you like your own gaff, your apartment?"

"It's okay. Sonia likes it. So it is what it is."

"Any of them pyrite cracks? Fire safety 100%? Floods yet? Leaks, mildew? Doors hang right?"

I could guess where he was going with this. He winced and sat upright, raising and lowering his arm like a robot warming up.

"Was that you saying that Tony Cummins laundered money in the building racket?"

"No. That's you speculating. At least you're starting to think."

He edged forward on the stool and readied himself to get up.

"Where is all this leading?"

"Why're you asking me? Isn't it your job to figure that out?"

He slid off the stool. For a few moments he looked like he'd just stepped on board a small boat.

"Go disappear that car of yours," he said then. "Your mobile too, obviously."

"How do I stay in touch?"

"You don't. And go all the way with that mobile too – battery, SIM, the whole thing."

"Is this general advice you give everybody?"

"Enough of the smart-alec stuff. You come out of the DART station there, you'll see me sitting in a car. An old Beemer, a white Beemer. But before you even go near the DART, you have a job to do. In that bag of yours, you are going to bring me something."

He paused as though overcome with a profound notion.

"Nothing's for nothing," he said.

"What 'nothing' do you have in mind."

"What it is, is a token. Proof we're on the same side here – just for this, one time and one time only. Why is because the stakes are high. I need to know you're going out on a limb here same as me."

"What is this? You're like The Riddler or something."

"I told you already, you're not thinking straight. If you were, you'd keep your gob shut. You'd get it. You'd see the gravity of the situation here. Because I'm about to do something that I swore I'd never, ever do. So when I tell you what it is, have your brain on. Like I said, one time, and one time only. Are you hearing me?"

"What's to hear?

"OK then. How it goes is like this. You bring with you a certain item. Now, before you rear up, don't. Yes, you do know the one I mean. That item that'd get you the sack and a date with the beak and a stretch in the big house."

He needn't have waited. I knew right away.

"That's mad," I said. "You're cracked. Stupid."

"My oh my. You ungrateful bollocks. Who's stupid here? I'm the one's sticking my neck out. So get over your high dudgeon there. Bring that item – and enough for a couple of clips."

I was suddenly a millimetre from going spare on Spots. For being so underhand. For breaking an unspoken agreement we'd always kept to. He knew this too, I could tell.

"That's when I'll know you're serious," he said. "You'll have a ball in the air same as me. Otherwise? The door's over there."

On his feet now, he rested for a moment, breathing shallow.

"How do I know you have anything? Give me a specific."

"All right. That I can do. You like to go on a drive, don't you?"

"A drive where?"

"The Ward. Have you ever been out that way?"

"The Ward. Why The Ward?"

He looked down his nose at me.

"Like you don't know why. Is that how you're going to be?"

"I know Jenn Cummins lives out there."

A knock on the hall door interrupted us. A fireman: he wanted Spots.

"I was in me twenties before I ever set eyes on the place," he said, ignoring the request. "Hard to believe, and it only a few miles out the road. There's not much in the way of entertainment out that way, but at least there's a pub. A quiet enough part of the world there still. But from what I heard, it wasn't that quiet there last Monday night. No sir."

"Because?"

"Well who knows. That's the issue. The word I have was there were cars racing around like mad. Not for long mind you, but long enough for someone to see them. Now one of them, believe it or not, was a cop car. An unmarked cop car, and it was after the other car. A Golf, he thinks. The person who told me this, he came across bits of trim, later on. Trim, you know, when you bang a car into something you shouldn't be banging a car into?"

"An accident, you're saying."

"No I'm not. Accident is doing something not on purpose."

Someone was pushing open the front door. Mr. Fireman again. Spots glared at me.

"You want to just keep on asking the wrong questions, or....?"

If there was such a thing as an angry smile, Spots had nailed it.

22

Ma answered on the second ring: no, there was no bother about me being late. Everything was still 'grand.' Then I phoned Áine. She was somewhere between impatient and annoyed. Just keeping in touch, I told her. Her response: "Ooo-kaaay." Answering a nonsensical question, as it were.

"So when I call again," I added, "it'll be off a different number."

She wasn't going to waste another *oooo-kay* on this one.

"Did you get through to Bernie Cummins yet?"

I told her I hadn't, but I'd keep trying. I asked if she'd connected with Mary Enright again.

"I did. And she's not happy. She's not talking."

"How come?"

"She says she's already told us everything she knows."

"What about that bloke, her chauffeur, Corcoran?"

"I talked to him. One slick boyo."

"What's a one slick boyo?"

"Well, for one thing, he gave me the whole put-in-in-writing routine."

"What does Mary Enright do that'd rate getting into this agency of his?"

"He did tell me that she was 'not current.' But he said he knew her years ago, and when he heard she slid into the drugs, he wanted to help her out."

"An act of charity? From a lawyer?"

"He didn't use that word – look, leave it for now. I'll work on it later. Look, where's Bernie Cummins right now? Is she headed down to Portlaoise?"

"I don't know where she is. I'm assuming she's at home."

"Well do you want a hand tracking her down?"

"I'm not trying to track her down."

"To phone her, I'm saying. This stabbing, it pushes everything up the list."

"Áine – "

"Will you just get on it, for Christ's sake?"

It wasn't an actual yell. It was near enough, though.

"We could lose this." She had softened a bit. "We've got to keep it moving. OK?"

I took my time with a reply.

"I heard you. But waving a stick at Bernie Cummins isn't going to get us anywhere. And by the way, how do we know she's not in hospital right now? Are you going to butt in on that?"

I could tell that she had plenty more sharp advice to throw at me. But she held back. I asked her for the latest on Tony Cummins.

"He got stitches, he's okay. We're just waiting to make contact, see if he's finally ready to open up. Let's say he asks for you though. What then?"

"He'll hardly be needing me if he's decided to come over."

I had forgotten to fill up the change I kept for toll money. Driving off the edge of the damned quay into the Liffey while I tried to get to my trouser pocket? I pulled in to the side of the road.

"I need time to sort this stuff out, this personal stuff. I'll be in touch."

"Wait," she said. "I need specifics here. We do, I mean."

"I'm working my end, but it'll take time."

"What does that mean, 'it'll take time'?"

"It means that I may have to look for other sources. Other ways and means."

"Which are?"

"Which, I have to tell you, unfortunately, Áine, are none of your business."

*   *   *

It took me a bit of time to get over that contretemps – which was weird.

Why the hell should it matter to me that I'd left Áine Nugent in a dander? I was the bloke out here in the thick of it, the brave soul trying to hold it together after getting targeted.

A flood of sunlight broke from under the mush that had been lying over the city, carving sharp lines and shadows everywhere. For these few first moments, it made the place fierce strange-looking. We were still in Dublin though: that Liffey beside me was proof. My last sight of it slid across the mirror, a rippling bright blue and sparkling like a heap of broken glass. As bad as things were getting here, seeing that made it hard to imagine leaving the place.

I noticed, and me coming up on Merchant's Quay, that the knot in my shoulders had eased. The headache had drained down to bearable too. I get hold of Ma again. She sounded downright giddy now. She told me that she needed to make a stop and buy a cake or a bottle of something for the Minogues. I took a hard line: she had to wait until they got well out of town, to Galway even, first.

"You know it's a farm, right? Out in the middle of nowhere?"

"Sure, what odds," she snapped back. "Amn't I glad to get it at all?"

Crises let Ma come into her own. I sometimes forgot that. I told her I'd be out to get her within the hour. Whatever came after a few days in culchie-land with the Minogues, we'd worry about later, when the dust settled. Her take on that? 'Grand, sure.' Was she into the sherry, I wondered.

I lowered the windows and let the breeze run through the car. People actually looked different, acted different, with sunshine. A sort of blitheness had come over them. One of Sonia's faves started up on the radio. She liked to sing the chorus, for a laugh. '*I still haven't found what I'm looking for.*' Right, Sonia. You nailed that one, so you did. She was almost proud of the fact that she hadn't got a note in her head. I loved that about her.

When I hit John's Road I left the Golf in second to give the engine some work, only drawing it back to law-abiding speed for the lights at the South Circ. The more-or-less found its own way down to the turn in to the apartment. That sunny mood had followed me right to the turn into the forecourt. I could feel it evaporating now, and the jumpiness soak in again.

Aside from the fella from the third floor operating a bucket of sudsy water and a cloth on his car, the place was deserted. I eyed the corners and the doors as I keyed in, and I made my way to the stairs. A faint, reassuring stink of cigarettes hung in the stairwell. Habit made me wait a bit before stepping out to my floor. The hallway as empty as it should be. It was probably a radio that I was hearing, that steady hum that ran and paused like speech. Pushing open the door to my place – our place – I immediately picked up the scent of Sonia's perfume. It was still there somewhere.

I was never a great packer. There was no folding needed for this anyway. Years ago, I got in the habit of taping my passport under the middle drawer, the one I blocked from coming out all the way. There was a cost to that 007 stuff: the contortions to get at it involved resting my noggin on the actual floor. It was a good opportunity to note that a serious hoovering job was needed back here – sometime. Sure, I thought, sometime like maybe never.

My fingers settled on the passport first try, and then the sellotape loop that I'd used to attach the plastic cover. As designed, one tug and it was free. It was too bloody free: down it went. Somewhere in there, I heard it fall on its edge. It had slid right against the wall too. Cursing wasn't going to entice it out. The only solution would involve undignified wriggling and groping.

Sussing out a not-too-dirty spot on the floor to rest my head, I planted it there and began a sideways survey across the floor of the hallway and kitchen. Then I stopped. My breathing stopped too. My heart did the exact opposite.

Joinery: the name for things fitting properly. Well there was a lot of shite joinery done here in the boom. Every dog and divil called himself a builder. Even legit builders weren't anywhere near as picky as they should've been about where their materials came from, or what was in them, or who was putting them together. The worst of it was the pyrite. Peoples' door jambs started going bockety was the first clue. Then it was cracks in the walls, and cracks across the ceilings. Now there were buildings being evacuated. Not every single bit of joinery in our apartment was done according to cocker, but compared to other places they were minor. Also, for long, happy weeks and months, the only joinery I was interested in was with Sonia.

But now I was ridiculously grateful for our little share of crap joinery. It had allowed me to catch sight of a shadow breaking that line of hallway light at the bottom of the door. One person out there, I decided – I hoped. If this was the real deal, it'd be the driver outside and two pros at the front end here. I stared at the door handle and the deadbolt. I'd paid an arm and a leg for that hardware. I'd put in a sleeve for the longer deadbolt too, to tighten it better in the strike plate. Short of someone hitting the door with one of the door rams we use, that lock was going to hold.

The light, or the shadow, moved. There wasn't a sound. Not so much as the slightest scuff of a shoe or a sleeve brushing against a jacket. I was getting a cramp now from craning my neck up to watch. I broke my stare at the door handle and drew my arm back slowly across the floor until my fingers found the edge of the holster. I breathed in deep and slow and tugged out the Sig. The soft tick of it releasing sounded like it'd break the frigging sound barrier. I waited.

Still nothing. The floor was not a bad place to be, but there was one problem with it. If someone was going to try to batter down the door, they'd quickly cop on that said door wasn't going to budge. If that was the case, they might let fly with shots through it. Just imagining that was enough to prod me into planning a move. I tucked in my elbows and began a roll out. I got an elbow back under me right away and then I was up – up on one knee. It was enough. I had a steady-enough stance and clear lines. I looked back at the living room. That sharp band of sunlight by the couch where I sat to play my pathetic video games – it might as well have been a mile away.

Somewhere in this small, empty universe a phone began to ring. My phone. The ring tone sounded different. It was coming from my jacket pocket. Said item I had parked on the back of the chair before I'd begun my floor maneuvers for the dropped passport. The quiet between rings vibrated in my head. In one gap, I thought I heard a squeak. I'd heard that sound plenty of times before. It was the sound of the piston release on the door to the stairs. A new one had been installed after Christmas. It had a slower release and it gave off a peculiar gasp like someone about to cry.

More time crawled by. Bit by bit, the world began to soak back in. The hush and sigh of the city that you forget is there. The dull clump of train shunting, a sound I had come to like. Someone beeping twice on a car horn. I tried to estimate how much time had gone by since the last ring on my mobile, when it had gone to voice mail. I couldn't be sure. A nearby sound startled me then: the fridge taking its normal spaz as the compressor fired up. My resting knee hurt now.

Straightening up was like trying to get free of wet cement. It took work too to unlock my death-grip on the Sig. I was immediately side-tracked then by my finger cramping as I let it out from inside the guard. But things did seem to be returning to the way they had been, still and familiar. Sugar bowl and kettle. The knobs on the presses, the unwashed dishes. All the delph there, lined up for days now.

I edged over sideways toward the chair. Grabbing my jacket, I held it out at arm's length like it was a bag of dog-shite, and I followed it back along the wall to the new roost I'd sussed out, a spot next to as much serious metal as I could find, the cooker. I let the jacket onto the floor there and crouched down, and I listened. An impossibly long minute passed. I slipped out my mobile and checked it. There was something reassuring about seeing Macker's name on the missed call. Talk about timing. The comforting glow of annoyance and nostalgia lingered. I pocketed my mobile and prepared for my next move – the spare bedroom. It was actually a study room for Sonia, Sonia the late-night exam swot. It was also where, in a genius move, I had put my ballistic vest.

Again I waited. Listened, waited, and waited some more. In the end, all it took was a one-step dart across the passageway into the bedroom. I took my time lining up the two sides of Velcro before pressing them home. The vest felt tight and confining, just the way I liked it. That false sense of security, sure. But whatever. It was time get beyond looking for places to curl up and hide. There'd be no foolhardiness as regards the hall door. No, the further I got from it, the better. I'd head for the sliding door out to the balcony. 'Balcony' was a bit of a misnomer. It was a three-foot-deep standing-around place where you could jam a couple of chairs and pretend we had OK weather. Opening it in one go made a racket like Copper Faced Jack's at full tilt. It'd be inch by inch so.

Nothing stood out from the background soundtrack of mid-afternoon Islandbridge. A banging, hammer against metal, echoed. Trucks snoring and snorting as they headed up Johns Road to the M7. Birds singing their little hearts out somewhere. And, intermittently, a scratching sound.

A short step got me to the side of the wicker chair, the one that Sonia just had to have, and I scanned the court below. The scratcher was Frank, aka Frank the unofficial gardener. Also Frank the Man Who Couldn't Sit Still. And why would he really, this widower, a retired train driver who had bought in here to be near the yards where he'd worked for decades. At this particular juncture Frank appeared to be farting around with those ornamental grasses along by the wall.

He must have felt eyes on him. He straightened up, rubbing his forehead with the back of his hand and looking around. It took him maybe five seconds to glom onto me.

"The hard man, Tommy. How's tricks with you."

Jesus, Frank: wake the dead. I managed with a neighbourly nod. No mean feat when you were shaking. As I retired from view, I saw his gaze stray a little and the smile contract. Frank might have missed that I was wearing a ballistic vest. They do look like a waistcoat after all. But Frank had spotted what I had neglected to pay attention to this past minute or so, the pistol I was holding.

*   *   *

A sudden, savage headache had swooped down on me and fastened in a tight band around my head. I had just taken my first, exploratory step out into the hallway – the result of the half-arsed plan that my addled mind had spat up. *Just make a bit of noise, that'll scare them off.*

I began with shoving the kitchen stools about and moved on to poking the umbrella around next to the hall door. The finale was tossing my coat out into the hall. There was no deafening fusillade. Just a coat lying in an empty hallway, in full compliance with the laws of physics. The sight of it put me in

265

mind of one the weird postcards that Minogue used have over his desk. Some famous dead painter.

Did getting the shite scared out of you really make you think clearly? My current state of mind told me no. Things kept moving in and out of focus. Still, headache or not, I was relieved to be pulling in by the curb outside Auntie Mary's.

Ma was bright-eyed, keen and lively. Too lively.

"Sure it was time for a bit of a change anyway," she said.

This observation arrived after a longish period of saying nothing. I had deflected all her questions. She had gotten the message.

"We'll call it a challenge. Think positive. Right, Tommy?"

"Fair enough."

"Maybe it's a sign actually, something like this happening."

Ma and her signs. I wasn't going to touch that one. I got off the M50 at Goatstown. Out here was very confusing, the roads. The turn for Kilmacud Road wasn't too far, if I remembered right. From the corner of my eye, I saw Ma sag in her seat.

"Tommy. Something I said earlier. I wish I hadn't said it."

"Your gangsters speech?"

"It was the wrong thing to say. I wasn't thinking."

"'Do what you have to do?' There's plenty'd go along with that."

"That's not the point. I know you, Tommy. *That's* what's got me worried."

Madame Sheila, fortune teller. She'd jinx me yet. I wondered how long it'd take her to find out about the fire at Spots' place. She'd tear into me for not telling her here now.

"Whatever you're thinking of doing, don't do it. All right?"

I refused to look over.

"Don't be worrying, Ma. I'll behave myself. I swear."

23

Kathleen Minogue was foostering around in the boot of their Renault when we drove up. Ma smiled when she saw her. Why wouldn't she. She's a Dub, Kathleen – *Fizzbra all de way*. Minogue was apparently doing something in the shed. A bit early to be dipping into the gargle, I thought.

He was actually fixing a rake. Who fixed a rake in this day and age? But he always had been a bit of a fog inspector. He'd gotten a bit jowly, a bit more grey in the thatch too. The eyes had that hint them still though– right this way to the Department of Mischief.

"You." He said it like he was lost for a proper curse word. "You have got me worried, so you do."

I caught him up on the fact that I had now backed out. That I was now changing abodes, but on my own. He wasn't impressed.

"There's no armed detail taking care of it? No watch?"

"Boss, I'll be grand. Honest to God. I have what I need."

He wouldn't need a translation: I'm armed. But the doubt stayed.

"If I was your C.O. still, you'd be getting a right good talking-to."

"Easy does it there hardman. You're talking to a Garda Sergeant now."

"Whether or which. Look, you don't owe them anything."

"Owe who?"

"The OCU crowd. And you don't owe the Cumminses either, the wife I mean, Mrs. Cummins. And you certainly don't owe a favour to your mother."

'Owe'- the word went skittering about my mind. Did I owe Christy Cullinane? Did I owe the someone who'd run my mother out of her own house? A different kind of 'owe' maybe. I looked around the garage while he finished screwing in the head of the rake. What a place. Wooden-handled

267

hand tools, a machete. Bits of farm implements that ought to be in a museum. Empty bottles, shelves of books, ..an old Martini ashtray? Big, useless-looking rocks. Metal grabby things.

"Boss. Another favour? Can I park in your garage while you're away?"

Up went the eyebrow.

"You're ditching your mobile, and now you're ditching your car?"

Kathleen's arrival derailed this eyeball match with her husband. But then somehow it all worked out. In a matter of minutes, I was in the weird position of standing in someone's driveway and waving them bye-bye – with the key of their house in my hand. Ma looked chuffed. 'An adventure.' The relief was like high pressure air let out of my chest.

I got the Golf in with about two millimetres to spare, but getting the garage door down still took a bit of finesse. I checked the lock on it twice, and shouldered the strap of my runaway bag. I remembered that the shops out on the Kilmacud Road were a roost for taxis at this time of the day.

Being out on foot in these open, suburban spaces got to me immediately. I felt like I had become prey. I passed a house decorated with frayed nylon tarps stirring in the breeze. Old scaffolding lay scattered about like it had fallen from a plane. Stalled in the middle of a renovation? Not what I'd have expected here in the so-called leafy suburbs. There were two shops closed too, one with a receivership sign in the window. An empty double-decker flew by. Where was everyone? I should've gone the other way instead, I thought, a longer walk to the Luas station. My hand kept going for my mobile, kept banging into the extra battery next to it. I beat myself up again for forgetting to get money out of the wall.

Then came a reprieve: a taxi, a real live vacant taxi, pulling in next to a newsagent ahead.

*   *   *

I was bloody starving by the time the DART pulled into Howth station. I was also ready to murder a pint or two...or ten. I put it all down to the sea air. Or maybe it was the sight of Dollymount Strand. It set me thinking of the times we'd gone out here, the four of us. I hadn't been out to Dollyer in years. Da always brought Cheese and Onion crisps, and Cokes. Naggins of vodka too, but that I only twigged to later on. Ma wouldn't give us the crisps and the Coke until we'd eaten our sandwiches. That used to drive Terry up the walls.

As for Howth itself, it was one of those places I never quite got. I always wanted to like the place but I just couldn't bring myself to. Howth people were definitely different – that I knew – but how exactly I couldn't figure out. Maybe it was the Viking thing, history, all that. Fishing boats from here went as far as Norway. There'd been gun-running here, and smuggling, and talk about the 'RA landing Semtex and AKs back in the day.

Mad, steep, narrow roads twisted up from the old village, and up onto Howth Head. 'The Hill of Howth' Ma called it, like it was The Hills of Rome. There were plenty of millionaire pads hiding behind hedges up on said Hill. For ordinary mortals like me and Sonia, Howth meant a walk along the cliffs and then a pint afterwards. The walk was her idea. For an hour or so, all you had to deal with were the sea and the clouds and the path ahead through the gorse. You could forget you were in Dublin – in Ireland actually.

If quaint and dainty had been my thing, then the DART station at Howth would've been right up my alley. I was one of maybe a couple of dozen people getting off. A lingering glance from the bloke behind the glass put me back on edge right quick. I adjusted the strap over my shoulder again and tucked my elbow in tighter to steady the bag. That was to guard against the handgun and ammunition in the bag from spilling out of it all over the floor of this quaint and dainty station.

Fishy smells and sea decay carried across the road from the harbour. There were few enough cars around. The only one occupied was a Beemer, a 520 no less, but a good number of model years back. Paint peeling on the roofline? Behind the wheel and silhouetted against the windscreen was a hefty-looking driver, wearing glasses. The lights flashed once and I heard the engine start up. A small, dark cloud of exhaust rose behind. Diesel, of course: a Spots Feeney fetish.

Nothing was said as I hefted the bag in the back seat. Spots pulled away from the curb and aimed the Beemer in the direction of Howth village. There was a different bandage on his arm now. He missed third gear but found it in time before he took a sharp turn up a hill. I knew this road. It led up by that pub place on the main street, the Abbey Tavern.

"Got everything?"

"Everything?"

"Don't be a smart-arse. You know what I mean. You brought it, yes?"

"You mean the 'it' that'd get me five to seven? And only if a get a sympathetic beak?"

"Lose that comedy thing, I said. And you totally kicked off your mobile. Yes?"

"Correct. Dead to the world. Look, isn't there a chipper around here?"

"Fish and chips, are you mad? You think we're on our holliers?"

"I'm starving. You know how I get."

"Forget it. I have grub at the place. Sangers, and that. So no bellyaching."

This excuse for a road – a laneway really – turned out to be a two-way. Stopping to let a van go by meant pulling in tight enough to a hedge to have it scrape along the side of the Beemer. Then we were at a junction and coming into a more built-up end of things.

"We need to get something straight," I said. "The deal was I bring that Beretta. OK, but that's all – bring it, I mean. There's no way I'm actually going to let you have it."

Spots worked the wheel to make another turn. He stepped hard on the accelerator for a quick dart up the next hill. We passed a terrace of labourers' cottages strung out like the carriages of a train. Howth cop-shop slid by to our left, sprouting its antennas and aerials. We came to the Howth I knew better, the big gates and the tall hedges and the houses behind the trees. Money Howth.

A quick glance in the mirror and Spots pulled a hard left. Not even a thought about using the brakes. My head hopped off the glass, the Beemer's right wheel boinked the curb medium-hard, and Spots straightened it out again. I didn't need a map: we were going around in a circle.

"A question," he said. "About Mrs. Cummins. Bernie."

"Not a chance. I already told you too much."

Without a by-your-leave, he stood on the brakes. Old Beemer but damned good brakes. Spots waited a bit, chewing his lip with his eyes locked on the mirror. Apparently satisfied, he reversed into the laneway. St Nessan's Terrace, the place was called.

"It's her minder I'm talking about."

He stared ahead, rowing the stick over and back across the gate.

"What about him?"

"Name of Blake, yes?"

"You tell me."

He let off the brakes and the Beemer rolled down onto the roadway. We were now heading back the way we had come.

"What do you know about Blake? You familiar with him?"

"Hah," Spots said. He seemed a tad less tense now. "Do your own homework. What did your copper computer say about him?"

"He reported his car robbed? A twelve year old 520 Beemer, manky but solid and er.... well loved?"

"I'm going to take it that you know what you're dealing with."

"Look. This spy type caper you're at. How much more of it?"

"As much as it takes, is how much. You prefer I was just as thick as you are? As careless?"

We were coming to a proper road. I could see ahead enough to believe that we were back at the main street. For all I knew, we might even be headed back to the DART station.

"Don't bother playing the fog inspector with me. I'm asking you for a reason."

I elected silence. The peculiar items of wear and tear along the dashboard caught my attention again. He wouldn't be mad enough to use a robbed car? He knew enough about Blake, I decided.

271

"All right. Him and Tony Cummins go way back."

"Well we all know that. C'mere to me, what's his nephew's name?"

"How would I know?"

Spots shot a quick scornful glare my way. Then I got it.

"OK. Wild guess. He's married to Jennifer Cummins?"

"Maybe you're not quite as thick as you look."

We were approaching to a big church, and shops. That famous hotel went by to our left. It looked empty. Spots was still looking in his mirrors every few seconds. He reached under his jacket and slipped out a yellow sticky note, and held it out. Something about the sight of it made me hesitate.

"It's is a Dublin number," I said. "So?"

"OK, Mastermind. So tell me who does it belong to."

"You tell me who. Because clearly you already know."

Spots dug out a mobile and handed it to me. The back was off of it.

"We're going for a bit of a drive. Not too far. Just to Coolock, say."

"Any logical reason? We're out here to be out of sight, are we not?"

"It's a technical issue. Coolock is a good enough spot. Fill in the missing bits yourself."

I knew. Spots had always had a too-keen interest in how the mobile phone system worked, specifically how calls were relayed and tracked and traced.

"I have got a technical issue of my own. I need something to eat, and now."

Spots made no comment but when we got to Sutton Cross, he pulled into the car park for a Centra. I bought chips and what were called 'sausage rolls.'

"I'll give you a battery when we get there," Spots said. "And you make a call."

"Call who?"

"Whoever you need to, to get the owner of that vehicle."

"Why would I be doing this?"

"Because you need to catch up, is why. Because you wouldn't take my word for it."

"You think I'm just going to get someone at work to key it in, and give me the results."

"I do, yeah. What kind of a Sergeant are you anyway?"

He didn't wait for me to finish eating. Within a few minutes we were onto Kilbarrack Road. Just before we saw the lights for the Malahide Road, he pulled the Beemer into a side road alongside a bit of a green. He slipped out a battery from his pocket and held it out.

"You need this immediately, tell them. Immediately if not sooner."

The best would've been Kilmartin, who was in Traffic, or Murtagh. But they'd be wondering.

"I don't have my numbers with me. They're on my mobile."

"Just get on with it."

I remembered Macker's mobile number. For some reason, it went to voice mail. The short message that I left there had three curse words. Spots wasn't impressed.

"What's that about? You're a Sergeant, aren't you? Can't you just get it done?"

"Give it a minute," I said.

I had underestimated Macker: it was seventeen seconds. I didn't remember him sounding so friendly before – and that was even after I dropped my big ask on him. Fair play to him, he just said yes. Still, I knew he was gumming for info.

"Ask me no questions and I'll tell you no lies," I said.

There was no overdone witty retort, which surprised me.

"How long a wait?" Spots asked.

I figured he already knew about the woeful delays on PULSE. It had been like this since day one. The whole system needed a swift kick in the arse.

"As long as it takes," I said.

Yet again, Macker was quick on the draw.

"Joseph Gerard Blake, Rialto," he said. "That sound right to you Skip?"

"Maybe. Look, I have to go. Thanks and all."

"Wait, wait. This is to do with your new thing?"

"That's right, my new thing. Look, the next question, don't ask it, OK?"

Macker gave one of his donkey-style laughs. Spots had heard it, surely.

"I'll be in touch, Macker. Best I can do."

Spots right away tore off the cover and ripped out the battery. I reached for the 7 Up. It was going to be the hard stuff soon: I needed something.

"So. That registration number you gave me. What's the story?"

"It happens to belong to a car that was seen tearing around one night recently."

"What kind of tearing around? Joyriders? Boy-racers? Robbers? What?"

"Calm down. It was one night in a certain area of Dublin. That car, and another car. Now the other car, it just so happens that it was .... a cop car. An unmarked cop-car."

"Says who it was a cop car?"

"Listen to you. A neck on you like a jockey's bollocks. It doesn't matter 'says who.'"

"Tell me again what went on then."

"It was two cars, going like the clappers, and one's a cop car. An unmarked cop-car."

He hit the accelerator hard. This Beemer was a tank, all right. I resumed my mopping-up operation with the flakes from the sausage roll while I turned over notions in my mind. Spots' whole secret agent rigmarole was beginning to get to me. Phone switching, car switching, coming to Coolock to get a cell tower there? I didn't even want to think about his demand for an absolute bona fide in the shape of The Alternative.

"This pseudo car-chase," I said then. "What's the real deal?"

"Well," he replied, after a highly passive-aggressive delay, "it occurred in a certain part of Dublin."

"Where? Ballyer? Finglas? Where – and when?"

"A nice, quiet spot. A place, as the saying goes that's far from the maddening crowd."

I knew: of course I knew.

"The Ward."

"It took you long enough."

"Jennifer Cummins' place?"

"Who said anything about that?"

"Don't be acting the maggot. Was it?"

"Anything's possible – anything. Don't you know your quantum physics? A thing in two places at the one time? It sounds totally haywire but you can't argue with science."

"Who gave you the tip on the car?"

"Someone who likes to be helpful, is who."

"'Helpful.' Why do I have a problem believing this?'"

"You're fierce quick to judge people. Captain Disaster here?"

I almost laughed. Maybe it was a kind of hysteria by then.

24

We headed back to Howth through Sutton Cross. Two planes out over the
Irish Sea caught my eye. The nearer one was wheels-down for a landing.
The far was doing that trick where it looked stationary. I let a fantasy live a
few moments: Sonia was on the first one. She'd seen the light, and now she
understood. I'd hear the key in the door, and there she'd be. She'd have a
little speech ready: *look, Tom. I had to get out to get back in. But now I'm
back, and* –

"That's the thing." Spots had adopted a strange sing-song tone. "Building
relationships."

His words pinched something in my mind.

"A complex matter, let me tell you. Complex and contentious."

"Since when do you talk like that?"

"Me? Everyone talks like that now. How is that news to you? Even
youse coppers do it, especially your propaganda wing. All that serving the
community, stakeholder, partner bollocks?"

"But why are you telling me this? Like, here, now?"

"Because cultivating relationships is a thing I do rather well."

"Is this out on Blu-ray already? So's I can skip through it?"

"Oh you're funny, Tommy. Funny in a thick way. But I'll tell you anyway.
There happens to be a bloke, a bloke who did right by me. A bar man. Not
an easy line of work at the best of times, as you well know. So one particular
evening, I was in a pub. Imagine that – I know, right. Now before you ask, this
bloke doesn't work there anymore. Anyway. I had a task to do. To coax a party
to leave this particular pub. Him and the mot he was with, and get him in the

car with me so's I could return him to the bosom of his loving family. Well he didn't want to be coaxed. You see?"

I made futile guesses at what Spots charged for this.

"So this chap working there, he sees my conundrum. And, very diplomatically, he informs me that he hopes I have somebody keeping sketch for me outside. Why's that, says I. Because, says he, there's two heads waiting outside. These were not just any two heads, you can be sure. No sir. They were intending to knock the head off of my client. Whether it was words said earlier, or his mot had set him up to be fleeced – whatever. Maybe he richly deserved a good clatter for all I knew. I mean a client is a client, but I'd have to say this guy was a massive loolah. Always on the lash, always. Going out of his way to look for trouble. That kind of a loolah. A self-destructive thing, is my belief. Now remember, this was back at the height of the boom. The coke flying, the hotel orgies, the exploding nightclubs. A lot of people let loose, a lot of poor judgement, a lot bad behaviour -"

He braked hard for a bus late with a signal.

"So think about this," he went on. "Remember – this barman, he didn't have to tell me a thing. No, this was a gift, free gratis and for nothing. But, of course, people are people. They have their reasons for doing something, or for not doing something. But so what? Let's say that this client that I was trying to keep out of hospital, or court, or maybe even a graveyard, let's say the management in that pub wanted him out. Say he was being a serious pain in the hole in that pub. But management, they didn't want a scene where he'd get a few digs or a proper hiding in the process. You see? So that bloke behind the bar, he saved the management and me a good bit of bother. What did I do then? I informed the client about the two heads waiting outside to break his snot. End result, he turned as meek as a lamb. I got him and his mot out the back in short order. Everybody's happy. You see?"

"Very touching. Was any of what you just said true?"

"What in the name of God kind of a question is that?"

He gave me a withering look. He seemed genuinely put out.

"The two skangers outside," I said, "that was a put-on, right? To get your bloke to hurry out."

"Er, no? I'm making a point about relationships. Bear with me. I go back to that pub a bit later on. A couple of weeks after the fact, say. But I don't see the fella who gave me the billy that night. So I ask about him. A fella tells me he works out at a pub out ....?"

"Wild guess – The Ward."

"That's twice you got it right. So what do you know about the Ward?"

"Not much. Why would I want to?"

It was like Spots hadn't heard me.

"It's an old name," he announced, "this Ward business. A historical thing. Did you know that The Ward goes right to the border of Meath?"

"No. Tell me why I should care."

"Why? You don't get it? Think, man – think. You know your geography, don't you? For example: The Ward is near enough the airport. For example: It also happens to be near the Belfast Road. Do those facts give you any notions?"

"Maybe they do."

"Well they should. Back to my helpful barman. I make a point of going out to this Ward place a few weeks later. And sure enough, there he is. A gaff called the White Horse Inn. Do you know it?"

"No. But I might have heard of it once."

"It's actually a kip, to tell you the God's honest truth. But there he was. It freaked him out that I'd found him. He never said so outright, but he had money issues. So my little brown envelope was well received. Did you ever notice money has that effect?"

"He's onside now, is he, your man in The Ward?"

"No, and by the way, that's not how things work. As a matter of fact, he was only a few days from taking a powder. He'd just gotten his year thing for Oz, his permit, visa. So he was jacking it in and making a bee-line for the airport. So he's gone."

"Brilliant. Australia's definitely short of barmen. I don't think."

"For your information, Mr. Know-it-all, he's actually an architectural draughtsman. But he's like everyone else in this frigging country who doesn't have a cushy number in the civil service or the Guards – he actually has to work for a living. Anyway, my point is, he mentioned to me that this White Horse Inn place has its fair share of colourful characters."

"Colourful. You don't mean Hollywood stars, I take it."

"Yeah well I don't mind 'colourful,' I have to say. Not to knock around with now, but for prospects. Long story short, he told me about this car race shemozzle. He was out having a smoke, thought it was joyriders flying by. He knows his cop cars though, the antennas and that. It was one of those standard issue Nissan jobs, newish. The other car, he got some of the reg off of it. Now there's a weird one, he said to himself. Because, a few days later, guess what car's parked outside the White Horse?"

"And the owner of this vehicle is...?"

"You tell me. You been great OK so far."

"Blake."

"Cor-rect. So that was Blake's car tearing around that night along with the cop car. Who was driving the cop car, you're going to ask? That I do not know. Anyway. Later on, my bloke he sees bits of plastic lying all over the road. Trim, bits of glass, the type of stuff you get after a prang."

"Come on. This is all a bit mucky."

"Mucky, you say. Well my lad knew that Blake does be there to that pub once in a while. And when he does, he sits and he has a pint with...?"

"His nephew. Liam Murphy, Jennifer Cummins' hub."

"There's hope for you yet. Now, back to geography. The car park there is a kind of a, well for lack of a better word, meeting-place. Fellas picking up labour for day jobs. Other matters too, as you might imagine. Equipment, tools, that sort of thing."

"All completely legal activities, you'll be telling me next?"

"Well they don't be going there to receive Holy Communion, do they. But it so happens that Blake drops by around the tea-time. Which is when Liam Murphy drops in too. Interesting, no?"

Howth Head slid across the windscreen and took up a steady position to Spots' side. A giant sleeping on his back.

"Enough of this carry-on," I said. "Fill in the missing bit here."

Spots shook his head and slowed for the lights ahead.

"Tell me something. Are youse tailing Blake? Surveillance?"

"What in the name of God kind of a question is that?"

"OK, so you're a copper, you're not supposed to blah blah. I have that speech on tape. Now: are you tailing him yes or no."

"Jaysus, I don't know. And if I did –"

"–Fine then. Missing pieces, you say. Try this. Did I say to you that Blake was in the pub that night of the car thing? No, I did not. What I *actually* said was, Blake goes there the odd time, at tea time, i.e. daytime."

"Daytime, night time – you're making no sense."

Spots' eyes held mine for way too long.

"Can you not crash the car but," I said.

"It wasn't coppers chasing Blake. It was Blake chasing coppers."

*   *   *

"Are you getting this yet? I thought you were on the ball."

"I get the words. What's behind them, I'm not so sure."

"It's all a spoof to you, is it? Me going to all this hassle just so's I can palm off porkies on you?"

"You might know something. Whatever it is, though, you're keeping it to yourself."

"As a matter of fact, I do 'know stuff' as you call it. I know some bastard set fire to my place, my car. I know Christy's funeral is coming up the Monday. And I know how he was kilt too. Your Ma's been put out of her home – I know that. Something else I know? Somebody wants you to keep that thick, interfering head of yours out of their business. Is that the kind of stuff you mean?"

I focused on the car ahead.

"'Somebody,'" I said. "In plain English, what are you saying?"

Spots rearranged his grip on the wheel and eyed the edge of the bandage where it met his palm.

"Here's a bet for you," he said. "Fifty, that this peculiar car episode does not feature on your system, your what-do-you-call-it, PULSE. You won't find hair nor hide of it. You know why?"

"It wasn't logged?"

"And why wasn't it logged?"

"Because, duh, it never happened? Because your fella made up a cod of a story to get on your good side again i.e. reel in more of your dosh? Or maybe, because there's no bloke in the first place?"

Spots tossed all this off with a grunt. Howth in all its glory had taken up the full windscreen now. What was wrong with me that I couldn't like this place?

"Are you ditching me back at the DART station there?"

"So help me God I should do exactly that."

He turned in off the road in front of a fancy apartment block. Producing a card from his shirt pocket, he took the Beemer to a ramp down to what I assumed was an underground garage.

"This is it?"

"This is it. What were you expecting? A badger's den?"

"A so-called 'hideout,' smack dab in the middle of a very visible, very fancy-looking block of apartments?"

Sonia had pointed this place out before. The floor-to-ceiling windows that looked out over the Harbour had her fairly entranced. These places would've gone for upwards of a million.

The Beemer was swallowed up in the tunnel.

"What, we're going to be burglars now?"

"'Investment expert' is the same as 'burglar'? Good one."

I surrendered to the pathetic air-quotes.

"Where's your 'investment expert?' Under a bed in Bolivia?"

"Not that it's any of your business, but he has a problem that a lot of people have – the wandering mickey syndrome. He got hot and heavy with someone he picked up in a night club. But the official girlfriend found out. So what did she do?"

"She snitched him to the wife."

A ghost of a smile told me Spots enjoyed recalling this folly.

"Just so. The wife, she went Balooba. Pulled out all the stops."

There were few enough cars parked in here. A fair few of them of were serious motors. A Range Rover down a bit on its tires and coated in dust. A Lexus in similar order. Lexus, Merc ...Merc again. We were in the secret Irish province of Lichtenstein.

Spots had his usual trouble maneuvering up out of the seat. I stayed put on my side and looked the other way. As short a walk as it was to the lifts, it revved up my case of the willies. I set my mind to noticing details: panels in the lift that looked like real cherrywood. That light pepperminty scent all about. Spots had a key ready. He mashed the third floor button. The lift slowed and then jerked to a stop. For a high-end gaff, the doors were a bit scrapey opening. Pot lights cast soft-edged, almost glowing, circles onto the hallway and drew a dull sheen from the patterned walls.

We passed some dried plant efforts set in tall, skinny holders. A little badge on one door, in the shape of a yacht: 'Carpe Diem.' Spots continued his bockety progress to 310. His key slid in like butter. Before pushing open the door, he gave me the no-go signal. I glued my back to the wall and looked up and down the hallway. After a quick but not quick-enough-for-me walkabout, Spots motioned me in. The place was a kip, an empty neglected-looking kip. It smelled of stale milk. Not a stick of furniture. The curtains, or sheers to give them their correct name, were thicker than I expected but I bet the view would be something, all the same.

"Lap of luxury? Not."

"It'd be like you to bellyache, all right. Second bedroom over there."

He might have been technically correct about bedroom. He was clearly wrong on the matter of bed. Instead, there was a cardboard box with a picture of a chesty young one lying on a lilo, on a beach. I put down my bag and headed back out to the kitchen. Spots was opening a laptop on the kitchen counter. The polished granite felt clammy. He fiddled with his hotspot yoke-e-me-bob, checked a switch on it and then held it up to see which lights were on.

"You're forgetting something," he said. I took up a spot near the fridge. It wasn't a bottle of holy water, I knew. "Just pony up. A deal's a deal. Eh, the ammo too. All of it."

"What do you actually want it for? We never discussed that."

"I told you already. It's proof you and me are on the same team. *Quid pro quo.*"

"Your way of saying you can blackmail me with it."

"Bullshit. Call it a security deposit then."

"Security? You know I carry a sidearm. That's good enough."

"'Sidearm,'" he said, wrinkling his nose. "Well good for you and your 'sidearm.' Have a nice day then."

"You plan on settling some issue with a gun? On my watch?"

He turned my way. There was a fake patience in his eyes.

"Come here to me, Einstein. They'd be a lot more used to carrying a gun than I would."

"'They?'"

He glanced back at the laptop screen.

"How do you think they set fire to my car? And don't say 'matches and petrol.'"

"I don't know. They got into the garage somehow?"

"Somehow? You like to keep playing the slow learner here? OK, let me come at it a different way. Tell me something. Who knows how to make a bomb and attach it to a car?"

"Who said anything about a bomb? Is there a forensic – "

"– bomb, device, timer – *whatever.* Look, nobody got into that garage. I have locks and stops on that garage that'd have the FBI running home crying to their mammies."

"At least wait until they tell you what they found."

"Uh uh. Waiting is not healthy. I'm telling you, someone got to me car somewhere else, some other time. They put something on it, or under it, that'd go off later on. That's not amateur.

"But why go to that trouble?"

"Do you think I know? I got a phone call – Caller ID blocked by the way, Sherlock, but that's another story – a half an hour before I find out me garage is on fire."

He waited for me to connect the dots.

"That phone call," he went on. "It's a bloke I don't know. Dublin accent, but it wasn't dragged along Kimmage Road for flavour. He's telling me he's in a tight spot. Says he got my number from someone who swears by me. Can I pick him up city centre and drive him out to Naas? He has to meet somebody there. Five hundred on the spot, says he. That sound attractive to you?"

"Attractive, I don't know. It has a dodgy feel to it."

"Do I have to spell it out for you?"

"You were being set up, you're saying."

"Right. Me behind the wheel of when this thing'd go off."

I didn't know what to say. There wasn't much to argue with.

"And it's you and your thicko carry-on has got me into mess."

I returned his glare. Thirty four years, I thought, since Senior Infants. Who could you trust these days. He turned away then and busied himself working on an internet connection. I had slid the bag into a cupboard next to the dishwasher.

He was online when I got back. I placed the plastic bag with the Beretta and the extra rounds on the countertop. He pretended to ignore it. Not so much as a hint that he knew I had just put my neck on a chopping block.

"There," he said, and nodded at a map on his screen. "That there's the White Horse Inn. See the car park? Bits of ould lorries and that parked to one side? More a dump than anything else."

The satellite view filled in slowly. It was all woods and fields out there? In Dublin?

"The Ward, it's like a rabbit warren all the little roads and that."

"Where are all the houses and stuff?"

"Money talks, did nobody tell you that? The locals, you can be sure they keep it that way too."

He poked gently at the screen.

"So there's the Airport, right there. And that's us here now, Howth. Malahide's over there." His finger wandered uncertainly before he dabbed at the screen again. "The Murphys' place, Jenn Cummins like, it's maybe a mile from that pub as the crow flies."

The crow? The whole area here was still in a no-man's land in my mind, where surprise and bafflement couldn't exist apart. Spots began to fiddle with something on his laptop. I looked out through the sheers again. The harbour was right there. Picturesque, sea view, people coming and going – Sonia'd be absolutely mad about the place. So had I just stumbled into a solution? Had destiny sent me here to even the score? To let me grab a win at last? Or maybe I had just caught Mackeritis. His hankering for crisis-discount bargains had attached itself to me.

Still – what a view. That bumpy little island was Ireland's Eye and behind it, a proper island, Lambay. Some mental indigestion had been building in me, and now it inched into clearer view in my mind: Spots' guff about 'a bomb.' You couldn't think 'bomb' and not think IRA. Did that mean I should rethink Hynes' lousy effort at a Nordy accent? Maybe. But if it had been a bloody bomb, Spots wouldn't be here. He'd be in flitters somewhere, or in an operating room, or in hiding. So all this carry-on, this secret agent type drive-around drama of his: just to misdirect me? A big part of Spots' M.O. was getting you to underestimate him. The man shouldn't be walking, shouldn't be cold-turkey drug-free. He probably shouldn't be a free man – alive even, come to think of it.

Christ: it was a bit late to be trying to second-guess things.

I let go the drapes, and watched them settle and fall still. That feeling had crept back, the one that I figured was warning that I was getting closer and closer to walking off the edge of something. I drew one of the curtains aside again. Yes, there was a problem with my Sonia-Howth fantasy. Yes, the view was great but I had entirely overlooked the big picture. Swish and all as this gaff was, it was actually the wrong side of Howth altogether. It faced north.

25

Spots was now in pronouncement mode: I was to drive. I actually didn't mind. I figured it'd be a change from thinking too much – or too little. Hoped.

Soon we were skirting Baldoyle. Then, as easy as that, we were into Donaghmede. Darndale we got through handy enough to boot. The magic kept working all the way out to the N2.

"A few miles to the turn-off," Spots said. "The Ward. St Margarets is another name from it."

I pushed the Beemer a bit in third. It was ancient, but it had a lot of poke left in it all the same.

"You've had this tour planned for a while."

Even if I had put it in writing, he'd have ignored me.

"Another sign'll come up," he said, "for the M1, the Belfast Road. Then the Bypass. Take the Bypass. You'll see the sign for St Margarets soon enough."

The curving ramp on to the M50 cambered enough that I could leave it in fourth. The satellite really hadn't lied: fields and hedges and overgrown ditches closed in around us right away. A sign came up: Derry 215. Not that far when you thought about it. Not far enough. A sign for St Margaret's came up soon after. I geared down for the inevitable roundabout.

Then it was narrower roads and thicker hedges, and even more trees. Ivy then, oceans of it, rooted in what I guessed were old stone walls buried in the banks running along to both sides. Whitethorn and blackthorn began to elbow their way into the party. The, but Every now and then a gap or a fenced gate flashed momentary views of small, grassy, hemmed-in fields. A horse standing in a meadow. The gable end of a wall. A barn. A billboard type sign appeared, with holes. (something) residences ... unrivalled splen... (dour?) and unpara... (something else) elegance...

A plane came in low over the hedges, so low I actually ducked.

"Told you," I heard Spots say just before the roar of the engines caught us.

On we went, slower, deeper into this overgrown-jungle corner of the county Dublin.

"You're scared of planes now, are you?"

Signs of trouble in paradise arrived on the roadside: bags of rubbish in the ditches, a good number split open. Spots hadn't stirred in a while. I wondered if he'd noticed a single thing most of the way here. He looked like he was meditating, or something.

"Turn in there. Yep, that one. It's a short cut."

He knew short-cuts here? I mentally filed it under Suspicious.

As though we hadn't been on a narrow enough road already, we now entered what could only be described as a green tunnel made of ivy and thick, scruffy hedges. The trees too were doing their damnedest to hide any remaining bits of sky.

"Tell me there isn't hobbits living here."

"Don't mind about hobbits. More like knackers hereabouts."

I'd wondered. Roads like this were ideal for the older tinker style anyway. The new ones, the dangerous, ganged-up, mad tinkers, they tended to favour spots nearer to facilities. They needed somewhere to park their SUVs and their rigs. I pulled in tight against a hedge to let a lorry go by. A northern registration. A tax move, I figured. Another hint of tinkers in the vicinity.

"Go over the plan again," I said. "But this time, put in the bits you left out before."

He shifted in his seat, setting my nerves on screech again. It wasn't much use reminding myself how we had gone over loading and unloading a dozen times and more, back in the apartment in Howth. How did I know Spots hadn't slipped that clip back into the Beretta and forgotten, or elected to forget, about the safety catch? Madness, what I had done. Absolute madness.

"What's hard about this," he said. "You're telling me that you have never done something like this before? OK. You go in, and you pretend you're a normal person. You buy a drink. You look around. You listen. You talk – the weather, football, whatever."

"But this isn't just any old pub out here in the boonies, is it."

"That's your third time asking me. Same answer: why are you asking me? Wouldn't youse know that? Your 'intel?'"

I had been running the name of the pub over and back in my mind. The White Horse Inn. I just couldn't recall hearing it come up in briefings. That didn't mean it wasn't on the radar with some section, though. Maybe it wasn't a venue for actual transactions or deliveries, what we'd call a clearing-house. It could be just a venue where heads liked to show for the chat, or to float deals.

Deals... God, where to start. It ran the gamut – whatever made money. Weapons, robbed cars. Hijacked lorries and cargoes. Illegals, prostitutes willing and not willing. Drugs, money for drugs, ingredients for labs. Fellas on the run, fellas needing documents, fellas needing cover and hide-outs. That dive out the Naas Road that we raided last year? Talk about a clearing house. We fetched up a million and a half street value of cocaine, lab equipment for meth – we never did find out the destination – and seventy something grand in cash. We also pulled out a Mac10 from under a blanket in the back of a brand new €70K-plus Lexus. That gave us the willies, big time.

"Liam Murphy. Is he building still?"

"Tommy? Newsflash: no builder in all of Ireland is building anything. It's called 'the crash.'"

I braked hard for a scatter of potholes. Rounding the curve, we came up on three caravans and two vans. There were no mounds of rubbish though, no half broken cars, and no horses. I spotted two big, name brand generators next to the caravans.

"Now don't be surprised if you see a few tinkers in that pub."

"In the line of criminal endeavours, you're saying?"

"Well what do you write in your reports? 'Knacker crime' or 'Traveller lifestyle?' Wait, don't bother telling me."

A gap opened in the bank along my side and a surprise mansion appeared behind iron gates. For Sale. A sign for a T junction stuck out from the tangles of growth.

"How old's that picture of Murphy you showed me?"

"It's the same as I told you before – five, six years ago."

In the picture that Spots showed me, Murphy had a semi-Afro head of ginger hair and a beard that put him square in Braveheart territory. He had on a tux, at some wedding.

"All right. Who else am I looking for again?"

"That's what we're here to find out. Keep an ear open for certain accents."

"What, Norn Iron you're talking about?"

Spots didn't answer. He was perusing an old Sat Nav.

"You're close now," he said. "After this bend."

Another big house loomed out from a gap in the bank. There was a paddock and freshly creosoted, horsey type fencing. The greenery quickly closed in again. The next bend ahead quickly unwound and suddenly the overgrown bank and trees were no more.

A long, skinny car park with a building at the end... The White Horse Inn. Not so much scruffy-looking as it was tatty-looking. I saw two vans, four, five cars. An older dinged and dusty Lexus SUV off to the side. There were Dublin and Meath ones, and on one of the vans. A Sprinter with ladders and all sorts of power gear, Kildare reg. No tell-tale yellow regs from the North.

"Not too near now," said Spots.

I parked in sight of the door of the pub and looked around. It was second nature for Spots to be on the lookout for CCTV as well. I soon found the bubble housing of a camera by the line of the gutter. Spots opened the glove compartment and took out a pair of glasses and something else. A moustache? I had to laugh.

"Will you give over. This is no joke."

I watched for a while.

"What're you waiting for," he said then. "Just go, will you."

"Say Murphy doesn't show."

"Stop your fussing. He's there, or he will be there."

"How do you know that?"

"You're out of order asking that. Remember, it was it you came begging for help."

I gave him an eyeball tussle for several moments.

"Christ Tommy, just git, will you? I don't want to sit here and get eyed by every dog and divil that comes by."

"What's to worry about?"

"Just go. I'll be ready, no problem."

"'Ready' means what?"

"What do you think? Ready to take a powder if you come out there on the trot."

He turned his head a little and nodded toward the open space across the road.

"I'll wait in there."

Beyond the half-dozen cars was a semi-organized jumble of half-ruined lorries and trailers and rigs. Flat or almost flat tires had left them leaning and sagging and squatting one way or the other. So this was what had become of those mad monsters that were the bane of everyone's life during the boom, as they raced around at warp speed, whisking diggers and what-have-you all over the place? Here they were helpless looking, like abandoned toys huddling together for comfort. 'For Sale Or Lease.' Sure. Not bloody likely.

"Don't be worrying, man. I'll be down there. OK?"

I'd been trying to ignore that curdling in my stomach. Now it felt like there wasn't enough air in the car. I reached again for some calm. This was a pub, I thought, not a gangster HQ. I'd come here of my own free will. And I wasn't expecting anyone here to cough up Gary Cummins' whereabouts, fate, destiny or choice of toothpaste. It was only my mind holding me back.

And then I was out. Just as I set foot on the tarmacadam apron that joined the car park to the road proper, a car with two fellas in it pulled in, and rap pouring out the windows. I tacked off to the left a bit and foostered around in my pockets as though for a mobile. They were thirsty fellas. The car had barely stopped before they heaved themselves out of it and made a bee-line for the pub door. I moved on. A lot new-looking power tools lay strewn about the back seat of their car.

The varnish on the door to the pub needed a serious refresh. Mind you, there wouldn't be much headway unless the kick marks across the bottom of the door were dealt with first. I pushed it open just in time to almost collide with an oul lad in dungarees and wellies. He pulled up like he had been interrupted in a ballet move. I held open the door and stepped aside.

"A gennelman an' ash collar."

A culchie accent. For a moment I was confused. Dublin city centre couldn't be more than ten or twelve miles away. His shoulder almost grazed my chest going by. Floothered he was, and he was going to drive in that condition? I watched him through the open doorway. A pick-up was pulling in outside now, a not-so-new rattley diesel with a Meath reg. The oul lad hove to. He managed a lame-looking fist-pump. It was enough to nearly send him on a wobble.

"Come on Rooney!" he called out.

It was a work truck, not a suburban statement, and it had no shortage of scrapes and gouges to prove it. I saw handles of a wheelbarrow sticking up over the cab, two shovels, and a machine for tamping down gravel.

"In the net, ya boy ya!"

The driver's window slid down. The Rooney bit made sense now: He did actually did look like Wayne Rooney, a Wayne Rooney who didn't shave and had a mobile stuck to his ear. Sure enough, there was a Man United item at the top of the windscreen.

"Fifteen mill a year? Can't get it in the net? Sell the fecker! *Get rid of him!* Jaysus!"

I was never much on the football, but even I knew Wayne Rooney was having a crap season of it. Not money-wise, of course.

"Right, Liam?"

Ireland was never short of Liams. Not all of them'd have ginger hair, though, or that heavy ginger fuzz happening. The driver let down his mobile and waited for the oul lad to get around the edge of the bonnet. Said oul lad was clapping his hands and rubbing them and walking at the same time. It looked like he was having a fit. He latched on to the side mirror to steady himself.

"You'd do better than that overpaid, useless... *bollocks*! They'd sign you in a flash!"

A rule of booze is that it's only the gargled ones that appreciate their own jokes. This 'You're the spit of Wayne Rooney' thing had been going on a while, I surmised. The Liam bloke rubbed his forehead and bashfully looked around.

A belch burst through the cackles. The oul lad fell to coughing again.

"In the net," he gasped." That's all. *For Jaysus sakes, just put the bleeding ball in the bleeding net.*"

I'd been holding the door with my foot while I employed my usual go-to: faking a sudden, imaginary preoccupation with something I'd forgotten. Yet I knew that this Liam bloke had scoped me out. A last look through the closing door showed me the oul lad meandering off down the road. An exhaust pipe rattled as an engine was switched off, and before the door met the jamb entirely, I heard the sharp ratchet of a hand brake yanked up.

I was right-away immersed in an orchestra of all-too-familiar smells, of beer and mildew and B.O. backed by that flowery stink of cleaner leaking in from the jacks. This place was a step back in time i.e. just a pub. No plush corners, no fancy glass or vegetation, or spiff blackboard with Catch of the Day or 'Carvery.' Zero espresso either. A quick look-around had also led me to believe that there were around about a dozen or so persons on the premises. Nobody here caught up in the rush of modern life then.

I hadn't lit on any sign of posh, but I didn't pick up a dosser / skanger vibe either. Mostly working fellas, it looked like, or at least fellas who knew how to work if they had to. That laughing pair who had tumbled out of the rap-and-power-tools filled car, were the youngest here. Almost definitely stoned. The only woman, late fifties or early sixties, with a red, outdoor face and wet eyes, was deep into it with a bloke who had the look of a jockey run to fat. Down two steps to wherever that flower-type carpet led to might be other customers.

I doubted it. Any 'action' here this time of day resided with the fellas at the bar.

Sky Sports was on. Some panel were talking about football, while pictures of stars who I probably should know appeared and disappeared behind them. The fella behind the bar looked to be a fit for what Spots described to me i.e. the owner, 'Pa Joe'. He had a vaguely unhappy, maybe out-of-order-intestinally look to him. He broke off a halting conversation with a guy sporting a grey pony-tail and a denim shirt to offer a non-committal nod.

"What can I get you, boss."

I ordered pint of lager shandy. Any lager, but with 7 Up. A quick uplift of the eyebrows as he turned away hinted to me that he didn't get many such namby-pamby orders. I started assembling coins on the counter top, and I waited, and I listened. Some head on the panel declared that Manchester City had a worrisome injury list. Furthermore, he was gutted by the team's loss to so-and-so. Gutted? The country was on a trolley, and this guy was 'gutted' by a football result.

Pony Tail surfaced from picking up a shopping bag by his feet.

"So Jimmy boy," said Pa Joe, half-way through topping up my Budweiser with the 7 Up. "Back to the books with you, is it."

Pony Tail seemed tense. I wondered if he had made me.

"I'd better," Pony Tail said, and sloped off. Pa Joe placed my shandy on the counter and lifted Pony Tail's empty glass, and wiped the counter beneath. I tried harder to filter out the guff on the telly. So far I couldn't pick up any of what the three blokes further down the counter were talking about. And where was Mr. Liam Probably Murphy? What had held him up outside?

Pa Joe leaned in and wiped the counter next to me.

"I'll tell you this much." He stopped wiping and stepped back and dropped the cloth onto some shelf or sink below the counter. "A lot of fierce well educated people in this country. You know?"

Was there a different accent here in this part of Dublin?

"You said it, all right."

"Desperate the way things is going. A lot of stress out there, a lot. Not a speck of work."

"The building trade, you're thinking of?"

"That too of course," he said. "Now Jimmy there, the lad who just left? Jimmy worked a JCB. The money?"

"Great while it lasted."

"I'm telling you. Not much on the horizon now but."

He had wet eyes but they weren't clear at all.

"How about yourself?"

"Little enough," I said. "I try to spread myself around."

Pa Joe stopped wiping and waited. Something about his face put me in mind of a dog.

"Locksmithing," I said. "I started but I never finished. I do electrical, plumbing too."

"You can never know enough plumbing. That's what they say."

His eyes left leave mine for an arrival behind me.

"Liam ould son. The minute I say 'plumbing,' in you come."

It was Murphy. He took up a spot at the counter a few feet from me. I edged aside a bit and gave him a quick once-over and a nod. In his return nod I saw a repeat of his earlier effort to see if maybe we had met before. He turned his mobile in his hand, over again and again, like a dealer with a pack of cards. He had the dried, calloused paws of a man in the building trade.

"Plumber, did I hear you say?"

So Murphy had ears then. The voice was a surprise. A bloke this size, and such a soft voice?

"Well I can do enough of it. But it's really locks and alarm systems is my thing."

"Alarms," said Pa Joe. "You're in the right country for alarms."

That was my chance to divert. I came up with a few considered curses for our leaders and statesmen and, of course, our bankers. Pa Joe smiled thinly in a putting-up-with-it sort of way.

Murphy took his pint from the counter and ambled down toward the three men. They'd been attentive since he showed up. Which said to me they had been waiting for him. Looking for work, I wondered. There was only the odd word out of them now. They spoke only after Murphy has said something. But what he was actually saying to them, I had no clue. All I had was the back of his head, and their eyes on him. One of them ticked my box for possible trouble on the horizon: the blondie-fair-haired one with baby blues floating like egg yolks on bloodshot whites.

As well as my acting skills and well-honed intuition, I had minor fiddling and juggling abilities to fall back on. There was a beer mat to toy with, my change on the counter to rearrange. Two more blokes, younger, arrived. A boisterous pair. It wouldn't be the first drink they'd had recently. I kept an eye on Murphy in the mirror, but all I was getting was a profile as he lifted his glass every now and then. He had finished with talking, it seemed. He looked more inclined to listen now. He also looked distracted. Which, I was beginning to believe, was a tell that here was a man just going through the motions. A man with more than chit-chat on his mind. The phone too, the way he kept rolling it in his hand.

Pa Joe began a slow patrol up and down the bar. He stopped once in a while to wipe under a glass, to rearrange a beer mat, to listen in to one of the new arrivals rabbiting on about some car he has that was driving him mad with repairs. Minutes passed, and the ads come on again. I could feel the shandy beginning to do its sly work. I was coming down from taking a longish go of it when I caught an eye on me. It was that blondie-headed one, Mr. Baby Blue. He looked away immediately but it was too late. You simply cannot hide the fact that you're keeping an eye on someone in your side vision. The more you try, the more obvious it is.

Pa Joe was back then, doing more unnecessary wiping.

"Living around here, are you?"

"Not yet, no."

I could tell he wasn't sure whether to go with this 'wit' or not.

"It's not up to me," I explained. "You go where the job takes you these days."

This seemed to appeal to him enough to stop him wiping.

"So you're looking for a bit of work then, are you."

I posed a question with my eyebrows. He nodded toward the group around Murphy.

"Doesn't hurt to ask," he said.

"That's Liam Murphy then, just came in?"

The eyes stayed on me for a bit.

"You know Liam do you."

"I know the name is all. A mate of mine, he worked for Liam, back, you know."

He started moving the cloth around again.

"Wife and kids?"

"No. Not yet. I'm a slow starter. That's me Ma talking."

He stopped wiping and stood back. I waited for a question but all I got was a stare. There was most definitely a change in the air. I noted Liam Murphy lifting his phone to his ear. I further noted that he hadn't dialed a number, but used one from his contacts. The men with him seemed highly interested in the surface of the bar in front of them, an empty glass, or even the view down toward the lower lounge. I took another go of my shandy, and caught Mister Blue Eyes glancing over again. When I ventured back toward Pa Joe, I was met with the same unwavering stare.

"Tell me. What's a man need to call himself a locksmith?"

"Ah I can't tell you. It's top secret."

His stare grew heavier.

"It's apprenticing. You pick it up on the job mostly."

"And the plumbing? Or was it electrical work you said?"

I took another slow sip of the shandy and looked up at the telly.

"You get them mixed up, that'd be a disaster. Wouldn't it?"

The telly only seemed to be louder. That was because nobody was talking now.

"They teach you that palaver down in Templemore, did they?"

I slid my coins off the counter.

"Well, Mister Locksmith? They've got youse Guards learning to pick locks now?"

"I don't know if you're you running a pub here, or a circus."

To call Pa Joe's eyes hostile would be incorrect. It was more triumph, and disgust.

"Hard chaw are you? Mr. Plain Clothes? Or just a spoofer?"

"Check them tablets you're taking. Sounds to me like you got the wrong ones."

"Hit the road pal. While you still can."

I looked down the bar toward Murphy and his crew. This time, Baby Blue Eyes made eye contact. Murphy had finished his phone call. He was making a point of not looking my way.

"And don't be in any rush back," I heard Pa Joe say.

I pretended to casually finish my pint but I focused on the space around me, and my path to the door. Pa Joe's words were for others' consumption but they followed me as I edged off the stool.

"Can you believe it? The cheek of them? Hassling decent people. Unbelievable."

26

No Beemer?

A cold wave washed up my spine. The bastard – he got me to go into that snake-pit and then promptly done a bunk. Left me here with no phone, no wheels, no explanations.

Then, through the windows of a parked car, I caught sight of a red bonnet. A few steps more and I saw it was the Beemer. I headed over.

"How'm I supposed to see you all the way over here?"

Spots righted himself in the seat and made a long, slow blink, and studied the dashboard. The pound shop specs gave him the look of a sleepy geezer.

"That was Liam Murphy in that pick-up," he said. "Right?"

"It looked like him, all right. The oul lad called him Liam."

"Tell us, what's the story inside?"

"What, in there? Why do you think I'm out here?"

Spots did an annoying eyebrow thing, and shrugged.

"I got made, is the story. The owner bloke, Pa Joe? There's a contrary bollocks if ever – "

"- What else, though. What else did you see."

A lorry came around a turn in the road, squeaking and lurching. Spots watched it passing, followed it until it disappeared.

"Well?"

"Well nothing. What're you keeping from me here?"

He massaged his eyebrows as if to concentrate harder.

"There you go again," he said. "The drama. The notions."

"Something's going on. You've got something up your sleeve."

He stopped massaging and looked down at his fingertips.

"'Something' this and 'something' that. What happened to that mindfulness thing you said you said you were trying?'"

"Who told you to bring me here? Who?"

"Who-who. Listen to yourself. Jaysus, Tommy. Really?"

"You've got some angle going here."

"Says the fella whose place was *not* set on fire. Says the fella comes to me looking for -"

"– OK, how much were you paid to bring me here then?"

"Paid? What I'm hearing here is you losing the run of yourself."

Maybe it was the earnest gaze or the gentle tone, but I felt the rest of my accusations weaken then. Or maybe Spots' telepathic talents were at work: *I'm here now, amn't I? You think I'd have waited until now to pull some stunt on you?*

"This is one weird dump here. There's a bad feel to the whole place."

Spots maintained his mild gaze.

"Liam Murphy," he said. "What was he doing in there?"

"Forget Liam Murphy. What gives here? Level with me."

"Was he having a pint? Chatting with someone?"

"I saw him make a call. Look, let's get the hell out of here."

Spots nodded thoughtfully. He looked at his watch and reached for the ignition.

"We'll go up the road a bit first," he said. "Have a little think."

Well, it was something. Away from here at least.

Maybe five, six hundred metres back the road, Spots slowed by some signs: Trespassers Prosecuted, No Dumping. Between the signs stood a padlocked swing barrier blocking a grassy track that vanished into a rake of lilac and fuchsia run wild. Between gaps in the foliage I made out anti-tinker trenches and beyond them, an old pebbledash house adorned with bonfire marks and blocked-in windows, and ancient, H-Block graffiti. A collapsed roof crowned the ensemble, joists clawing up through the leaves like grey bones.

He reversed in until I heard a clank – the barrier.

I listened to the coolant gurgling and the steady ticking from the block, and the birds. The shandy had made me fierce drowsy. And I needed a leak. A car passed along the road as I found my spot. The birds in these parts were serious noise merchants, but the faint smell of lilac was good enough compensation. That other smell in the air was pig shit, I was sure of it. I did not like the look of those trenches, not one bit.

"I'll tell you one thing," I said then, mission accomplished and me pulling the door shut again. "You know your way around here, so you so. Interesting."

"You think so, do you."

"Yeah I think do. You knew to park here, for one thing."

"I see a place, I pull in. You see a big theory in that?"

"I don't need a theory. I can tell you sussed the place out already."

"Eh, come here. I have a question for you. You're a man of the world, right? You'll have the answer, I'm sure. OK. What do women look for?"

"Stop it. Look, the item I brought, I made a mistake. Give it back to me."

"In a husband, I mean. What does a woman look for."

"Stop changing the subject. Where is it, the bag?"

"The bad boy thing makes sense. Think about it a minute."

"Just gimme. I'll settle for the important bits for now."

Spots looked at me like I was a lab rat that had just recited the Our Father, in sign language.

"We're calling this off," I said. "Where is it?"

"Whoa there. Contrary's one thing, but going back on a promise?"

"What 'promise?' I wasn't thinking straight. Give me the firing pin at least."

"My point is," he said, reached out to pluck a leaf, "that bad boy thing? That's evolution at work. Supposedly, like. The bad boy, he carries the genes for survival. Right?"

"Look, I'll drive. Hop out you, and I'll take the wheel."

Spots only seemed to slip deeper into thought.

"That's all that progress is," he said. "Really, when you boil it all down. Going out on a limb. Reckless carry-on even. Like a controlled madness really – that's evolution for you. Not pretty."

"I'll drop you off at the pub and you talk to Murphy yourself. First you tell me where –"

"– I'd consider it. As long you don't come crying to me after."

"After what? After sitting here like gobshites, with no plan?"

"There is a plan, Doubting Thomas. Hey, does your Ma still call you that?"

"What is 'a plan'? And what's with all this yapping anyway?"

"The plan? All right, I'll tell you. The plan is, we wait."

Neither of us spoke for a while. I ran through possibilities again in my mind. Shove Spots out the door. Impossible. Just root around and find the Beretta, and head off on my own. And miss whatever it was that Spots believed we'd get here?

"That oul lad," he said then. "Three sheets in the wind and all. But that Wayne Rooney business, what did that tell you?"

"I don't know. That the oul lad has a drinking problem?"

Spots tapped his temple twice. His face had taken on a grimly patient expression.

"Some copper you are. What it should tell you is this: Liam Murphy is not a man to go losing his rag."

A notion began to glow feebly at the back of my mind. The words were not there yet.

"Furthermore, it also says that people laugh at Liam Murphy behind his back. Why? Oh they're way smarter than him. That's what they *think*, these local yokels here. But you know the funny thing?"

"He got to marry Tony Cummins' daughter."

"Well aren't you the clever boy."

"Stop this riddle shite. What exactly are you driving at?"

"Ah, your favourite question. Your only question, half the time. God, but it's a dirty business you're in. But that's the whole law-and-order caper for you.

Yes, seeing the bad in people. You should try to see the good instead. Hard, I know, but you have to try."

This was not a Spots Feeney I knew. Was he stoned?

"Oh yes," he went on, "fierce clever people, we are. We look at Liam Murphy and we see ...? We see a gobshite. Nice fella and all, but a gobshite all the same. But someone knows better. Better than all of us clever people. Sees something that we don't."

"Jenn Cummins you're talking about."

"Correct. The joke's on us, Tommy. We're the real iijits – we are. And do you know why?"

"The meek shall inherit the earth?"

"You're close, actually. Though I know bloody well the way you said it, you don't for a second believe it. Well here's the answer: it's because the Liam Murphys of the world, they're the ones who come through in the end."

He looked down the bonnet, gently nodding his head.

"All we are's genes. That's the order of business in life. So, all that cleverality from people? All the PhD, diddly-aye-day relativity quantum how's-your-father mahogany gaspipes? A cod. A complete cod, every bit of it. That doesn't run the show at all. No. The important stuff, the really important stuff? All behind the scenes."

Behind the scenes. The phrase hit the wrong note with me.

"See Tommy, she got it, Jenn did. She copped to it. Not consciously, now. But what does that matter?"

"I'm driving. You can keep explaining the meaning of life on the way."

"So she went and she found herself – *recruited* I should say – a nice, ordinary, decent bloke. No, he's not in line for Oxford. Didn't invent the Internet or anything. Not Mr. Excitement, or the wittiest wit either, for that matter. What he is not, though, is her oul lad version two. No way Jenn's going to follow in her Ma's footsteps. You can bet your bottom dollar Bernie Cummins made damned sure of that."

If you could've put rueful and ruthless together in one expression, it'd have Spots name on it.

303

"And that's the be-all and end-all of it," he went on. "They didn't need some expert's advice or heart-to-hearts, or deep sessions with a shrink – saving your presence now and no offence intended. It's not about the fancy talk and the tall foreheads. No, it's evolution, plain and simple."

"You sound like a fella I work with. He doesn't make much sense either."

"Fair enough. So you think I'm talking shite."

"Sour grapes is what I'm thinking. You never got to shift Jenn Cummins. Saving your presence et cetera."

Whistling softly once as though he'd dipped his toe in freezing water, he stretched out his arm on the window frame and began to poke the wing mirror.

"OK," I said. "I stayed for the speech. But now we split."

"I hear you. OK, but there's one condition."

I waited.

"I'm after putting myself out a considerable amount here. All right? So it's only right and proper that you bear with me a bit longer."

"What's 'a little bit longer?'"

He looked at his watch again. I did not like the way he seemed to be timing the minutes here.

"Twenty minutes. Then, if there's nothing, OK, we split."

The dopiness from the shandy had kicked in now in earnest. It'd be no great hardship to remain sitting here amid fresh greenery and the sounds of birds. I'd hold my whisht for now.

The next time I looked at the dash clock, fourteen minutes had passed. Karma bonus. I sat up.

"A deal's a deal. Time to skedaddle."

Before Spots could concoct an answer, his eyes skipped toward the road. I heard it now too. Another thing about motorbikes that put me on edge? You hear them a long way off, but you can never really tell how far away it really is. This one, I couldn't even tell which direction it was coming from. It sounded like a biggish engine, and he or she was keeping the bike in third – maybe even second – for engine braking on the bends.

"Does that mean something to you?"

I looked over. Spots wasn't in receiving mode.

"Did you hear what I said? A motorbike."

His answer was a finger raised to his lips. Head tilted then like a dog trying to learn English, he looked up blankly between the leaves. The motorbike picked up speed again, but did not gear up. I caught a flicker between the leaves as it passed the end of the lane: full-face helmet, low handlebars. Shiny exhausts. From Spots came a peculiar, noisy swallow. I noticed a dull shine on his forehead now, more waxy-looking than proper sweat.

"You're expecting someone?"

He made another one of his trademark slow blinks. The motorbike slowed again and I heard the light clank of a gear escaping the clutch. After a few short revs, the engine fell quiet. Spots reached for the ignition key.

"Who or what is that?"

"Fair question," he said. "Let's go take a little gander then."

He worked the Beemer around the ruts back out toward the roadway. He didn't seem to care a damn about the branches scraping along the bodywork. The last of the foliage parted, and then we were out.

It was one of those café racer types, some version of that vintage look that people seemed to be keen on now. He or she had driven it down into a far corner of the car park, or pseudo car park, right to where it ended in that truck park aka graveyard. Notions skittered through my mind. Some fella out for a run on his motorbike. He was taking a smoke break, before slipping in for his pint. But why park out there? Maybe this whole decrepit trucks-and-diggers scenario here was the backdrop for a photo shoot thing. So where was the photographer, and his or her gear set up? A buyer then, a prospective buyer, out to inspect some rigs. Dream on – this stuff would never sell. I had been trying to avoid the obvious – the other merchandise, the items you'd find in demand in every corner of the country. Well, if it was a drug deal, I had a conundrum on my hands. Take a pass, or step in with the badge?

He, she or it began to take off the helmet. The slim build was telling me it was a girl, but I wasn't seeing curves and bumps. After a pause to get the edge by their jaw, the helmet detached completely. I had seen enough.

"Keep going," I said to Spots. "Don't stop."

"Why so because?"

"He'll recognize me, is why. Go."

Spots let Beemer roll on uncertainly in third. We came upon a gate into a field.

"Who is he?"

"I'll tell you later."

I could tell this did not suit Spots. I ignored the repeated turns of his head my way.

"So you saw Murphy's pick-up," he said then. "Right?"

"What about it?"

"The state of it? Scraped, along the side? All banged up?"

"Wait a sec. You're thinking Christy? No – that was a van."

Spots had been concentrating on something in the mirror. He cursed under his breath, yanked the wheel and pulled back out onto the road. A brisk reverse followed, and the Beemer headed back toward the pub.

Murphy's pick-up hadn't moved The motorbike was exactly where it had been too, leaning on its side stand. Motorbike man had placed his helmet on the seat and lit up his smoke. He had a phone to his ear now. He turned when he heard the Beemer, watched it approach.

"That's close enough. Turn around."

"Where do you know him from?"

"None of your business. Turn, for Christ's sake."

Spots tapped the brakes and squinted at the motorbike fella. The fake moustache twitched as he chewed on something.

"Wait a sec. Do you know that guy?"

Spots said nothing.

"You do know him. Where from?"

"Cool it Tommy, will you. You're so jumpy here."

He turned the wheel a tad and let the Beemer roll on. Motorbike man let down his mobile, took a drag on his smoke, and flicked it away. The Beemer stopped. Spots looked over.

"Hold everything," I said. "This is all a cod, what you're doing here. Answer me. What is that guy to you?"

"If I knew him, I'd say so."

His voice had dropped back into a weary-sounding monotone.

"I don't believe you."

"Go and ask him then, why don't you. But you better do it quick because that guy, he's not staying around."

I swore and I climbed out.

Motorbike man looked different out here. He was a lot more interested in Spots than he was in me. Even as I drew closer, it took an effort for him to shift his eyes my way.

"How's it going there. Nice bike, by the way."

He darted another look toward the Beemer. Did Spots's moustache and glasses ensemble have a hypnotic power over him?

"I saw you there over at Hynes' place. The Fast Lane?"

He was not inclined to talk. I heard the Beemer in motion again. Spots was parking it? Motorbike man looked puzzled too.

"You know him, the fella driving the old Beemer there?"

A tightening around the eyes signalled that he'd had enough. He reached for the helmet.

"Massive coincidence seeing you here, all the same. You know?"

He grabbed the helmet with both hands. I reached out before he could raise it. There were weird flecks in his eyes. He was older than I had thought too, wiry rather than skinny too.

"Let go of it. And get out of my face."

"What's your hurry? What're you at here? Hide and go seek?"

"I've got nothing to say to the likes of you."

"Well Jaysus, that's a bit rude. The fella you're supposed to be meeting, aren't you going to phone him at least?"

He pivoted away, pulling the helmet with him, and he raised it again. Half way up, he stopped. I'd heard the tires squeal too. Now I heard an engine being pushed hard. Almost on cue, a newish Carina flew out from behind a hedge.

307

The driver hit the brakes hard before turning in, skidding and shuddering as it came to a stop. As far as I could tell, it was just the driver aboard. I tried harder to make him or her out. When I looked back at Motorbike man his face was much altered. It was the look of someone whose brain was trying to catch up with what his eyes were telling him.

"Is that your date?"

He flicked a look from me to the idling Carina and back. His eyes seemed bigger now, or they stood out more.

"The fella with you," he said, his voice catching, "in that car."

"What about him? Come to think of it, he's acting peculiar too."

His eyes slid back toward the Carina. He shaped up to say something, but there was nary a word.

"You don't one bit look happy. What ails you?"

Again he seemed about to talk. This effort ended in a mouth half open and his upper teeth gumming on his lip. Then he ran.

I heard a handbrake pulled up hard. The Carina shifted on its springs as the door opened. Out stepped Blake. He took a few steps in a heavy plod, and stopped. He didn't seem to notice the bloke quick-stepping toward him. It was me he was interested in.

I heard a few mumbled words: 'another one.' '... I swear...' Blake swung a look toward him but quickly re-latched those fish eyes back on mine. There still hadn't been so much as a flicker of recognition. Motorbike Man had stopped talking. His arms hung out a little, hands opened as though he'd lost his balance. That prickling chill along my spine arced to my scalp.

You don't think of your brain as being dangerous. After all, it's the item that moved us on from throwing spears at dinosaurs. But the brain needs time. And the thing about time is that time is actually a liar. A fickle, spiteful thing, is what it is. As for thinking itself, the pinnacle of creation, you'd wonder why we bother to do it at all. It's more a sabotage machine than anything else. The way it jumbles up *shouldn't* and *won't* and *can't*? X can't happen, you think – oh God no. This, even as X is happening right before your very eyes. But then it piles on more. Yeah well OK, it tries to tell you, if X ever happens, it'll happen to someone else. No way in the wide world can it happen to you.

Except it bloody-well can. What Motorbike Man yanked out from inside his jacket wasn't any mobile phone. You didn't pull back a slide on a mobile phone and then aim it at someone.

A heavy, rolling wave crashed through my chest. And by Jesus the guy was fast. His hand twitched almost immediately. I saw the flash as a fizzing whistle cut the air next to me. Something made a sharp, thump on metal behind me, and a millisecond later came the report. A cold fact that no mental process could sidestep hit me full on then: whoever this fella was, he wasn't just some wild young skanger playing hardman, firing off a gun. He was firing off his shots in a steady, measured manner.

It wasn't training then. It was absolute blind panic.

My flat-out dive to the asphalt didn't register as pain, or even discomfort. It was just the whoof of breath pounded out of my chest. I even heard myself groan in useless protest at the delay in getting out my Sig. Just as I brought it around, a sheet-flash of pain erupted on the side of my face. Another impact sent tiny pieces of asphalt needling into the back of my hand. I rolled away toward the cover of something that I'd been only dimly, incidentally, aware of – this collection of half-abandoned bangers was now the one place in the world in which I desperately wanted to hide.

An engine came to life nearby, revving high. The shots stopped. A desperate hope flared up in me: that was the Carina, and was Blake on the move. He'd scoop up this maniac off the motorbike, and they'd make their getaway. I eased my hand from over my injured eye and let my fingertips trace over the cheekbone. There were fragments of something embedded in the flesh.

I just had to know. Holding my breath, I coaxed up the eyelid a titch. There was light – murky and blurred and bleary, but light nonetheless. Through the scratchy wet film I made out shapes, and even colours. I was about to tease it up a bit more but reflex took over, clapping shut the eyelid again. I looked down at my fingertips. Whatever was overflowing my lashes and pooling in the corners of my eyes was clear. But my relief vapourized in an instant. I was still out here, still exposed. Every pore screeched at me to scarper, and now.

My best move was to get cover here in this junkyard. I sized up a one, a sorry-looking DAF, and I launched into a full-on, one-eyed scramble toward it.

Time immediately threw its nastiest trick at me, marooning me for timeless moments in wide-open space. Then the cabs and doors and panels of the trucks were closing around me. My fingers and knuckles met hard with a bumper and a moment later, my shoulder collided with the top of a wheel. That should have hurt, I thought. I scrambled back up on one knee and pointed the Sig one-handed back in the direction I'd come, and let off three rounds quick-and-dirty. Up on my hunkers then, I scuttled left, half-creeping and half-falling around to the back of a trailer. I nestled in under the end of it and leaning back against a bumper I swept the Sig through the gaps and overhead.

A little jet of hope lit up again. I had cover here now. They knew that I could shoot back too. And surely to God someone in that pub had to have heard the racket by now. But my mind had run ahead of itself again, frantic to slap a happy ending on things. I was waiting – expecting actually – to hear tires squealing as Blake and his sidekick made a getaway. But I'd heard nothing like that. What I heard now instead was an engine down to not much more than an idle. Blake was staying put....? Worse, way worse. That faint sound that I'd been hearing suddenly had an explanation. Those little ticks and pops were the sounds that tires made as they rolled slowly over cracked tarmacadam. This was Blake, getaway car ready to go, keeping pace with that head-case as they closed in to finish the job.

My scalp lifted with fear. I set my hand on the bumper to push off but a sudden shriek of tires and an engine roaring full-on made me drop back down. The hulks around me only amplified the racket. I looked down the gap in time to see the Carina swaying and veering and turning broadside to me as it went by – with a red Beemer attached. The cars seemed to be actually wrestling, the Beemer jostling and elbowing the Carina like it was trying to to throw a leg up over its bonnet. It ended moments later in a grinding crunch loud enough to count as an explosion.

And then – nothing.

No banging doors, no shouts, no running footsteps – but no shooting, either. One engine was still running, clanking a bit and making a flapping noise. I tried to steady my breathing, only for my hammering heart to fill up the quiet instead. That starburst of relief bursting in my chest came of knowing that I was not on my own out here. It had to be Spots in the middle of all that mayhem. Better yet, Blake was on the receiving end of that hammering too. Not something you'd walk away from. Rage surged in then. That weedy little bollocks on the motorbike had had the gall to shoot at a Guard? Well the shoe was on the other foot now, by God.

But some part of my brain still had contact with sanity. Its message was as convincing as it was simple: no mad moves here. Things might have turned my way now, but adrenalin heroics were a no-go. I was an injured, one-eyed copper in unfamiliar terrain. As for support, I didn't even know what shape Spots was in – or Blake, for that matter. What I needed to do was to not do something stupid. Motorbike fella had surely gotten the message now too. If he had a brain at all, he'd be doing his best to get the hell away from here. Well let him. We'd find him soon enough.

Two loud cracks exploded this fantasy, rattling and reverberating between the lorries behind me. Somebody yelled, I couldn't tell who. A withering dread had closed over me. Another gunshot – a louder, deeper-sounding one – split the air. A quick volley of two shots followed, the second louder than the first. I wedged myself deeper in behind the wheels and tried to make sense of it. Had I gotten things backwards? Spots up close most definitely qualified as a hardman. But he was still a guy who was held together by pins. He'd have taken the bigger hit in that bang-up. So those gunshots meant that Blake was still in good-enough working order to get into the fight. Those shots might have given motorbike man an opening too. Any moment now he'd pop up right next to me. I forced open my bad eye again. Still nothing. Just that same blurry mush and enough bits of grit to make me quickly close it again.

Everything around me looked more dangerous by the second. Could your mind actually scream at you? Mine was. It was yelling at me that I was in a trap. I edged out a tad to plot a move. A loud crack sent me back so fast my arse actually bounced off the ground. Scrambling back up, I dived or lurched sideways, frantically looking for the darkest, dimmest place that I could find. Back on my hunkers again, I forced myself half-under the bed of a tipper lorry and madly fanned the Sig across every bit of space around me. Where that shot had come from, or how close it had come, I couldn't tell. Spots, I thought. But yelling would only give me away. Same for him – and that was if he was in one piece. But if he wasn't, and if those shots had actually come from Blake, I was truly on the losing end now. There just had to be a place to disappear into. The panic had crowded everything out and whole body was twitching. I tightened my grip on the Sig, bobbed a couple of times and braced my knees for the launch.

And right away stopped. Something had bobbed up out of the chaos. I looked down at where my fingertips were tightly pressed to the ground. A mad, impossible longing took hold of me: if I could only magically vanish under the tarmacadam here, out of sight and safe. Mad, sure, but it had left a not-mad notion in my mind. I ducked down until my head was inches from the ground and looked across the ground. They had plenty of clearance, all right. Any sinking or collapsing would've happened already. They'd been parked here for ages. Scooting along in there, maybe rolling even, I could cover ground. Once I'd gone a good ways, I'd up and do the unexpected and make a mad, zig-zag sprint for the side door of the pub. That point of departure would be sixty, maybe eighty feet away too. Nobody was that good with a handgun.

There was something weirdly reassuring about being on all fours down here. A memory of carefree childhood play? Sharp patches of light cut between the shadows and dark outlines of wheels and axles, and fallen or dumped junk. In the middle distance, an irregular slice of glare opened out to greenery so intensely coloured it seemed to be glowing. Yet the more I looked around, the darker and more crowded with obstacles it looked in here. The spaces looked tighter now too, more confined. And what if Blake or the mechanic fella copped on to my move? The most I'd be able to do then would be to wriggle away somehow. Another trap in the making.

Dithering was not an option. Every muscle and sense was screeching at me to get on the move. A moment from getting back on my hunkers again, I caught a flicker near one of those patches of light. Had it been just a speck of something in my eye? The eyelash itself maybe? The moments ticking by made me feel like I was up to my neck in boiling static.

But then it happened: a denim leg ending in a black boot slowly emerged from behind the curve of a tire. He was backing away. Heading back to his motorbike? Whatever was going on out there with Blake, it didn't matter a damn to him. He wouldn't be taking orders from Blake. This fella wanted out.

So why was he walking backwards?

Because he wasn't going anywhere. He couldn't. Getting out to his motorbike meant he'd be out in the open, himself. And this was the guy who was had pulled a gun on a copper. Not just to scare me off either: he intended to use it on me. For that alone, he'd be looking at ten to fifteen. Leaving me to come after him was a risk he wasn't willing to take. His answer? To lead me by the nose, draw me closer to his bike. The moment I'd get up to take a look, he'd be waiting – him or Blake. Maybe him *and* Blake.

Yet this little mental preview had not left me paralyzed again. It had thrown me right through fear, into outrage. Bad enough that this guy was trying to shoot someone who'd done him no harm, someone he didn't even know – or he did know me and he was still willing to do for me. Now he was playing me for a gobshite too?

My mind cleared. I sank back down again. Settling my forearms along the oily ground, I drew my support hand up and under and reset the end of the grip on my palm. I loosened my arms a bit then and plotted him another backwards step. I had already drawn in a deep breath. It was time now to let it out, slow and easy.

To my absolute astonishment back came that leg. I fired.

There was a loud pop and an even louder hiss, and some enormous undercarriage lurched and sank lower between us. I stopped at three. I'd seen him dropping and reaching down for something. He was trying to wriggle away. My eye burned from the effort to keep him lined up. I squeezed off another shot, and then another. Panic swept back in: I had only four rounds left.

But he was still there. Had that been some mad mirage from my imagination, thinking that I'd seen something fly up, or scatter, off him with that second shot? I lowered the Sig a bit and rubbed at my eye, and stared again. His head was tucked in, but a part of his forehead was turned toward me. I closed my eye and massaged it a bit, and tried again. Not a budge out of him. He was hurt? I stared until the burning became too much again. Next time when I looked, something had changed. I took a couple of slow blinks. It was a line on his forehead. A dark, crooked line reaching down from his hair. And, unless my one eye had given up on me now, it was getting longer.

And just as I made myself process this again, the line started again but this time lower and moving faster now.

A cold, heavy current washed through me. Bit by bit the world came back. Suddenly I had a pain worse than the stinging on my face and cheek. My shoulder: it had been grinding into stones, or gravel. I shifted a little to dislodge them and ran my fingers over my face again. My eyelid was even more sticky now and when I slid it up, everything was still wet, still blurry. The watery blood on my fingers reminded me of the scrapes and cuts we collected when we flew off our bikes or took headers in the yard trying to prove we were Man United material before the bell rang.

A sound of shuffling threw me into a spasm, twisting my upper body to bring the Sig around to where the noise had come from.

"Tommy?"

It sounded like Spots, but a hoarse, fogey version of him.

"You in there? Can you hear me, Tommy?"

"Yeah I can hear you. What's going on out there?"

"Nothing's going on. It's sorted. Are you all right?"

"What do you mean 'sorted?' Is Blake there?"

"He's here, all right. But it's OK."

"That shooting –"

"No, no. That's finished now. Look I'm coming right next to you. So don't be doing anything mad with that gun. All right?"

The figure blocking part of an overcast but still blinding sky looked like an older version of Spots, slumped and drawn-looking and pale. Bits of the crap disguise moustache were still stuck on.

"Easy does it," he said. "You're hurt. I'll give you a hand up."

"The other fella, the motorbike fella?"

"That madman who was chasing you? Yeh. He's over there."

He paused to clear his throat. His eyes were down to slits. It was like he was sleepwalking, or over-sedated.

"Looks a goner to me, Tommy."

"You said Blake -"

"Don't mind about him. Look, you're safe to come out."

I wanted to ask something but I couldn't assemble the words.

"Come on out. I swear."

It was way too quiet. I got slowly onto my knees and waited for the woozy light to stop its pulsing. That was when I noticed the Beretta held loosely and carelessly by his side.

"What are you doing with that?"

"What happened your face, your eye? Jesus."

"Shut up about that. What did you do, I'm asking you."

"We need a plan, Tommy – a plan. You hear me?"

"You used it, didn't you. You lunatic."

He angled his head and squinted at me for several moments. Then, without a word, he backed out ahead of me into the yard, tugging the bits of moustache off his lip. What I saw out there in the yard then left me gaping. Some giant, raging kid had squeezed Blake's Toyota and the Beemer together into one new something. All around it, bits of glass and plastic caught the light.

"Is that Blake in that car?"

Spots eyed the ground between us and nodded. He cleared his throat again and stretched his neck a bit.

"Tommy. Listen to me." His tone matched his gaze, a confusing mixture of exhaustion and concern. "You're after getting a fierce knock on the head, so you are. You're shook. Concussion for sure."

315

"No it isn't -"

"- And you were out of it for a bit too."

"No I wasn't. Lookit, this is a Guard you're talking to!"

"You think I'm blind, do you? Look, I'm just trying to tell you something."

His face had taken on a bit more colour now. There was a light in his eyes now, as though something glowed behind them.

"Listen to me, Tommy, for once. If you are thinking that we're just going to let them bastards take us down, you have got another thing coming. Because that is just not going to happen."

I didn't want to look down to where he held the Beretta. A numbness had settled like a blanket on my mind. It was refusing to make sense of the contradictions coming at me. Spots Feeney with bits of a ridiculous disguise still pasted to his face. A Spots Feeney seething with anger, but with something else that I couldn't be sure of radiating out too. Exhilaration. Maybe even joy?

"You think you know what happened here, Tommy? Do you? Well you don't. All you are thinking of is – whoa, where are you going?"

27

I took my time getting up, bracing my hands on my knees and waiting for the sky to swing back up to where it belonged. Notions kept trickling into my mind but wouldn't stick around to make any sense. I straightened up more and risked a few steps.

"Hey hey hey," Spots said. "Where are you going, I said."

Beyond Spots was that gapped hedge that marked the turn in to the carpark. The pub was further away that I'd thought. But surely to God somebody had heard the shooting at least? I saw a gun now, a black semi-automatic. A Glock. Of course it was a Glock. The status item, the hardman's statement. But what was he really? A mechanic? I gently toed the pistol away a couple of feet. I didn't want to see : I had to see. The mind immediately commenced its trickery. That blood coming steadily from under his head – that was movement, wasn't it? And movement meant life. I stared at his eyelashes. Any moment now they'd flutter and open. He was concussed. He was resting.

"There's no point. All right?"

Spots' tone was so transformed that I had to look over.

"You had to," he said. "You had no choice, none."

The full heft of things fell on me then. I'd taken this man's life. That lucky shot to his leg, wouldn't that have been enough? He hadn't been coming at me then. But I had still I let off two more rounds. I'd aimed them all too, insofar as you could ever 'aim' a pistol. There was no denying it. So I must have intended it. But maybe ...? I should at least check for vitals.

"No, Tommy. No. Nothing you can do."

I looked back at the Toyota. The passenger window was out in a heap on the ground and even from here I could see the trails of blood that led like drawn lines from a spray of blood on the headrest. I re-worked my grip of the Sig for a low-ready walk, and headed over.

"Tommy?"

"Shut up. Not another word out of you."

I could still smell cordite. Swollen from the gunshot, Blake's eyes stood out like small glassy islands. He looked like he was reminiscing, or daydreaming. The entry wound was right where his eyebrow started. A baby finger-wide path of blood that flowed down from it over his nose and mouth continued to drip steadily onto his belly. It had had streaked Blake's right hand too, and the pistol still held in it. I'd seen a few of these Kel-Tecs before, but here it looked like a toy. A dainty little purse gun? It was almost unworthy.

I looked around the wound again. I couldn't make out burns or residue. But what could a more-or-less one-eyed copper who was maybe off his head actually see? Still the thought forced itself on me: Spots swotting up amateur forensics to know that he'd need to shoot from as far back as he could, to avoid the giveaway signs? And so cool, calm and collected that he'd taken his time and aimed so well? The answer had to be yes.

"That could just as easy be me – or you."

Yelling sent daggers through my eye. Spots wasn't having any of it.

"No way," he said Spots then. "No way. You hear?"

"I know what you did."

"What was I supposed to do? Let him do for me? And you next?"

With that jerking stride that he'd used for so long I'd forgotten there ever existed a Spots who'd actually walked properly, he drew in close. He was breathing heavily but holding back on the exhale.

"This is what happened, so listen. That lunatic on the motorbike? He did for Blake. Yes he did. They got into this huge big row, it got out of hand, and then they went haywire the both of them, shooting."

Why was it only now that I noticed latex gloves sticking out of his pocket?

"You knew this was going to happen. You planned it."

"Plan? You're mad. How could anyone plan this? Here, sit down before you keel over."

I shoved his arm away. The effort made the light swell and pop softly around me.

"Maybe I was an iijit before," I managed, "but now I get it."

"You get what? You get a twenty stretch? Losing everything, you get? Destroy your Ma, your Sonia? That's what you get?"

He tilted his head and pinned a look of deep concern on me.

"Go through it again, OK? That fella, he turned on Blake. Then he tried to make a run for it. But you caught him in time, so you did, and you settled his hash there and then. You'd no choice. It was him or you. You had to do it. You had to."

He stepped back then and after looking around, he began to wrestle with himself. But the way he was swapping the Beretta from one hand back to the other alarmed me.

"Point that away, or put it down – and hit safety on it first."

Spots ignored me. He elbowed out of his shirt like it was on fire. All right, I thought: maybe I really was gone mad.

"What the hell are you doing?"

"What does it look like I'm doing. Look, this was infighting, see? *Infighting.* A feud. Savages, they are. OK?"

He kept throwing looks across the hedge toward the pub, grunting out words as he stripped.

"This massive row, we just stumbled on it. Bad luck is all."

A half-smudgy eagle tattoo on the right side of his chest was new to me. He paused in his contortions and nodded toward where Motorbike Man lay. I didn't want to look any more. Things were beginning to seem more and more distant.

"He knew you were the law." It was like he was talking to someone next to me. "That's why he freaked. I seen right away how he turned his sights on you. So I came to your assistance, see. Tried to head him off with the jammer. To distract him, discourage him, whatever. I had to. Got that?"

I thought of the old Beemer that he'd brought. Heavy, solid.

"But how did you know, though? To come to this place, how did you know?"

Spots waved away the question.

"He goes for you – nearly nails you by the way – but, fair play to you, you go back at him. You make him go between them lorries and things – and, well, what happened happened. Got it? Tell me you do."

"I can't go along with that... shite. I can't."

"That's right you can't." He lowered his head a little and glared. "That's exactly what I'm trying to get through to you – *you can't*. You can't let those two put you in jail for the next how many years of your life."

My head was clearing a little. Lights were blinking in the old memory bank too.

"I saw you eyeballing him," I said. "The motorbike fella. You knew him. I saw it."

"Maybe I did, maybe I didn't. But I'll tell you one thing, he knew me."

"Blake too. You knew he'd come out here. Because you made it happen."

Spots was squeezing some liquid into his hand: disinfectant? Clenching his eyes tight, he began to wipe down his face and neck. Part of me admired the speed, the sureness. The sheer brazenness.

"Blake, I said. You got him to –"

"I know what you said. I'm not deaf. Don't you get it yet? I just saved your life."

He wasn't angry. He was baffled, even hurt.

"Look, Tommy, look." His tone turned soft. "Any second now, someone's going to come out the door of that pub. Or someone's going to come by in a jam-jar, or a tractor or something. We don't have time for debate here. I'm getting myself sorted here. You've got to as well."

He took extra care with his hands and forearms. Then he dropped the bottle onto the clothes he had dumped on the asphalt, picked up a stainless steel water thing and unscrewed the stopper. The smoke, or vapour, coming off the clothes was mesmerizing. I watched the material darken and then lighten at the edges of the holes as they widened. They grew and met and grew again.

"The Beretta," I said. "You set me up here too."

Spots glanced over. He seemed pleased to hear the calm in my voice.

"Fantasy, man," he said. "I only did what needed doing. That's all."

With that, he reached into the boot for a plastic bottle of what might be water.

"Premeditated murder. And you wanted an accomplice."

He spun around.

"That's enough out of you," he growled. "You are your 'premeditated' shite."

"I'm a copper. It's not just a hobby."

"A copper, are you? Well tell me this, Mister Copper. Where were youse when he came at me, all those years ago? Where were you then?"

His expression remained frozen, contorted by rage.

"Well? Did youse arrest him? Did you even question him back then? Did you? No, you did nothing. Not a thing."

He saw that I didn't get it.

"Blake! The Blake who did that to me – *that* Blake! The bastard I been thinking about every single day. Eighteen years, *ighteen*! Eighteen years, seven months and twenty-five days."

He turned to the boot and yanked out the bottle of water. I touched the wet mess on my cheek and looked down at my fingers. It was almost all watery now.

"There was no barman," I said. "No tip. All bullshit. Right?"

Spots' eyes narrowed in disgust. The little pile he had made of his trackies and T shirt had collapsed into a sodden lump. He stopped dowsing it and tossed the empty bottle into the boot. Pulling out a bamboo stick then, he poked it at the congealed and still-smoking mass. He tested the weight on the end of the stick before he carried most of it to the back end of a collapsed sander truck. After two dry runs to get a swing going, he fired the bundle off the end of the stick in under the chassis. And repeated: a lighter load this time. Then he stumped back.

"We're out of time. We have to go."

"There was more to this than you having a go at Blake."

He abruptly shut his eyes and then snapped them open wide.

"Tony Cummins," I said. "How much is he paying you?"

"Christ, listen to you. You get a bang on the noggin and you can't stop raving. Hallucinating."

"Did he hire you first? Before he dragged me into it?"

Slowly then, like he was still not quite awake, Spots recited a short series of numbers and letters. A registration number.

"Go check that out," he said. "Then go do your roaring and yelling at somebody else. Where it belongs."

I grabbed at his arm but he immediately twisted it away.

"Don't ever, ever do that."

As though taken aback himself, his face suddenly eased.

"An Avensis," he said. "Newish. An unmarked cop car."

Whatever he read on my face, it wasn't a message he wanted.

"You've got to get it together here Tommy. Look, there's no crime happened here."

"There's two men killed here, not fifteen feet from me."

"So what? Don't you get it yet? You're the copper, Tommy – you're the white haired boy here! You done your job! See?"

A wave of something pulsed up through me, and I got a chalky taste in my mouth. Spots was talking again.

"I'll tell you one thing. No way I'm going to swing for any of this – no way in the wide world. We're going to do this right."

"Do what?"

"That gun you never had? This Beretta, yeah. It's going on the motorbike fella."

He didn't wait long for a reaction.

"I'll do it," he added. "Now, before you start telling me stuff, just listen. I'll get all them shells – every single one. I will. I'll wipe everything and I'll move around whatever needs moving around. I know what I'm doing here, OK? I do. But there's one thing I need to know. I have to know you'll carry your end here."

He nodded toward the hedge and the pub beyond.

"It starts with you going back in there and sorting them out."

Too many notions were coming at me: words'd have to wait.

"You go in there to that crowd in the pub and you plant the story with them. You keep it simple. Say it a few times too. That's what works. That's all I'm asking you to do. All right?"

Again he waited, but no more than a few moments.

"Christ, Tommy. Do I have to spell it out for you? It's basic psychology, man. Power of suggestion. OK? One more time: these two headers had this massive row out here. A falling-out. They went bananas and started shooting. Push the feud angle, the double-cross. That's the stuff that sticks in people's minds. Conflict, fighting, we're hard-wired to focus on that stuff. See?"

I leaned out and looked around the end of the truck cab. There was a partial view of the side wall of the White Horse Inn, the side where they had a big drink ad mounted.

"That's right. You barge in there like a lunatic." His voice was a strained whisper now. "That won't be hard for you, will it?"

I knew Spots was trying to get us to normal, but it was as though there was a glass wall between us.

"And plenty of shouting and yelling too, OK? Wave that gun of yours around – freak the living shite out of them. Tell them it's a lock-down type of thing, and to get under the tables and stuff. Nobody comes out – nobody, not a sinner. No eyes at the windows, nobody trying to peep through the hedge there."

Did he expect a reply, I wondered. It seemed not.

"Get the show going. Cops, ambulance, firemen– the whole shebang. Helicopters, jet planes, for all I care. The more mental it goes, the better. But here, you've got to follow the plan."

He was listing a little to one side now, breathing deep and massaging his shoulder. I didn't see any cuts or scrapes. But I didn't like the way he kept looking at my wonky eye, though.

"One last thing, Tommy. It's important."

The change of tone, to me sounded like second thoughts.

"I can't stay here. It won't look right. There has to be an out."

I couldn't land on a question, much less string the words together for one.

"Stop – I know what you're thinking. Just listen. This is why you've got to make 200% certain no-one sees anything here. Soon's I've got this sorted here, I'd doing a bunk. I have to, OK?"

"Do a bunk," I managed.

"Exactly, good. Because, what does a normal person do when bullets start flying? He runs. He runs like the wind is what he does. I did what I could with the car, see? But, Jesus Mary and Joseph, a shooting? That's madness entirely. What's a man to do? So, being a normal human being, which is to say bleeding petrified, I'm going to leg it out of there as fast as I can. OK?"

"No it's not OK. And stop asking if it -"

" – Now where do I go? Me car's banjoed. It got wrecked when I went at your man, when I was coming to your aid –"

"Stop. You didn't come –"

"Pay attention here!"

His finger hit hard against my chest a second time. Then he raised his arm and pointed the finger square at my nose.

"Get this right," he said. "The last thing we need here is some holier-than-thou shite out of you. Any other day, any other place, maybe. But not here, and not now. Because you owe me, pal."

I focused my good eye on the trembling finger.

"OK? So there's fellas running around with guns here. Were do I go? I run in to the pub, is where. But I'm scared shitless, so I am. I don't run in the door of the actual bar or lounge. No, no, no – I hide somewhere in there. That's not being a coward, that's human nature. It's self-preservation. Perfectly normal."

I stopped shaking my head. All that had done was made me woozy again. But I didn't need much working brain power to grasp that Spots had put plenty of thought into this.

"There's a door around the side of the pub. Soon's I have my little thing here done, I'm heading for that door, and rapid, like."

He gave me a solemn yet almost friendly look.

"You'll be doing your bit too," he said. "Keeping them all doggo there on the floor, like. Code red or whatever? So when I know it's safe, I'll come out into the bar proper. So to anyone there it'll look like I was in the back of the place all along."

"Hold your horses there," I said in the quiet that followed. "You think I'll just go along with all this."

Spots levelled a stare.

"As a matter of fact I do, yeah."

I looked back again in the direction of The White Horse Inn.

"And Tommy? Don't be getting any brainwaves here."

The tone made me look over.

"Like you get to thinking some notion that it's me's the problem here and you being the law, you think you have to go a certain way on this. That would not go down well at all. I'm not the problem. I never was, and well you know it. You live in the real world, you know right from wrong. You get it. Right?"

How much time passed then, I couldn't be sure. All I knew was that it was now far too quiet.

"Now go do your thing, or we're bunched, the pair of us."

I did not look back, not once.

The pain flared as I walked, gathering in a big expanding ball, ready to pounce and take over completely. Maybe ten feet from the door, I saw it crack open a little. I reset my grip on the pistol and brought it to low ready, and I yelled out to whoever was on the far side of it to get back inside. It was the red-haired one backing away when I pulled open the door. His eyes darted from the mashed side of my face down to the Sig. He backed further, toward the bar. People were very still, and staring. There was too much glare in here. My good eye was straining so much it hurt.

"Everybody down, on the floor. There's shooting going on."

My head might've been a bit astray but sudden shifts in posture, and hands darting out of pockets, immediately had me sweeping the pistol over and back.

"Away from windows and doors. Get under something, behind something."

I waited until the noise died down enough. Cut-off groans and soft gasps lingered

"Stay down 'til I give you the all-clear. 999 on the way."

I found my way around a table to where Redser had taken his dive. A hint of the cockiness remained, but fear had drained his face of colour. He reluctantly eyed the carnage on my face.

"Remember me, do you? Good. Mind how you answer this. Liam Murphy – where'd he go?"

Redser said nothing but sent his eyes straying toward the bar.

I headed over to get a gawk at whoever has ducked or huddled down there. Somebody started with fright as I peered over and I heard sharp intakes of breath. They were packed in tight here, all right. Big anxious eyes beamed my way. Two fellas were texting, a third whispering into his mobile. Behind them, with his face turned away like he was looking into that dim space around the kegs was Mr. Liam Murphy. I parked an accusing stare on him. All that came back at me was a mute, wide-eyed blankness.

"Stay put there. Me and you are going to talk by and by."

"But who's out there?" It was the geezer I'd noticed earlier. White as a sheet. A candidate for a heart attack?

"Just stay low. Nobody's getting in here."

I put a warning eye on Murphy before shifting it back to Redser. I edged back toward the door then, and picked my spot. Any straying eyes or quick peeks would see me at the ready, both hands on and finger over the guard. I tried not to imagine what Spots was doing out there. But I couldn't help it. I could almost hear him, cursing and grunting as he maneuvered, stooping and foraging and arranging.

"Everybody listen." My voice sounded so strange in here. "Don't stir, any of you. Now, I need to know something. Listening? Anyone hear anything about trouble brewing around here? Threats or that? Rumours?"

Nobody had answers, of course. I wouldn't have known what to do if there had been. I caught sight of myself then in a corner of a mirror then. It took me a moment to recognize the battered-looking apparition with blood smeared down his cheek.

"Come on now. Any spats or feuds? People falling out with one another over something? Any talk about bad blood? People arguing and shouting?"

The zero response mood was holding firm.

"People coming by, asking after somebody? Fellas sitting in here, people you don't know, waiting for someone? Parked cars just sitting there, people looking around?"

I wasn't sure how long more I should keep this up. Or could.

"Ah come on now. Someone must have seen something. No? Heard something then. Anything?"

I turned to the old teacher trick. Redser would be my stooge.

"Yeah you. Just locals here? Nobody else? Not what I heard."

Redser poured as much insolence into his eyes as he dared. Like it mattered to me. I looked from face to face.

"What, are ye all too scared to say the words? 'Fellas down from the North?' No? Foreigners? Anybody...?"

The distant sound of siren gained strength, faded and came back stronger. A quick, scurrying sound put me in a crouch and aiming down the hallway beyond the bar.

The figure approaching had his arms half up and a wide eyed look on his face. Spots looked genuinely scared. So he should be.

"Am I OK to come out now?"

I looked beyond him to the door. He knew the layout here. Knew where the back door was. Knew how to get in on the sly.

I looked back, and his stare had changed. Relief, of course, but something else too. Contentment, I'd maybe have called it, if I had to put a word on it.

A quiet pride, even. But it wouldn't have been a stretch to wonder if it wasn't actually triumph.

28

Some things hadn't changed: a shooting call still got serious response. A shooting call with a copper in the picture meant slews of people showing up, many of them arriving in a fierce hurry.

I thought I was ready for the sight of the ERU heads storming into the pub: but no. But nobody could be ready. The shouting, the side-step dance they do to gain ground – just the sight of these aliens in balaclavas all got up in black and loaded with badges and kit and belts, jabbing and sweeping those short-barrelled H & Ks – that was more than enough. Everyone just froze, breaths held, like a magic spell had been cast. As well as a complicated kind of relief, I also felt another huge rush of weirdness. This was a film in re-run, I thought. But somehow, as well as being caught up in the middle of the craziness happening here, I was in the audience too?

Things were soon sorted, though. The sight of an ERU kicking Spots' leg gave me an oddly pleasant feeling. He was well aware of me staring at him, but he wouldn't look over. Which only made me even more sure: he had known what was going to happen here. He had strung me along. But how? I still didn't want to admit it to myself. No. The pills, the quirks, the occasional questions about the shrink, the minorly off-the-mark reactions he'd noticed in me – Spots had known all along. He'd seen an opening.

The paramedics were waved in right quick. The bloke treating me turned out to be a bit of a card. A Donegal fella with that odd accent they had, and no translations offered either. Dabbing antiseptic and poking around with his fingers, he informed me that I should go and buy a rake of Lotto tickets. A vague nausea had settled on me. I felt hyper but wasted too, like jet lag but without the jet.

He stopped dabbing. Something about lotto?

"If you're not in you can't win," I tried. "That it?"

He must have seen enough glimmers of sense. He went back to his well-intentioned torture with the gauze, and his quiet, semi-humorous monologue about ghost town Dublin with the zero traffic delays and weird peace and quiet that gave him the jitters.

Liam Murphy sat slumped in a chair across from me all the while, his jaw hanging a little as he tugged uselessly on his stubby fingers one by one, over and over again. The slightly pained, far-off expression reminded me of someone after receiving Communion. Nothing could pry him from his trance. Not the mad racket off two-ways turned up high. Not even the armed-and-deadly coppers stalking stiffly by, guns at the ready.

The head ranking copper, somebody Ryan from Finglas station, a Sergeant nonetheless, returned. He had made calls, I surmised. While he waited for the paramedic bloke to call a halt to his dabbing and swabbing, he dropped his jaw and rubbed his chin along the flap of his ballistic.

"All right," he said, pausing to cock an ear to the chatter from the two-ways, "tell me again. You're off-duty. Or you're on leave?"

"Sort of both. I was working a lead here. On the QT like."

Even to me it sounded preposterous. He looked over at Spots.

"A lead," he said. "And this Freely character here?"

"Feeney. He drove me here."

"He drove you. And you're armed. Drug Squad Central, Dublin Castle. But working an OCU case. While you're on leave."

"She vouched for me, right? Áine Nugent, that sergeant you talked to?"

On this elementary question, Ryan remained mute.

"The thing is," he went on, "I happen to know Éamonn Nolan. You're telling me that this here is one of his operations. You and this Freely person here. Is that it?"

"Feeney, right. It's complicated. Hard to explain all in one go."

Ryan's jaw, or his chin, resumed its side-to-side wandering and stretching. I'd seen cows do the same. Masticating, I believe is the word. Whatever about cow talents, if Ryan's eyes had been lasers, Spots'd be cinders by now. Said lasers detached from Spots and landed back on me.

"Complicated," Ryan said, almost poetically.

The opening doorway whisked his gaze over. One of the ERU crew stood there, and and nodded, and let it shut. Ryan looked back again at Spots.

"And those two outside," he said to me. "'Not part of the plan,' you said?"

"Right. Most definitely wasn't expecting things to go haywire."

"Haywire? Do you know the both of them are dead?"

Even if I had had the patience to explain more, or the will, I doubted I'd get by what was fixed in his mind now.

"Like I said, it's an active investigation. At a critical stage."

He flicked a doubting look over toward Liam Murphy.

"Critical, I see. And you absolutely must pursue this now, you're telling me. You only. No support from your unit or the say-so from your C.O. or -"

"The longer I'm stuck talking here, the closer we get to losing the thing."

I turned to the paramedic before Ryan could reach for some official phrase than said 'no.'

"I'm grand for the next while anyway. Right?"

His response was an exchange of looks with Ryan. I got up from the chair. I right away noticed Murphy raising his head. His eyes drifted from face to face but they didn't stray my way.

"You drive us over to your place," I said to him. I heard Ryan say something to me about waiting for Nolan, or for someone. "There's a fella coming with me, I believe you know him."

Spots, I saw now, was staring hard. Murphy's eyes came slowly to life, but it was to me they turned.

*　　*　　*

I'd never been in a pick-up truck in my life. Pick-up truck? Crumlin?

I watched Murphy clearing space for us, wondering if he was aware of just how edgy the ERU fella standing next to us was. Maybe the ERUU guy knew better than I did. The model of the reliable, decent husband and father was the Spots Feeney version of Liam Murphy. The same Spots Feeney had minus 100% of my trust right now.

Calmly and methodically, Murphy toted the power tools out of the back seat and around to the bed of the truck. A circular saw that looked to be in rag order, a drill bigger than I was used to seeing, and one of those reciprocating saws. Then he began rearranging the stuff cluttering the floor. Boxes of nails and screws, a small heap of galvanized yokes that had a masonry vibe to them. Lengths of electrical cable, and extension cables. Loose tiles and small tubs of compound or glue took their places between and around various trowels and sticks. He pulled a few half-crushed water bottles and cans from the ensemble and tossed them in the back. The wrappers off bags of crisps and bars of Aero and Crunchies he squeezed into a loose ball and shoved in under the driver's seat. No cigarette packages, I noticed. One battered roll of toilet paper, unused, he rolled up and shoved down between the seat and the transmission tunnel.

He drove slowly and carefully, like a learner doing his road test, eyes locked on the road ahead and frowning all the while, as though this driving business was the hardest job in the world. This calm and leisurely jaunt had to be the ultimate proof of just how weird things had turned. Like nothing had happened back there. Like we were just three mates coasting along a narrow country road, taking in the bushes and trees and ditches and what have you. All to the accompaniment of a slow and very, very peculiar monologue coming from Spots. Part thinking out loud, part reminiscence, part yarn – there was no term for it. What came to mind was a thing I saw a while back on Discovery. Some famous woman in the States, a weirdo if I remembered right, calming horses down.

A girl's name kept coming up: Maria. There was talk about a pony, and Disneyworld and Barbies and Princess Somebody. On and on it went, Spot's voice rarely rising above a murmur. This was Spots Feeney, I reminded myself. How in the name of God would he know this stuff? Sure, he had a daughter of his own, Jessica, but Jess was fourteen or fifteen now, well beyond this dolls and mermaids carry-on. Actually, I had already picked up from Spots that Jess had turned into a bit of a strap. Put it down to the hormones and what-have-you, fair enough, but there would've been genes lying in ambush for her from the start.

I kept eyeing Murphy all the while. So this was the man who got to take Jennifer Cummins to the altar. That wedding had been held just as Spots was finishing his first set of operations. When he was trying to get his head around the notion that he'd been maimed for life.

The disconnect finally got to me. We had just turned onto a freshly finished asphalt drive.

"Wait a minute," I said. "Are youse two mates, or what?"

Neither answered. The road twisted sharply by a stand of trees. That seemed to bring Murphy out of his minor trance. He looked across at Spots.

"Not a word to Jenn," he said. "Right?"

"Fair enough," Spots said.

"I'll be the one tells her. You hear?"

Another 'fair enough' from Spots. Murphy searched me out in the rear mirror.

"What about him?" he asked.

It wasn't easy for Spots to turn around, to give me the eye.

"No worries there. He's down with it."

"And they don't know yet," Murphy added. "You know?"

"Right," said Spots. "Neither Tony, nor Bernie. So there's that at least."

Murphy nodded a few times. He seemed to relax a bit. Not me. Spots' answer had set my mind on spin cycle. How would he know to say that about the Cumminses, that they were in the dark over this? I thought of the nonsensical yarn that Spots had put my way, the back-to-front car chase that had persuaded me that it was worth a drive out here in the first place. Had Liam Murphy phoned Blake that night? Had Jennifer?

"Not in a million years," Murphy said then.

"I can imagine," said Spots. "Well, I mean I can't imagine."

"If you'd told me..." Murphy began, but shook off the rest unsaid. Spots performed his sympathetic nods again.

"Thing is, Liam, we need to settle it. You know yourself, like."

333

The road opened out. The wall of hedge began to give away in places and some serious haciendas began to reveal themselves.

"Nice along here," Spots said. "Very nice."

"Well it *was* nice," Murphy said. "But after this?"

It was driving me mad the way the pair were talking. They were like two oul lads reminiscing. But here I was, a sworn Garda officer who had just been shot at and nearly done in, relegated to spectator status.

"Eh, where exactly is this new house of yours?"

I might as well have been talking to the wall.

"Your name comes up still," Murphy said to Spots. "Not every day, of course."

"Well I'd be worried if it did."

Murphy didn't react. In the mirror, I saw his forehead crease in a frown.

"You know I never actually asked you," he began to say. Spots brushed away the rest with a weak wave of his hand.

"God no," Spots said. "There never was. No, no."

Murphy seemed to quietly savour this.

"The fact of the matter is, Liam, it'd never have worked. No."

Murphy glanced over as though to check he had heard right. The tone of tender regret had me on the back foot too. Because it had come from the bloke known to me as Spots Feeney.

"It took time to get the divils out," Spots added, quietly. "A lot of time, in actual fact. But there had to be a parting of the ways."

We passed a showy-offy set of gates, big cast iron ones with gold tips on the ends, hung on pillars under two rearing concrete stallions. Mother of God.

"I forget," Spots said. "How old is she now? Fourteen, is it?"

"Fourteen is right. You remembered."

"Holy God, time flies."

"April fourth, four in the morning. Four, four, four."

The big heap of a house behind the railings would be spot-on for Henry Tudor to set up home in. If he was half-Mexican maybe.

"She has a grand life here," Spots said. "Lucky girl."

Murphy gripped the wheel tighter. His jaw slid over and back.

"Anything else," he said. "*Anything*. Money, Jen's rings – her car even. *Anything*. Then, well you know."

This was too much. They were taunting me, it felt like.

"Then well you know *what*?"

"Nobody's talking to you," Spots snapped.

Murphy geared down and let the pick-up down off the asphalt and over a small gully lined with crushed stones. The track in had two channels, deep enough to set the pick-up wagging side to side. We passed pillars for what was going to be a gate, standing amid small piles of finishing stones. Murphy took it slow in second. A house slid out from behind a clump of conifers: exactly the type of place that'd have the heritage crowd spluttering – a cross between something in Surrey and one of those Desperate Housewives places. There was sod in, and the beginnings of landscaping too.

"Jesus, Liam," said Spots. "The other place, that was something. But this? Wow, man."

"You like it? It should be finished and ready by July. Jen's birthday, like."

"The tenth?"

Murphy shifted a little in his seat. Amused or annoyed, I couldn't tell.

"You'd get millions for a place like this. Not a doubt in my mind. Millions."

This was fantasy. Even builders didn't believe that one. I tried again to keep a lid on things by mentally rehearsing the massive bollicking I was going to give Spots. Not alone had he kept tabs on his old flame 'Jenn' Cummins. He was actually on friendly terms with the man Jennifer had ended up marrying. And now, it sounded like Spots had even been a visitor to their home.

Murphy had slowed to a crawl. It wasn't enough to prevent me getting heaved me across the seat as the truck leaned and corrected itself. He brought it to a stop well short of a circular driveway. Resting his forearms on the wheel then, he lowered his chin onto his wrist and stared. It was like this was his first sight of the house.

Patience was never my strong suit. Spots had my number though, and set a high-beam warning eye on me again. The wait went on. Exhaust soon began to find its way into the cab.

Eventually, Spots stirred.

"Liam," he said. "Something I have to ask you."

Murphy maintained his stare at the house.

"Is he here still? Or is he, you know, gone?"

Murphy straightened up slowly, licked gingerly around his gob, and shifted into first gear.

"Liam? Tell us what we're going to find here."

If I'd had to describe Murphy's expression, I'd have been useless. Dreamy. Baffled. Doomed. Relieved? Spots nudged him on his forearm and Murphy let the stick back into neutral.

"Gary's here," Spots said. "Isn't he."

Murphy's gaze went back to the house.

"Look," he said. "It wasn't my doing. No way."

Spots knew to wait.

"She has to find out eventually, I know. Just don't tell her where, though. OK?"

"Don't tell her where what," Spots said.

"It's the one thing she really wanted, that cellar. A wine thing."

"A cellar. In a new house, a cellar?"

"A basement, yes. It's a stick-built house, like the Yanks do."

A sudden burst of sunshine lit up the colours. The big window put me in mind of a church, a cathedral even. Sparkles winked at us from silica dust on the stone around the hall door.

We drew in alongside the steps. I got out first, complete with aches and pains, and I slid the Sig down alongside my leg.

"Anyone else about?"

Murphy looked at me like I had asked him a riddle.

"No," he said. "I have the keys."

Sunshine flooded the hallway like a film set. To me, the place looked awful close to finished. The only clear sign that there was more to do were a mitre saw and odd lengths of trim and a few large tiles set on a saw horse by the staircase. That was travertine, I decided. Dull-looking and very pricey. Said staircase alone probably cost more than my apartment. Polished wood grain curved up like the branch of a tree. Everything was so high up, so bright. Sharp tangs filled the air: plaster, varnish, paint.

Spots made his way in. He seemed indifferent to the finery.

"Show me this cellar place," I said.

Murphy headed for a passageway next to a doorless entry that led to the kitchen. There was a second staircase there, L shaped and plain enough. Cellars were the very last places I wanted to go, but the impatience was like a hand on my shoulder pushing me down after Murphy. A dank, stale, cement-y smell came on stronger as we descended. But there was something else in the mix too. Murphy stopped at a heavy-looking, unfinished door. He was already fingering through his keys.

"Just put the key in," I said. "Don't turn it."

The look he threw me was the first real sign of normal. I brought the pistol up and gave him a one-eyed, knock-down stare.

"Go back over there and sit on the floor, facing me. Sit on your hands too."

"I told you," he said. "This wasn't my idea at all."

"Whose idea was in then?"

Murphy looked at the floor. I took a step back. My heart was already doing its mad rat-a-tat.

"Put the key in, and go sit off over there like I told you to."

He lifted his gaze and turned it toward Spots. A sharp, cold suspicion went through me. Cahoots? I took another step back. A quick tightening around the eyes and a look of muted surprise told me that Spots had noticed right away.

"Talk to him," I said to him. "Any thick move out of him, it comes back on everyone."

I watched Murphy's hands as he worked the key into the lock. Then I waited until he had let himself down completely to the floor in the corner and tucked his hands under. He looked like a huge, awkward kid who'd just gotten in trouble in school. The key turned easily enough, no locksmith skills required. I gave Murphy another warning eye and I pushed down the handle.

It didn't help that the god-awful stink was familiar. I didn't even have to think about holding my breath. In the dim light I saw a plastic pail and what looked like a big water bottle, and something in the corner, something like a sleeping bag or a bundle of clothes. The room was about the size of my apartment kitchen. The state of the place reminded me of a nest. A fouled nest.

"Where's the light?"

I heard something that might have been a whisper. The clothes-pile in the corner stirred. I pinched my nose hard. The stink here was almost like a living thing itself now. The movement stopped. A sound like something rolling across a bare floor came from the pile of clothes. It turned into a groan. I looked back out the doorway and across at Murphy.

"Where's the bleeding light, I said."

Murphy didn't bother to look up.

"I took the bulb out."

The sound of chain pulled across concrete drew me back. There was an arm out now and the hand reached up spreading open and trembling. The groan gave way to gasps and then some hoarse voice and words I couldn't make out. A pale, stubbly face appeared, with dark stains and streaks. It took me a second or two to see that those were not sunglasses at all but yellow and grey coloured swollen eyelids. It was like a close-up of some insect head, I thought, or some rare nocturnal creature.

"Am I alive," it said.

"Are you Gary Cummins?"

The sobbing seemed too much for him. He shook and he buckled and with a clink from the chain, fell back slowly back into his nest. It wasn't much of an answer, but it was enough.

29

A sit-down with my C.O. was the last thing I wanted. It was probably the last thing Delaney wanted too. That didn't stop him from waving me into a chair, though.

"I see the face is on the mend," he said.

"They did what they could, I suppose."

Delaney possibly aimed for a smile. It didn't get much beyond a twitch of his mouth. He wouldn't have much to smile about anyway. The raid had been put off. Three days back, four of our high-values went off the radar. Poof: vanished. How or why, nobody knew yet. Delaney, I heard, was livid. Two off the team even got into a huge barney that night too – in a pub, where else. A lot of tension. There was talk of disciplinary too.

"And it looks like you survived your session with Big Mac."

"Barely. It went the full fourteen."

Delaney was still sort-of willing to pretend he was amused. He knew that Chief Super Martin McNally, the semi-legendary Big Mac, hadn't gotten his job by winning a bonnie baby competition.

"I added it my CV already. Next to 'working an op with the OCU.'"

Sure, it was on the high side of cheeky. I just didn't want Delaney thinking I'd forgotten. A call interrupted his next conversational offering.

I eased back in the chair and tried to think of other matters. The scab on my knee was beginning to separate. There were tiny bits of gravel or something under the skin there still. I took a quick, discreet gander at my phone. No email from Áine. Why would she cancel, though. It was her asked for a meet. The thought of her stirred up that heavy, go-nowhere restlessness again. I upped my efforts to divert.

My mind skittered back to yesterday's session with McNally. I had arrived to his office braced for things to go south. It wouldn't have been the end of the world. I'd had Oz on my mind more lately, and Sonia of course, and a vague an probably stupid notion involving both. I had also become aware of a dense, undigested ball of something festering away in the back of my mind. Those shifts with Macker had left their mark, right enough. It wasn't al his quirks and mental trickery. No, the only problem with Macker was that he was right. We really were well on the way – well on the way to being banjoed. Things were too-far gone. Even if we pulled out of this crash/crisis, the insiders would just flip the switch on the old merry-go-round, and me and all the other Joe Soaps would be lined up to get fleeced and codded all over again.

Anyway. McNally.

He had a pretty solid opener: a copy of the Garda oath slid across the table to me. It was the full ceremonial one too, with the fancy calligraphy; the self-same one you take home the day you're sworn in. A copy of the Regulations followed. Then, a copy of that poxy values and standards declaration that we all had to sign. He made a point of arranging them side by side and carefully squared to the edge of the table. My first thought: bullshit, incoming, in large quantities.

Was I familiar with the documents, McNally wanted to know. Reasonably familiar, I told him. After a few ambiguous-looking nods, he reached down beside his feet for a manila folder. Print-outs, OK. He placed them one by one on the desk and rotated each around my way. He needn't have bothered. I'd put in enough years on the Squad to be able to read the likes of these upside down and written backwards in ancient Mongolian.

He might actually have read my very thoughts because, like he was about to play an invisible piano, he then laid two big meaty sets of fingers on the edge of the table. The Regulations spoke for themselves, he declared. As did the Oath and the declaration. He waited then for a bit of solid eye contact that'd tell him I was on board. Might he offer me a summary of the other documents?

First came the map and the diagrammatic, the scene reconstruction. The examiners remained puzzled, Big Mac informed me. This evidently arose from trajectories and triangulations and suchlike, and the various paths of the involved parties through that car park slash yard out near the White Horse Inn. It was noted that the location was visible neither from the road nor the public house. Compounding this were difficulties with the sequence of events. McNally's timed hesitation before 'difficulties' wasn't lost on me. Blake had arrived at the location to find a party named Lunney in conversation with Sergeant Malone. According to a log of text messages, Mr. Lunney had in fact been summoned there by Blake, the object of which might have been to assist Blake in containing a situation with a kidnapping victim.

'Contain.' I doubted McNally meant to be sarcastic. No, it had the ring of true Garda reportese. Expecting that it'd just state things in plain English would be a sure sign that I had lost the run of myself: Blake had phoned this Lunney guy to meet him for another job - to do for a nosy copper. Lunney, the prize hit-man who had been so carefully groomed by his IRA sponsors. Lunney, the go-to for setting fire to cars. For running s human being down with a van. This came-out-of-nowhere psycho -

McNally had stopped talking. How long had I been zoned out?

Dropping his gaze back to the report, he moved his lips around like he had swallowed something unexpected and shuttled big culchie head over and back while he tried to scan through the stuff. He signalled that he had found whatever he had been looking for with a slow and solemn nod.

Blake, he went on, may already have had some dispute with Lunney, or with Lunney's associates, or sponsors. He may even have suspected Lunney of informing on him to Malone, or of being a Garda informer generally. Lunney, believing that Blake presented an imminent threat to him, immediately produced a handgun and discharged it at Blake, following up with several more shots at close range.

McNally paused at that and began a study of his fingers. Maybe he had forgotten how many he owned. I knew not to trust the calm that I was feeling. I had learned the hard way that this so-called calm was actually a warning sign that some part of me was already in reckless territory.

With all his fingers presumably accounted for, McNally felt he could resume. The aisy-Daisy culchie tilt I had heard in his voice earlier had drained out now. Blake, he went on, had been shot inside his vehicle. Shot four times, including one delivered at point blank range into his right temple. This obliged investigators to consider the possibility that Lunney had in fact come to that location expecting threat from Blake, or even with the express purpose of murdering him perhaps even directed so by as yet unknown persons.

McNally turned then to the ballistics report. I remember how he looked down his nose while he read, like his glasses were an impediment that he was keen to be rid of. The environment had presented unique difficulties. Bullet fragments had been widely dispersed and unrecoverable. While several complete slugs had been recovered from the scene, all were flattened and further distorted by impacts, however. Those recovered from Blake did indeed test as having come from a firearm recovered on scene, under Lunney's body, a Beretta semi-automatic pistol. Upon searching Lunney's effects in his apartment and at his place of employment, investigators did indeed uncover an ammunition cache. None of those rounds was for use with the recovered pistol.

Having brought forth these conundrums, McNally peered up from his pages. Did I have questions at this point? I did. I had about a million, actually. No, I told him. He turned then to a summary of Blake's criminal record. It was, predictably enough, dense. But the one-page summary on Lunney contained only the basics – birth, education, Social Protection involvement, bank stuff and so forth. McNally planted a finger on the three letters N.C.R. printed in caps at the bottom and lobbed a quick, questioning glance my way. Was I taken aback to see that, it meant. Taken aback that we'd stumbled over Lunney, a completely off-the-radar killer, by chance? I said that I was. Taken aback was putting it mildly. Especially when I'd copped on that the bloke shooting at me in that car park was by no means an amateur.

He proceeded instead to his next items. Lunney, he told me, was now being looked at as the 'mystery hit-man' who had been hitting Dublin hard the past eighteen months to two years. What was called in the trade a cleaner. Furthermore, we were now close to putting Lunney behind the wheel of the van that had run Christy down too, a van stolen with suspicious ease. Possible connections to other crimes were also emerging. There was some involvement with dissident or disaffected IRA figures in Dundalk. A contract killing on behalf of a Lithuanian gang. A firebombing of a house in West Belfast.....

He scanned the rest of the paragraph and let down the page, and looked at the window behind me. So, he announced, in relation to Misters Lunney and Blake, it was possible that several questions would remain unanswered. 'Would remain unanswered.' A nice, short, tidy-sounding string of words, that. All-in-all, a phrase elastic enough to hold up every pair of knickers in Ireland.

His gaze shifted from the window to me. Neanderthals walk amongst us yet, I thought. His face had settled into the look of a man waiting for a bus, a bus that he already knew would be late. Fair enough, I remembered thinking then. This was Big Mac as much as admitting that he had to hold his nose concerning the business. A truce, right? Sleeping dogs and so forth. Job done, ship's name is Murphy, here's your hat and what's your hurry. But then I detected what looked to me to be a faint hint of amusement in his eyes.

That was what probably did it.

Well that was too bad, I told him. His reaction was an ever-so-slight tilt of the head, followed by a not-bad impersonation of an Easter Island statue. Too bad – I went on – because what was actually needed were answers about what led up to that day, beginning with this question: had Garda officers gone beyond just collaborating in a criminal conspiracy, to actually initiating one?

I paused at that to see if McNally was in receiving mode. A look of mild interest had entered his eyes. Was he daring me to spell it out? Well he had come to the right man. In I jumped. It was one thing to conceal the assault, kidnapping and imprisoning of Gary Cummins. But, had Garda officers actually obstructed the investigation of other serious crimes? One such crime was the sexual assault, or the attempted sexual assault, of a minor. A minor made even more vulnerable by her condition.

Big Mac had apparently spotted a mark on his desktop that needed removing, and had been methodically rubbing a knuckle over a small section of it. Another hint that, even at this stage, I should leave things well enough alone? I was angry, but this time it was a cold, lucid anger.

I launched right into the Blake side of things then. Garda officers had allowed Blake to continue unhindered a drug-dealing enterprise that he conducted with Corcoran and Hynes, and very likely with the co-operation of IRA gangsters. Garda officers had conspired to obstruct a Garda investigation by concealing a data trail from at least one of Gary Cummins' mobile phones. At least one Garda officer had misused Garda resources in assigning staff to investigative tasks that were known to be dead ends. In other words, this 'team' that had been struck for Áine and me was a big, expensive fake. A Garda officer may have even directed Jennifer Murphy to make herself unavailable by leaving the country for a 'holiday.' That same Garda officer had helped orchestrate, or at the very least turned a blind eye to, a dog-and-pony show with Mary Enright expressly for the purposes of misleading Gardaí in a criminal investigation.

MvNally's desk restoration task came to a halt and he flicked a look slantways at me. There was nothing remotely agreeable about it. It was a closer, a warning. And if I was thick enough not to pick it up, his tone of voice carried it too. If I was suggesting that serious lapses in judgment had occurred, he said, it would be difficult to disagree with that. I could also rest assured, he added, that there'd be no commendations handed out over the affair.

Lapses, I thought. Judgment. Commendations...? I had cut down on the pills, but words or phrases still stick to the inside of my head like Velcro. Did 'lapse in judgment' describe the fact that Nolan had as much as handed Blake an invitation to go after me? Our big genius strategist had screwed up so badly that even one of his officers believed that she had to intervene? Not that she could admit to that, though. That'd get her the sack, for one thing. It'd be charges too, criminal charges. What could she say in her defence anyway? That, as insane a scheme as it was to tip off Spots, she felt it was her only move? Things were so off-the-rails that only a desperate move like that would keep Malone out of harm's way?

But what a gift she had handed Spots. Revenge with a capital R – and by God he had jumped on it. I'd already concluded that he'd gotten the go-ahead from Tony Cummins too. And then, to put the tin hat on it, he had delivered his revenge under the nose of, and maybe even enabled by, a Garda officer. Maybe my imagination was working overtime here, but the look on McNally's face now said that he knew exactly what was going on in my head. He knew I wouldn't put that out there about Áine Nugent. And, as much as I wanted to tear the face off Spots, now basking and basting himself on some beach in Spain – he *said* - I wasn't going to throw him to the wolves either. Well, I decided, if McNally was going to play mind games, the least I could do was slide a few notions his way that the traffic here went both ways.

A rethink on the commendations might be in order, I said then. For this I received what I'd been anticipating all along: a cold stare. A case could be made for Jennifer Murphy getting some kind of a commendation, could it not? After all, she had prevented her husband from tearing Gary Cummins apart. So what if it had been Jennifer who'd phoned Blake in a panic to get him to talk down her husband from doing for Gary, and yes, that had set matters in motion. But how was she to know that Nolan was listening in? And how would she have known that Blake would go haywire later on?

McNally's response was a blink followed by a relaxing of his features into a mildly hostile, mildly enquiring expression. I did a quick see-saw in my mind. Big Mac here was a) maybe now just realizing that he hadn't been briefed on highly inconvenient details or b) watching me dig the hole deeper, the hole I'd be falling into soon enough. What odds, I figured. Might as well be hung for a sheep as a lamb. The fur would be flying good-oh here soon enough anyway.

Nolan, I ploughed on, must've figured he'd won the lotto that night of that back-to-front car chase. He'd been trying to get to Tony Cummins for ages. He had a tap on Blake's phone. He heard that panicked call from Jennifer: she couldn't hold her husband back from tearing Gary limb from limb. Liam Murphy, a man who had done nothing more than be an ordinary, decent husband and father. This Gary Cummins SNAFU had landed Blake in his lap. He had raced out to the Murphy's house ahead of Blake, where he confronted him. The game was up. Nolan was on the inside now.

Nolan had been pressuring Blake for months already, pushing the line that Tony Cummins was having serious doubts about his loyalties. That to me said that Nolan knew about what Blake was up to with Hynes and Corcoran, supplying drugs to what was left of the country's jumped-up celebrities and suchlike who could still afford their Celtic Tiger style diversions. Had that information gone to Pulse? Routed as a tip to Drugs Central, anonymously or otherwise...?

Big Mac was taking his Easter Island role back on tour again. I noticed an incline in one McNally eyebrow, however. It was either a sign of genuine interest or the calm before the storm. I opted for the former. For Nolan, I went on, the timing couldn't have been better. This latest screw-up with Gary was the last straw for Blake. Everything was on the slide with him. He knew that rowing in with Corcoran and Hynes in a drugs business was not a sure thing. He'd seen how the IRA operated, how they made you an offer you couldn't refuse. Or worse. Hadn't they moved in on Hynes, even placed one of their prize pieces in there?

Which led to taking a hard look at Hynes and Corcoran. It was all fine and well for them to be claiming now how terrified they were of Blake, or Lunney, or whoever was arranging the furniture in the background. Well why didn't one of them pick up the phone to the Guards? And whatever about Hynes, Corcoran in particular should be getting pinned to the wall in a much more serious fashion than I'd been hearing about. Any copper with a head on his shoulders would look at him and his 'talent agency' and see it for what it was – a cod. Corcoran was an insider. What he was selling was access to a network, to money and celebrities. To bigger and better things. Like blackmail. Like extortion. Like taking over businesses.

That sort of thing was out of Blake's league. All right, he'd have thought, he might be on their good side for now. He even had pull with them. There were signs enough of that on Lunney's phone, with those texts that came from a burner found in Blake's flat. Apparently, Blake could and did call on Lunney's 'services' when he wanted. But he'd have known that he could never turn his back on Lunney. The same as he'd have known that sooner or later the IRA would want a middle man or do-for out of their way.

All this piled on top of other issues for Blake. The years were passing. The walls were closing in. If he wasn't busy enough looking over his shoulder all the time to see if Lunney had gotten the word from on high that he, Blake, had outlived his usefulness, could he even trust that Corcoran or Hynes wasn't screwing him? Or that Hynes wouldn't finally crack and run to the law? Corcoran? As for Nolan pushing at him with the line that Tony Cummins was considering doing for him, Blake couldn't be sure that was bullshit. So he had to have been wondering. All these years taking care of stuff for Cummins? Where was the gravy? Here he was, no trust, no money, no prospects - and now the Guards were poking hard at him too. So yes, he was looking for the door out. Yes, he'd deal. Yes, he'd keep Gary's whereabouts hush-hush. Once Tony Cummins talked, Nolan would disappear the woes that he was holding over Blake's head.

Again: did Blake believe it? Who knew. He went with it. And Nolan hadn't just scooped up Blake that night. He had Gary too, and by God he was going to use him. To top it off, he even had the threat of a charge on Liam Murphy, which for Bernie Cummins, that was an absolute no-go. It'd tear up Jennifer's life, and Maria's, the Cumminses' only save from the family wreckage. Nolan reckoned he had Tony Cummins well-and-truly over a barrel. Except for one simple fact – he had underestimated Tony Cummins big-time.

McNally had left Easter Island and returned to rubbing invisible blemishes from the desktop. That told me that he was willing to sit a while yet, and pretend to listen to me rabbit on a while more. But sooner or later, he'd lower the boom. And what then? Off to lunch with the other brass, was what. This whole thing was headed under the wallpaper. Nolan? Shuffled, reassigned, fed to a new section – whatever. A rap on the knuckles, for show. In other words, we were just going through the motions here. Well, I'd give it one more go.

Christopher Cullinane, I said. Did that name mean anything to him?

To my surprise, McNally nodded. Well somebody had lit the match that led to that. Someone had taken a run at Tony Cummins in jail – which by the way was attempted murder. Someone, and not just whoever had come at Cummins with a knife, had set that in motion too. A man's home had been firebombed. A Guard and his family had been threatened. They had been forced out of their home. Sure, go after Blake and Lunney for any and all of this. But who was it gave them the lead in the first place? Where had that information come from?

McNally was holding to a vow of silence, and he had moved on to a new activity: stroking the edge of his ear with his little finger. That new faraway-half-daydreaming look of his didn't fool me. He for damned sure knew where I was going with this it – straight for Nolan. Nolan and his go-boy, Quinn.

That, it turned out, would be a step too far. I watched Big Mac's operations on the ear wind down and then cease. He drew himself up ramrod straight in the chair and, resting his forearms heavily on the table, clasped his hands together. For several moments, he studied both sets of knuckles in turn. With that accomplished, he laid his hands flat on the table and planted a stare on me. I waited and he stared. He waited and I stared back. Finally, he let his hands trail back to the edge the desk whereupon he withdrew them from sight.

The moment I tried to have my spake again, his arm shot up. I was presented with a large palm. He slowly lowered it and turned to his briefcase, and drew out a single sheet. It was three or four lines. There was a space for two signatures. I began reading. Confidentiality... acknowledgement... affidavit... Affirmation? I'd heard of this form. I'd never actually seen one.

The sing-song, culchie accent had made a come-back. He spoke slowly and deliberately, with a peculiar warmth that was hard to tell from sarcasm. Thanked me for my observations. The valid concerns about operational strategy. Explained that matters were under review as a result of this operation. A need to remember that I'd not been privy to the planning of the operation. Many open files that needed to be addressed, including murders and ongoing, large-scale criminal enterprises. The Garda Síochána facing myriad challenges at the present time, especially the expansion of criminal activity with international reach....

My eyes must have glazed over. He waited to be sure that I had rejoined the planet before presenting the main course. In order to take advantage of evolving opportunities, Inspector Nolan had made decisions that he believed would further the goals of the operation overall. 'Under review,' I remembered thinking. 'Evolving opportunities.' Did words mean anything anymore?

And now, McNally went on, it was time to remember my oath. A key part of that oath was the duty to keep confidential police matters ...confidential. A matter of utmost importance. A sacred trust in fact. Upholding the law was the foundation of society. Confidentiality meant no exceptions – zero. Not colleagues, not friends, not even family – and especially not a journalist. 'Nobody' covered a nobody from Justice, a DPP of a nobody, or any nobody calling himself barrister or solicitor – even a nobody delivering a bench order.

He waited a bit, maybe for me to reflect that his 'humour' was deadly serious. Or maybe it was so's I could memorize a list of nobodies that'd trigger my vow of silence. His eyes went a bit beady. I was not to contact members of the Organized Crime Unit. This was apparently grievous enough in Big Mac's mind that he asked if I understood. I told him that I did. I did not tell him that I had good hearing, and that I understood the English language probably a damned sight better than the fat-fingered culchie Neanderthal sitting across the table from me. Nor did I tell him that I was set to meet Soon-to-be-Inspector Áine Nugent in town, a meet that she had asked for. Above all else, McNally said then, extruding a bit of genuine menace from his eyes, 'nobody' meant a certain Mr. Feeney. The Mr. Feeney who, though not known to be helpful to the Guards, had apparently been so helpful to me that I had let him accompany me to The White Horse that day.

He then reached back into his bag and drew out a photo, and laid it down on the table between us. There was a surprise factor, all right. The telephoto surveillance shot of Signor Feeney – or a sweaty-looking non-existent identical twin – had him in sunglasses in a café somewhere. Somewhere not Ireland, like. That photo was taken yesterday afternoon, McNally informed me. Did I happen to know Mr. Feeney's current whereabouts? I told him that I did not. But I could tell that McNally wasn't having any of it. I had been to Spain myself, had I not? So maybe I recognized the locale in that picture? I was never one much for poker, but I bet McNally was.

So I told him the truth. That the place looked awfully like The Black Cat, whatever the name was in Spanish, Gato something. El Gato Negro, he said quickly, like we were talking about a favourite film. Was I sure it wasn't O'Donohues? There was a glint in his eyes now. As if he didn't already know that O'D's would be the last place Spots or I would go. I told him that was unlikely. McNally nodded as though we were in complete agreement: *why of course a Sergeant in the Drug Squad would want to take his holidays in*

Estapona. Especially in a pub heaving with gangsters, mug-shots of whom we circulate on our watch lists almost every single day of the year. Perfectly normal...

I recalled marvelling at how many little mannerisms McNally had. His next one was poking together the tips of his fingers on each hand, and appearing to be quietly pleased to discover that they actually met. Concerning Mr. Feeney, he said, investigators had developed several theories, all of which centered on whether Mr. Feeney was key to the shooting out at The White Horse. Key, he repeated, hoisting his eyebrows, as in a possibility that Mr. Feeney's involvement came at the behest of one Anthony Cummins.

He very wisely let the notion float out there a while. I didn't bother to pretend that it was news to me. As a matter of fact, it had been on my mind morning noon and night since that day. But, it turned out, McNally had more on his to-dos here than chatting about Spain or Nolan, or even Spots Feeney.

For all that, he continued, it was for the most part assumed that whatever Mister Feeney's involvement in this had been, Mister Feeney would in all likelihood have kept any such arrangement from me. Unless, of course, there was another possibility. McNally didn't need to put in the long pause. I could tell where this was headed. Unless, he went on, Mister Feeney hadn't in fact pulled the wool over my eyes concerning his involvement. Which was to say that there had been no wool needing pulling. Because, went a theory, Mister Feeney had already recruited Detective Sergeant Malone some time ago.

With that he began drumming lightly, even cheerfully, on the edge of the desktop. I should've known something of this nature was coming. But the very fact that McNally had even aired this notion told me there'd be no trapdoor snapping open under me. Not here anyway, and not now. If I really was under the scope, I'd have been done over by now.

The drumming stopped. McNally had a questioning look. A bit far-fetched, didn't I think? I said nothing. It was clear enough to me that McNally had a plan. What he wanted to know now was whether Sergeant Malone here could be trusted to go with the plan. And if I couldn't? Well, those theories he had just mentioned so casually, they'd be back. He did not need to put in words that in that event, he personally would see to it that they bit big-time.

I looked down again at the copy of the oath. I wanted to say something about it. Something grand. Like, I hadn't signed it just to get that parade jacket with brass buttons on it, or even to make Ma proud. I'd signed it because I wanted to be one of the good guys, which to me did not involve sworn, ranking Garda officers the likes of Nolan throwing the rule book down the jacks so's they could run their own show and cause untold mayhem in the process. As for trust, Nolan and Quinn had just driven a coach and horses through that. Between the pair of them they'd made a pig's mickey of the whole OCU too – just when we needed it more than ever. Not alone that, but Garda brass had let Nolan get away with behaving no better than the gangsters we were supposed to be nailing and jailing. And all this at a time when not a day went by now that we didn't get another sign that things were unravelling out there. Not to speak of...

That was as far as my mental rehearsal got.

My mind had slid off elsewhere. Courtesy of those damned pills again, I was sure. It had slid in the direction of Nolan and Áine, actually. Nolan, I'd heard, was holding firm to his story – he had no idea Blake would go to the lengths that he did. Were the brass going to let him away with that? Jesus wept. You could walk into any pet shop and ask a goldfish, and the goldfish would tell you that Blake was a dangerous proposition. You don't put a rat in a corner unless you want to get bit. And if anyone should've known that Blake was a rat in a corner, it was Éamonn Nolan. He was the one put him there.

I watched McNally pluck a biro from his tunic pocket and place it on that sheet, the affirmation thing. He wanted this thing put to bed. Books balanced and signed off, sorted and filed away. They – the brass – had done their sums, their profit and loss summary. On the minus side was their star copper in an elite Garda unit and now, by God, their star copper had overstepped. On the plus side, a gangster of long standing was now deceased. So too was a stone-cold psychopath by the name of Alan Lunney. Also the plus-plus side, it looked like Tony Cummins was ready to play ball. And really, who could deny that Bernie Cummins getting her son back was a plus?

I concluded my study of the wall. McNally's eyebrows slid up in a mute enquiry, and he nodded down at the form. I picked up the biro and did a fast, careless signature. McNally turned the form his way and signed it. He folded the sheet once, and tucked it into a file folder. Then he stood up, and extended a hand. Whether from reflex or confusion, I shook it.

I went straight to Ryans after. By two o'clock I had sunk four pints and three small Vitamin Js. I wasn't even angry, but the confusion was thicker than ever. I had also composed and deleted upwards of a dozen drunk-man versions of a long, stupid email to Sonia. None survived, thank God but -

- Delaney's call was ending.

30

Delaney replaced the receiver like he was handling a valuable heirloom. He wrote 'Estonia?' on the bottom of a sheet in his day timer, stared at it for a few moments, and flipped it shut.

"Sorry about that. You take it when you can get it, I'm afraid."

Whatever that meant. He rubbed his eyes and sat back.

"OK, the Big Mac treatment. Not exactly hail fellow well met, is he. So let me guess. The Oath and the Regs, all laid out? Confidentiality form? Bless me father for I have sinned?"

"'I can neither confirm nor deny....'"

Delaney had only so much fake congeniality to spare today.

"This whole Gary Cummins business," he said. "You know what sticks in my mind?"

No I didn't. I let my eyes out of focus.

"The girl," he went on. "The daughter. She's Downs, right? I mean, Jesus Christ."

Delaney had three kids. His eldest, a boy with glasses, might be of an age with Maria.

"His niece. *His own niece?*"

Even if it was a real question, I had no answers.

"What's the Murphy fella's first name again? The father?"

"Liam."

"I tell you this much. I'd have wanted to as well. It's a fact."

A spiky quiet followed. So Delaney couldn't find words either. Mary Enright – after she had opted to be a mite truthful – had put it about that Gary was warped in that regard. Whatever about Maria, I didn't want to think of what Jenn Cummins had gone through. What she still was going through. All she had done was leave a smiling and giggling Maria with her uncle Gary. Let down her guard and gone out in the car for a half an hour. Well, it was a miracle that Gary Cummins survived at all. I'd gotten a sense of what Murphy could do. The only one who could've stopped him was Jennifer.

Delaney took a while to loosen his frown. I liked Delaney. Even with that MBA guff of his and the teacher-man way of him sometimes. He had what I never had, patience.

"The main thing is you came back to us in one piece."

What I didn't say: says the C.O. who'd dispatched me over to Nolan with indecent haste?

"And you're not up on charges. So far, anyway."

The steady look told me it wasn't chuckles he was aiming for.

"Boss? If there's something you know that I don't...."

"If you're asking whether Chief Superintendent McNally and I spoke, well I'll tell you – yes we did."

Delaney's blank expression helping. I gave him my thicko look.

"I believe you paid a call on the OCU," he said next. "After?"

The pass card that Nolan had given me had been deactivated. I'd kicked at the door a few times. The response was five OCU coppers. Their arrival thwarted my plan to tear in there and knock the living shite out of Nolan or Quinn, or both.

"You wanted a meeting with Éamonn Nolan, is it?"

"Something along those lines."

"I see. Well here's a thought for you now, Tommy. Stay away?"

I tried focusing on that photo I had seen online, that one of Hong Kong at night. Jesus, it was like the inside of a video game. How could they live like that?

"Now Big Mac wasn't in a position to say a few things, so I will. At the end of the day, Éamonn Nolan's only what we made him. No more and no less. And that, in my opinion, needs saying."

I had most definitely not expected that one.

"Boss? Now offence now, but I heard that one already."

Delaney didn't bother asking. I told him anyway.

"'So Nolan may be a bollocks. But he's our bollocks. End of.'"

"Really? I'll say it again then, Tommy. It's all of us, we're all in this. This mess didn't just come out of nowhere. We've got a situation where a first-class Garda officer got to the stage he got to because, well, this is Ireland we're living in. And by that I mean...? We let ourselves down at every turn. Sell ourselves short. In-fighting, backstabbing, all that. Foreigners see it, and they play it to the hilt on us. I'm saying Nolan deserves better. Fair enough?"

This was a Delaney I did not know.

"Look," he said then, "is it any wonder people get fed up? I just hope to God someone has the guts to come out and say that when it matters. Call a spade a spade. Cause and effect, that's all. It needs to be said. Transparency and all that? Well let's see it in action."

I didn't want to argue the toss. But Delaney was puffing up Nolan to be a victim here?

"Fed up," I said. "Well which one of us isn't fed up?"

Delaney had no answer for that item, of course. Who would?

"We get the arrest," I went on, "they get bail. We get the conviction, they get probation. We go for their assets, they sandbag us with lawyers. Numbered companies, shells, trusts, brass plate ghost corporations. Every bit of pretendy, complicated, double-jointed shite invented by humankind. And then, when we do manage to wade through that – finally – and get them up in front of the beak? A tsunami of bullshit. Constitutional cases. Procedurals, charges of harassment, improper searches, illegal seizure claims, the European Court of Human Rights -"

"- which is exactly my point, Tommy -"

"-we all know the score, Boss. But we're not all up in a heap over it. What if I told you I was so fed up that I set up a team to fake an investigation? So's I could keep running my own game."

Delaney made a maybe-maybe not wag of his head.

"We'll see what becomes of him above in Sligo," he said.

"Sligo. You're serious."

"Just read the briefing this very morning, so I did. There's a whole rake of violent burglaries going on up there. Rampaging through Mayo as well, and up into Donegal. Wolf-pack, they're calling them, the way they're picking on out-of-the-way farms and the elderly. Violent? Jesus, it's is nothing to them. Gives wolves a bad name, if you ask me. But Éamonn Nolan's just the one to go toe-to-toe with them. Wouldn't you think?"

No. What I was thinking about was meeting Áine Nugent later today.

"So anyway," he went on. "I didn't ask you in this morning to listen to me gostering away. No, I need to know something. I'll put it plainly. I know what I sent out – who I sent out, like. I think I do anyway. I'm just not sure who I'm getting back."

It took me a few moments.

"Boss. Is this an audition? To get me job back?"

"Don't look at it like that. I'm saying that people talk, and like it or not, that matters."

"The people doing this talking, what do they be saying?"

"Here's one: 'Gotta hand it to Malone. A1 job. Air-tight.'"

"Not Sergeant Malone? Just for my Ma's sake?"

I caught the quick flash of anger at last. A forced smile followed.

"You're the limit, so you are Tommy. Look that wasn't a compliment, the 'gotta hand it' bit. And well you know it."

"Can you tell them – these people – to come say it to my face?"

Delaney let the silence drag on.

"People are going to believe what they want to believe," I said then. "That's on them, not me."

But it was like Delaney hadn't heard me.

"Look at it from other side a minute, Tommy. What's at the net result of all this? This Blake fella, a serious, life-long career criminal was coming over. But now he's brown bread."

"'Coming over?' According to who? To Nolan?"

"That mechanic guy too. That nutter? An arrest would've put light on several open murders. That's all that's in the wind now too. Inconvenient for the forces of law and order, to say the least. So you've got to wonder who's happy over the way things have turned out. Or relieved, at least. You can see that, can't you?"

I debated not answering. I quickly lost that debate, however.

"No offence Boss, but to me it sounds like you believe that shite."

"Believe? Hah. Not until I check everything. And then I check it again and I still don't believe it. I'm saying I can't just dismiss it as gossip. This stuff affects us here. It comes down to trust. Morale. Now I have to say it, Tommy. This Cummins thing is on top of the other stuff. OK?"

Not OK. Delaney let another instructive silence linger.

"Specifically, Tommy, that roof incident, your man falling -"

"- Joey, Joey Gilmore. What about it."

"We know you were cleared, Tommy. Of course we know. And that shooting out in Dalkey? An awful, awful thing. Again, you're in the clear. But I have to tell you, people see stuff like this going on and they wonder. This is human nature we're talking about. You can't just switch it off."

I had no answer for Delaney. At least he hadn't come up with a 'nothing personal.' Yet.

"So that's where I am coming from, Tommy. Now it so happens that I have a pretty good idea of what you can't talk about. What you signed with Big Mac? So here's what I propose – I talk and you listen. Why, is because I need you to know what's doing the rounds here about this latest episode. Fair enough?"

I hadn't had a headache yet today but one was on the way.

"I'll take that as a yes. OK. Here's number one: 'My God but that Tony Cummins is one hell of a smart operator.' You get that? 'Look how he covered all the angles, Cummins. A master stroke!'

He waited. For effect, of course. I had nothing to say, though.

"But that doesn't really hold water, does it. Not when you look closely at it. Not in my book anyway. There's too many bits hanging off the end of it. Tony

Cummins paying someone to go after a Guard? Really? Now we all know there are some real nutters out there, and more dangerous by the day, but I just can't see the likes of Tony Cummins giving a go-ahead for that. Can you?"

Something about the expression 'go-ahead' pitched me back to those moments in the car park. That steady, relentless shooting from Lunney. It couldn't have been much more than five or six seconds. I'd thought that I was a goner.

"Then there's the Feeney angle," I heard Delaney say. "What you might call a type of an iceberg situation? You only see the bit of it at the surface? I mean, you've known this guy since you were kids. But how well do you know him? Like really know him? That's the question. Did Feeney get word that Lunney had set fire to his place? So he set him up in turn?"

Another flash of memory lit up: that expression on Lunney's face when he asked about 'the other fella' in the car that day. Was that him realizing that Spots had sussed him?

"Well he's hardly going to tell us now, is he. But I'd say your pal would know how to carry a grudge though. As for the question of who was behind the wheel of that van that ran over ... Sorry, his name slips my mind. Culligan?"

For a moment I was sure that Delaney did it to provoke me.

"Cullinane. Christopher Cullinane."

"Right. My point is this. Do we have a bit of a repeat scenario here? Feeney getting run over himself, I'm referring to. It was a good number of years ago, of course. And it couldn't have been this Lunney fella, of course. Lunney'd only have been, what, seven or eight years old the time. But Blake though? Now that would get a man thinking, I say."

He looked down at his phone.

"That yard," he said then, raising his gaze again. "Out by that White Horse Inn place? I went out there, you know."

I tried to hide my surprise. Delaney didn't seem to notice, or care.

"Yep, the curiosity got the better of me. Quite the place. Car-park? More like a junk yard than anything else. But I'll tell you what I noticed right away – no angle of view from that pub. None. Matter of fact, a few feet into all that junk, you might as well be in a maze or something."

He massaged his hands like he was working soap into each fold.

"So what's a copper to think," he went on. "Well obviously, he might suppose that that's the very reason that Blake or Lunney picked the venue to meet. Handy, but still out of sight. Just what the doctor ordered really. Or, you might suppose something else."

I had a pretty good idea what was coming.

"You might suppose that it was Feeney picked that place, and for the exact same reason. After he did his recce, to set it up there."

He sat back and stretched. He followed it up with a couple of neck extensions and a sigh.

"Éamonn Nolan," he said next. "Always three moves ahead, Éamonn. Right? So you'd think he'd see all this coming. Feeney coming into the picture, I'm talking about and, of course, your good self. Not the sort of copper to overlook that."

It was issues like this I'd be putting to Soon-to-be-Inspector Áine Nugent.

"Anyway. Ever heard the expression, 'the rule of the gods?'"

"It sounds familiar. Was it on Discovery?"

Delaney's face immediately reddened. I felt half-bad about it. There were only so many jabs I'd soak up before returning the favour. But – fair play to him – he reissued his mildly amused look.

"Not quite," he said. "No, it's about the thing they call hubris. Pride and so forth."

Ah, I thought. Good old begrudgery. You could always depend on it in Ireland. Nolan getting comeuppance like this would please a fair few people. Delaney too, I shouldn't wonder.

"A bit of a cliché now," he went on, "but a sharp reminder all the same. Never underestimate the bad guys. Right? The reach they have, even from inside prison?"

"True for you."

He turned thoughtful. A sign this'd be over soon then? I made a diplomatic shuffle of my feet to move things along.

"You know, Tommy," he said, landing back on the planet, "I have to say this. I was impressed how you kept it together. Very impressed, I can tell you, at how you kept your wits about you."

The smile looked way too genuine.

"I mean there you were, smack dab in the middle of a complete shite tornado, with everything going completely haywire all around you. How could a man handle that chaos, I wonder?"

If life was really a cartoon, he'd have no trouble reading my thought-answer: pills, apparently.

"So when you ran into that pub, the White Horse place, well nobody'd be expecting anything like a logical line of thinking at that point. To be so coherent, and on the investigative trail, like. Would they?"

The smile set tight but Delaney's gaze was cool.

"'Anyone here hear a row?' 'Any set-tos here recently?'"

At least he wasn't putting on a Dublin accent.

"'Anybody hear of feuding going on between two blokes here?'"

If I tried too hard, he'd see I was faking indifference.

"You put a lot out there. In-fighting, feuding, double-crossing, reneging – all there."

I studied the bottom of the window frame.

"I wasn't in the whole of my health when I ran in there," I said.

"'Ran?' I'm not sure I heard about a 'ran.' Read it, I mean."

It was as clear a signal as I was likely to get that Delaney had gone over the case – minutely. He tried to liven up his smile. It only made him look like a vampire, or a lunatic.

"Look, whatever way you made your entry, you can bet your bottom dollar that every pair of ears in that pub was tuned to whatever you were about to tell them."

The stare slowly dimmed. His expression eased into something resembling humour.

"So did you like that?" I said nothing. "Almost an accusation, isn't it?"

"Depends on how you take it, I'd say."

"Let's say whoever says such a thing, they piled it on."

"Like?"

"Like 'That's exactly the type of questioning that'd have the beak tossing the case before it got started, and giving the Guard a tongue-lashing into the bargain?' Like 'Planting responses is exactly contrary to practices we're expected to apply?'"

"Planting. That'd be quite a thing to say, all right."

"But people aren't like vegetables, are they."

This was Delaney being funny? Or more proof of missing cues, and the addled feeling every now and then? Those pills had to go.

"You were off duty anyway," he went on. "And ... Well you know yourself. Extenuating circumstances. Covers a multitude."

"Right. 'Everything going completely haywire?'"

And there it was, a millimetre below the surface: anger. But he quickly covered it up again.

"Well my point is, that's the class of thing you may have coming at you, Tommy. Better get used to it. So *Bí ullamh*. 'Always prepared?' Were you ever in the Scouts? The Cubs? *Bí ullamh*?"

I had an overwhelming urge to laugh. Boy Scouts? I thought again of Macker. The Yeats recitations and the culchie talk and expressions. The endless mental poking and probing and pinching he did. All the while him and his missus were on the make, waiting their chance to pounce on a house next to the DART. For the right price, of course. The proverbial deal that some gobshite – broke, jobless, in over his head – just could not refuse. Áine Nugent, another culchie, always prepared to do what she had to get ahead.

"Tommy?"

"Sorry. Scouts,was it you were saying? No, no. I never got that far."

Delaney stretched again and looked away.

"Anyway," he said next, "whatever else it did, this whole business gave us a good look into corners that are long in need of it. That's something, isn't it? Yes, we'll see where that takes us."

I wasn't going to ask what 'corners' he meant. As if that stopped him.

361

"'Nobody knew,'" he murmured. "Remember all that? Which gets me back thinking about this Corcoran fella again. Mr. 'Talent agency.' You know he's got more baggage than Dublin Airport?"

I nodded. No need to share my view that, like in the airport, there was plenty of baggage went missing too. Had any bright spark investigated that, about Corcoran? Like, what *else*, duh...?

"You know he set tons of legal maneuvering in motion too, right? He knows how to work things, you can be sure."

He looked down at his watch again like it was a deadly snake.

"Scum of the earth," he muttered, to the watch.

"Nice timing anyway," he said. Clenching his eyes then, he yawned into his fist. I could only wait. "The big one. Out Friday."

He let me imagine I'd fooled him with my show of bafflement.

"The Inspectorate? Holy God, Tommy. Don't tell me you're after forgetting about this much-awaited initiative?"

A sarcastic Delaney was a Delaney that I couldn't really figure out. But a shrug would hardly incriminate me.

"We got briefed on it the other day. Four hundred and odd pages, the final version. Buzz word count well up to par too, let me tell you. 'Don't waste a crisis'? Heard that a thousand times lately?"

"You hear it around a good bit, right enough."

"Plenty of runners-up too. Outside the box. Re-tool. Stakeholders. Buy-in. Leverage resources. Empower, take ownership, elephants, rooms – every MBA cliché in the book."

Whoa. This from the C.O. with the MBA? Today's version of Delaney was most definitely doing a number on my head.

"And all this, mark you, while the country's going to pot."

He drew in a breath through his nose. I saw the effort he made to let go of something.

"Interesting times," he said, exhaling. "Chinese, right?"

"I do believe so."

His ambiguous half-smile, half-grimace re-surfaced. He uncovered his watch again. The time seemed to surprise him.

"Back to McNally," he said. "There was one item he wanted to share with me. Just the one. He said he found you... 'interesting.'"

These air quotes, they followed me everywhere. Diabolical.

"He asked me to pass on a piece of advice. When the time was right, of course. Something for you to think about while you're on your holliers?"

"You know me, boss. Love getting the old bit of advice."

Delaney's eyes seemed to freeze up. I didn't care. He waited a few moments before imparting what I then realized had probably prompted this useless meeting in the first place.

"Superintendent McNally said, and I quote, 'fine and well to be interesting. But be sure and tell Malone not to get *too* fucking interesting.'"

31

'Café Capri' – yet another overpriced Italian-style joint.

Well, Áine had picked it. A tired-looking bloke with circles under his eyes kept glancing over from his spot behind the counter. It started out as annoying, but it soon began to give me a touch of the heebie-jeebies. Did I know him? Did he know me? Had I maybe done him for something years ago? Or maybe there was something weird-looking about me that I wasn't aware of. Like I looked a bit... mad?

All in the mind, I told myself. Just to be sure, I repeated it twice more. The week off would help. All this imagining, this plotting connections where there were none – it'd go away, and it'd stay away. It had bloody-well better. No way was I going to let the Summer go by with me still feeling that I couldn't trust things not to go unexpectedly skew-ways at any given moment. Mind you, I wouldn't be the only person in this country thinking that.

I concentrated on the view outside. I might well be the only person here who knew we were actually cheek-by-jowl with the East Wall. A good idea on paper to bring restaurants and the like down here: the bling and the blags, a stone's throw apart. If there were stones needed throwing, East Wall would be the place to get that particular task done, and done right too.

I checked the time. It was early yet. My mind wandered back to the Italian business. Firenza, Café Capri – people were mad for anything Italian. Was it because of the Catholic connection? Hardly. Great talkers, of course. Fiery. Singers, stylers, all that. Italians were past masters at the old nudge-nudge, wink-wink too. Those Italian coppers at the conference last year? To me they came across as full of themselves. Sure enough, one of them, a sergeant but with a title that sounded like superintendent, got arrested a month after.

I hadn't bothered to look at a menu. Why would I pay a tenner for a plate of noodles? I had a different sort of menu on my mind anyway – what to expect from Áine Nugent. She was hardly coming here just for the *craic*. Maybe she'd had a change of heart. Maybe she'd finally decided that I deserved answers. More to the point, that I deserved to hear it from her. Spots could come up with cover stories until the cows came home, about how he'd gotten the low down on where Gary Cummins was. The anonymous, helpful barman, now unfortunately inaccessible in Australia... somewhere?

I began observing the seagulls. Such totally brazen feckers. So god-awful loud too. They had a cocky walk to them too, with their chests out. And they never appeared to be one bit concerned about anything. No sleepless nights worrying about getting put out of their homes or losing their jobs, or watching the place coming apart at the seams. They just carried on doing whatever they liked. Fly, scavenge, scream, eat, shite. Fly, scavenge, scream, eat ...

Had she actually phoned Spots? No, she couldn't have. Texted? Emailed? It didn't matter how. What I really wanted to know was how and when and why had she finally pushed free of the Éamonn Nolan gravity field. The thinking side of her had surely known that Nolan had lost it. Known too that, with Quinn to tell him what he wanted to hear, Nolan was actually dangerous.

How hard it must've been to take that step. What had finally pushed her over the edge? Was it hearing about the rounds of ammunition at Ma's door that did it? Learning that Spots' place had been set on fire? She might have known that Blake was off the leash and freaking, and doing things his way no matter what Nolan'd tell him to do or not to do. Well, whatever it was, she must have decided that Nolan would not, or could not, control this anymore And here was the strangest thing: I just couldn't bring myself to be mad at her. I just couldn't.

I sank back again into the what-ifs. What if I hadn't seen them that night, Nolan like a mad king on his throne and her on her knees for him. How long would that image stay glued in my mind? Why, I wanted to ask her. Did he force you? No. We were back to the old human dynamics, the continuing conundrums. It was useless me trying to stop myself feeling that I owed her something. Yes, I had picked up enough on how the OCU jungle operated, yet I still hadn't cared enough to try to do something about it. I could use the excuse that all I'd gotten was someone who wasn't on the level with me. But that was a cop-out. I just didn't take the time to get by that and to see what was really going on there – a woman just trying to do her job around the OCU gorillas, and getting the worst of it. No, I hadn't protected her from that.

A sea gull began screeching nearby. It seemed to be shrieking at me alone.

I started then: somebody was suddenly beside me. Sunglasses? Áine. Jesus! I hoped she didn't see the fright she gave me.

"There you are," she said. "*Far niente* and all that. Is that the way?"

"I don't know. I haven't looked at the menu yet."

"I mean hanging around, nothing to do. In a nice way, though."

She took a slow look-around of this bit of pretend Italy. She had colour, and she looked younger. I certainly was not about to make a comment about the blouse. Really, if I had a titter of wit, I'd have been lying poolside at that hotel too, the one Spots goes to when he feels the need for a cure for his various issues. Or I might be nervously working through the crowds in Hong Kong, on my way to a surprise rendezvous with you-know-who.

We had Johnny Depp's twin for a waiter? Áine ordered an Americano.

"They have Americanos in Sligo-o? Things I never knew."

She put her mobile on the table and looked around. The light this time of year was magic, all right. It wouldn't be dark proper until eleven.

"So you finally got your time off. Where are you headed?"

"Off to sunny Crumlin, is where. A bit of tiling, a bit of painting."

"Little jobs of work for your mother? That's nice."

I said nothing. I was actually embarrassed.

"Relaxing, though. Right? 'Mindful painting' or something?"

"Oh Jaysus don't talk to me about that mindfulness caper. Please?"

They call it a Mona Lisa smile. A balloon inflated where my heart should be. I waited for her to meet my gaze. She knew – I was sure of it. Then I saw her draw back in her mind. Had I put her off? But how?

"You're back to the running, you said."

Sure enough, she'd switched effortlessly to colleague mode.

"Well, I'm trying to. But the Phoenix Park is bigger than I remember it. I'll tell you that for nothing."

"You're not bumping into any wildlife there, I hope."

"Deer you mean, is it?"

"Don't mind the deer," she said. "It's the primates I'm talking about."

Ha ha. I sometimes wondered if I'd meet OCU heads out for a run. They'd hardly be liable to listen to me telling them it wasn't me who huffed and puffed the OCU house down, or put Golden Boy Nolan into the ditch.

"And your pal, Vincent, is it?"

"Here look, don't call him Vincent whatever you do. 'Spots.' But you know that already. You're just sticking close to the script here. Right?"

She looked at me the way a patient teacher looked at a serial messer. I darted a few secret-agent glances around the place and gave her a shifty look.

"Oh you think this is a set-up?" she asked.

"Did I say I did? Check the tape after, why don't you."

She seemed genuinely taken aback.

"You're paranoid," she said.

"I am, am I. Well maybe paranoia is actually healthy. Because that's how a fella should be, especially after he's been to a funeral. Maybe I'm making up for the paranoia that Christy Cullinane should've had but didn't, and that was why he ended up the way he did. Of course, to the genius running the OCU, Christy would have been just a – "

"You're just making yourself angry. Deep down, you know that's not how it went at all."

She wasn't wrong. I could think of nothing to say.

"I said paranoid," she added. "I didn't 'out of your mind.'"

"Me? Hah. You were out of your mind, what you did."

She looked up at the furled umbrella between us.

"You're under a lot of stress, I imagine," she said. "A tough spot to be in."

"And you're Mother Teresa here to help me out. Fantastic."

I still got no hint that she was about to fly the coop, though.

"Look," she said. "There's no set-up. Nobody asked me, or ordered me ,to come here. Surely you'd get it that I'm actually taking a chance coming here."

"In sunglasses. International intrigue style. Go on out of that."

She did what I'd noticed women did rather too well: change the subject.

"So where did he go again?" she asked. "Spots? Spain, d'you reckon?"

I waited until she met my gaze.

"'Spain, d'you reckon?' Get up the yard Áine, will you. As if you didn't know that as well. Here, I'll give you a laugh. About one hour ago, I got shown a photo of him sitting in a bar there the other day. Message delivered, like."

Her head inclined for a question but it never came.

"You had no clue what he'd do with that information?"

I could tell that she had expected this to come up.

"But you do know that I won't say another word to you about it here," I went on. "Because no matter what you say, I can't be sure this isn't a set-up."

She was very still. Maybe she did the mindfulness thing, and never said?

"He had a not-bad story cooked up," I said. "Did you help him with that?"

Even with the tint I saw that her eyes had gone blank.

"The barman used to work at the White Horse, did him a favour et cetera? Conveniently gone to Australia? Great timing or what. Well, he had my number anyway. He strung me along nicely, so he did. It looks good on me, you reckon?"

Her eyes were on the move again. She trained her gaze on the far corner of the place, and she adjusted the sunglasses a bit. Then I saw it.

"Who did that?"

She locked her stare on where it had wandered off to.

"Áine? I said, who did that."

She made a brush-off gesture with her hand.

"Was it Nolan?"

"Stop it. OK? Just stop it."

She turned a little, but she wouldn't look at me.

"I didn't come here to listen to that," she said.

"He figured it was you that slipped that message to – oops. Did he?"

Her lips tightened. For a moment I thought she'd up and skedaddle.

"Because you knew it had gone too far. Not 'it' – *he* had gone too far. Éamonn I-make-me-own-rules Nolan. He'd well-and-truly lost it. Hadn't he?"

I could tell that she had settled on waiting me out.

"Well I hope you nailed him for it, Áine. You better have."

Something about her stillness told me otherwise. I waited a bit.

"Look, I said then. "If you don't –"

"Tony Cummins."

"What about him?"

"How do you know that your pal wasn't working for him?"

I stared into where I estimated her pupils were.

"You're doing the same thing everybody else is doing," she said. She moved in over the table more. "The same question: how did Tony Cummins know."

"Who says he knew?"

"That's just it," she snapped. "Nobody knows whether he did or not. Did he suspect Blake was up to something? Or, did somebody actually tell him?"

"Enough with the questions. You tell me. Who else knew what Nolan was up to, with Blake? You did. His butty Quinn did too. So now, tell me that Tony Cummins has a 'shield' right in your outfit. Go on, try that one on me."

She sat back. It was an answer of sorts.

"Come on, Áine. I'm an easy mark. You could tell me anything, so you could. I'm the thicko who can be led around by the nose."

She looked away again. Adjusted her sun glasses again.

"Wait, maybe I've got it all wrong. Maybe you came to apologize?"

The sunglasses slid around my way again. I could barely see the shape of her eyes in there.

"For not replying to four voice mails I left you? The emails?"

Maybe she was actually glaring at me. I pretend-glared back.

"We were ordered not to be in communication with you."

"Well Jaysus Áine, even when we *were* working together – *supposedly* working together – it turns out you weren't communicating then either."

I might have been imagining the start of a smile. But whatever it was, it was whipped away right quick. Something had shifted, all the same. The atmosphere maybe? I couldn't be sure, but it felt like a truce.

"Look," she said. "I knew that you'd clued in. Mick Quinn told me. He saw you came back that evening for something and, well, all the rest of it. Me and Éamonn I'm talking about."

"Why would I care about that? Adults, and all that jazz?"

Even with the sunglasses, I knew right away that she knew better.

"By the by. On the subject of Quinn. Are you in touch with him at all?"

She didn't answer. In fact she was making a point of showing she wouldn't.

"Because I want a message passed on to him. Tell him that if he ever crosses my path again, on the job or off of it, I'll give him the hiding he deserves."

It didn't make me feel one bit better, saying that. I felt stupider actually.

"OK, let's do a rewind," I said then. "You came here to apologize. Yes?"

"Apologize for what, exactly?"

"How's about for the whole OCU outfit. Throw in one for how the brass screwed up, into the bargain?"

"You have some imagination, is all I can say to that."

"Says you. Nolan didn't work in a vacuum, you know. There's a thing called oversight. So who above Nolan decided to stay blind to his shenanigans, or to look the other way?"

Her nostrils caved as she drew in a breath and then held it.

"Nolan never entered Blake in the system. You know that, at least?"

I doubted she was playing the gom here. There were still coppers who kept their informants to themselves. The killing in Donegal had torn the lid off that grand old tradition, and the brass had come down very hard on it after . It was document your tout on Pulse, or else.

I grew tired of waiting.

"OK. Lack of response means I've got it right so. Someone gave Nolan the go-ahead to use Gary to nail Tony Cummins. Leverage, extortion, call it whatever. Be interesting to see who gets to carry the can for that. You reckon?"

She didn't reckon. Instead, she took off the sunglasses and carefully folded them. I tried not to stare at the ping-pong-ball sized welt up under her eye. She looked boldly at me. Just like that, my anger vapourized.

"What," I said.

"How do you know it wasn't Blake made the approach to Éamonn?"

"Ah. So that's what he trying now, is it. God there's no end to it."

She turned to study a passer-by. A lonely enough sight it looked too.

"You and Nolan," I said. She shook her head slowly but did not look over.

"Uh uh," she said. "I'm out. I got the move. The one I wanted too."

"Fraud – oops: The Garda National Economic Crime Bureau?"

"You remembered. I like the old name better."

"Fraud, yeh. A bit ironic, though. And you after bamboozling me?"

She let her gaze trail across the table and then sent it up between the walls of glass. The sky was like cold tea, flat and milky.

"Mrs. Cummins' back in hospital, I believe."

It looked like she had addressed her remarks to the heavens.

"That she is. She took a turn there last week."

I knew this and more about Bernie Cummins because I had a Ma who wouldn't stop telling me things. How grateful Bernie was. Sure, it was nice to hear. What was nicer to hear, but in a very complicated definition of 'nicer', was a message that purportedly came from her husband. It came to me second or third-hand via one DeeMan, aka David Collins, a short, heavily-tattooed mug who appeared to have used every minute of his sentence to lift the heaviest lumps of iron he could find. Tony Cummins, I was informed, wanted me to know that he had put out the word. 'The word': Blake's demise was not down to me. This... acquittal? judgement?... was coming to me from an inmate recently released after a lengthy sentence in our country's high security prison. As if I needed another reminder that we were living in upside-down land.

"OK, why are we here," I asked her. "Just to chew the fat, is it?"

She eyed the screen on her mobile and turned it over again.

"You know Éamonn's taking full responsibility. Right?"

"Not right, no. Because it's not like he had a choice. The wheels came off, remember? Crash bang boom, and up the creek big-time."

She looked out a gap that offered a bit of a view of the Liffey.

"Thomas? Can you take a break from being a contrary..."

"Áine? Only if you stop treating me like one?"

"Look. It is what it is."

"It is what it fecking isn't, you mean. Look, this isn't some debate. Christy Cullinane was murdered. My Ma was run out of her house in fear of her life. A mate of mine had his place torched. Not to mention the fact that it was me, like a complete gobshite, who ended up walking into a mad shoot-out with two dyed-in-the-wool killers. Does any of that register with you?"

She took a deep breath and let it out in a meditative manner. It bothered me more and more that I just couldn't snap into the state that I wanted to be in, was entitled to be in – being seriously pissed off.

"Of course it does. Why do you think I'm here?"

"Well that's not what I'm hearing. All I'm hearing is some guff about Nolan, how he just slipped up here a bit. This is the fella who made his rep for being on the ball and taking down a bunch of serious gangsters when no-body else could. Ah but sure, says you, he just slipped up a little. A tiny bit, ah yes. So what if he massaged the rules a little bit. Jaysus."

"You're talking like he broke the law. He didn't. And you know we have to fight with our hands tied behind our backs. Don't pretend you don't know that. But at least Éamonn got results."

"Results. I see. You mean the madness that day out in that car park?"

"You think he wanted that? He's gutted about it, if you want to know."

"Gutted? I see. Like he had no clue how crazy it all would get. No clue."

She narrowed her eyes and kept them like that.

"What next," I said. "Claim he was fierce distracted? Stars in his eyes?"

No, I shouldn't have. The colour left her face. It only made the welt stand out more. Her nostrils went in and out a few times. She moved her jaw about like as if to get the feeling back there after a dig. Her next words were delivered in a low, neutral tone.

"And he said to tell you that he respects what you did, no matter what."

She stared at the table for a while then, like it disappointed her. I wanted to ask just how much deep shit Nolan was in on the home front, with his wife. As he bloody should be.

"Look, about ..." she paused and let a vague, doubting look drift by me. "You don't get it. Everyone in the unit would go to the wall for Éamonn."

"Áine? Don't you see? That's how it goes with people like him."

She had a distant look now, tinted by frustration and anger.

"That's their thing – getting people to go to the wall for them. And the wreckage, afterwards? Meh – whatever. They've moved on. That's not a bug. It's a feature."

"Look," she said. "Come on. People aren't stupid. They know."

I had a good notion of what she meant. I'd keep it to myself.

"They know what really happened out there," she went on. "And they know how it's being handled too."

Out there. Handled. Sometimes it was like words had claws. But just as I was about to tell her how far out of the loop she was, and what I thought of the stupid gossip she was letting herself get taken in by, I lost heart. I had copped on to something. She was hurting a damn sight more than she was letting on.

Her eyes had wandered off to another study of architecture, or something. I joined in. Then I felt her eyes light onto me.

"So how's your mother," she said, brightly. "I meant to ask."

"Ma's grand. She was down the country a few days. Took her Amy CDs with her for good measure too."

Áine Nugent had a smile like I'd never seen before. I felt like I'd suddenly been caught in a slow landslide.

"You're serious," she said. "Amy Winehouse."

"'No, no, no,' Drug Squad, son's a copper... I know. What can I say? Except she likes her R and B, Ma does. The Sixties and all. Life goes on, right?"

"Any Winehouse down on the farm. In Clare."

"Hey it's not just Clare – it's the *wilds* of Clare. Really. That's what my mate calls it. And him born and reared there."

How could a smile change somebody so much? Had I sleepwalked through the past few days? I was staring, and I knew it. She was looking away now.

"A bit of an eye-opener all around then," she said.

"Don't be talking. The time of her life, she had."

Áine turned back. The smile was gone now. Something sank in my chest somewhere. She looked down at the table top.

"So after your holiday in ..."

"...in Costa Del Crumlino. Yes?"

The smile wasn't coming back. Was I right back to mis-reading everything?

"What then?" she asked.

I had no proper answer. Life With Macker days were over and done with at any rate. Not a moment too soon either. It had become a bit of an endurance contest really. The Q and A routine, the mental trickery, all the quirks and the round-the-corner wit – that I wouldn't miss. I had Macker figured out. It was just a cod. An act. Behind all the guff was a decent bloke, a fella just could not cover up the fact that deep down, he was actually a softie. Maybe in the wrong line of work, truth be told. Anyway. I hadn't heard a peep out of him since I'd blocked his texts. Maybe that was a bit drastic. I'd text him before the day was out. Maybe even go for a pint. I owed him that much at least.

"Back to the Drug Squad, is it?"

"That's the plan in anyhow. If they'll have me, ha-ha."

Áine's face was different now. I might even have imagined that she was blushing. How come it was only now that I noticed that her eyebrows were blond at the edges?

Rain? Just like that? It bloody was. Heavy, hard-hitting drops too.

She got to the canopy first. There we stood, watching Johnny Depp the waiter scurry around. I stole a glance. She was watching rain hopping off the railings. But that was no raindrop coming down from her left eye. She wasn't much concerned with hiding it, however. She dabbed at it like it was a cut.

"You think you have things figured out," she said. I could barely hear her, with the rain, but I didn't want to say so. "You know? In the job a good while now? All grown up?"

"I'm not so sure about that," I said. "I found out that career was a verb too. But it can turn into a verb too. There's days, I tell you..."

The beads of rain hanging and dropping from the railings had absorbed her attention. I reached for a smart remark, but found absolutely nothing. I was looking at her wrist, and the way the skin moved as she flexed her fingers. Her eyes had grown intense. My heart leaped into the old two-step again.

"I hope I'm not being nosy now," she began. "Your fiancée –"

My god-damned phone. I had forgotten to turn it off.

The shrink's office, was my first thought. I'd asked to bump the appointment to this week. I wanted out.

Delaney? I dithered. I was on me holliers, for the love of God! But maybe he was calling to tell me that Drugs Central now had no place for me. I couldn't – I wouldn't – hide. I stepped back until I was almost catching some of the rain still flemming down.

What Delaney told me then, it made no sense. They were just words. I let them go by my mind like I had just heard something meant for someone else, or heard something that didn't have to do with me. But a part of me knew. And it also knew that this refusing to believe Delaney couldn't last. He repeated himself only once, at the end.

"I'm sorry Tommy. I just felt you needed to know. He thought you were the bee's knees. He said that to me, he did. Told me he never had such..." He was gasping now, and losing it. "That's all I can say right now. I'm sorry."

Johnny Depp had given up trying to rescue things off the tables and promoted himself to staring at the drops pip-popping on the table instead. Everything around me had turned strange-looking, and useless and ugly. The urge to grab tables and toss them was almost too much.

Áine had taken off the sunglasses and she was staring – that much I registered. But my mind was still nailed to that DART station. Booterstown? Christ. A mickey mouse station, just a non-entity of a stop on the way out the Southside proper. Wasn't there some bird sanctuary thing there? All those stations out there had pedestrian bridges over the tracks. So there'd likely be fair decent views from one of those. Macker could take a last look at the sea, or the mountains, or the grass or whatever with him?

I wanted to yell. At Áine, for that confused look on her face. At these people here too, for worrying about something stupid like a shower of rain. Couldn't they see what was going on right under their noses in this careless, messed-up country? What gave them or anyone else the right to expect cops to do the impossible? To push them so far that they couldn't take it anymore?

But then everything caved in. All I knew was that I had to get out of here. The shower had passed its peak. Between the slaps of my shoes splashing down in the puddles and sheets of rainwater, I heard Áine Nugent's voice fading behind. What happened, she wanted to know. It ran back to her first question and she repeated that one too: what's wrong?

As if I had an answer to that one either.

The Tommy Malone series is preceded by the Inspector Matt Minogue series..

'Matt Minogue, the magnetic centre of this superb series... and Brady's tone of battered lyricism are the music which keep drawing us back to this haunting series...'
New York Times

johnbradysbooks.com